Whisper to a Scream

Susan Ann Wall

Whisper to a Scream
Heart of Jupiter Publishing

Paperback:
ISBN-13: 978-1941852125
ISBN-10: 1941852122

Ebook:
ISBN-13: 978-1-941852-11-8

Cover
Foreground Images:
© Themalni | Dreamstime.com
© Konradbak | Dreamstime.com
Background Image: © Deb Heathe
Design: Heart of Jupiter Publishing

Lyrics used with permission of Jon Bon Jovi.

Dedication

This book is dedicated to Jon Bon Jovi.
Thank you for the thoughtful love songs, the inspiring anthems, and the healing power of every single lyric and chord.
Your music has seen me through happy times and difficult days and I'm so grateful I was able to share it in this story.

Chapter 1

Dry County
The promise has run dry
Where nobody cries
And no one's getting out of here alive
-Dry County, Bon Jovi

Shame.

It slithered up her spine and down her arms, surprising Skye Everhart with its ferocity. She'd felt nothing but pain for eight long months. So apropos to finally feel something else now.

"Call me next time you're in a jam," Finn drawled from behind her. The satisfied amusement in his voice had always made Skye want to punch him in the face. Funny how time hadn't changed his smugness.

Swallowing a good dose of disgust and once again leaning on the solid oak desk for support, Skye couldn't bear to look at him. "There won't be a next time," she muttered, shaking off the growing shame with a shudder.

Clothing rustled from across the small room, followed by

the distinct sound of a zipper. Skye's mouth filled with saliva, a repulsive flood that threatened to bust through the dam she'd made with pursed lips and a clenched jaw.

She would not hurl, not here. Not ever.

What was that saying? Necessity is the mother of invention? Yeah, that was it. Skye reminded herself of the circumstances that had brought her here.

She swallowed hard and took a deep breath. *Necessity,* she thought, an internal mantra that would get her through the rest of this repulsive transaction.

"I prefer cash, but for someone like you, I'm willing to compromise," Finn said.

Someone like you. The words echoed around her head, the whisper threatening to fade into a memory she just couldn't face.

His breath on her neck pushed the memory aside, inspiring a different kind of shudder, the kind that brought bile and another flood of saliva. Before it had traveled far, Finn smacked her ass. The vibration sent a stabbing cacophony down her right leg and up her side, a brutal reminder why she stood in his living room. "This was fun."

For Skye, fun didn't describe what had just transpired, but as he placed the unlabeled orange bottle on the desk in front of her, relief pushed aside all signs of self-deprecation.

"There won't be a next time," she insisted, gripping the bottle as she folded her arms across her chest and turned to face him.

Finn smirked, as if he knew Skye would do whatever it took to get what she needed. He pinched her chin between his thumb and index finger, reigniting the shame of what she'd just done. "There's always a next time, darling. Always."

Skye jerked from his grasp as the sting of bile fought for purchase. She'd push him away if she stood a chance of escaping unscathed, but his large, tattooed frame was all muscle and strength while metal screws and unforgiving scars held together half of

Skye's petite body. Any muscle built up in twelve years of army physical training had turned to mush in the eight months she'd spent in a hospital bed.

"Help yourself to a glass of water," he said, nodding toward the kitchen. "There's something stronger to wash it down with in the cupboard next to the stove."

"I'm fine," Skye lied. The shame was enough to deal with. It would morph into humiliation if she acted like a junkie getting her fix in front of the man who had provided what he called 357s. Skye had heard the street name and even though that wasn't the caliber of ammunition she'd used during two tours in Afghanistan, the term made her twitchy for more reasons than she would ever acknowledge.

Twisting the cap, Skye eyed the contents. "How do I know this is what I asked for?" Though she approached Finn, trust didn't accompany the bargain. He'd been a sleaze bag in high school and based on the limited interaction they had in the last few days, that hadn't changed.

"I'm a business man. I guarantee my product." His thumb brushed against her lips. "A satisfied customer always comes back."

The implications of that statement made Skye's stomach roil. She didn't like Finn, hadn't liked him since he'd proved what an ass-hole he was during their junior prom over a decade ago. Unfortunately, necessity never made a good bargain.

She knocked his hand away. "I won't be coming back." This was a one-time deal. Once connected with a doctor at the VA clinic, her prescription wouldn't run out and she wouldn't find herself in this situation again.

The corner of Finn's mouth lifted into a smirk that had melted the panties off nearly every girl at Sunset Valley High School all those years ago. Now it held a knowledge that made Skye want to hurl all over his tattered t-shirt and worn jeans. He still had the classic bad-boy look, but she wasn't a hormonal teenage girl who swooned just because the hot guy with a leather jacket and

3

motorcycle smiled at her. No, if she came back to Finn for another transaction, she would be something far worse.

I won't be coming back, she told herself on a whisper in her mind, hoping Finn saw the determination in her eyes.

"Don't forget about the concert," he reminded her, as if he understood the silent declaration. "I'm not sure that pretty little ass of yours can handle my bike for three hours, so you can pick me up. Just text me with the time."

Skye hoped he forgot about that part of the bargain. When approaching him about her predicament and asked to pay him later when the government straightened out her pay, he'd gone into negotiations that rivaled those of warring countries trying to reach a peace treaty. In a moment of weakness, Skye not only agreed to trade sex for the prescription meds, but also offered Finn the extra ticket she had to the upcoming Bon Jovi concert in Montreal.

"I'll be in touch," was all she could say, those words leaving a bitter taste in her mouth.

"I look forward to it," he responded, the charm so thick and fake you could wade through it. When Finn stepped back, his arm waved in an invitation to leave. "I have other business, so you'll forgive me if I don't show you out."

So much for the fake charm. That was fine with Skye. She didn't need an escort and hadn't expected any courteous gestures from the man who had a love 'em and leave 'em reputation back in the day — and probably still did. After screwing the cap back on the bottle, she stepped forward, swallowing a wince as the pain shot up her right leg. No way could she let Finn know how much she needed the pain killers. He was a predator and Skye refused to be his prey.

The limp proved impossible to hide, though, even under the black and white striped maxi skirt that covered the scars. The doctors at Walter Reed assured her with time and physical therapy, the limp would disappear. They'd also promised the pain would subside. As she reached the kitchen door, the pain shooting around her body like rogue fireworks, Skye wondered if pain and shame were the only things she'd ever feel.

Sighing, she mustered up whatever strength remained to get to her car. The four steps down the porch may as well have been four hundred. Walking up the steps had not been easy, but it was a walk in the park compared to what she had to push through now. Without a railing to hold tight to, Skye wished the cane she refused to use wasn't across the driveway in her car.

"Need some help?" The question echoed with more knowledge than Skye was comfortable with. Of course she *needed* help, but want trumped need and she did not *want* help.

"I'm fine," she said, not turning. The steps were daunting, but she'd rather face off with this new nemesis than see what must be a cocky smile on Finn's face.

He witnessed her weakness and Skye didn't like it. When her prescription had run out a week ago and she couldn't get her next appointment moved up, she started looking for an alternative. Two days ago she'd discovered a solution, in the form of an ex-boyfriend who promised he could get what she needed. Skye was a skeptic at heart, but Finn had come through.

She swore she'd hide the pain so he wouldn't know she was as desperate as an addict. She had to move — now — before Finn discovered just how vulnerable she was.

Sucking in a breath, she stepped down with her left foot, dragging the right behind until it landed with a thump on the step below. The pain shot all the way up her leg and spine like an exploding mortar. Rather than cry out, Skye focused on getting her footing so she could manage the next step.

Finn chuckled from the kitchen door, fueling her motivation.

With her left foot planted firmly on the next step below, Skye repeated the drag and drop drill. She sucked in a couple shallow breaths to fight off the cry battling to escape.

She wasn't so successful on the third step.

"You should have had a 357 first," Finn drawled. He may as

well have said, "I told you so."

Her eyes stung with unshed tears by the time she dragged her right foot to the dirt. She wouldn't cry, hadn't since waking up in Germany and wouldn't after all these months. Crying changed nothing, nor would it make the pain go away.

It was only about twenty paces to the car. Twenty paces was nothing. Even with the pins in her leg and the scars on her torso, she could low crawl that distance.

Twenty paces. That's all. She could do this.

In Igor-like fashion, she dragged her right leg more than stepped with it and soon realized her assessment of the distance proved not just inaccurate, but completely off the mark. Just like the first twenty paces at that first physical therapy session, the distance dug into the depths of hell.

Since this was Sunset Valley and locking your car wasn't required, she tugged the door open and fell into the seat with all the grace her injury didn't allow. Finn still stood in the doorway, one side of his mouth angled up in a glib smirk. With her left foot on the brake and her right leg bent to keep her foot clear of the pedals, Skye put the car in gear and lifted her foot off the brake as she used the cane to push on the accelerator. She ignored Finn and the pain shooting up her right side as she skidded out of the driveway.

It was a short drive from Finn's to her parent's house, but Skye took the scenic route. The sun, surrounded by endless blue, sat high as she coasted into a quiet fishing spot by the river. She twisted the cap off the bottle again, tossing two pills to the back of her mouth and taking a long drink of iced tea. With the windows down, the cool April air soothed her battered soul. After spending two tours in the dessert in the last five years, she loved the cold.

As a kid, she couldn't wait to get away from Sunset Valley. The town was too small and the people too nosy. Skye had developed an aversion to people being all up in her business. In the army, she'd been harassed for being so private, but as the daughter of the high school principal, she had grown up with the whole town knowing every move she made. As an adult, only her closest friends were privy to her personal information, but not even those friends knew about the man who had won her heart.

No, no one knew, because if even one person disclosed that bit of intel, it would have meant an Article 15, or worse, a dishonorable discharge.

A lone tear streaked Skye's cheek and she closed her eyes, putting on the proverbial armor before any more rogue tears escaped. For eight long months she'd kept the tears locked up like artillery in the weapons depot. The pain from the explosion kept her mind off the ache in her chest. Even when the Vicodin kicked in to bring the pain to a manageable level, it created enough of a fog in her brain to keep the reality of that single moment from seeping its way into her head.

Some secrets were meant to be kept, even after they'd died.

Chapter 2

It doesn't matter where you are,
doesn't matter where you go
If it's a million miles away or
just a mile up the road
Take it in, take it with you when you go
Who says you can't go home?
-Who Says You Can't Go Home, Bon Jovi

Humiliation.

It joined the party like a long lost friend just back from the war.

Coming home was supposed to be a way to regain some control of her life, to burn off the fog Skye had been living in since regaining consciousness in Germany, and maybe, just maybe help her learn to live with the pain.

But, parking in front of her parents' house and seeing Noah Carbonneau sitting on the front porch churned up the humiliation she'd managed to stomp out at Finn's.

Skye realized now that coming home wasn't going to be the walk in the park she'd hoped for. Not that she had any other choice.

Once her parents found out she was being released from Walter Reed and medically discharged from the army, they would have dragged her back to Sunset Valley — kicking and screaming — if she hadn't agreed to move home.

After living alone in a hotel for a week with no nurses, doctors, and who the hell knows who else checking on her every five seconds, Skye realized how difficult the path ahead was going to be on her own.

The quiet town she'd grown up in was normal. You didn't have to carry a weapon here, or wear a flak vest that wouldn't protect you from a buried IED anyway. Mortar fire didn't echo at night. Running water and toilets were the norm and no one would expect you to work eighteen hour days, six days a week.

So, yeah, she'd come home, to grab a little piece of normal. The problem with that plan lay with the man sitting on the porch, the man who had once been her best friend.

After parking the car, Skye closed her eyes and sucked in a few deep breaths. It was a feeble attempt to get her thundering heart under control. You'd think five years would erase the humiliation, but just seeing Noah ignited it with a vengeance.

To add fuel to the fire, he was going to see her like *this*.

The doctors had advised her not to use crutches. The cane was all she'd need and at some point — with hard work and physical therapy — she wouldn't need the cane at all. Skye lived with the constant ache, not those all-knowing doctors. Pain throbbed as much with the cane as without, so why suffer the humiliation of needing it? When it got bad enough she couldn't walk without assistance — like now because the Vicodin still hadn't kicked in — she preferred the crutches. While a cane spoke of a disability, something long and enduring, crutches spoke of an injury, something quick and temporary that didn't bring with it the emotional fog. Crutches made people curious, but there was no pity. Skye despised pity.

Unable to calm her nerves, she stuffed the orange bottle into her camouflage backpack, grabbed the crutches, and pushed out of the car with as much grace as she could manage under the pain. With the pack secured on her shoulders, she closed the door and let the crutches lead the way.

As a girl, Skye skipped or cartwheeled up the canopied walkway. She'd climbed the old maples countless times, spending hours perched on the branches, avoiding her mother and hiding from her brothers. Noah had spent hours in the trees with her, the two of them always strategizing some plan to break free of Sunset Valley. Noah had outgrown those plans, choosing to stay and breaking Skye's heart in the process. She could deal with a broken heart, but the humiliation prickled as she hobbled up the walkway.

Noah stood and approached with slow, guarded steps. Skye wanted to believe he hesitated because of what had happened the last time they saw each other, but that wasn't Noah's style. The truth was so much harder to swallow. Skye was broken now, the shattered pieces of her body fused and stitched and screwed back together. She'd never cartwheel or skip up the walkway again, never climb the old trees. She may not even be able to look Noah in the eye.

He'd always kept his dark hair short and his beard neatly trimmed, showing the tight line of his mouth. The faded jeans and a dark t-shirt were a lot like Finn's but didn't scream bad-boy. Noah had always been one of the good guys. Her heart betrayed her, jumping into double-time as Noah's narrow mouth lifted into a welcoming smile. "Hi," he said when he came within a few steps.

It should be that simple, two friends saying hi to each other after a long time apart, but it wasn't. Nothing between them would ever be that simple again.

"Hi," she responded, surprised she could manage that one syllable through her constricted throat. Despite the tension and pain of her injuries, Skye held eye contact. Noah needed to see that she was still strong, determined. Whatever was going on with her body and inside her head didn't need to be worn on her sleeve.

"Let me take that for you," he offered, holding out his hand.

"I can handle it," she snapped. Secure on her back, the weight of the pack offered a counter-balance to the forward lean, but the bigger issue would be accepting help she didn't need.

"I know you can handle it, Skye," he muttered, the annoyance clear in his voice. "That doesn't mean you have to."

This is how it would start. A simple gesture, just carrying the pack for her while she hobbled up the stairs, but it wouldn't end there. Skye didn't want help, didn't need it. To get back to normal again, she had to do it on her terms.

"Why are you here?" she asked, stopping at the bottom of the porch. Three steps, the same number to climb up as she just climbed down thirty minutes before. Going up was easier, especially with the crutches, but Skye had little confidence in her remaining strength to lift her battered body up the three steps. Confronting Noah seemed like a good delay tactic.

"Your mom told me to give you a few days to get settled. I wanted to go to D.C. to see you, but—"

"Why are you here?" she asked again, turning to him.

"Skye, come on. It doesn't have to be like this. I didn't mean to hurt you."

"I've got things to do. Thanks for stopping by." She turned and took a deep breath. She could do this. The anger pulsing through her veins was enough to get her moving.

On the second step, Skye didn't quite get the balance right on the crutch and nose-dived onto the porch, muttering a string of curses that would have made her platoon-mates proud.

"Skye." Noah moved to her side, trying to turn her. "Are you all right?"

"I'm fine," she snarled. "Back off."

He didn't. One thing they had in common was that Noah could be just as stubborn. "Take off the damn backpack and let me help you," he demanded.

Skye shrugged the pack off and tossed it on the porch before

11

dragging herself up and sitting in the spot where Noah had been when she'd first arrived. He settled in the spot next to her.

"Is this where you tell me this wouldn't have happened if I'd let you carry the pack?" she asked.

"You know I'm not the '*I told you so*' kind of person."

"Oh, you so are," she laughed. "You might not say it, but you think it."

He nudged her with his elbow, a sweet smile relaxing his face. "I'm glad you're home. Glad you're safe."

Skye couldn't say she was glad to be home, or glad to be safe. She should have died in Afghanistan. Instead, she lived with the burden of being the lone survivor of an IED explosion that killed the three other soldiers in the Humvee.

As the driver, she was responsible for their safety and therefore, responsible for their deaths, including the man she loved — the man who minutes before the explosion had proposed.

"You look good," Noah said, giving her another nudge. "A little skinny, but I hear hospital food is the pits."

"Hospital food is gourmet after what I had to eat in Afghanistan." Her appetite was the issue. Skye had never been a dainty eater. She swore she had some Mexican heritage because she could put away a plate of tacos, burritos, or enchiladas like nobody's business. With the daily physical activity the army required, it wasn't unheard of even after basic training to put away a few thousand calories a day. Food in Afghanistan wasn't gourmet, or even very good, but beggars couldn't be choosers. It wasn't until her hospital stay that she'd dropped about twenty pounds, not that she needed to. Circumstance provided a potent diet.

"Why don't you come over tonight? I'll throw some steaks and corn on the grill, have monster baked potatoes."

Such a basic meal, but aside from Mexican food, it was Skye's favorite and she'd never known anyone who could grill a steak as perfectly as Noah.

"I—"

"No lame excuses. I'll even pick you up and drive you home. Better yet, you can crash in my guest room."

Just like old times. Noah acted like nothing had changed between them, like Skye hadn't risked it all and lost.

"Don't you have a girlfriend to get jealous of me hanging out at your place?" It was a low blow, but Skye had no other ammunition.

"You know I don't."

"What makes you think—"

Once again he didn't let her finish. "This is Sunset Valley. You don't have to live here to know what's going on. I know for a fact your mother kept you informed of my relationship status."

Ever the hopeful one, her mother. Amelia had always asked why Skye and Noah weren't more than just friends. If Skye thought about it enough, which she had since there wasn't much else to do during the limited downtime in the desert, she'd chalk it up to timing. They were like a pendulum: when Skye had a boyfriend, Noah was single and then the pendulum would swing the other way. Neither were single at the same time, but it didn't seem to matter. They were close, best friends. Not even jealous boyfriends or girlfriends could compromise their friendship.

"I've been a little too … busy …" not the right word, but the easiest without giving away any secrets, "to stay abreast of your relationship status." Of course she knew all about Noah, because not even the humiliation had made her stop caring about him.

Noah turned, putting his arms around her and tugging her close. "It really is good to have you home," he sighed.

Skye melted into Noah's arms. For just a moment, she wanted to be normal, to be friends again, to feel that little bit of something more that always echoed between them, but neither one of them could catch.

She was about to lose herself in the security of his arms when he pulled away. "Why do you smell like men's cologne?"

Well, shit. Skye wasn't prepared to answer that question.

Fortunately, she was quick on her feet, at least mentally, because as her leg reminded her, the Vicodin *still* hadn't kicked in. "I ran into a few people at the drug store today. Old friends. All the hugging, you know."

"All the hugging? Like who? Who'd you hug so hard you're wearing his cologne?"

She could try to tell him it was none of his damned business, because it wasn't, but that would put her on the defensive. Noah would recognize it right away.

"I ran into Finn," she said, hoping that truth would be enough for Noah.

"Finn? You ran into Finn at the drug store?" Noah chortled. "How fitting."

"What the hell is that supposed to mean?" Skye bit out before she could think better of it.

"Scott Finnegan is trouble."

Skye snorted. "You said that back in high school when he asked me to the junior prom."

"And I was right, wasn't I?"

Not wanting to give Noah the benefit of being right, she shrugged.

"He's even more so now. You need to steer clear of him. I'm not kidding, Skye."

If Skye could get up and walk away, she would, but her right side throbbed enough to keep her ass firmly planted on the porch. "I don't need you telling me what to do, Noah Carbonneau."

"You know Luke is the police chief now, right?" Noah asked, referring to his cousin who was a couple years older than them. Luke had been in the army, too, only recently returning to Sunset Valley to take over as police chief for Noah's dad.

"So?" Skye asked.

"There's an investigation going on. They haven't been able to nail Finn, but Luke is sure he's dealing drugs."

Skye tried to hide her surprise at Noah's knowledge of

14

Finn's extracurricular activities. Of course, it had only taken her hours to scope out that information. People here for the long haul would already have a clue. "Well, sorry, but it didn't come up in conversation."

"But you got close enough to wear his cologne?" Noah's disapproval forced the shame she'd battled an hour ago to creep back up her spine.

If she admitted to what she'd done, she may as well admit why. Skye didn't want anyone to know how much pain she lived with, how she relied on the Vicodin not just to mask the physical pain, but to keep the emotional storm locked up tight.

"Finn always liked to bathe in cologne, seems that hasn't changed." Skye grabbed the crutches and pushed herself up until she stood on the step below. "Thanks for stopping by," she dismissed Noah, desperate for a shower to wash away the surging shame and stench of desperation.

Noah picked up the backpack before opening the kitchen door. After Skye stepped inside, he set the pack on the table. "I'll be back at six to pick you up for dinner."

He leaned in and kissed her cheek, the same chaste gesture that had become habit over the course of their friendship. It was so normal, and yet it felt so awkward after what had happened the last time she'd seen him. Maybe this was the path to healing. Maybe the humiliation would fade, along with the pain.

A wave of peace washed over Skye, the first indication that the Vicodin was finally working its magic. With it the awkwardness dissipated, leaving Skye wishing Noah wasn't walking out the front door.

Chapter 3

If there's one thing I hang onto,
That gets me through the night,
I ain't gonna do what I don't want to,
I'm gonna live my life.
-Have a Nice Day, Bon Jovi

Purpose.

Noah hadn't had one in so long he had wondered if he ever would again. When Skye left five years ago after being home on leave for almost a month, he'd lost his sense of purpose. He'd lost everything.

Man, she had the worst timing. If he hadn't been with Maddie at the time, he'd have taken Skye up on her proposition.

And, if he had left with Skye, maybe now she wouldn't be recovering from a combat injury.

Noah wasn't one for regret. Seeing Skye in so much pain broke his heart, just as the look on her face had when he'd told her he loved Maddie and wouldn't leave Sunset Valley with Skye. Even now he couldn't regret his decision. He had always loved Skye, always, but she had never given him any indication that she loved him more than as a friend, at least, not until that moment.

At the time, Noah thought he was in love with Maddie Carson. After two years of trying to make it work, they both owned up to the lack of chemistry. Then Maddie, being the psychotherapist, told him his feelings for Skye were probably the underlying issue and he wasn't going to be able to be intimate with anyone until he dealt with that.

So he had, accepting that he didn't just love her as a friend, but that he was in love with her and always had been. With her home now, he embraced those feelings and the renewed sense of purpose in his life.

For the last eight months he'd been preparing for this. Based on what Skye's parents had told him, Noah had started researching post-traumatic stress disorder. Amelia had described Skye as sad, and Ken had described his daughter as moody. They both claimed coming home would make her feel better, but Noah didn't think it was that simple. After all the reading he'd done, from medical and psychology journals to blogs and forums, he worried Skye had PTSD. Knowing her stubborn personality, she'd never admit it and never get help.

Skye had always been stubborn. It was clear that hadn't changed. Dammit, if she had only let him help, maybe she wouldn't have taken a dive going up the steps.

Seeing her inspired his new purpose, though. She was hurting, not just because of what had happened between them — which he was determined to make right — but the physical pain from her injuries was obvious. She had tried to hide it, even downplay it, but Noah knew Skye. What she might be able to hide from everyone else she couldn't hide from him.

Noah had no doubt she needed help and because she'd never admit it, that gave him purpose. He was going to help whether she wanted him to or not.

As if his car had also been tasked with purpose, the Camry led him straight to the one person who could offer sound advice, maybe even encouragement. Though his intimate relationship with Maddie had ended a few years ago, they had remained friends and she'd already helped him get educated on what Skye might be dealing with.

The twenty-minute drive to Lilac Ridge where Maddie lived and owned a psychotherapy practice flew by. When Noah didn't spot her truck at the office, he hoped to find her with the horses at her parent's house. As he pulled into the driveway, he was happy to find her beat up F150 parked next to the barn.

As he approached the opening to the barn he called out a "Hello," not wanting to surprise her.

Maddie's dad leaned on a pitchfork outside one of the stalls. Hank Carson was a large man, formidable in appearance, even intimidating if you didn't know him. When he saw Noah, he offered a friendly smile. "Noah, this is a surprise. Maddie didn't mention she was expecting you."

Noah shook hands with the man, noticing a tighter grip than necessary and taking it for the warning it was. "Hank, good to see you. Maddie's not expecting me. Is she around?"

"She's in the paddock with Crystal," Hank said, referring to the horse Maddie's parents had given her for her thirteenth birthday.

Noah made his way through the barn to the back where a large door offered access to the paddock. "Hey," he said quietly, hoping he didn't startle her or the horses.

"Noah?" she asked when he stepped through the doorway.

"Hi, Maddie. Sorry to just drop in. Wow, you look great." She'd lost a lot of weight since he'd last seen her. "Not that you ever didn't look great," he stumbled. She was a beautiful woman, fun and passionate and Noah had loved her when they'd been together.

Dressed in worn jeans and a sweatshirt, her hair pulled into a pony tail, she continued to brush Crystal as he stood in the doorway, offering him a concerned smile. "Thanks. I gave up chocolate, joined the gym, and lost thirty-six pounds. I've got nine more to go." She'd always been an open book, which was one of the things he'd loved about her. He didn't have to try and read her or figure out what was going on inside her head because she'd just tell him outright.

"Congratulations," he said. She was a self-proclaimed comfort eater and had admitted to him that every time her brother deployed, she gained fifteen pounds. Her brother being in the army was one of the things they had in common and it had probably kept them together for so long.

"Thanks. So what brings you by? Is everything okay?"

Noah shook his head. "Skye's home."

Her eyes widened. They had talked on the phone and chatted online several times over the last eight months about Skye. "How is she?" Maddie asked.

Noah shook his head again. "Not good. She's in pain and carrying a heavy load of angst on top of it."

"That's expected," she said. "Come here, say hi to Crystal." Noah wasn't comfortable around horses. Because he and Maddie had been together for so long, he had at some point gotten used to being around them, but it had been a few years.

He moved slowly and when close enough, Maddie grabbed his hand and placed it on Crystal's neck. "Just pet her. She won't hurt you," she insisted.

"I know. I remember," he replied, stepping up to the horse.

"Do you remember Noah, sweet girl?" Maddie asked the horse. Crystal moved a little, as if stepping toward him and Maddie laughed. "Yep, she remembers you. Stand your ground, Noah. She's moving closer because she remembers you like to keep your distance."

He looked at Maddie then, who wore an amused expression. "I take it that comment has dual meaning?"

She winked at him in her playful way. "You pet her, I'll ask the questions. Did Skye talk about her injuries at all, about what happened in Afghanistan?"

"No, and I didn't ask. I didn't want to push her."

"That's a good idea. Was her angst directed at you because of what happened last time she was home? Or do you think she's moved past that?"

Noah shook his head. "She wasn't happy to see me. I think she's probably embarrassed, which is stupid."

Shaking her head, Maddie had a stern look of disapproval. "Don't undermine her feelings, Noah. She risked your friendship because of how she felt about you and it backfired. She's a strong, stubborn woman and probably sees that as a failure. Strong, stubborn women don't deal well with failure."

"I've tried to make things right." He'd called, texted, messaged her on Facebook, but she'd first ignored and then blocked him. He'd even sent care packages while she was deployed — both times — and they all went unanswered.

"We both know it's not that easy when it comes to Skye. Didn't you once tell me she held a grudge like a mafia boss?"

Noah laughed at that. "Yeah, I just hoped she wouldn't do that with me, given our history." Being best friends since childhood obviously wasn't the magic formula for not being the target of one of Skye's epic grudges.

"Any signs of PTSD?" Maddie asked.

Shaking his head once more, he felt like a bobblehead, but at least this time it was a positive response. "Nothing obvious, but I only spent ten minutes with her. She's coming over for dinner tonight, though."

Maddie's brow lifted in surprise. "Really? How'd you manage that if she's angry with you?"

Noah smiled. "I didn't give her an option. When she tried to decline my invitation, I told her I'd pick her up and offered my guest room. I know she hates living at her parent's house."

He could see the disapproval on Maddie's face. "Noah, you need to be careful about forcing her to do things. I know this is her home and where she grew up, but she's been a soldier for ten years.

Soldiers who have served less time or those with no combat experience have trouble acclimating to civilian life. I know your intentions are good, but be careful they aren't self-serving. Pushing Skye can inflame the situation, not make it better."

Skye had been a soldier longer than ten years. Some days it seemed longer, some days it seemed like she'd just left yesterday. "I want to help, prove I'm an ally, a friend."

"Just a friend?" Maddie's sympathetic smile soothed the guilt that question inspired.

No, not just a friend. Noah wanted what Skye had asked for five years ago.

"I'm sorry I hurt you," he told Maddie.

She shook her head, moving closer to him and resting a reassuring hand on his shoulder. "You didn't, no more than I hurt myself. I suspected for a long time Skye was the barrier we couldn't get past. If I'd been willing to accept that sooner, maybe you wouldn't have been hurt, too."

He abandoned the horse, taking Maddie's hand in his. "You're a good person, a good friend. Thank you."

"Anytime. I hope things work out for both of you. Remember, it's good to be persistent, but don't be pushy."

"Thanks. If I can talk her into it, would you be willing to see her, you know, professionally?"

Maddie shook her head. "I have no doubt she needs a therapist, but given our history, she's not going to trust me. I'll email you a few names, therapists I trust who have more experience with PTSD than I do."

"Sounds good. Thanks again." Noah stepped back toward the barn.

"Noah," Maddie said as he reached the door. He turned to her. "Having PTSD is like being trapped inside a tornado. The storm swirls all around you, but even the loudest scream is as effective as a whisper, so most sufferers don't bother with the scream. Given Skye's stubborn nature, she's going to internalize it.

21

She's dealing with the horror of the explosion, possibly guilt and maybe even shame. She's going to question everything she's ever believed in and doubt her ability to survive. None of this will go away overnight. It could be with her for years, maybe even the rest of her life."

"I know," Noah said, having learned all that from his research.

"Many sufferers feel like a liability to their partner, which is why so many relationships fail for those with PTSD. If you're planning to take things further than friendship, you need to be prepared for that."

Maddie's warning dropped like a cinder block on his chest, tearing his next breath from him. He tried to push the aching weight away, but it was relentless because of the truth behind that simple statement.

Noah couldn't be just friends with Skye. Ever since she'd admitted to being in love with him five years ago, he'd merely been existing, not living. Seeing Skye today pumped some life back into his soul and he wanted more. He wanted to help her heal and wanted to love her the way she deserved to be loved.

To do that, he had to do what Skye had done the last time he'd seen her. He had to risk it all. Noah just hoped this time the timing was right.

Chapter 4

Love is like fingerprints
They don't wash away.
I left mine all over you.
I take the blame.
-That's What the Water Made Me, Bon Jovi

Compromise.

Skye had never liked the word or the concept, but it seemed to be the only stable thing in her life.

A long hot shower offered only a short reprieve from the pain, but Skye would take what she could get. Against her wishes, her parents had fitted the upstairs bathroom with handicap bars next to the toilet and in the shower, as well as a handicap seat for the shower. Skye didn't want the help. Normal people didn't need these things. If she was ever going to be normal, she had to function without them.

That's why there were three towels spread out on her bed. She couldn't stand up to dry off, not after all the physical activity she'd exerted today and with the Vicodin making only a meager attempt to mask the pain. She could, however, lie on the towels and let them absorb whatever water hadn't air-dried.

With the two pills she'd taken after leaving Finn's and the hot shower, the pain dropped to a tolerable level but the medicine would soon wear off. She had a good regimen of alternating between taking one pill and then two, about every three hours. Which meant it was time to self-medicate. Since the last dose hadn't worked so well, she opted to double up on this one. Skye couldn't hang out with Noah and let him see how much pain she lived with. He'd insist on trying to fix everything, but Skye was too broken for even Noah's noble intentions.

She hobbled over to the bookshelf where she kept the stash her parents didn't know about. They'd tracked the pills too closely, worried about the addiction they claimed to read about on the Internet. They didn't understand what she had to deal with and Skye was too old to succumb to such monitoring, so she'd split up the bottle from Finn. She put enough in the regular prescription bottle to last until her next appointment if following the recommended daily dosage — no more than eight tablets per day. She kept the rest in the unlabeled bottle and stashed it behind her Stephen King book collection on the bookshelf between the two windows that looked west.

The sun had dropped below the silhouette of the mountains, the sky aglow with a million shades of pink and orange. Skye supposed the colors here weren't so different from Afghanistan, but the sky in Sunset Valley seemed more tranquil, not tainted by an endless war or countless, senseless deaths.

During that last deployment, sunset was always the time when Rafe made an appearance. Under the guise of needing an end of day briefing, her platoon leader would insist they leave the windowless tin building and get some air. He'd been deployed enough times in his career — first as a non-commissioned officer like Skye, then later, after completing Officer Candidate School, as a first lieutenant — to appreciate things such as sunsets and cease fires and soldiers returning uninjured from patrols. Every day someone didn't die was a small victory in First Lieutenant Warren's platoon and most days, he chose to celebrate that victory with the NCO whose simple name reminded the LT to keep looking up.

"If only one of us had been looking down," she sighed, swiping at her tear-soaked cheeks.

A knock on the door brought Skye out of the tragic reverie. "Skye, honey, are you okay? You've been in there a while."

Skye was going to go crazy under her mother's watchful eye. "Don't come in, Ma. I'm not dressed."

"I can help if you need it. You don't have to be embarrassed."

"I'm not embarrassed," Skye insisted. "I just don't need any help." Basic training had ripped any modesty from her twelve years ago. If there'd been any left, it blew away with the desert sand in Afghanistan during her first deployment and washed down the drain like hospital disinfectant after her last deployment.

What Skye didn't want her mother seeing were the scars. Amelia had gone ghost-white when seeing Skye's right leg in the hospital. She'd pass out catching even a glimpse of the burn scars that wove an intricate pattern from hip to breast. Plus, if Amelia saw the tears, there'd be more worries, and worse, questions. Skye knew all the answers, but wasn't ready to share them.

"Okay, well, Noah is here. Don't keep him waiting too long."

Noah.

His name was a sigh in her mind. Skye had wondered how she'd react to seeing him the first time. As much as she wanted to avoid him, Sunset Valley proved too small and Noah too persistent.

Except for that fleeting moment when her heart betrayed her, there was nothing but the whisper of humiliation he'd tamped out with his casual greeting. Skye supposed that had a lot to do with Rafe. He'd been the cause of her racing heart for the months leading up to the explosion. He'd helped put the shattered pieces back together, showed her that love didn't have to be on a swinging

25

pendulum — even if it did break the rules.

Slipping on loose-fitting boy-shorts panties, because they were the only underwear that didn't inflame the burn scars, and a red maxi skirt because she didn't want to deal with the rub of denim tonight, Skye managed to get dressed without toppling over. It was a small success.

She laughed, surprising herself. Normally when Rafe marched through her mind, the tears threatened, but now she seemed to be adopting his survival tactics.

Every small success should be celebrated.

Still unable to manage a proper bra, and grateful for small breasts that didn't require one, Skye tugged on a loose sweater, letting it fall around her hips. April in Sunset Valley put a chill in the air. She wasn't sure what she'd manage for a summer wardrobe. Maybe she'd move to Alaska to avoid having to show too much skin.

Skye snagged a couple pills out of the secret stash, careful to line the books up like soldiers in formation when she returned the bottle to its hiding spot. Skye had learned in high school her mother liked to snoop. She hadn't been smart enough to hide the birth control pills somewhere less obvious than the nightstand drawer, but after Amelia discovered them, Skye went to greater efforts to hide the cigarettes she'd experimented with at seventeen. Amelia still found them.

With the water she kept next to the bed, Skye swallowed the pills, then ran a brush through her long hair. One of the many things she didn't miss about the army was wearing her hair up. Skye didn't mind the routine or the uniform, or even taking orders from officers who had less time in and less experience than she. It was the nature of the beast. The best officer she'd ever had in her chain of command had been older than her by a year. Being prior enlisted had worked in Rafe's favor as platoon leader. He was respected because he knew his shit, plain and simple, but also because he wasn't just a good soldier, he was a good man. The kind of man you fell for even though you weren't supposed to.

Skye took a deep breath and fought back the tears once again. She missed him, his smile and his laugh … his touch. It had been tricky, and risky as hell, but somehow they'd managed to steal a few moments here and there while the war continued around them. Their first kiss was stolen in the shadows of twilight, a tentative question that melted Skye's heart and connected them so completely. Rafe laughed after, admitting he'd wanted to kiss her for weeks but worried she'd give him a black eye if he tried. Without laughing, Skye told him she'd have introduced her knee to his nuts because it wouldn't leave a physical mark that could get her in trouble.

On one of those occasions when joking around, Rafe told Skye he loved her. The words were so unexpected that Skye was sure it had been her imagination, but then he'd pressed his lips to hers and said it again.

Footsteps padding up the stairs brought Skye's focus back to the here and now where it belonged. Rafe was gone, killed because of Skye's carelessness as a soldier. She didn't deserve those heartfelt memories.

"I'll be right out," she said, wiping the tears.

"You decent?" Noah asked.

She didn't want him in her room, not with evidence of her crime streaking down her cheeks. "No. Don't come in."

"You never take this long to get ready," Noah laughed. "What are you doing in there?"

Skye had never been a primper. She liked simple clothes, didn't bother with make-up except mascara, and let her hair do as it wished. When growing up, Skye would rather be out having fun than worrying about what she looked like.

"I'll be down in a minute," she insisted.

The door handle lowered before the door opened a crack. "I'm coming in. I don't care if you're naked."

Skye turned away before Noah walked in. Her eyes stung, so

she knew they had to be red. Her face was probably splotchy and her nose a shade Rudolph would wear with pride. Crying never looked good on her, just one of many reasons she avoided it.

"You want to talk about it?" Noah offered as the door clicked closed. He knew her too well. Even after five years with no contact, he still knew her. He had never let her hide, and that obviously hadn't changed.

"I told you I'd be down in a minute."

"Skye, I know you think you have to handle whatever it is you're going through on your own, but you don't."

Her mirthless laugh echoed in the room as she turned to him. "What do you know about it? You've never left the tranquility of this town. Not everywhere in the world has perfect sunsets or crimeless streets, or—"

"No, not everywhere is as nice as home. I'm not so naive that I don't know that."

Skye hated herself for lashing out at him, but anger was her only defense and it put a wall up around the pain. She couldn't tell Noah what she'd done, what she'd lost, couldn't bear his pity, or worse, his blame. Most of all, Skye didn't want to hear that she'd get through this, that everything would be all right. Three soldiers were dead because of her. The man she loved had died and Skye couldn't even go to his funeral because no one knew, no one could know, that she'd fallen in love with her platoon leader.

"I don't think this is a good idea. I should just stay home tonight." Noah didn't deserve her anger. He'd never done anything except be honest. Five years ago that honesty broke her heart, but it wasn't his fault. He was a good man, just like Rafe.

"You're not staying in this room and feeling sorry for yourself," he said, his words as harsh as hers had been. "Maybe you're not ready to talk about what happened, but you sure as hell aren't going to stop living."

Skye wanted to argue, to tell him staying in this room wasn't avoiding life, but the truth burned as bright and persistent as the sunrise on the edge of morning. "You can't fix me, Noah," she said, wishing she could collapse on the bed and never wake up.

"You're not broken." His stern voice resembled a drill sergeant commanding a new recruit to do one more push up, but the words fell short of the truth. Skye was broken everywhere, in body and spirit.

The metal pins and woven scars were proof of her broken body. The hollowness in her chest and the fog she longed to lose herself in provided the proof of her broken spirit. She couldn't escape the pain, not even here in her childhood home, with her childhood best friend.

She hadn't touched Rafe in months, but he was there, his fingerprints forever burned into her skin, his death the scars marring her frail body. The reminders would never go away, no matter how far she ran.

"I am broken," Skye whispered, dropping her head to avoid looking at the man who had once been the most important person in her life. "You should get away while you can. There's no hope for me."

Noah closed the distance between them, gripping Skye's arms in his firm hands. The touch wasn't meant to be intimate, but it sparked a tingle of awareness, rendering Skye's broken body needy and confused.

"Look at me," he demanded in a soft whisper. When Skye didn't comply, he gripped her arms with a possessive hold and raised his voice. "Look at me, Skye."

Skye looked up expecting to see sadness, even disappointment in Noah's blue eyes. Instead, she saw the love they'd shared as friends for as long as she could remember.

His expression softened, the tight line of his lips curving into a warm smile that spoke more than his words. "There's always hope. Always."

Chapter 5

There's hope I know
Out on that lonely road ...
-Brokenpromiseland, Bon Jovi

Hope.

Skye had clung to it more than once in her life. More than once it burned her.

Last time she was home, she'd risked it all, telling Noah the truth and hoping he felt the same.

During that last deployment, she'd hoped twelve months would pass without tragedy.

When she awoke in the hospital in Germany and learned of Rafe's death, she'd hoped to die too.

Hope only led to heartache and loneliness and broken promises.

Now, sitting on Noah's porch, the word continued to echo in her mind like the lyrics of a song that touched your soul. A tiny piece of her wanted to reach out and pull it close, demand it live up to her expectations. If nothing else, Skye was a realist. Hope would only ever lead to disappointment.

"How come you aren't using your cane?" Noah asked as he flipped the steaks on the charcoal grill.

"I don't need it." Skye tried to speak casually, to hide the surging anger. Looked like her mother had given Noah a full report of what she should and shouldn't be doing according to the all-knowing doctors who didn't have a damn clue.

"You were on crutches this afternoon," he pointed out, looking over his shoulder.

Skye shrugged and Noah went back to babying the steaks.

He had a great house, a small ranch style with a walk-out basement. Skye sat in a wooden rocker of the porch built over the walk-out. She remembered this house from when they were kids. It had been in shambles and Noah bought it for next to nothing, investing more money into gutting and renovating it than into purchase price.

There was a path through the woods to the river about half a mile away and another path that led to the old railroad tracks that had been converted to an ATV trail. Sitting on a hill, Skye enjoyed the view of the lake sparkling in the distance under the twilight sky.

Part of Noah's renovations included the porch. The recessed lighting had a dimmer switch for ambiance and the built in speakers played Bon Jovi — no surprise — at a low level that still allowed for conversation.

Skye closed her eyes and let the music ease into her mind. She'd been harassed in Afghanistan for listening to Bon Jovi. People who didn't follow the band would say things like, "they're still together?" or "you like 80's hair bands?"

Early in her career — she cringed at the word, knowing her beloved career was now a failure she'd regret for the rest of her life — Skye had defended her love of the band and the music. As she grew older however, gaining experience in how to handle difficult and unwanted situations, and learning the power of tact and silence, she'd shrugged off or ignored the comments. People who didn't love the music didn't understand its power, the connection it provided to something larger than life.

For Skye, the music had always been a symbol of hope, guiding her forward when the world tried to knock her down. She had continued to listen to Bon Jovi even though it reminded her of Noah. He was the only person she knew who loved the band as much as she did.

"Can we listen to something else?" Skye asked, not wanting to tango again with hope. She was in too much pain to dance. Nor did she want to give hope any power since it always seemed to let her down.

Noah hit a button on the remote and it skipped to the next song.

"I meant different music," she said.

Noah looked at her like she had three heads. "You don't want to listen to Bon Jovi?"

Skye shrugged. "Not really."

"Why not?" he asked, clearly perplexed.

"It's kind of juvenile, don't you think? Then again, I guess that's normal for you. You cling to the past as if you don't have anything else to hang on to."

Skye swallowed the bile that rose in her throat. The hateful words came out of nowhere. She was as shocked to hear them as she was disgusted to have said them. Now that they were out, she couldn't take them back, but she also wouldn't apologize. Noah had forced her here. She didn't want his company, didn't want to push away the hope she couldn't embrace. Skye just wanted to go to sleep and wake up eight months in the past, to a time when she could change the course of her future and keep Rafe alive.

When the hurt played across Noah's face, Skye wanted to dial back to that time five years ago, when she'd laid her heart out in front of him and he'd pushed it aside. She wanted to go back to that time, to change the event that destroyed their friendship.

Noah tossed the spatula on the table next to the grill and crossed the porch to where Skye braced herself for a fight. He loomed over her, but Skye wasn't intimidated. She knew Noah, knew his gentle soul. He would never hurt her, at least not physically. She was too broken and scattered for him to hurt her emotionally.

"I remember the past so I can learn from it. You can try to ignore it all you want Skye, but that isn't going to help you move forward."

"Choosing not to dwell on it isn't ignoring it," she argued.

"Spin it however you want. That doesn't change what you're doing?"

"And just what am I doing, Mr. Righteous?"

He continued to loom over her. It was unlike Noah to fight back, even more unlike him to take the offensive like this.

"Have you talked to anyone, Skye, about the explosion? About the pain you're in?"

"I'm fine," she spat. "I don't need to talk to anyone." Nor did she want to. Skye didn't even want to remember that horrific day, she wasn't about to relive it by giving it a voice.

"You're not fine. You can barely walk. Your parents are worried that you're over-medicating. You never come out of your room, a place you despised when you lived here, so you're hiding instead of dealing with—"

"Dealing with what? My injuries? You talk like you know something about it? Have you ever been in an explosion, Noah? Have you ever been in a vehicle that was shredded to pieces, along with the people inside it? No, you haven't, because you've never left this stupid town."

Noah laughed, a mirthless sound that told Skye she'd hit the target. "What pisses you off more? That you were forced to come back here or that I didn't leave with you when you asked me to?"

Skye choked on the sob the memory inspired. She had never been the type to nurse a broken heart with tears. When hurting, she liked to break things. As a teenager, she had a special baseball bat perfect for hitting bottles. It had started out as target practice, hitting

33

rocks at the bottles, but it had grown into a direct assault where she'd lash out directly, striking the bottles with the bat and shattering the heartache into a million pieces that got lost in the dirt and grass.

That changed with Noah because he didn't qualify as some stupid guy. He was her best friend, her soul mate. When she'd told him she was in love with him and asked him to leave with her, and he'd said no, he loved Maddie, she'd cried all the way back to Fort Carson. How ironic, given that Carson was also Maddie's last name.

Unable to bear the anger and hurt on his face, she looked away, toward the lake where darkness had taken hold and turned the water to a mysterious shade of gray.

"Goddammit," Noah murmured, storming back to the grill. Skye recognized the sound of the opening lid and the scrape of the spatula. When the cover dropped closed, she jumped, a dead weight filling her chest.

"Shit," Noah cursed louder this time, his footsteps light as he moved back to where Skye held her head high. "I'm sorry."

The microburst of anger replaced the regret, followed by a surge of smoke and ash from a dormant volcano rushing to the surface and propelling her out of the chair.

"I didn't mean to startle you," he explained.

She didn't want his apology, or his sympathy, and it was obvious that's the turn Noah had taken. "I'm fine," she snarled, focusing on the anger as a way to ignore the rising pain.

His hand touched her cheek, a gentle caress that shot straight to her heart and angered Skye even more. She knocked his hand away.

Noah's lips curled between his teeth before he took a deep breath. "We both know you're not fine, Skye. You can try to ignore it, but I'm not going to."

Coming here was such a bad idea. Noah liked to fix things. He always had. He always went for the girls who were wounded and needed rescuing. Once they were fixed, he always got his heart broken.

"What do you want from me? To go sit on your girlfriend's couch and let my soul bleed until she declares I'm fine?"

Noah shook his head. "Maddie isn't my girlfriend. I'm not with anyone. I haven't been with anyone in a long time."

"I don't care," she said, turning from him so he couldn't see the truth and so she could try to ignore it. Because she did care and until this very moment, hadn't even realized it.

Skye didn't want to care. Caring led to hope and hope led to broken promises and shattered lives.

The air thickened as Noah's hands landed on her shoulder and moved down her arms before wrapping her in an embrace she didn't want but needed more than her next breath.

His arms were strong, his body solid, his touch warm. Skye thought she'd gotten over him, that falling for Rafe had patched the hole in her heart Noah had left, but standing here, letting his strength and warmth pour into her, she realized getting over Noah wasn't as simple as loving someone else.

"I'm sorry," she muttered. "Being home is … weird." It wasn't the right word, but it was safe and it kept Noah outside the wall she didn't want him or anyone else to get through. "I'm bitchy and you're an easy target."

"It's okay to let it go, Skye. You don't have to be an army of one when you're with me."

She smiled, knowing he quoted Bon Jovi lyrics and not the army's old motto.

"Been to any concerts lately?" Skye asked, choosing a lighter topic so she didn't have to make any false promises.

Noah stepped back. "Since they haven't been on tour, no, but I have tickets for the concert in Montreal in a couple of weeks. You should go with me."

She plastered a fake smile on her face, hoping he bought it but knowing he didn't as the concern furrowed his brow. "I have tickets, and someone to go with."

"Who?" he asked, surprised and if she had to guess, a little hurt.

Skye shook her head. She'd been to Montreal before. The arena was big enough that she and Noah probably wouldn't be seated near each other. He would have bought the most expensive tickets, right near the stage. Since Skye couldn't stand for long periods of time, she'd bought 200 level tickets so she could sit and still see the show. If she worked the right strategy, she wouldn't see Noah at all and wouldn't have to tell him who she was taking. "No one you know. Someone I know from the army."

The lie left a bitter taste in her mouth and she took a long drink to wash it away.

His eyes narrowed as if he recognized the lie. Skye breathed a sigh of relief when he didn't push for the truth. "Well, maybe we can get together before the show for dinner."

Skye nodded. "Yeah, maybe."

Noah returned to the grill, pulling the steaks and corn off the fire and bringing them to the large table that could have seated her entire squad.

"I have an apartment in the basement," he said as he dropped one of the steaks on her plate. "I've been using it for storage, but you're welcome to live there. You might be happier there than at your parents' house."

Skye looked at him, searching for a hidden motive in that offer. Her parents were good people. She loved them and appreciated their support. Skye had always been independent and since she was the only daughter, her parents had always tried to reel in that independence. While her older brothers seemed to have all the freedom, Skye felt like she'd been raised under martial law. It still felt that way.

"My pay is screwed up," she told Noah. "I can't pay rent until that gets straightened out."

He smiled. "I'm not worried about the rent."

"I'm not a charity case," she argued.

Noah held up a hand. "I know. What I'm saying, is we can square the rent once your pay gets straightened out."

The offer was appealing. Having her own apartment would give Skye the independence she didn't have now. She hated being under the microscope and even though Noah would also try to keep a watchful eye on her, they wouldn't share any common space. She'd have her own kitchen, own bathroom, own living space.

"Thanks. Let me think about it," she said, only because she didn't want to seem too anxious. There were still old wounds to mend and Skye had to decide if her freedom was worth exposing those scars.

Chapter 6

With these two hands
I can tear down walls
I can build a bridge,
I can break my fall.
-These Two Hands, Bon Jovi

Paranoia.

It had crept in like an undetected insurgent, burrowing its theories into Skye's brain until she dangled on the edge of reason. Now, she had reached the point where even the slightest shift would send her toppling off the cliff, falling into an abyss of accusations and a reality she couldn't face.

It had been less than a week since Noah offered his basement apartment. As Skye stared at the half empty bottle of pills, moving out of her parent's house and into Noah's seemed the lesser of two evils. Amelia hovered and fussed over Skye every waking moment. Skye had taken to pretending to nap just to get a reprieve.

She had another week until the appointment at the VA. The pills she had left were not going to be enough to get her through. When she'd discovered that little predicament a few hours ago, she'd decided to take control back from her mother.

While Skye couldn't prove Amelia had disposed of the pills, she also couldn't blatantly accuse the woman of taking them either. That accusation, if false, could reveal too many truths, truths Skye wasn't ready for the world to know.

Somewhere deep inside, where the combat wounds hadn't reached her soul, but the scars kept her strength from creeping out, Skye knew Amelia hadn't touched the pills.

She just wasn't strong enough to accept what that really meant.

So, she blamed her mother, because it was easy and on the surface, it made perfect sense. Amelia had come into Skye's room and taken the pills while she slept.

The anger bubbled up. Skye never should have waited to move out. While she'd been going for self-preservation when it came to Noah, a small part of staying at her parents' was to spare hurting their feelings, particularly Amelia's. Skye was sure her dad wouldn't care about where she lived as long as she had a roof over her head. Unless of course, he had helped Amelia steal the pills, as a way to keep Skye under lock and key, to monitor and control her every move.

Skye stuffed the bottle back in her bag and sent Noah a text, letting him know she wanted the apartment and she'd be there in an hour.

She didn't have much to pack, just some clothes and essentials. Her household goods wouldn't arrive until the end of the month. Skye had planned to put everything in storage until she was on her feet again, so really, moving out now just saved that hassle and expense.

Everything she wanted to take fit into two army duffel bags.

Skye weighed the pros and cons of taking both of them in one trip to the car or taking two trips. Physically, it was six in one, half a dozen of the other. One trip with two bags presented a challenge, but two trips down and up the stairs could prove just as draining. Two trips would also give her mother more time to whine over Skye's decision.

One trip it was.

She lifted the bags, happy for their equal weight and hoping the even distribution kept her balanced.

She took the stairs one slow step at a time, breathing through the shooting pain up her right leg and trying to ignore the way the burn scars on her torso tugged so tight they threatened to unravel.

There were fifteen steps and she counted them one at a time just like she'd counted paces in the field.

By the time she reached the bottom, she panted as if just finishing the final sprint of a two-mile run for the army's physical training test. From experience, Skye knew it was ten paces to the front door, three across the porch, down the three steps, and another twenty paces to her car. She wasn't going to be able to do them without taking a rest, so she dropped the bags and focused on breathing.

"Skye, what are you doing?" Amelia asked from down the hall. Skye had hoped to get out without facing her mother. She had planned to call after settling into Noah's apartment.

"Noah offered me his basement apartment. I've decided to move in there."

Her mother's eyes widened with horror as she looked at the bags at Skye's feet. "Were you just going to sneak out?"

Skye shook her head. "I was just taking my things to the car."

"Did you just carry those bags down here?"

"I'm fine, Ma. I need to build my strength. That was a good exercise."

"That was stupid, Skye. You're not ready for that kind of physical exertion."

The ongoing argument irked Skye. Her mother wanted to coddle her and she had been making Skye crazy with the constant pestering and concern. Skye knew how to pick her fights. Engaging her mother in this one would be as useless as engaging insurgents who had you out-manned, out-gunned, and out-maneuvered. Sometimes retreat was the better option. Live to fight another day.

"You promised, Skye. You promised to come home and let us take care of you."

Skye had broken promises to her mother as a child because that's what children did. This, however, was not breaking a promise.

"Ma, I promised to move home, to Sunset Valley. I didn't promise to live in this house."

"You promised to move home, Skye. This house is your home."

Skye couldn't believe Amelia succumbed to tears over this. It wasn't like she was going off to war. She was moving across town, to her own apartment, like a grown-up.

"This *was* my home. I'm an adult now. I need to be out on my own. I'm too old to live with Mommy and Daddy." On a normal day, Amelia brought out the worst in Skye. She wasn't sure what normal looked like anymore, but it couldn't be this.

Her mother had fallen into a full-blown temper tantrum. "I'm calling your father," Amelia declared.

"Go ahead, Ma. I'll see you later."

"Skye, please," she pleaded.

Turning to face her mother, Skye almost fell over at the sadness on Amelia's face.

Skye blinked back her own tears as she realized what Amelia must be feeling. "This," Skye swept both hands down her broken body, "it isn't your fault."

Amelia shook her head. "But it is. I drove you away. You joined the army to get away from me. I never should have let you go. It was too dangerous. I thought you'd serve your four years and come home and maybe then you would want to be here."

"You didn't drive me away," Skye sighed. It wasn't a total lie. She had never wanted to stay in Sunset Valley. The town was too small. She didn't have the grades to get into college and her parent's didn't have the money. The army had always appealed to her. It offered a steady paycheck and travel. While she didn't like that the travel included two rotations in Afghanistan, she had enjoyed her time in Hawaii and Germany.

"Kids grow up, move out. It's the natural order of things."

"But you're the baby," Amelia cried. "My baby girl."

Skye hated being referred to as the baby, but she didn't want to argue with her mother. No doubt news of the explosion had been painful for her family to endure, as had seeing Skye in that hospital bed at Walter Reed, covered in bandages and hooked up to all of those monitors. She was back on her feet now and while that was more painful for Skye than the time in the hospital, this burden was hers to bear — her penance, so to speak. If she'd been a better soldier instead of a lovesick fool, the explosion wouldn't have happened. She'd be back at Ft. Hood. Everything would be normal.

Unsure how to comfort her mother, Skye said the only words she thought would help. "I love you, Ma, but I need to do this. I need to rebuild my life, my way." She picked up the two duffel bags, hoping the weight provided balance while hobbling the short distance to her car.

Because she'd been spending so much time in her room hiding out from her mother, Skye wasn't in a lot of pain, but that didn't make the front steps any easier.

"Can I at least carry your bags?" Amelia asked from behind Skye.

Even before the explosion, Skye wasn't one to ask for help. Now, dealing with these injuries, she was even more determined to do everything on her own. The task ahead seemed impossible. Falling down the stairs with the two bags in hand and with her mother watching would be beyond humiliating. Amelia's plea offered Skye an out that didn't force her to ask for help. Instead, she'd be helping Amelia cope with the sudden departure.

"Sure," Skye said, bending both knees and swallowing the

painful cry as the pins in her thigh and hip reminded her they were there to punish her for being an irresponsible soldier.

Even the scars on her torso pulled as she set the bags on the steps.

"What can I do, honey?" Amelia asked.

"I'm fine," Skye barked, straightening her knees and stepping down. She almost stumbled on the last step, but caught herself and kept walking, blinking away the tears and breathing through the pain while counting the steps to the car.

Amelia placed the two bags in the trunk as Skye bore the pain of lowering herself into the driver's seat. Skye smiled as her mother stood there. She didn't want to burden Amelia with her pain, nor did she want her mother weighed down with guilt. Skye put the window down. "I'll talk to you later, okay?"

The tears pooling in Amelia's eyes pushed Skye to put the car in gear. She had never been good with tears, not her own and not other people's, especially her mother's.

After pulling onto the street, she drove to the intersection and turned left, stopping at the shopping center on Main Street. She pulled into a spot in an empty corner of the lot and dug for the bottle of pills stuffed in her messenger bag. Skye couldn't remember how long it had been since the last dose, but if the pain offered any indication, it had been hours. She popped two in her mouth and swallowed.

At this rate, she would need to see Finn again. Since her pay hadn't been straightened out, Skye shuddered at the thought. His hands on her, in her, it was like being touched by the devil himself. Finn would like that analogy, but it made Skye sick. It might be hell, but she'd find a way to survive on the pills she had because no way could she walk down that treacherous path with Finn again.

Chapter 7

We stared at the sun and
we made a promise
A promise this world
would never blind us.
-In These Arms, Bon Jovi

Promises.

They meant everything to Noah and while he'd never broken any with Skye, he had hurt her and to him that was just as treacherous.

Hoping she'd accept his offer, Noah had enlisted his cousin Luke's help last Sunday to move the guest bed into the basement and get all the items he'd been storing down there moved into the loft over the garage. Now, Noah rocked in the chair on the patio, his fingers tapping on the hard wood while waiting for Skye to arrive.

When her car pulled onto the lawn, he smiled with surprise. Even though he'd told her to park down there, he didn't think she would. Skye was stubborn that way, and would have used the excuse of preserving the grass to hide her own self-preservation.

As she came to a stop and leaned her head on the steering

wheel, Noah bolted out of the chair to where she parked, nearly tearing the car door off its hinges. "Skye," he said, but she didn't respond.

"Skye," he said more loudly, giving her shoulder a shake.

"I'm fine, Noah. Back off."

There was that word again, *fine*. She said it often, too often, and Noah hadn't believed it a single time. She'd been through a lot, more than he could imagine, and was trying to cope with the aftermath of it all. Based on what little he knew about the explosion and her injuries, she was far from fine.

"What do you need?" he asked, hoping she'd swallow that stubborn pride and let him help.

She leaned back in the seat and looked up at him, a haunting smile sending a shiver up his spine. "Noah, hi," she said as though she hadn't just told him to back off.

Her pupils were constricted as if the sun shined down from a cloudless sky, but the weather was quite the opposite, the thick clouds bringing a darkness that made it seem like early evening rather than mid-afternoon.

He didn't dare ask if she was drunk, or worse, high, so he leaned into the car and pressed a quick kiss to her cheek, breathing in to try and detect the smell of alcohol.

He caught the spicy orange scent of her hair and a powder smell that might have been deodorant, but no alcohol. The long, slow breaths didn't seem right either. "You seem out of sorts," he said as he stood. "Are you okay?"

As her eyes narrowed, the warm smile faded. She just stared at him before shaking her head. "I took a pain pill when I left the house. Sometimes they make me a little loopy. I'm fine."

The words were spoken at a slow pace, deliberate, maybe thought out. Could be from the meds. Amelia and Ken were concerned about prescription drug addiction because the doctors at Walter Reed warned them of the risk. As Noah thought about the first day he'd seen her, when she claimed to run into Finn at the drug store, his concern grew.

"Let's get you inside," he insisted, holding out his hand.

"I can do it," she said, smacking his hand. Noah took a step back, giving her a little space but keeping his proximity close enough that he could step back in to help if she needed it. Once she was standing, she seemed to take a moment to test her balance.

Then she gave him a look that told him to back off.

Noah wanted to take her hand, but he figured she'd just smack it away again, so he ambled off, letting her come up next to him.

"Do you have anything with you?" he asked.

"A couple duffel bags. They're in the trunk. I'll get them later."

Noah would get them before she had a chance, but he didn't bother to tell her that knowing it would only trigger her stubborn attitude.

"It's a studio style apartment. I didn't want to build walls because of where the windows are, but otherwise it has everything you need."

"I'm sure it's great," she said, smiling at him again.

Skye had the most beautiful smile he'd ever seen, but what he saw now was not the natural smile he had loved. It was almost lethargic.

He held the door and followed her in, directing her through a doorway to the left. "Oh, Noah, this is fantastic."

"Thanks," he said, proud of his work. When he'd bought the house, the basement was just concrete. He'd built the wall to block off the stairs and built a wall to close off the boiler room and another to close off the laundry room. "I need to install a door, but I only come down here to do laundry, so I can just give you advance warning until I get the door up."

A small kitchenette, equipped with a sink, stove, and refrigerator occupied one corner. He'd set the bed in the back corner. "The bathroom is back there," he said, pointing to the corner opposite the bed. "I built it there to help insulate the rest of the room from the boiler noise."

"You did all this on your own?" she asked.

"Luke helps when I need it. He renovated his old man's place, too, so between the two of us, we figure out how to get the work done."

"I like it," she said, turning to him with sleepy eyes and that haunting smile. "Thanks again for offering it."

"My pleasure. It'll be nice to have you around. I've missed you."

The Skye he had known and loved his whole life wasn't outwardly affectionate or generous with affectionate words, but those who made it to her inner circle were blessed with a reserved affection that made the recipient feel special. She'd never been afraid to tell Noah she missed him or loved him, at least until admitting she was in love with him. Once she'd done that, and Noah hadn't reciprocated, she'd shut him out. He hoped his declaration now wouldn't push her away or rekindle the bitterness.

"I've missed you, too." The quiet words should have thrilled Noah, but without the beautiful smile, they filled his heart with worry. Skye focused on the room instead of looking at him. "Thanks for the bed. My household goods should be here by the end of the month, if the army doesn't screw that up too."

"No worries, Skye. No one is using it."

"It's been a busy afternoon. I'm going to take a nap."

Noah wanted to hug her, to pull her into his arms and convince her everything was going to be fine, but he reeled in the urge and let her step to the bed. "I'm just upstairs if you need anything."

She waved without turning and fell onto the bed. Noah stepped out, but instead of going upstairs, went to the car to grab the bags. When he came back, she was in the same position, lying on her stomach, her left foot hanging off the bed.

"Skye," he nudged, not wanting to startle her. She didn't

move.

He crossed the room to check her breathing and found her head turned to the right. Her breaths were still slow, but that seemed normal for someone sleeping. Amelia had told him Skye took Vicodin. He'd read up on it and drowsiness was a side effect, so he figured that's what had made her so sleepy.

Returning to the car, Noah grabbed her purse from the front seat and removed the keys from the ignition. On his way back in, he snagged a patio chair, unwilling to leave her alone.

A couple hours later, she started tossing and turning, muttering words he couldn't understand until she sat bolt upright, screaming, "Rafe!"

Noah bolted across the room, dropping onto the bed next to her. He put his arms around her and she tried to fight him off, kicking and screaming.

"Skye, wake up. It's me, Noah. I've got you. You're home now. You're safe."

She stopped flailing, but Noah didn't let go of her shaking body. He kissed her temple, continuing to whisper reassuring words as he held her.

"Shit," she muttered after a while, pushing out of his hold. She stumbled as she stood, as if her leg had given out. Noah caught her, earning himself a glare that would have sent a T-Rex running for safety.

"You okay?" he asked.

"I'm fine," she said.

Noah laughed with frustration. "You need to come up with a better response, because I'm not buying any of your *I'm fine* bullshit."

"Fuck you, Noah. How's that for a response?" She pushed out of his hold and limped across the room to the sink where she splashed cold water on her face.

"How long was I out?" she asked.

"A couple hours."

She turned to face him, water dripping from her face. "You've been watching me sleep?"

Noah nodded. "I wanted to make sure you were okay."

"That's kind of stalkerish, don't you think?"

Was that a joke? Skye had a great sense of humor, dry and sardonic, but he hadn't seen it in the small amount of time they'd spent together since she'd come home. "New hobby of mine," he retorted.

"Maybe you should find a hobby that won't land you in jail or with a boot in your crotch."

He cringed at the thought. "I'll keep that in mind. Are you hungry? It's almost six."

She seemed surprised by that. "I could eat if you're grilling."

"I've got chicken," he said, happy for her suggestion. It was one less battle he'd have to fight with her.

"I'm just going to grab a shower and then I'll come up. You're not a peeping Tom, too, are you?"

"Just stalking," he laughed. "I brought your bags in. I'll see you upstairs when you're ready."

She nodded and smiled. It didn't reach her eyes, but also wasn't the haunting smile that had worried him.

Noah fired up the grill and pulled out the chicken and the vegetables he planned to grill beside them. He also hit the Bon Jovi playlist he'd put together for Skye. It included all her favorite songs with a few additions Noah thought might get through that stubborn exterior and reach the reasonable person inside.

Dinner was almost ready to come off the grill when she appeared. Noah suspected the timing was deliberate, a means to avoid conversation, but she was here now and he hadn't had to convince her to be, so that was something.

"Do you think we can eat inside?" she asked.

"Sure. Not a fan of the rain?" The porch was well protected, but not warm. He planned to buy the outside heaters, but hadn't worked that into his budget yet.

"The cold bothers my hip," she said and the small admission floored Noah.

When he brought the food inside, the table was set and she sat in the chair facing the door. He was about to tell her she didn't have to set the table, but knew that wouldn't be well received, so instead just placed the platter on the table and took the seat facing her.

"Dig in," he said.

Skye did, devouring everything on the plate as if she hadn't been fed in years. Last week, she'd picked at the steak. Since she'd never been one of those women who worried about her size or denied herself food, he'd been surprised to see her so thin. Maybe she just needed a good meal prepared for her.

Since Noah loved to cook, he was happy to be the one to do that.

They ate in silence, each of them clearing their plates. "You want dessert?" he asked, knowing a tub of Ben and Jerry's waited in the freezer.

Skye laughed and shook her head. "No, I'm good. I haven't eaten like that in ..." Her words trailed off and that beautiful smile faded.

Noah reached across the table and took her hand, but Skye jerked it away. "Don't," she snarled.

Pulling his hand back, Noah smiled. "Do you remember when we were fourteen? We hiked up to my uncle's hunting cabin in the woods?"

Skye chuckled, turning her left hand over and tracing the scar on her palm that matched the one on Noah's right hand.

"We listened to *Blood on Blood* and cut our hands."

"And promised to always be friends, to always be there for each other, no matter what," Noah reminded her.

She stopped tracing the thick scar and clenched her fist, prompting Noah to get up from his chair and stand next to her.

When he held up his hand, she just stared at it. A range of emotions swept across her face so fast Noah couldn't identify them all, but he saw the hope and couldn't ignore the fear that seemed to linger.

"We promised," he reiterated.

She looked up at him then. "We're not fourteen anymore. We're not kids."

"No, we're not, but I'd still hike up to that cabin with you and cut my hand again."

Skye shook her head and looked away as if she didn't believe him. Maybe she didn't want to. "Look at me," he whispered.

To his surprise, she did. Tears pooled in her eyes, her anger so potent it nearly brought him to his knees. "I hated you," she whispered. "I poured my heart out and all you could say was that you loved Maddie and couldn't leave."

Her words did bring him to his knees. "I never meant to hurt you. I loved you, Skye. I loved you so much it hurt. Every time you left, it ripped my heart to pieces. Then I found Maddie and the hurt was bearable, because she was hurting too. She understood because her brother was doing exactly what you were doing."

"I got over you, you know. I got over you and found someone else."

Noah's heart dropped into his stomach like the dead weight of a brick in water. Her parents had never mentioned anyone, and he was sure they would have. "Are you still with him?" he asked, his stomach turning as she scratched at her ring finger. He hadn't noticed a mark there, but she'd been in the hospital for eight months. They might not have allowed her to wear a ring, so a mark would be long gone.

Then he remembered the name she'd screamed during that nightmare. *Rafe*.

She shook her head, tears streaming down her cheeks.

"Do you want to talk about him?" he asked, selfishly hoping she didn't. The last thing Noah wanted to know about was a man in her life, but they couldn't get past this barrier without each of them sacrificing something.

"No, Noah, I don't want to talk about him. I don't want to think about him. I don't even want to remember him."

Chapter 8

Now your pictures that you left behind
Are just memories of a different life,
Some that made us laugh,
Some that made us cry,
One that made you have to say goodbye.
-Always, Bon Jovi

Avoidance.

It stayed by her side as she stomped off to the living room, the only weapon Skye had against the assault of feelings and memories threatening to crush her heart and destroy her very soul.

It took effort, every second of every day, not to think about Rafe, but being around Noah stirred the memories and the hurt and so much more.

Her anger ratcheted up a notch when she crossed the room and saw all the pictures on the sideboard against the wall.

Her senior portrait. Her army portrait. Snapshots of her and Noah. It looked like a shrine, a hopeful, humiliating shrine.

He moved across the open space, his steps slow but sure, holding up his scarred hand. She knew what he wanted. Skye couldn't give it to him.

"Stop it," she demanded.

"No. That promise wasn't a stupid stunt by two kids. We sealed those words with our blood because we loved each other, just as we always had. Maybe you don't want to give me another chance with your heart, Skye. Maybe I don't deserve another chance, but we promised no matter what, we'd always friends. Always."

"I know what we promised," she sobbed, hating how easily he broke her down, leaping past her walls with ease.

"I'm not going to back down because you're stubborn and think you need to do this on your own."

Skye turned back to the pictures. She had the same ones and for a long time they'd been on display. She'd even taken one on her first deployment. When that deployment finished without incident, she packed all the pictures up, ready to move on with her life. She'd gambled with her heart and lost, but that didn't mean she couldn't pick up the pieces and glue them back together.

She was strong, after all. Strong and independent. She could survive on her own. If only she'd stuck to that mission, instead of letting Rafe steal her heart.

Her hip throbbed, the pain pulsing down her leg. She was stupid to leave the pills downstairs, stupid not to take a couple before coming up. She thought after a long nap and a hot shower she'd be fine, after all, sitting didn't bother her as much as standing and moving around.

"What is this?" she asked, waving at the pictures. "What do you see when you look at all these?"

"I see us," he said.

"I see history," she hissed. A history that had gotten her nowhere except alone.

"I see friendship, hope. Most of all, I see love. You said it, Skye. You said all those years you'd been in love with me, but you were too scared to risk our friendship for it. You were too scared until you were looking down the barrel of a gun."

"That's what I said," she muttered. She had buried those words and the memory that accompanied them so deep it had become a blur, a memory she could tolerate but didn't have to acknowledge.

"What I didn't say was that it was the same for me. I first realized it at our junior prom."

"Junior prom?" she asked. He had a girlfriend then, one of the many girls he set out to rescue from a tragic life. Skye couldn't even recall which tragic girl it was, but remembered they broke up that summer.

"I was pissed you went with Finn."

Skye winced at the name, more recent memories of Finn pushing to the surface, bringing with them the shame of what she'd done.

"So you were pissed. Finn's an asshole. Everyone was pissed I went with him."

"I was more pissed than anyone, not because I knew he was a prick, but because I was jealous. He got to dance with you, hold you, take you home and kiss you goodnight."

Except Finn didn't take her home and kiss her goodnight. He'd left in the middle of prom with another girl, leaving Skye humiliated and alone. "We both know that didn't happen," she added.

"No, and as much as it killed me to see you so hurt, I was relieved. It was the first time I'd ever been jealous of anyone. I knew why, it wasn't just who you were with, it was that you were with someone. I wanted you to be with me."

"Why didn't you..." she couldn't even finish the question. How would that have changed things for them?

"Why didn't I say anything? I was terrified. I didn't think you felt the same way. You always went after the jerks, the stereotypical bad boys. I wasn't even on your radar."

Noah had always been on her radar, but there were so many factors against them. Not only were they always on a pendulum, but

55

Skye was too scared to risk their friendship. Noah had never even hinted at wanting anything more than friendship, so she kept those feelings locked deep inside. She wanted him in her life but had never been willing to gamble on their friendship for the sake of something more. At least not until that first deployment.

A different kind of fear had pushed her to lay her heart on the table. If she'd gone to Afghanistan and not come home, she at least wanted Noah to know that her love had gone so much deeper than friendship. It raced through her veins, as if he'd somehow gotten in that day when they'd sealed their promise to each other with a blood bond.

The humiliation was what rushed through her veins now, shame and guilt hot on its trail. Skye wanted to run, but avoiding it now was futile. Everything she'd worked so hard to bury dug its way to the surface. It pumped through her so hard and fast that when she looked at the photos on the shelf, she only saw red. There was no hope for her and Noah because there was no hope for her.

Screaming to release the pressure, she swept her arms across the shelf, sending the framed pictures flying across the room until they shattered on the floor.

"Jesus Christ," Noah cursed. "Don't move."

Skye shook herself out of the chaos, startled by the destruction. Shards of glass trapped her. With no shoes, she could either stay put or bleed all over Noah's floor.

"Goddammit, Skye. Do. Not. Move."

"Noah," she said, stunned by what she'd done.

"Promise me. Promise me right now that you will not move an inch."

Her head still shook. Skye pressed her fingertips into her skull to still the madness.

"Promise me, Skye," Noah pleaded.

She opened her eyes to see the terror on his face. "I promise," she said, breathing through a sob of her own terror.

People always called her stubborn. While Skye would never

describe herself that way, she didn't disagree with that assessment. She wasn't violent, though. A little temperamental maybe, but never destructive.

She caught a glimpse of herself in the glass cabinet filled with pictures of Noah's family and trinkets. She didn't recognize the face staring back. "I don't even know who I am anymore," she muttered.

The swooshing of a broom had her turning to see Noah clearing a path through the living room to the kitchen. After rolling the shard-covered throw rug, he leaned the broom against the wall and stepped up to her, reaching for her left hand.

Noah peeled her fingers open, loosening the fist clenched so tight her knuckles screamed when the blood rushed back to them. He traced the scar before pressing his lips to it.

Whatever stubbornness Skye had been harboring melted, a rush of something she didn't want to acknowledge surging through her. Noah placed his right palm to her left. They'd cut their palms to mirror each other, specifically for this purpose. It was their own secret handshake, and while it had seemed so innocent at fourteen, as their fingers wove together, it now whispered of intimacy, a new promise yet to be spoken.

Skye's entire body shook at that revelation. Intimate promises meant no secrets. Since she couldn't tell Noah any of the secrets locked in her vault, she'd have to break any promises made to him now.

The tenderness in his eyes almost shattered her resolve, but Skye drew in a deep breath, calling forth every ounce of strength she could manage, and pulled her hand from his.

"No," she whispered, unable to give any real voice to her decision. With another deep breath, she looked him in the eye. "I'm not the person I used to be. Afghanistan changed me, Noah. I'm broken beyond repair. You can't fix me and I'm not going to let you destroy yourself trying."

Stepping around him, she didn't care if she had to walk

across glass to escape. Skye didn't look back, knowing hurt filled his eyes.

"You're not broken," he said when she reached the basement door. "You're wounded and wounds heal over time."

She shook her head. Maybe the combat injuries would, but she'd always wear the scars, evidence that she'd failed the man she loved and the soldiers who depended on her to get them home. "Not all wounds heal, Noah. I don't expect you to understand that, but you do need to accept it."

Now Noah shook his head. "You're not a quitter. Neither am I."

With his smile, hope crept into her heart. Skye didn't have the strength to push it aside. Instead, she used it to get down the stairs and into bed where she sobbed until the memory of Noah's lips on her palm faded to the blackness of sleep.

Chapter 9

Don't be afraid to breathe,
Don't be afraid to hurt,
Don't be afraid to need.
-What About Now, Bon Jovi

Pain.

As if insisting Skye have a co-pilot, it throbbed and pulsed from knee to ribcage, keeping a steady beat that made it difficult to move, let alone drive a car.

The pain rode shotgun as a constant companion, but when she could take the pain meds, it sometimes hopped in the back seat. She'd learned, however, that she couldn't take any pills and drive. Since the VA hospital was an hour away, pain meds weren't an option today.

Well, unless she asked for help.

Asking Noah was out of the question. He seemed to have taken the hint that she wouldn't be his pet project, but if she gave him an inch, he'd be sure to take a mile. Skye couldn't bear to spend all that time with her mother. Amelia would insist on talking to the doctor personally and getting every grave detail so she could nag and nitpick over Skye's care.

There was always Finn, but asking him for help came with an even greater price.

That left two choices, Vaughn and Riley. They weren't overly protective for older brothers. Skye established early on in childhood that she could take care of herself. They had gotten along as well as siblings did when growing up, dishing out the appropriate brotherly torture and torment. She had no doubt either of them would drop what they were doing for the day and take her. The trouble lay in admitting she needed help.

She'd never been good at it. Asking for a ride, though, that shouldn't be a big deal.

Hitting Vaughn in her contacts, Skye hoped he could skip out on work for the day. "Yo, Sarge, good morning. Reveille's playing a little early isn't it?"

Vaughn had called her Sarge ever since they were kids because he claimed Skye was bossy and tossed around orders like a drill sergeant. Skye hated it as a kid, but had grown to find it endearing. Now it made her chest ache.

"Hi, Vaughn. I have an appointment at the VA hospital today. Do you think you could drive me? It's at nine, so we'd need to leave by eight."

"Hey, I'd love to."

"Thanks. I really appreciate it."

"It's not a problem. I'd love to spend some time with you. It's been too long."

Skye hadn't been home in five years, not since she'd humiliated herself with Noah. Since arriving in Sunset Valley three weeks ago, she'd kept a low profile, only seeing her brothers the first couple days. Skye despised the worry on their faces, so made efforts to avoid them, mostly by pretending to sleep when they stopped by her parents' house.

"Are you sure? I'm not pulling you away from work or something important?" she asked. Vaughn restored old cars and motorcycles out of a shop he owned in town.

Vaughn chuckled. "This is killing you, isn't it? Big, bad Sarge asking for help."

Skye sighed. "I knew this was a bad idea. Just forget it."

"Too late. I'm already heading out the door. You're at Noah's, right?"

She sighed again. "Yeah. How'd you know that?"

"This is Sunset Valley. Everyone knows."

Skye hated small towns and because her father was the school principal and Noah's father the police chief, they couldn't get away with anything while growing up.

And boy did they try.

"Be ready in twenty. I'll take you to the truck stop for breakfast."

Skye knew arguing with Vaughn would get her nowhere because no matter what she said, he'd be at her door in twenty minutes. Skye's stubbornness didn't hold a candle to Vaughn's persistence.

True to his word, Vaughn stood outside her door fifteen minutes later. He would have done well in the army with that kind of promptness. The army drilled into Skye in basic training, and reinforced timeliness at Ft. Polk, her first duty station, no matter what time you were told to be in formation, you were expected to be there ten minutes prior. Skye always thought it ridiculous spending so much time standing around waiting so that you could formally stand around and wait, but it was the nature of the beast. Since she'd lived that life for a dozen years, she'd been ready to go before her brother knocked on the door.

"You're not going to let me in?" Vaughn asked as she stepped outside. "Come on, Sarge. I want to see your new digs."

"There's nothing to see. It's an empty apartment. If I'm lucky, my household goods will arrive this century."

Skye didn't have a lot, but she still wanted her stuff. It would make the barren basement feel like home.

"I'll just scope it out when I bring you back."

Since Vaughn was taking her for breakfast, Skye opted to wait to take the Vicodin to avoid tossing it into an empty stomach. That meant the pain impeded her movement enough that she walked like Igor to the car. "I can't believe you still have this clunker," she laughed as she dropped into the '69 Shelby GT 350.

"Don't talk about Connie like that. You'll hurt her feelings." He had named the car after the 1969 Playmate of the Year when he learned she had received the same car when claiming the title. The car was a wreck when he bought it in high school, but he'd restored it and treated it better than his girlfriends. That explained why he was single.

"You read *Christine*, right? Or at least saw the movie since you never learned to read?" she joked.

"I don't care about your war injuries. I'll take you down just like when we were kids," he warned, giving her a nudge.

Skye held on to the humor of the moment instead of grappling with the anxiety her *war injuries* inspired. "I can still plant my knee in the family jewels," she said. As a kid, her only defense against two older brothers was to fight dirty. It turned out to be a good life lesson too.

Vaughn cringed as if she'd done just that. Then he cupped himself. "Don't worry fellas, she didn't mean it."

Skye smacked his arm. "Oh for the love of … do not grope yourself in front of me."

"I'm actually beside you, not in front of you."

"We haven't even made it out of the driveway and already I regret asking you to drive me. I should have called Ma."

Vaughn laughed then. "I'm pretty sure you would have thumbed it first, maybe even sold your soul to the devil before asking Ma."

Well, he was right about that and while his comment about selling her soul made Skye's stomach turn, she knew her brother didn't mean anything by it. Yes, this was Sunset Valley where everyone was in your business, but there's no way anyone could know about what she'd done with Finn. Vaughn wouldn't let it slide if he did know. He'd been the one to break Finn's nose after he'd ditched her at prom.

Skye reclined the seat, settling into the most comfortable position she could manage with the pain. She focused on breathing, drawing in a long breath through her nose and releasing it through her mouth.

"You okay?" Vaughn asked.

"Fine," she sighed, so tired of people asking. She thought leaving Walter Reed would give her a reprieve, but then her mother asked a million times a day, as if that was the only phrase she could utter.

"Is that what you're going to tell the doc today?"

Without turning, Skye glanced at Vaughn, but his gaze remained on the road. She had no idea what to say to the doctor. Mostly, she would put forth every effort not to scream when he asked how she was doing, the medical equivalent of asking if she was okay.

"According to Ma, 'fine' is your favorite word. She's not buying it. Neither am I."

"I asked for a ride, not the Everhart Inquisition."

"Well, you're in for a treat, then, because we're picking up Riley."

"Shit," Skye muttered, eliciting a chuckle from Vaughn. "How is it both of you happen to be free today?"

"You probably wouldn't believe me if I claimed it was a mere coincidence, huh?"

Skye shook her head. "Not in a million years."

Vaughn chuckled again, but didn't offer an explanation. He turned off the main road toward Riley's house. When they pulled up to his small cabin tucked in the woods, he sat on the front step.

"Hey, Sis," Riley said as he climbed in behind Vaughn. "Oh, man, the back seat sucks. We should take my Jeep."

"I won that coin toss fair and square," Vaughn retorted.

Skye didn't know how, but they had obviously manipulated this situation. "I hate you both."

"Ooh, I love this game," Riley said. "Where we say the opposite of what we really mean. I hate you, too, Skye."

Oh, brothers, it was going to be a long day.

Twenty minutes later, Skye struggled to get out of the old Shelby. It was low to the ground, but the pain was bad enough she couldn't push herself up. "We should have taken the Jeep," she muttered. It would be far easier to slide down from the Jeep than pull herself out of this beast.

"Told you," Riley said as he and Vaughn came around the car.

"It's the opposite game, dip-wad. She doesn't mean it."

Both brothers held out a hand. Swallowing what little pride she had left, Skye grabbed each of them and nearly bit a hole through her lower lip as they tugged her up.

"Jesus, Skye, aren't you taking something?" Vaughn cursed.

"I was … waiting to eat," she said, pinching her eyes closed to try and survive the stabbing pain in her hip and the burning throb in her side.

"I told you breakfast in bed was a better option," Riley offered.

"That's Noah's gig, not ours," Vaughn countered.

Skye's eyes snapped open. "What the hell does that mean?"

"Nothing," Vaughn muttered. "Let's get some grub so you can take your meds."

Vaughn and Riley tried to help her walk, but Skye shrugged them off. This wasn't the worst pain she'd ever experienced, though it defied the one to ten scale. Since that was close to normal, she could manage to get to the restaurant on her own.

"Did you bring it?" Riley asked.

"It's in the trunk," Vaughn responded, pushing the key into the slot and popping it open. He pulled out a cane.

"I don't need that," Skye bit out. She had left it at her parent's house

"It's either this or our arms. Your choice."

Skye started toward the restaurant, but couldn't even lift her right leg.

"Give it up, Sarge," Vaughn said.

"Don't call me that," Skye snapped.

"I've always called you that," Vaughn insisted.

"And I've always hated it," she lied. She didn't like it as a kid, but it grew on her after joining the army. It was only after she'd come home, battered and broken with scars that would never heal that Skye had started to despise the nickname. The army had turned its back on her because of the one mistake she'd made in twelve years of active duty. Even though Vaughn meant it as an endearment, it reminded her of everything she'd lost.

"I think this is one of those mood swings Ma warned us about," Riley joked.

Skye spun on him, falling to the ground as her bad leg gave out.

Both brothers muttered a string of curses that would have had Dad threatening to get out the bar of soap.

As she sat there in the dirt, her ego as bruised as the rest of her body, she realized it would have been better to take a Vicodin on an empty stomach than suffer this humiliation in front of her brothers.

"Are you okay?" Vaughn asked, crouching as Skye made every effort to blink back the tears and bury the pain.

"Stop asking me that," she demanded.

"It's a legit question," Riley said, crouching on the other side of her. "You just took a nice digger."

"Which I wouldn't have done if you two had accepted the fact I can make it to the restaurant on my own," she pointed out.

Riley got the mischievous look in his eye that told Skye more trouble was coming her way. He looked at Vaughn. "She says she can make it to the restaurant on her own."

"Don't be an ass," Vaughn said, ever the responsible brother. "We're not leaving her here in the dirt. Grab an elbow."

Riley did as told, snickering as he gripped her arm. Vaughn got a firm hold on her other arm. "On three," he said and commenced to counting.

Only they didn't wait until three. On two, they both hefted her up and Skye screamed out.

"Ah, so it does hurt," Riley chided.

"Don't tease her. She's vulnerable," Vaughn added.

"Go to hell," Skye snapped, trying to shrug out of their hold.

Neither of them let go. "It's either us or the cane," Vaughn said.

Skye despised the cane more than she hated the pain. The pain was punishment for breaking the rules and screwing up, for killing three innocent soldiers. She had to live with the repercussions of those careless actions, but the nature of pain was personal. She could hide it, mask it so no one had to know about it but her.

The cane though, acted as a symbol of that pain, a cracked door to let the outside world see blood on her hands. She couldn't use it.

"Let's go," Skye said, taking one labored step forward. Her brothers held her steady, slow, measured steps moving them all forward.

They made it inside the truck stop and had to walk through the store to get to the restaurant. Skye was grateful to be seated right away.

"You are one stubborn ass woman," Riley said, shaking his head as he sat on the other side of the booth.

She didn't bait him with a response. Riley always had to have the last word and Skye wasn't in the mood to play that game.

Both brothers opted for the all you can eat buffet because they were Neanderthals when it came to food. Skye didn't want to risk standing, so ordered a combo breakfast from the menu.

Since they were family and manners weren't a requirement, Vaughn and Riley dug in before her food arrived. Skye nabbed a piece of bacon from Vaughn and a sausage link from Riley. They both complained about her stealing their food, giving her even more satisfaction.

When her food arrived, Skye took two Vicodin. If she was going to be dragged around by her brothers, she would rather be comatose than conscious.

"What's your poison?" Riley asked, nodding at the bottle that didn't have a label.

"Vicodin," she said, popping them in her mouth and washing them down with a swig of OJ.

"Potent stuff," Vaughn muttered from beside her. She was trapped in the booth which she figured was another of their strategies.

"Sometimes," she said, though with the pain surging since the fall in the parking lot, she didn't think it would be potent today.

Riley picked up the bottle. "Why isn't there a label?" he asked.

"I peeled it off," Skye lied.

"Why?" Riley persisted.

She grabbed the bottle and stuffed it back in her messenger bag. "So nosy brothers would ask stupid questions."

Vaughn laughed, earning a scowl from Riley.

"So, Sarge," Riley emphasized. "You figure out what you're going to do with the rest of your life?"

"Ri," Vaughn warned, giving a couple slow shakes of his head.

"Did Ma put you up to this? Is that why you manipulated this whole situation?"

"Ma didn't put us up to anything. She said you had an appointment and might need help."

"A ride. I needed a ride. That's hardly needing help," she

corrected.

Riley laughed. "Spin it however you want, Sarge."

"Don't call me that," she said, kicking him under the table with her good leg.

"Ow," he complained. "Did you just kick me?"

Vaughn laughed again. "Lay off her."

It was nice to have one brother at least a little bit on her side. "Thank you," she said.

"No problem," Vaughn replied, scooping up a forkful of scrambled eggs. He paused before shoveling it into his mouth. "So, have you figured it out yet? You can't hide out in Noah's basement forever."

"I'm not hiding," she said.

"No?" Vaughn asked. "Because you've been there for a week and Noah says he hasn't seen you. Speaking of, what the hell happened between you two?"

"Nothing happened," she said.

"Nothing," Riley cut in. "Is everything that comes out your mouth a lie?"

Skye dropped the fork on the plate, her appetite gone. She crossed her arms, scowling at Riley. "What exactly is your problem with me?" she demanded.

"Five years, Skye. Five years you were gone. You were home, everything was good, then you left two days early without even a good-bye and we've spent all that time keeping Noah updated on how you're doing. Now you're living in his basement but still not talking to him. What the hell happened?"

"Nothing," she insisted.

Vaughn chuckled next to her. "Did they teach you to master the one word responses in Afghanistan? *Fine. Nothing.*"

"Fuck you," Skye muttered. "There's a two word response for you."

Now Riley laughed. "You have to admit, that was a good one."

And they claimed Skye was moody. "Noah and I disagreed on something. That's all you need to know. As far as the rest of my life, I haven't thought about it."

The lie served as a bitter reminder of this new life she'd been forced into. She spent most of her days sprawled out on the bed, staring at the ceiling while contemplating the rest of her life. In truth, she had no real world skills. She'd been taught to analyze battlefield data, communications, insurgent activity and movement, equipment images and locations, all to predict what the enemy might do next and strategize the allies' next move.

There was no application for that in corporate America, even less of an opportunity in a small town like Sunset Valley.

"Have you talked to Dad? He's good at career stuff," Riley suggested.

Their father had been a guidance counselor before becoming a principal. "No, I haven't talked to Dad," she answered, speaking in a complete sentence instead of giving a one word response. She wasn't ready for her father's inquisition and inevitable judgment.

Before the explosion, Skye had a plan. She had eight years left in the army until eligible for retirement. While she had taken a few college courses, she hadn't focused on it because she wasn't sure what she wanted to do once retired. There was plenty of time to figure it out, at least until a well-placed IED stole that time from her.

Noah's job fascinated her, but she couldn't see herself taking pictures of buildings. She wanted to do something more creative, but didn't think photography would be very lucrative.

"I need to get my medical and discharge issues straightened out. I don't want to get a job before I know what my physical therapy schedule is going to be like." It was an excuse, but a valid one. Skye hoped it would be enough to appease her brothers, and her mother, since she suspected they were going to report this conversation back to her.

When they arrived at the VA hospital, Skye tried to get her

brothers to leave, but they insisted on escorting her in and waiting. It turned out to be a long wait. Thirty minutes after her scheduled time, a medical assistant finally came to get her and then it was the same rigmarole she'd grown accustomed to at Walter Reed. The same questions, the same exam, the same disapproving glances from the doctor. The icing on the cake came when Skye had to beg for a new prescription and endure another lecture about the risks of addiction, ya-da ya-da ya-da.

"I assure you, I don't have an addiction. I have pain. This is the only thing that helps," Skye explained.

Dr. Dillhole dropped his chin, peering at her over thick-rimmed glasses. Skye wanted to smack the condescending expression right off his face and given his slight build, even with a gimp hip and leg, she could take him down.

"I noticed you scratch your arms quite often. How long has this been bothering you?" the doctor asked.

Skye hadn't even realized she was doing it. "I don't know," she shrugged. It had been a while, long enough that it was more habit than bothersome.

"A constant itch is a sign of opiate addiction," he said.

Shaking her head, she refused to take the bait. She'd grown tired of the addiction lectures at Walter Reed. It seemed every VA doctor was required to read her the riot act. "Well, I just moved to a new place and my roommate uses different laundry detergent. That's when the itching started, so I'm sure that's the problem."

He held out a shiny card. "I'm giving you this pamphlet on opiate addiction. Share it with your family, boyfriend, whomever your close to. Have them look for any symptoms."

"Yes, sir," she replied, hoping that'd be enough to get him to let her go.

"Stop by reception and they'll get you scheduled for physical therapy at a clinic we work with in Sunset Valley."

Skye nodded, and after one more assessing glance, the doctor let her leave.

She tucked the pamphlet into her messenger bag and stopped by reception, leaning on the counter as the receptionist called the White Mountain Clinic to schedule her first few appointments. Her brothers hovered and when the receptionist printed her appointment schedule, Riley snagged it, snapping a picture with his phone.

"What the hell!" Skye complained, knowing his mission.

"I'm under strict orders, Sarge," he said, a thick slice of sarcasm on the nickname. "I'd rather face your wrath than Ma's."

Great. If her mother knew about the PT appointments, she'd nag Skye about it, maybe even insist on going … or sending Dumb and Dumber in again to make sure she got there.

"Come on," Vaughn said. "Lunch is on me."

"Damn straight it is," Riley agreed.

Skye rolled her eyes, grabbing the appointment list back from Riley and stuffing it in her bag with the other papers that would never again see the light of day. The only one she cared about was the prescription, but she had that secured in her pocket. She'd hit the drug store after Vaughn dropped her off. She didn't need anyone supervising this part of her medical needs, especially if her brothers were under orders to report back to their mother.

Chapter 10

If somebody sent you
An angel to save you
What would you tell him
To turn him away?
-Superman Tonight, Bon Jovi

Deceit.

The bile rose in Skye's throat. This was such a bad idea. She should have just given Finn both concert tickets. Skye could have gone with Noah. Of course, that would mean talking to him and she'd managed to avoid that ever since the night she'd wrecked his photo shrine.

"This isn't what I agreed to," Skye said as Finn got comfortable on the large bed in the Montreal hotel.

"All part of the deal, darling," Finn drawled, folding his hands behind his head and crossing his ankles.

Skye rubbed at her arms, trying to relieve the itch that continued to plague her. She really needed to talk to Noah about changing laundry detergent.

"I'm not sleeping with you, Finn," she said.

"Sleep isn't what I had in mind."

The man repulsed her. Skye wasn't sure why she'd ever been attracted to him back in high school, and chalked it up to stupid teenage hormones. Even though he was good looking, she didn't find him attractive at all. The smug way he carried himself was a complete turn-off, not to mention his choice of career.

"We came here to go to the concert. We should go grab something to eat before heading over to the arena."

Skye had planned it down to the minute so she didn't have to spend any more time with Finn than necessary. Her plan had included driving home after the concert. After arriving in the city, Finn revealed his deceitful plans.

He shot off the bed, making Skye jump back. The movement inspired a shooting pain from hip to toe, but she breathed through it, not wanting to give Finn the upper hand.

"You can't hide from me, Skye. Try all you want to be the stoic soldier, but I know what you really are."

"And what is that?" she snarled.

"A junkie whore."

"Fuck you, Finn."

His sinister smile sent a shiver up her spine, bringing with it a surge of regret for her retort. Skye knew better. Finn was manipulative and with him, she needed to choose her words carefully.

"You may have been a soldier, may have served your country, but you failed at that. Now all you can think about is your next fix and you're willing to do anything to get it."

"The army screwed up my discharge and the VA was slow to catch up. That's why I ran out of meds."

Finn cornered her, his hands moving up and down her arms. "I understand, Skye." His voice was different, the cocky undertones gone, replaced with a compassion that didn't fit the man. "No one else does, but I do. I'm not going to tell you to deal with the pain or accept the past."

He was full of shit. Skye knew it and knew she should break ranks and run from the madness, but his words still managed to get through. She needed someone to understand without having to talk about what had happened. Allowing her pain to have a voice gave it power, something she couldn't allow, but someone needed to hear her silent cries.

Pulling a bottle out of his pocket, Finn shook it in front of her. There was something comforting in the sound, like a rain stick that washed away every worry and regret, taking with it the pain and guilt.

"I'm giving you what you need, what you want. I'm giving you the chance to forget about it all. I'm giving you freedom."

Skye struggled to suck in a breath, ready to crawl out of her skin with need for what he offered. As she reached for the bottle, a voice deep inside her head screamed to stop, that the price was too high.

She pulled her hand back, as if that voice had taken control. Finn looked so damn smug she wanted to smack him. "I'm fine," she insisted through a scowl.

Finn didn't budge, keeping her pinned. "You're going to need a friend. When the world finds out what you are, everyone you love is going to shut you out." He caressed her cheek with the intimacy of a lover. Even though they'd had sex just weeks ago, there was nothing intimate about the act. It had been so long since Skye had felt the loving touch of a man, her soul pleaded with her to lean in to his touch, to accept what he offered. "But I won't, Skye. I'll be there, because I understand. I'll always give you what you need."

A more reasonable voice in her head whispered the warnings behind his words. Finn wasn't a friend. If anything, he was the enemy, a force that needed to be thrown from its corrupt power. "All I need right now is for you to get out of my face before your balls receive a direct hit from my foot."

Finn chuckled, but he wasn't stupid. He backed away. Skye

pulled one of the tickets from her messenger bag and dropped it on the bed as she headed to the door. "I'm going to get food. I'll see you at the show."

If she'd been physically capable, Skye would have found the stairs. Since the room Finn booked was on the eleventh floor and pain had already taken up residence in her hip and thigh, stairs would be the death of her. Instead, she called for the elevator and prayed Finn wouldn't follow.

After entering the empty box and counting the seconds until the doors closed, she was just about to breathe a sigh of relief when they opened again. Finn smirked as he stepped in. "I'm hungry, too. Dinner's on me, darling."

Skye would rather eat with an insurgent. At least then she'd be armed and better protected. With Finn, she felt exposed, like a gaping wound at the mercy of a relentless infection.

They walked in silence to the tavern on the first floor of the hotel, but Finn's words played over and over in her mind. She hadn't found comfort in anything since returning to Sunset Valley ... well, since waking up in the hospital in Germany. As manipulative as his words were, Skye clung to them, a shameful hope bubbling in her chest. Finn represented exactly what she didn't need. He would not only nudge her to the edge of reason, but give her a swift push off the ledge. Skye had managed to get her need for the painkillers under control since moving into Noah's basement, but Finn triggered that desire again. He was like an aphrodisiac, except it wasn't sex she craved, it was the fog, the thick cloud that masked her pain and muddled the memories that continued to haunt her.

He chuckled as they entered the tavern, as if he knew every thought bouncing around her head and what she craved. She didn't even bother to try to hide the limp because that only ratcheted up the pain and it's not like she could deceive Finn.

He *knew*. He *understood*.

The strange comfort Skye found in that put a spring in her

gimpy steps. Skye marched straight for the bar, desperate for a drink. Thanks to the Vicodin, she hadn't had a drink since she'd been home. Add eight months in the hospital and six months in Afghanistan to that and it made her absolutely parched.

Skye limped around the bar looking for an empty seat. The bar chairs allowed her to stretch out her leg and still have support so it didn't dangle.

She found a couple open seats at the corner, the perfect strategy to keep a little space between her and Finn. Living off frozen dinners for the past week had proved a necessity. Skye couldn't manage the strength or patience to cook and couldn't afford to dine out. If the army ever got her disability pay straightened out, she was going to eat out every night for a month.

When the bartender came over, Skye made her best effort to order in French. "Puis-je avoir la maison rouge, s'il vouse plait."

He smiled. "Bien sur. Et toi?"

"Uh, yeah," Finn muttered. "I don't speak French. I'll have a Jack and Coke."

After the bartender set off on his mission to get the drinks, Finn turned to Skye. "So you speak French?"

Skye shrugged. "Not really. I picked up bits and pieces of different languages in my travels. I went to France a few times while stationed in Germany." Taking four years of French in high school also helped.

"You've been to a lot of cool places, huh?"

Skye nodded, unable to speak as memories of the places she'd rather not remember burrowed into her brain.

"What happened to you? I heard you were in some sort of explosion?"

There were two schools of civilians: those who over-dramatized the war and those who had no clue about the actual mission. Skye didn't know which school she despised more because people from both schools were equal in their morbid curiosity. "Something like that," she said, taking inventory of the liquors behind the bar just so she didn't have to look at Finn.

Finn chuckled. "Yeah, I've heard you guys don't like to talk about it. PTSD helps keep me in business."

"I don't have PTSD," she snapped.

"Sure, darling. All you brought home were those pretty little scars on your hip."

The mocking tone ignited the spark of anger he'd inspired. Skye pinched her eyes closed, and took a long deep breath, holding it as the fire burned through every cell. While Finn missed the mark by labeling her a junkie whore, Skye had no doubt what he was: a merciless drug dealer. It would serve her well to remember that.

Remembering his occupation brought a healthy dose of shame because along with it came the memory of what she'd done in exchange for the Vicodin.

It was exactly what a *junkie whore* would do to get a fix.

Skye shook her head, refusing to believe she'd fallen that far. With the pain under control and physical therapy in the near future, it was only a matter of time before the pain retreated and surrendered. At least that's what the doctor promised.

And with Finn, it's not like she'd wanted to have sex with him. With her pay screwed up, her ATM card deactivated, and her checks packed away with her household goods, she had no access to her modest savings. So, they'd bartered. She'd refused to take her clothes off because the scars on her hip and thigh were nothing compared to the intricate pattern of burn scars across her torso. No one had seen them except the doctors and nurses. Skye planned to keep it that way.

"Talking isn't part of our deal," she said, hoping he'd take the hint and shut the hell up. "Why don't you watch the game?"

Skye didn't have a clue who was playing, nor did she care, but if Finn watched the hockey game, maybe he'd leave her alone.

He snickered, but seemed to take the hint. They ordered and ate without another syllable of small talk.

After hobbling to the arena, which thankfully resided only a block from the hotel, Skye was surprised when they weren't searched going in. She supposed life in Canada was a little safer than in the States, and a lot safer than in the Middle East.

Vaughn loaned her money to buy a t-shirt and she put it on over the one she wore to avoid carrying it. When they found their seats, she breathed as if just finishing an army PT test. The pain begged for something stronger than the ibuprofen in her purse, but Skye was determined to make it through this concert without the fog.

"These seats don't suck," Finn muttered.

They were in the two hundred level, at the back of the arena with the stage facing them. The seats were fantastic, but someone like Finn couldn't appreciate that.

"So who is Bon Jovi?" the girl behind them asked her date. "Is it the name of the band or the name of the person?"

Skye shook her head, resisting the urge to turn around and ask them what the hell they were doing there if they didn't know anything about the band, but it wasn't her battle to fight. Not everyone liked the band or appreciated the music like she and Noah did.

With her iPod among the things she'd left behind in Afghanistan, she'd been given one at the hospital. It shattered when Skye had gotten frustrated with therapy one day and fired it against the wall. She hadn't bothered to replace it, what with the army not paying her and all, so until moving into Noah's basement, she hadn't listened to the music in months.

As a photographer for a real estate management company, Noah spent a lot of time working from his home office. He always listened to Bon Jovi and the music wafted into the basement. Skye didn't mind. On her good days, it soothed her damaged soul. While she wasn't ready to make peace with Noah, she appreciated him sharing the music.

Her heart raced when the lights went out and the music started. She loved the adrenaline rush that accompanied the anticipation. Though this was Skye's sixteenth Bon Jovi concert, the shows were never boring. There was always something new, something exciting.

She would never forget the concert in Denver during the *Have a Nice Day* tour. Noah had flown out to go to the concert with her. They sat in about the same spot she occupied now, but in the lower section. Skye had been watching the stage and when the stage lights came on, Jon was nowhere to be seen. Confused, she yelled to Noah, "I don't see him."

Noah turned her head to the small stage just to the left. There he was, standing just thirty feet away, belting out *Last Man Standing*.

It had been her favorite song ever since, until the irony had been too much to bear. Skye would rather have been killed in that explosion than be the last man standing.

Chapter 11

I got what I wanted
I paid every cost
I'd give it all back
To get back what I've lost.
-A Teardrop to the Sea, Bon Jovi

Anger.

It vibrated on the surface of her skin, raising every hair on end, and threatening to go deeper.

Skye never should have agreed to bring Finn to the show. He didn't care about the music, didn't appreciate the performance, the energy, the feeling. People who didn't love the music didn't understand the connection or the power it had.

Finn was one of those people.

"Come on Skye, the show's over. Let's go."

Skye shook her head. She'd been to enough concerts to know it wasn't over. "They'll be back out for an encore. The show's not over until the arena lights come back on."

"They've already done an encore," Finn complained.

"Yeah, and sometimes they do two."

"You can't even stand up. We should go. I've got just what you need back at the hotel."

The anger swirled as bile lurched up her throat. "I'm driving home tonight."

It was going to be a long, difficult drive, but it was better than the alternative. Finn was muscular, strong, and she had no doubt he would take whatever he wanted, whether she wanted to give it or not. Skye might be broken, but she refused to give Finn that kind of power.

Before he could argue, the crowd erupted with cheers as the band took the stage once more. Skye uttered a silent, "told you so," and focused on the stage, letting the rhythm of the music beat out the anger.

Five songs later, when the band bowed, waved and left the stage, Skye wanted to mourn the end. It was the first time since waking up in the hospital that she'd felt alive, the music pumping through her veins, the words a poetic harmony in her mind.

Skye wished she'd shared it with Noah and not Finn. Noah would have been excited for the second encore, humming with anticipation the same way she had until Finn crushed out the excitement as if she was a spent cigarette under his boot.

After the crowd around them left, Skye pushed herself out of the chair. The ibuprofen barely took the edge off, but with the music echoing in her mind, she managed to limp rather than drag her useless appendage.

She and Finn filed in with the crowd, flowing down the escalator and out the doors. They had to walk around the building to get to the parking garage under the hotel. "The lobby is this way," Finn said, gripping her arm and trying to steer her to the left, away from the parking garage.

"I told you, I'm driving home tonight. You can come with me or find your own way."

"That wasn't part of the deal," he growled, pulling her against him.

Skye had taken enough personal safety training in the army to know how to defend against a personal attack, but she hadn't learned how to execute any countermeasures with a gimp leg.

"Let me go," she warned, every usable muscle ratcheting up for a fight.

Finn just chuckled, tightening his hold. "Pretend all you want, Skye, but you want this. You want what I have, all of it. You need me."

"I don't," she said with a confidence she hadn't felt since Afghanistan.

"Take your hands off her."

Skye closed her eyes, drawing in a breath that was equal amounts frustration and relief. She had hoped to not see Noah this trip, but hope had once again turned its back on her.

Finn released her arm but didn't step back. "We're just having a little chat. I was telling Skye we should go for a drink, but she's desperate to get me back to our room."

"Fuck you, Finn," she snapped, shoving at his chest. He didn't budge, but she stumbled back, landing in Noah's arms.

Finn snickered and Skye held her breath in order to regain a little balance. She shrugged out of Noah's firm hold, stepping aside.

Noah loomed on one side of her, his cousin Luke a formidable guard on the other side. Neither of them were huge, but as she looked back and forth between them, both standing with their feet apart and their arms crossed, she knew Finn would have no choice but to back off. He may have had the upper hand against her, but the intimidation surrounding her was enough to ward off the most sinister aggressor.

"See that boys, she's so wet for it, she's begging, right here for the world to hear."

Skye would have gone on the attack, but because of her gimp leg, Noah beat her to it. His fist made contact with Finn's nose before Luke got a lock on him and pulled him back.

"Son of a bitch!" Finn cursed, wiping the blood from his

face.

"We're not doing this Noah," Luke commanded.

"You may not be, but I am."

"No," Luke demanded. "You're not."

The ache grew in Skye's leg. She didn't want to stay here on the concrete and have this stand-off until she fell over, so she opted to be the voice of reason. "I'm going home. Like I said, you can catch a ride with me or you can find your own way."

"Fine," Finn conceded, wiping at his nose again. "I need to grab my stuff from the room."

"You're not riding with her," Noah growled.

"I can take care of myself," Skye countered.

"I don't give a damn," Noah said, an unfamiliar fury in his voice. "I'm not leaving you alone with this piece of shit for one second."

"Strong words," Finn drawled with amusement.

"Finn can come with me," Luke offered. "You go with Skye."

"No," Skye and Noah said at the same time. She looked at him, surprised at his declaration.

"He comes with me. We're going to have a heart to heart."

Great. Noah knew nothing about the situation between her and Finn, but he was going to try and fix it anyway. Fine, whatever. He could play out the hero and feel like he accomplished something and then maybe he'd leave Skye alone.

"Sounds like a party," Finn chuckled.

"Come on, Skye. I'll drive," Luke said, his voice and expression deterring any argument she might have waged. Skye limped into the garage, grateful Luke wasn't a conversationalist. When they reached the car, she got in the passenger side, happy to relinquish control. Since Luke served as Sunset Valley's police chief, he was probably accustomed to driving.

He maneuvered through the city with the confidence his job required. She appreciated his stoic silence. It gave her time to think about the show and forget about Noah and Finn's juvenile behavior.

As the bright city lights gave way to darkness, Skye shuttered. She'd been out in darkness like this before. While it always made her apprehensive, she'd never been scared. Soldiers were often stupidly brave, believing nothing horrible would happen. Now, though, the dark sent a shudder through her body. Clenched fists did little to tamp the shaking so Skye pulled her left foot onto the seat to hug her leg. It was her own version of the fetal position since she didn't have that much flexibility in her right leg.

"Are you cold?" Luke asked.

There should have been an easy answer to that, but Skye analyzed all of the possible follow-up questions or responses he might have and realized there wasn't an easy answer.

"A little bit," she said, opting for the lie because it seemed to open the fewest doors.

"It was August when I came back from my last deployment. I couldn't shake the chills until the following summer."

Skye hummed an acknowledgment, not wanting to encourage Luke to talk about his deployment because it might prompt him to ask questions she didn't want to answer.

"Noah said you won't talk about what happened, that you're not talking to him at all."

She grunted, again not wanting to encourage him.

"You getting help?" he asked.

"I start physical therapy next week," she offered.

"Good, but we both know that's not what I meant."

"I'm fine," she insisted. "Noah's bored. He's finished fixing his house and needs a new project. He thinks it should be me."

Luke glanced at her for the first time, just a quick assessing look before putting his attention back on the road. This was the first time she'd seen him since he'd left for the army all those years ago, a year before she did. Even back then, before he'd been military police, before he'd become police chief, he'd had that ability to strip you bare, exposing your soul and all your secrets. Skye hated it back then and despised it now.

"Don't put this on Noah. He loves you and just wants to help."

"That's the problem. I don't need help."

She rubbed her arms, wishing the incessant itching would go away.

Luke was quiet for a while, giving a quick glance each time she rubbed her arms. They made it through border patrol without incident before he spoke again.

"You've been scratching a lot."

"Yeah. I think I'm allergic to Noah's laundry detergent."

"That's one explanation," he murmured. She recognized his tone. He'd used the same one back in high school when he thought someone was full of shit.

"What the hell does that mean?"

"Did you know itchy skin is a sign of opiate addiction? Docs prescribed you Vicodin, right?"

With a shrug, she recalled the doctor's same words, but Skye had the meds under control. She wasn't dealing with addiction, she was dealing with pain, plain and simple.

"The VA loves to prescribe that shit," Luke went on. "Thinks it'll fix all the world's problems."

She laughed at his comment because her doctor wasn't so generous. He didn't want to prescribe it and she'd had to jump through hoops to get him to sign off on a refill. "They didn't make it that easy for me."

Luke gave her another one of those assessing glances. "He probably saw the signs, doesn't want to be responsible for your addiction."

"It's not an addiction. I'm in pain. I have pins in my leg and hip that feel like razor blades." Not to mention the burn scars. Numbness plagued her torso, but on occasion, when she moved just right, the shooting pain rivaled that of her hip and leg.

"What the hell were you doing out there, Skye? You were an

intel analyst, a desk jockey. You had no business being outside the fenceline."

"Desk jockey," she scoffed. "That's what our CO called us too. He was hard-core infantry, thought everyone should be out in the field. Thought us desk jockeys could do our jobs better if we knew what was really going on."

"Shit," he muttered.

Yeah, shit. "I didn't mind going on patrols. It broke up the monotony of the job and yeah, maybe it did make me look at the intel a little more closely before I filed my reports."

"You weren't trained for that."

No, but she had a good squad, a team that meshed well and always had each other's six. They never let her down. That burden was all hers.

Another long silence replaced the conversation, leaving Skye to drown in the memories of that last patrol. She didn't want to remember, but every car moving toward them offered a stark reminder of the bright light that flashed before everything had gone black. Skye breathed a long sigh of relief when they got off the highway and headed to Sunset Valley. At three in the morning, there were no lights, no oncoming cars to keep the terror brewing in her chest.

They followed Noah to Finn's house. "What are you doing?" she asked Luke.

"Making sure Noah doesn't do something stupid."

"Noah isn't the violent type," she reminded him.

"He's capable of more than you give him credit for."

Finn got out and shot Skye a smirk that sent a shameful chill racing down her spine.

"That man right there, he's trouble, Skye. He's into things that are going to land him in jail for a very long time. I don't want to see you get caught in the cross fire."

"I won't. It was just the concert. I don't plan to see him again." That was the truth. Finn could be poetic, his words alluring, but when Skye removed herself from the situation and looked in from the outside, she saw him for what he was, a manipulator who would say anything to keep her coming back.

She wasn't an addict.

She wasn't a whore.

She didn't need anyone to understand what she was going through because Skye was ready to put it behind her.

"You better stick to that. You may be a friend, but I won't hesitate to toss your ass in jail, either."

Chapter 12

> *Who's gonna save you*
> *When the stars fall from your sky?*
> *And who's gonna pull you in*
> *When the tide gets too high?*
> -Superman Tonight, Bon Jovi

Fury.

The energy pulsed through him like a drug and Noah gripped the steering wheel like a junkie, desperate for more. He imagined his passenger's neck strangled between his fingers and palm, ready to snap with a quick flick of the wrist. Noah wanted to sever the ass-hole's head with his bare hands and toss it out the window, leaving it to rot on the highway like roadkill.

He'd never decked anyone in his entire life. Thought about it a time or two, yeah — hell, yeah! But actually followed through with the impulse? Never.

He'd give a king's ransom in dimes to have the chance to do it again.

For now, Noah held tight to the steering wheel because

landing in jail on assault charges and letting Finn walk away wouldn't do a bit of good for Skye.

Noah couldn't ignore Finn's smug demeanor, despite the fact he had a bag of ice pressed to his damned nose. When Finn came out of the hotel with the ice, Noah wanted to snatch it so the bastard would suffer. Instead, he reveled in the thought that he'd disfigured the man permanently. If that was the case, Noah would be the one sporting the smug grin every time they crossed paths.

Finn was smart though, and hadn't uttered a word in the last three hours.

The long drive back from Montreal did nothing to quell Noah's fury. He had hoped Luke would take Skye home instead of following Noah to Finn's house. With an audience, he couldn't finish what they started in the parking garage.

After bringing the car to a stop in front of Finn's front door, Noah gripped the guy's arm before he could get out.

Finn glanced at Noah's hand before pinning him with a look that might be intimidating if every nerve wasn't gorging on adrenaline.

"I would have leveled you if the cop wasn't there to run interference," Finn warned.

"You would have tried," Noah countered.

"Get your fucking hand off me."

Noah shook his head. "Stay away from Skye."

Finn chuckled. "She came to me, man. I'm not one to turn a lady down, especially when she's desperate for it."

The fury surged again, a cataclysmic heat pumping through Noah, flexing every muscle and tendon in his body. He gripped Finn's shirt, tugging him across the console. "Stay. Away. From. Skye."

Undeterred, the ass-hole smirked like he'd just won the battle. "Hey, man, you need to have this conversation with your girlfriend."

Skye wasn't his girlfriend, another sore spot for Noah,

adding more fuel to his rage.

"Get out," he demanded, releasing Finn's shirt.

He didn't wait for the guy to even get in the house. Noah executed a three-point turn with a calm control that was a direct contradiction to the rage in his heart. Out of respect for his cousin, he kept his speed under the limit while making the ten minute drive to his house on Walker Hill.

Before Noah parked the car, he spotted Luke in the rear view mirror maneuvering Skye's car around the back.

After cutting the engine, he gripped the steering wheel, calculating his next move. He should let her rest, but Noah was still charged for a fight. During the week when he'd opted to give her space, she hadn't uttered a single syllable to him. He was done with that bullshit. While he wouldn't force her to talk about the explosion, they were going to hash it out about Finn.

Luke came around as Noah hit the front door. "You got your shit under control?"

"Not even close," Noah admitted.

"Then you need to leave Skye alone. You go in with guns blazing and you're just going to push her away."

"Did she talk to you?" Noah asked with a hope that calmed his raging temper. Pairing Skye with Luke had been intentional. Since they'd both served and seen combat, Noah thought maybe she'd open up to Luke. If she did, maybe the dam would break and she'd let Noah in.

"A little. Nothing earth shattering."

"I'll go easy on her," he assured his cousin. They shook hands and Luke thundered off on his motorcycle.

When Noah walked in the house, he was surprised to see Skye sitting in the recliner.

"Are you okay?" she asked.

The question shattered the fight in him. "I'm fine," he said and chuckled, realizing he answered in the same way Skye always did. "My hand is fine. The rest of me, not so much."

"I didn't ask you to fight my battles," she said.

"What the hell are you doing with him, Skye?"

"It's obvious, isn't it?"

Noah shook his head. She couldn't be saying that Finn was telling the truth. "Are you sleeping with him?"

Skye shrugged. "I don't think that's any of your business."

Like a match striking a metal strip, Noah's anger sparked back to life. He held up his hand, showing her the scar they shared to remind her of the promise they'd made to each other. "Like hell it isn't."

He saw the fury spark in her eyes now too. Maybe it was the wrong emotion, but at least it was something. "Fine. You want details? I'm happy to give them to you."

"A simple yes or no would suffice," he muttered, absolutely not wanting details.

"It's been a long time for me. Afghanistan for six months, the hospital for eight. I hadn't been with anyone for a while before we deployed. Finn's not looking for a relationship, neither am I. It's a perfect arrangement. He really knows how to make a girl scream."

Noah swallowed the fury, and yeah, the disgust. Nothing good could come of Skye being involved with Finn. Whether that involvement was as simple as a date to the concert or something as deplorable as what she'd just described, she would be the one who got hurt. It happened once already, back in high school. Skye held a grudge, something Noah knew firsthand because he'd hurt her too. Now, Finn's unscrupulous activities would not just hurt Skye, but destroy her. For the first time since he'd known her, she was vulnerable. Noah had to protect her.

Her words fell short, though. Skye held a grudge. She neither forgave nor forgot. Noah knew first hand if you hurt her, you would suffer her wrath the rest of your life. While he had hoped to be exempt from that given their friendship, he learned the hard way that hurting Skye had repercussions. Their friendship was the one thing that gave him confidence she would forgive him sooner rather than later.

Finn didn't have that advantage. He had humiliated her in high school, asking her to the prom only to leave her standing in the middle of the dance floor while he left with a girl who had been crowned the class slut long before prom.

No, Skye wouldn't give Finn a second chance.

"I don't believe you," he said. "If you're sleeping with him, why the scene in the parking garage?"

"He was an ass-hole during the concert. It was just payback."

"Is he giving you drugs?"

Skye shook her head but didn't meet his eyes. "Shit, Skye. What the hell is going on? This isn't like you."

"I'm living my life the best way I know how. You need to accept that, Noah. I'm too broken to fix. There isn't some great mystery behind the explosion. It happened. I got hurt. My body was stitched and stapled back together. The end."

It wasn't that simple. She was different, hurting in ways that had nothing to do with her injuries. "I don't think you're broken."

"We both know I am."

Sighing, he pushed has hand across his head, wishing he had hair to grip and tug. "Are you ever going to forgive me?" he asked.

"I did. I told you, I got over you. Moved on."

Those words ratcheted up the anxiety. He didn't want her to be over him. He wanted them to have a fresh start, to discover where their friendship could go, where their love could take them.

"I think you're lying, about Finn, about the drugs. I've seen you, Skye, high as a kite, and I know Finn deals. Luke is going to bust him. Sooner or later Finn is going to slip and get caught. Don't let that bastard take you down with him."

Chapter 13

I lost all faith in my God,
in His religion too.
I told the angels they could sing
their songs to someone new.
I lost all trust in my friends,
I watched my heart turn to stone.
I thought that I was left to walk
this wicked world alone.
-Something to Believe In, Bon Jovi

Regret.

Two days later, Skye's ugly words skulked through her brain, the memory of the hurt on Noah's face haunting her like the rest of the demons she couldn't escape.

Gripping the dog tags, she wished for a way to take it back. All of it. Opening her heart to Noah, only to have that risk blow up in her face. The months of secrecy with Rafe, of pretending not to be in love with her platoon leader. The giddy feeling after he had proposed while they were out on patrol. Those last moments, when she smiled at him instead of looking at the road ahead.

The tags were cold in her hand, sending a slow chill up her arm. It settled in her heart, slowing it to nearly a lifeless beat.

Death would have been so much easier than adapting to this new life. Skye had once believed in heaven, had grown up going to church and praying. As a teenager filled with angst, her first act of rebellion had been to stop going to church with her parents. She had still believed, though, in God, in heaven. She had believed until that moment when she woke up in the hospital in Germany.

It was shameful to just drop her beliefs like a cold, dead carcass. Even more shameful was how her life seemed to be unfolding since returning to Sunset Valley. First, screwing Finn in exchange for pain killers, then all of the lying. Lying to her parents about the pain was one thing, but lying to her brothers about the pain and everything else, and lying to Noah about her involvement with Finn, fabricating a relationship just to get him to hate her. It was all so shameful.

Shameful, but necessary. No one understood. Her parents, her brothers, Noah, none of them had served. They'd never been in a combat situation, never had to survive a deadly explosion that had killed everyone but her. The chaplain at Walter Reed and the psychiatrist she had refused to talk to had both tossed around the term survivor's guilt, along with PTSD. In her final days at the hospital, they'd warned her about separation anxiety and the resentment that would ride in its wake.

Skye had assured them both she was fine. Growing up with older brothers and then serving twelve years in the army had taught her to be a fighter. She was born battle ready. The United States War on Terror may no longer be her fight, but she stood ready to face her own battle.

The guilt was her cross to bear, punishment for letting down her squad and the man she loved. The anxiety would pass, just as it always did after being tossed into new and unfamiliar territory. Resentment had yet to set in. If it hadn't by now, Skye figured she'd dodged at least one bullet.

The shame though, that was unexpected and difficult to shake.

She couldn't take back her words. If she told Noah the truth, that she wasn't involved with Finn, it would only open more doors Skye couldn't let him walk through. Noah wanted something she couldn't give. Not now. Not with so many demons haunting her.

Her phone vibrated, a number Skye didn't recognize, but most numbers she didn't these days. She answered it, holding little hope for good news.

"Yeah, I'm trying to reach Staff Sergeant Everhart. Skye Everhart."

"This is she," Skye replied, more regret bubbling up at the sound of her former rank. She wasn't SSG Everhart anymore. The only insignia she wore now were the scars that labeled her a wounded veteran who had lost her way in the world.

"This is Todd from Coastal Movers. We had you scheduled for a delivery next week, but today's pack up canceled and your shipment is here. If you want it today, we can be there in two hours."

"Really?" she asked, hoping this wasn't some kind of prank. She wouldn't put it past Riley to pull a stunt like this.

"Yeah, really. You want it delivered today?" the man asked.

"Yes, today is great."

"Someone has to be there," he said.

This wasn't her first rodeo. Skye had moved enough times in twelve years to understand how it worked. "I'm here," she said. After confirming the address, she ended the call, her spirits elevated.

Delivery of her household goods offered a good distraction. Just one little problem: she needed to let Noah know.

On a positive note, she'd heard him leave that morning and hadn't heard him return. With no music wafting through the floor, he must still be gone.

Skye swallowed her pride, something she did more and more as of late, and sent him a text. A minute later Noah's response beeped in.

OK.

Annoyance gave way to a self-deprecating amusement. Vaughn had accused her of being a master of one-word answers. It was her own method of self-preservation, but now on the receiving end, she understood the frustration.

It was no less than she deserved.

Skye needed to figure out what to do about the guest bed set up in her apartment when the phone played the Bon Jovi ring tone she favored. *We Weren't Born to Follow* had become her favorite song since she couldn't bear to listen to Last Man Standing. The lyrics rang with a soul-deep echo of how she had lived life, how she wanted to live life again. She checked the caller ID, surprised to see it was Noah.

"Hello?" she answered.

"Hi, Skye," he said, the apprehension in his voice loud and clear.

"Hi."

"I just wanted to check in, see what a household goods delivery entails. Maybe you need an extra pair of hands?"

Such a normal question shouldn't have inspired a smile, but it was so typical of Noah, always ready to lend a hand. Plus, Skye was happy to hear his voice.

"The movers bring a crew. They unload everything, put furniture together, unpack if I want them to. So no, I don't need extra hands for that, but I do need to get your bed out of here so they can put mine together."

"All right. I'm on my way. See you soon."

"See you," she responded, waiting until the phone went silent to put it down.

She recognized this as an intended peace offering and whispered a silent promise to come clean about Finn. Getting the words out might prove difficult, if not impossible, but Noah was her friend — best friend — and he should know the truth — at least part of it. Even though she was too ashamed of what she'd done with Finn to admit that to Noah, he could at least know they weren't involved now.

With that honesty, though, Skye also had to be truthful about where she stood with Noah. She couldn't love him, not the way he wanted. Those feelings existed only in the past, dead and buried before she'd given her heart to Rafe. Even though Rafe was now dead and buried, she couldn't give her heart to Noah. That kind of love wasn't in the cards for Skye.

She had finished stripping the bed but hadn't figured out what to say to Noah when a knock at the door sent her heart plummeting into her stomach. Her stomach turned over when she found Luke standing on the other side. "Noah called. Said you need the bed out of here."

As Luke entered, a wave of disappointment hit her chest like a Tsunami. She dropped into the patio chair Noah had left in the kitchen the day she moved in. It was foolish to think Noah's call translated to a peace offering.

"He's on his way," Luke said, narrowing his eyes. "I was just closer."

"Oh," she said, embarrassed she was that transparent.

"You two hash things out the other night?" he asked.

Skye shrugged. "Something like that. What can I do to help?" She didn't want to talk to Luke about his cousin and didn't want to open the door to talk about other things that were none of his business.

"Noah keeps a toolbox in the boiler room. Can you grab it?"

"Sure," she said, glad Luke didn't tell her to sit her ass in the chair. She hated being useless.

The boiler room demonstrated Noah's tidy side, everything in its intended place. After spotting the toolbox, Skye hefted it up with a grunt, surprised by its weight. Holding it in her left hand, she pressed her right hand against the wall as she walked to keep herself steady. When she got to laundry room, another knock startled her. "Come in," she hollered and came face to face with Noah.

"Hi," he said, his eyes wide, as if he hadn't expected to find Skye there.

"Hi," she responded, winded from the heavy box and the proximity to Noah. The narrow space between the stairs and the laundry room accommodated one person without an issue. Two people meant very tight quarters.

"Want me to take that?" he asked, nodding at the toolbox.

The heat in the basement amped up several degrees and Skye found her breaths shallow and quick. She pushed her nerves and any other awry emotions aside and focused on the task. "I got it. Luke is already in there."

"Okay," he said and turned, leading the way into the apartment before letting her pass once there was room enough.

Noah and Luke greeted each other with the same brotherly affection they'd always shared. Neither of them had siblings, but as cousins they'd always shared a close bond.

Skye put the toolbox down on the bed and retreated to the patio chair. Noah wouldn't let her help, so there was no point even offering.

They leaned the mattress against the wall and flipped the box spring over. It was two pieces, held together by a metal plate and bolts.

"Don't just sit there," Luke drawled. "Grab the socket wrench and the 5/8 socket."

"I can get it," Noah offered as Skye started to push out of the chair.

"I know you can get it, but I need you to hold this box steady. Skye is capable of helping."

Skye choked on a laugh as she pushed out of the chair. There weren't many people who could order Noah around. Luke had always had an authority about him, even when on the other side of the law in high school. She knew he was trying to teach Noah a lesson that Skye wasn't helpless and appreciated the gesture.

Grabbing the wrench and socket, she put them together and handed the tool to Luke.

"Thanks," Luke drawled. "At the risk of sounding sexist, can you get some coffee going? It's too early for a beer."

The clock showed 9:30, so yeah, it was too early for a beer. "I've got a Keurig," Noah offered. "K-cups are in the drawer under the unit."

She headed upstairs, her steps slow and measured as a shot of pain reminded her with each step that it still owned her. Balancing most of her weight on her left leg, she was sorting through the different flavors when the two of them grunted their way up with one half of the box spring. "What flavor do you want?" she called down the hall.

"Caramel, if he's got it. Otherwise, I'm not picky."

"I'll have caramel, too," Noah called. Looked like he didn't think making coffee was too arduous a task for her crippled self.

"Two sugars, a splash of milk," Luke called.

"Wow, got a sweet tooth?" Skye joked.

"It keeps me balanced since I'm such a sour puss."

Skye brewed three cups of caramel, adding sugar and milk to Luke's as the two of them entered the kitchen.

"You still take one sugar and milk?" she asked Noah.

"Sure do," he smiled.

"We'll finish moving that beast. Keep the lane clear," Luke said. Then they headed back down the stairs.

It took them four trips to get all the pieces upstairs, but they stopped for coffee before assembling the bed in the guest room.

"Got any donuts?" Luke asked.

Noah laughed. "You are such a cop."

"And you grew up with one. There's gotta be donuts in this house somewhere."

Noah went to the pantry and pulled out a box of chocolate

glazed.

"Perfect," Luke drawled, grabbing two.

Skye took one, dipping it in her coffee before taking a bite.

"Just like old times," Luke laughed.

"Not quite. Autumn is missing. Do you ever hear from her?" The four of them had been like the four stooges growing up. Luke was a couple years older than Skye and Noah, and a year older than Autumn Clark. Just before she graduated, Luke joined the army, betraying his plans with Autumn. There were rumors that Mr. Clark had threatened to press charges against Luke for statutory rape, but Noah's father, police chief at the time, refused to talk about it. Autumn left after graduation and Skye never heard from her.

Noah choked on his donut as Luke scowled. "Her father has this whole town convinced I'm still bad news. No one will tell me where she is."

"How are your Sunday morning peace offerings going?" Noah asked.

"I'm breaking him down, one donut at a time."

Skye must have looked confused because Luke explained, "I bring fresh donuts from the bakery over every Sunday, along with coffee. He won't let me in the B&B, but he sits on the porch and we shoot the shit. Honestly, I think he looks forward to it. One of these days he'll tell me where Autumn is."

"Don't you have resources at your disposal?" she asked. As police chief, investigating and locating people was part of that job.

"I'm not going to use department resources for personal gain," he said, tearing a huge piece of donut with his teeth.

"Who the hell are you?" she laughed. The Luke Carbonneau she'd grown up with lived to test the limits of right and wrong.

"I grew up," he said after swallowing his donut.

They finished their coffee and donuts and got the bed put together, Skye playing her role as the surgical nurse, handing over tools whenever they needed one. It wasn't long after that when the moving truck showed up.

Luke and Noah worked alongside the three-man crew, unloading the truck in record time. All the furniture was assembled and arranged where Skye wanted it, but she opted to only have her kitchen boxes unpacked by the crew. She would deal with everything else.

Luke left when the movers did, leaving Skye alone with Noah and her life in boxes.

"I thought you said you didn't have much stuff," he said, looking at the wall of boxes.

"I don't." Looking at the brown cardboard that represented her last twelve years, it seemed pathetic, but Skye had never been one to have a lot of clutter in her life.

"All right, so where do you want to start?" he asked.

She smiled, hoping she wasn't about to hurt him again. "I appreciate all the help, but I can go through the boxes on my own."

"What, you don't want me seeing your unmentionables?" he laughed. At least he had a sense of humor about it.

Laughing with him, Skye shook her head. "It's not that, I just don't know what I'm going to do with all this stuff."

"We'll figure it out, one box at a time." He pulled a box off the top of the stack and read the label. "Bedroom? You want to handle this one?"

She laughed again. "Open it. If it's not underwear, you can put it away."

Noah used a box cutter from the toolbox to tear through the tape. "Damn, it's just shirts."

Skye rolled her eyes. "Second drawer down," she directed. He set the box aside and grabbed another.

"This one is addressed to you at Walter Reed," he said, setting it on the bed next to her.

Despite every effort, she couldn't avoid this box forever. She suspected it was her personal things from Afghanistan, sent by someone in the platoon after she'd been shipped home.

Noah tore through the tape before putting the box cutter on

the dresser and grabbing the box he'd already opened.

Skye peered into the box as if it was filled with explosives. Instead, she found an envelope on top of the contents, *SSG Everhart* written neatly on the front. After dropping onto the bed, Skye ripped it open and unfolded the handwritten letter. It was from Specialist Newton, one of the young soldiers in her squad.

Dear SSG Everhart,

I hope you are recovering okay. It hasn't been the same here since the explosion. Most of us are terrified to go out on patrols now, but Captain Smith still insists everyone in the intelligence platoon take a rotation. Sergeant Brown is our new squad leader and he's okay, but he's not as cool as you were. You were the best squad leader I've known in my three years in the army. LT Warren was the best officer, too, but I guess you already know that.

I volunteered to pack up your things and Sergeant Brown said I should pack up the LT's things too. I sent most of his things home, but there were a few things I thought you should have. I hope my analysis wasn't wrong.

And don't worry, I didn't tell anyone.

Take care and feel free to friend me on Facebook.

All the best,
SPC Melanie Newton

"What is it?" Noah asked.

Skye folded the paper and clutched it to her chest with one hand, picking the next item out of the box.

Rafe's dog tags. Everyone had a spare set. She doubted the one's he'd been wearing on patrol survived the explosion and appreciated SPC Newton sending the spare set. Skye slid the chain over her head, tucking the tags into her shirt. Putting her hand over them, she closed her eyes and remembered the man who had worn them.

Except she didn't want to remember. Remembering hurt too much. Opening her eyes, she reached for the next item, a selfie Rafe snapped with his iPod during one of their evening walks. He had said something to make her laugh, so Skye wasn't looking at the camera. Neither was he. He was looking at her, completely enamored.

"You look happy," Noah said, a hint of sadness in his voice that shot straight to her heart. A tear dripped onto the photo before she even realized she was crying. "Is that Rafe?"

Skye's breath hitched with surprise. "What?" How do you know his name?" She had told Noah there was someone, but had not revealed his name.

"The day you moved in, when you passed out and I stuck around. You had a nightmare and called out his name. Is that him?"

She wished it were only a nightmare. The warped memory of the explosion haunted her at random intervals. While she had zero memory of the explosion, in the dream, Skye remained conscious and watched as Rafe's body was blown to pieces.

"Yes," she whispered, answering Noah's question and aware of the one word answer. What else could she say? It would only hurt Noah if she explained who Rafe was. Even worse, Noah would look at her in a whole new way if he knew she was the reason Rafe had been killed.

She placed the picture back in the box, closing the flaps and pushing it aside.

"Screw this," she said. "This crap can wait. Let's get pizza, watch a concert video or something."

"Skye," he pleaded, but she held up her hand.

"Don't give me some pep talk about avoiding all this or facing it or whatever. I'll deal with it when I'm ready, not before."

He took the box and placed it back on the stack. Then in a gesture that surprised her even more, he held out his scarred hand.

Skye put her scarred hand in his and he lifted her off the

bed. "Let's make pizza from scratch," he suggested.

She nodded, loving that he'd proposed a distraction rather than trying to fix the situation. After slipping on her shoes, Skye followed Noah toward the stairs and away from the terrors of her past.

Chapter 14

The hands of time may tick no more.
Let darkness fall upon this door.
Now waves will wash up on this shore.
I won the fight but lost the war.
-Not Running Anymore, Bon Jovi

Chaos.

Reminders of what Skye lost lurked in every corner. Stacks of framed awards covered the dresser. Her Class A uniform hung from the bathroom door. Pictures from the last twelve years were scattered across the bed like dead leaves settling on a long-forgotten grave.

It was the purple heart that cracked her resolve.

The whispering ache spread, an unwelcome reminder of the scars plaguing her body. As the walls of the small apartment closed in, fast, shallow breaths seized Skye's chest. She had managed to avoid this for two days while methodically unpacking the boxes, but she'd left the ones that held the biggest threat of cracking her emotions for last.

Now, Skye knew that was a mistake.

Before she required a paper bag to control the rabid breathing, Skye grabbed her keys and messenger bag, letting the door slam as she double-timed it outside. She ignored the pain shooting up her leg with the fast pace because she needed air and distance from the memories, but most of all, she needed some closure. Time for a new mission.

Leaving all those memories in boxes would only taunt her. Skye knew that. She had to deal with all that stuff. A bonfire offered a tempting solution, but leaned toward impulsive and extreme. Someday she might regret burning everything. Living with the scars of her burned body weighed on her soul. There had to be a less extreme solution.

Her mother kept photo albums and scrapbooks. Dozens of books filled shelves in the hallway along the stairs in Skye's childhood home. Even now in the digital age, Amelia still printed pictures and put them into scrapbooks. Skye had always been more interested in frames, displaying pictures on walls to enjoy them and relive the memories. With all she'd lost, staring at those images hurt more than her injuries. While she didn't want them decorating her walls like old, faded wallpaper, she also didn't want to destroy those memories. Her mother's hobby seemed like the best solution.

Skye slid into the Honda, determined to kill two birds with a quick trip to Super Wal-mart. The shopping list on her memo app could be tackled while seeking out photo albums. She didn't plan to get all crazy with scrapbooking the way her mother did, but albums would be quick and easy. If she'd learned nothing else as a soldier, being practical would be forever ingrained in her habits. The battle for the last eight months of back pay still endured, but *retirement* pay had started coming in now that her discharge was official. The pay was less than expected, but enough to get by on a strict budget. At least until she figured out what to do with her life. Reporting for a self-inflicted pity party every day had gotten her nowhere.

The parking lot of the super store looked like a battle field, as many cars vying for a spot as there were leaving the lot. Too ashamed to use the handicap tag the DMV had granted her — thanks to Amelia's efforts — Skye trolled the lot until securing a spot next to a cart return stall.

She grabbed one of the carts, a strategy to keep her upright without needing crutches or a cane, and limped across the lot, keeping close to the parked cars as vehicles screamed up and down the lanes.

"It's just Wal-mart," she preached, trying to acknowledge that this was not a war zone. A retail store in a small town did not warrant the anxiety pulsing through her veins. There were no explosives here, no insurgents lurking in the shadows while waiting for the opportune moment to attack.

As Skye passed through the doors, she took in her surroundings. A group of people blocked the main aisle, laughing and chatting. To the right, the check-out registers buzzed with activity. Most were open, but lines formed behind every one she could see.

To the left, the bakery and produce area ran amok, people milling about, carts bumping, kids running around.

Having managed the crowd at the concert without any anxiety, Skye didn't understand why walking into this store surrounded her with an ominous cloud of fear. "You can do this," she encouraged and took a deep breath in as she set off on this mission. The grocery list was short. Maneuvering around other shoppers, she headed straight for an empty space in the produce area, parking the cart and tearing a few bags from the rack overhead. Her breaths shortened in length and increased in speed each time someone bumped her, so she worked as quickly as possible to get out of the busy aisle.

Things slowed down when Skye reached the meat section. Leaning against one of the freezers, she closed her eyes, ordered her lungs to be a bit more reasonable. Minutes or hours could have passed as she brought the anxiety to a halt. Checking her list, she made a mental note of everything she needed in this section and put the device down, focusing on the mission.

With haste, she collected each of the items before moving on to the next section. She had been in the store before and had the list organized by aisle, channeling the analyst and strategist the army had trained her to be. Skye wasn't here for a leisurely stroll. This was like any mission, she had an objective and focused on the most efficient way to achieve it. Civilians would make fun of the strategy, but since Skye despised grocery shopping, she found it effective in getting in and out as quickly as possible.

And so it went, dodging other shoppers while collecting goods in each aisle. Until a woman focused on her phone ran into her.

Skye's temper flared, but she made an effort to breathe through it and stay calm. "You shouldn't look at your phone while you're walking," Skye suggested as the woman scowled.

"It's a free country," the woman snarled.

Something Skye knew better than most. "I know. I spent 18 months in Afghanistan keeping it that way," she bellowed.

"Good for you, honey. Do you mind?" The woman angled her head, indicating Skye's cart blocked the path.

Skye gripped the cart and pushed by, the other cart making it difficult because the woman wasn't courteous enough to get it out of the middle of the aisle. When she managed to get her cart by the other one, the woman shoved her cart right into Skye's side.

Her eyes burned with tears as the stabbing pain exploded from her hip and across the burn scars. "You fucking bitch," Skye muttered, her steely control just a remnant with all the other shrapnel. If she had the strength, she'd let go of the cart and tear the woman apart.

But, if Skye let go of the cart now, she'd fall to the concrete floor.

"Thanks for your service," the woman said, giving a mock salute and stomping off.

"Oh my God, are you all right? That woman was a complete psycho," another woman said as she came up next to Skye.

"I'm fine," Skye said, tears pouring as the pain and humiliation made its stand against her will to lock it up. "I just need to keep moving."

Skye limped down the aisle the woman who had crashed into her came from. As fast as she could, she found her way into the baby section and pushed the cart into a corner, falling to the floor behind it where no one could see her.

"Oh, God, you're hyperventilating."

The woman tapped her fingers against a phone. Her garbled words were lost behind the ringing in Skye's ears. Unshed tears burned her narrowed vision. Hot and cold battled, sweat dampening her palms and neck.

"Just breathe," the woman pleaded. As if she had control of that. The pain throbbed, but humiliation and unreasonable panic took hold. Skye wished could float away, disappear like a cloud after the rain dried up. Instead, she gripped her good leg to her chest, closing her eyes and rocking like a child who had lost its mother.

In the blackness, orange flames came to life, consuming the meager hold Skye had on reality.

"Oh, God, she's shaking now. I don't know what to do," the woman whined. "She's on the floor, in the corner by the diapers."

Skye tried to crawl away, but the flames surrounded her, offering no escape. Screaming wouldn't do any good, so she huddled beneath the heat, praying for the fire to claim her quickly.

As the flames burned out, Skye opened her eyes, seeing a blur of dark blue approach from the other side of the cart.

"Oh, Jesus, Skye," she heard, the man's voice familiar but not comforting. He pushed the cart aside, not only freeing Skye from her self-imposed prison, but releasing the useless grip she had on the panic.

"Get away from me!" she demanded, her vision narrowing

so much she could have been looking through the sight of a rifle.

"Skye, it's me, Luke. Come on, you need to calm down. Take a breath in and hold it. Can you do that for me?"

Her head shook like a bobblehead, bouncing around with all the uncertainty crippling her. All she wanted to do was run, but the explosion had robbed her of that ability.

"It's an order, Skye. Breathe in and hold. Now."

Her body responded to the authority in Luke's voice. With a rhythm that matched the three-round bursts of an M4 rifle.

"Good. Now let it out, slowly if you can."

Without much breath to let out, Skye exhaled and sucked in another shallow breath, this one a little less on the rapid fire rhythm.

"Hold it," he commanded.

Skye counted off the repetitions. Her vision came into focus after fourteen, but it took twenty to get the breathing under control.

By that time, first responders formed a horseshoe around her position.

"The ambulance is here. Let's get you on the gurney," Luke said, his commanding voice replaced with a softer tone that put Skye on the defensive.

"I am not getting in an ambulance."

"Don't be stubborn. You just had a panic attack in the middle of Wal-mart. You need to get checked out."

"I'm fine," she insisted. "I just need a few minutes."

He sighed, the sound of frustration and resignation meshing with the ventilation system in the store. "Can you tell me what triggered it?" Luke asked.

Skye shook her head. The whole situation served up a good helping of humiliation. No way in hell could she give an after action review with an audience.

"I saw everything," the good Samaritan said from behind Luke. "This crazy woman crashed into her cart and then was super nasty about it. Then she deliberately ran into this poor woman. I don't know who the other woman was, but I took her picture."

"Do you want to press charges?" Luke asked Skye.

Press charges? For being run into with a shopping cart? "I just want to go home. Forget this happened." By taking a couple pain killers and drowning the humiliation in a six pack.

Luke crouched next to her again. "You can go home, but there's no forgetting," he said in a lowered voice. "You need to get this taken care of. PTSD is no joke."

"I don't have PTSD," she snapped.

Luke grunted and pulled out his cell phone. He walked away so Skye couldn't hear, but she had a feeling he called for back-up, and not the kind in uniform.

Ten minutes later, her suspicion was confirmed when Noah stormed past the first responders. "Oh, hell, Skye."

"I'm fine," she said.

Noah dropped into a crouch next to her, his assessing gaze raising her hackles. "I really hate it when you say that. Come on, I'll take you home."

Before she could insist on doing it herself, Luke and Noah lifted her off the floor. Pain shot up her right leg the same way it had when her brother tugged her out of the car and off the ground. The humiliation surged with a vengeance.

"Can you walk?" Noah asked.

"Yes," she snarled. "I told you, I'm fine."

"Forgive me if I don't believe you."

With Noah and Luke holding her arms in the same way her brothers had after the parking lot incident, Skye wondered how long she was going to have to endure these episodes. Moving to Sunset Valley meant life would get easier, but every experience presented a challenge she didn't know how to conquer.

Rather than hanging her head in shame, Skye hitched her chin up a little higher than usual. She'd fought in a war, for Chrissake. Twice. That should count for something.

"Where are you parked?" Luke asked.

"Near the carts." She nodded in the direction of the aisle

she'd left the car in.

"Not you," Luke scowled. "Noah."

"I'm behind you," Noah said. "You're not going to ticket me, are you?"

Luke laughed, still holding Skye's elbow even though she didn't need the assist. "Not this time, but don't make a habit of it."

As the two men shuffled her to Noah's car, Skye's instincts demanded fight or flight, but relief drowned out the impulse for either. She just wanted to get home. Going with Noah was the fastest way to make that happen.

She settled into Noah's Camry and even let him buckle her in. On autopilot, she reclined the seat a few inches and closed her eyes, hoping for the blackness and not the flames.

"Give me your keys, Skye, I'll have one of the guys bring your car home," Luke ordered. In the army, Skye didn't have an issue following orders, but Luke wasn't her commander. She swallowed the surging defiance and dug into the messenger bag on her lap to pull out the keys. "Get help Skye. This is some serious shit."

Offering a mock salute without bothering to open her eyes, Skye hoped that acknowledgment inspired him to back off.

After Luke closed the door, his words to Noah wafted through the closed window. *PTSD* echoed over and over in her head. The worst part, Noah agreed with his cousin.

She struck a little luck on the ride home though. Noah didn't utter a word until they pulled into the driveway. "Your place or mine?" he asked.

It should have made her laugh, but the reality of the situation cut a little too deep. She couldn't go back to her apartment, not with all those memories scattered around. "Yours."

He pulled up in front of the garage instead of driving around back. Skye managed to get in the house of her own volition and headed straight for Noah's bathroom.

The throbbing had subsided, but the anxiety remained. Skye

longed for the fog the painkillers brought. After taking a minute to reel in the anxiety, she flushed the toilet before digging into her bag for the pills. Two would do the job despite the compulsion to take three. In an effort to mask the sound of the pills rattling around while returning the bottle to her bag, Skye ran the faucet, then choked down the pills without water. All the while, she did her best to avoid her reflection. Months of being bed-ridden and having little to no appetite resulted in an appearance that bordered on the living dead. The panic attack probably pushed her closer to looking like the lifeless dead.

Leaving the bathroom, guilt rushed through every vein. If Noah knew or even suspected that she'd taken two pain pills, he'd go all drug police on her. The PTSD accusations were enough to deal with. When she found him in the living room reading a magazine, relief pushed the guilt aside.

"I'll let you rest," he said as Skye settled in the chair on the opposite side of the room. "But later we're going to talk about this whether you want to or not."

This.

The one syllable held too many accusations. Did it refer to her time in the bathroom or the panic attack? If he uttered the letters P-T-S-D again, she might dig deep for some of the self-defense skills acquired from years of training.

Instead of arguing that there was nothing to talk about, Skye opted to fight the battle later. For now, she just wanted to close her eyes and pretend this day never happened.

Chapter 15

I'm with you.
When hope is gone and all you want is the truth.
I'm with you.
You carry on when they say it's no use.
I'm with you.
If I got one thing, I got something to prove.
We all got nothing if there's nothing to lose.
I'm with you.
-I'm With You, Bon Jovi

Fear.

As Skye drifted off to sleep, it gripped Noah in a strangle hold that had him gasping for breath.

He'd been giving Skye space, letting her cope in her own way. What a mistake that had been. If today's incident offered any indication, she wasn't coping at all.

Even in sleep, she seemed tense, anxious. The white-knuckled fist should have relaxed, along with the shallow breaths, but just as the fear gripped Noah, the panic endured in Skye.

He remembered his time with Maddie, how she always burned aromatherapy oils. After a rough day, she chose lavender for its calming qualities. Noah made a mental note to look into that, maybe get some advice from Maddie about burners and stuff. That kind of thing might do something to calm his nerves too.

When a car pulled into the drive, Noah sprung up from his perch to peer out the window. His heart took a nose dive into his stomach at seeing the police chief's cruiser. Luke always called first, so just dropping in like this couldn't be a good sign.

Skye remained restless in her sleep. Noah stepped out the front door so as not to disturb her.

"Hey, man," Noah greeted.

"How's she doing?" Luke asked.

"Zonked out almost immediately."

"That was some serious shit that went down today. One of the witnesses videoed a good five minutes of it. I've never seen a panic attack that severe."

Noah had mixed feelings about not being there. While he didn't want to see Skye under that level of duress, he truly felt if he'd been with her, it never would have happened. "Thanks for being there," he said. Luke wasn't just his cousin, he was like a brother, Noah's best friend since they were young and the only person aside from Skye's brothers Noah trusted to protect her.

"I was two minutes down the road heading in the other direction when the dispatch came in. It's good I was that close. Took the EMTs another ten minutes to arrive on scene." Luke leaned on the cruiser, hands resting on the hood. Noah wished he could relax like that under these circumstances. His nerves were wound so tight, he worried he might launch into space like a rocket. Not even the warm mid-day sun soothed him.

"I'll to be honest, I don't know what to do. I want to shake some sense back into her, but I don't think that's going to do any good."

Luke shook his head. "She needs professional help —

counseling. She's dealing with a lot, the injuries, PTSD, separation anxiety. It's all normal given her circumstances, but she was the sole survivor of that explosion, so survivor guilt gets tossed into the circus."

"I'll talk to her, appeal to her reason," Noah said.

"Yeah, good luck with that," he grunted. "I've got her groceries in the cruiser."

"Really?" Noah asked. They had abandoned the cart in the diaper aisle. He hadn't even given the groceries a second thought.

"It wasn't me," Luke said, holding up his hands. "The lady who witnessed it stopped by the station, said she wanted to help, felt bad about what happened. So she bought Skye's groceries as a way to thank her for her service."

That made Noah smile and restored his faith in humanity. "Let's bring them around back. I don't want to wake her."

"She's at your place?" Luke asked.

"Yeah. I gave her the choice of where she wanted to go. She's sleeping in the recliner." Skye's choice inspired a hope that maybe she was ready to talk and admit to everything troubling her. Noah still clung to that hope.

They grabbed the bags and made their way around back.

"I found the woman who perpetrated the attack. She was checking out when I went back into the store. Skye said she didn't want to press charges, but I might have stretched the truth about that. Based on how white the woman got, I don't think she'll pull a stunt like that again."

"Good. She should be in jail, but I get why Skye wants to put it behind her."

"There's a little too much of that going on with Skye. She needs to stop ignoring her issues and face them," Luke added.

This wasn't news to Noah and he was doing his best to be there for her. It'd be easier if she wasn't so stubborn.

"What the hell?" Noah muttered when they walked into her apartment.

"Look's like Hurricane Skye unleashed in here," Luke murmured.

Noah put the bags on the table and made his way across the room. Photos were scattered all over her bed and dresser, frames filling one of the boxes.

Some of the pictures were snapshots of people, others were deliberate poses. Some included Skye, but most didn't. Then there were scenic pictures, mountains, the ocean, flowers.

"Did she take those?" Luke asked from over Noah's shoulder.

"I have no idea. They're really good." The photos were shot with the skill of an expert eye, the color perfect, the focal points framed with precision. "What do you make of the frames?" he asked.

Luke picked one out of the box, studied it, then did the same with another and another. None of the frames held photos. "If I had to guess, I'd say she took these pictures out of the frames. They're not new. There's dust and scratches."

"So what? Did she set off to buy new frames before shit hit the fan?"

"Possibly." Luke plucked a black box from the floor. "Or maybe she was planning something more extreme and destructive."

Noah suspected what the box held, those suspicions confirmed when Luke opened it to reveal a Purple Heart medal. "You think that sent her over the edge?"

"I'd bet my badge on it," Luke drawled. "This isn't the kind of honor normal soldiers strive to earn. With everything she's dealing with, I'd say she wanted to make all this disappear."

"Shit," Noah muttered, taking in the chaos. "What's worse, leaving this all out for her to deal with or packing it away?"

"Six of one, half a dozen of the other. It's a gamble, either way."

That wasn't helpful. "I can handle all this," Noah said. "You probably need to get back to work."

"Suppose I should. Make sure she gets help, even if you have to drag her kicking and screaming. I'd hate to see this develop into something worse."

Noah didn't need Luke to explain that. With Finn in the picture, *something worse* was easy to interpret. It seemed Skye already teetered on the edge of prescription drug addiction. Finn would do whatever he could to push her over.

After Luke set off, Noah put the groceries away before looking through the pictures. He didn't spot Rafe in any of them and the picture he'd seen the other day wasn't among the collection. Who the hell was this guy and why wouldn't Skye talk about him? She still loved the guy based on the way she held those dog tags and looked at that picture the other day.

Noah's heart cracked, filling his chest with the same jealousy he always tried to suppress when she had a boyfriend. They always seemed to be at opposite ends of a Ferris wheel when it came to relationships.

His jealousy wasn't fair to Skye, but Noah loved her, wanted to be with her, and she continued to push him away. Was it because of Rafe?

When his phone rang, it was a stark reminder he needed to respect her things and her space. He left everything where he found it and answered the call.

"Noah, this is Amelia. I was just outside working on my flower beds when Nadia Foster came home. She was just at Wal-mart and said Skye was taken away in an ambulance. I tried calling Skye, but she's not answering."

Noah took a deep breath to give himself a few seconds to decide on the best response. Amelia had a tendency to jump to conclusions, true or not, and based on his approach, she might not believe a word he said. "Skye is here. She's sleeping. There was an incident at Wal-mart, but she didn't need to go to the hospital."

"Oh my God, what happened? Is she all right? I'll be right over."

"She's fine, really. Like I said, she's sleeping. Don't come over. She needs to rest."

"But—"

"Amelia, please. I'll have her call you when she wakes up."

"Please, Noah, what happened?"

"A woman ran into Skye with her cart, deliberately. It caused Skye to have a panic attack. Someone called 911. Luke was first on the scene and called me. I brought her home."

"Home," Amelia sighed. "This is her home."

Noah didn't respond. This wasn't his argument and he knew Amelia well enough that even if he did try to argue the point with her, it would get him nowhere.

"I should come over," Amelia insisted.

"No," Noah said firmly. He knew of the rocky relationship between Skye and her mother. While Amelia meant well, Skye wouldn't see it that way. "She needs to rest. I'll have her call you when she wakes."

Amelia sighed and Noah hoped she was relenting. "Fine, but if I don't hear from her in a couple hours, I'm coming over."

"Okay," Noah said. He had no idea how long Skye would sleep, but made note of the time so he could call Amelia in a couple hours if Skye wasn't up by then.

Noah ended the call and went upstairs to find Skye still sleeping, a little more peaceful now than when he'd stepped outside. He went into the kitchen, unsure what the hell to do with himself. Luke had distracted him from the building fear, but now, with the terminal silence taunting him, it simmered below the surface. If he didn't find something to do, it would heat to a full boil again.

As he paced the kitchen, Skye stirred, nothing unusual, but in a split second she flailed in the chair like a fish out of water. Noah wasn't willing to let her ride it out. Crouching next to the chair, he shook her arm. "Skye, wake up."

Unresponsive, she still jerked around, so Noah shook her a little harder. "Skye, come on, wake up."

With a gasp her eyes opened. A sheen of sweat glistened across her forehead. Fast and shallow breaths made it seem like she'd just run a sprint instead of woken from sleep. Noah took her shaking hands in his, hoping to calm the chaos raging inside.

"You were having a nightmare," he explained.

She grunted and looked around wide-eyed, as if trying to remember where she was.

"What do you need?" Noah asked.

Pulling her hands away, Skye wiped her forehead and raked both hands through her pretty brown hair, pulling it all together and twisting it before letting it fall over one shoulder. "Coffee," she grunted when she seemed to get her bearings.

The request surprised Noah. He expected a standard answer, like *"nothing"* or *"I'm fine."* He smiled at the unexpected response, taking her hands again and giving them a gentle squeeze. "Any flavor requests or should I surprise you?"

She shook head, pushing a hand over her hair this time. When she smiled, Noah's breath hitched. "Surprise me."

Since Noah lived alone and worked from home, the Keurig proved a lifesaver, much more efficient than brewing a pot every time he wanted a cup of joe. He grabbed a white chocolate, a flavor purchased after Skye moved into the apartment, and brewed a cup.

Without delay, he crossed the room, holding the cup steady as Skye took it.

"Thank you," she whispered.

"My pleasure."

She grabbed his hand before he could walk away. "For the rescue too. You know I hate that, but I'm glad it was you."

As this door opened, Noah knew he would be an idiot not to step through it, but he couldn't just pummel her with demands about what happened. Instead, he chose a more subtle approach. "The woman who called 911 bought your groceries and delivered them to the police station. Luke dropped them off."

Skye's head shook as her eyes narrowed. "Why would she

do that? I don't even know her."

"She said she wanted to help, to thank you for your service."

Still shaking her head, Noah's heart ruptured when those pretty blue eyes widened and filled with tears.

"What's wrong?" Noah asked, squeezing her hand.

"I hate that, being thanked for my service. I never know what to say. It's not like I joined the army out of some overwhelming sense of duty. I joined to get the hell out of Sunset Valley."

Now Noah shook his head. "Your reasons don't matter. It's still a commitment, a sacrifice."

She tugged her hand away, anger narrowing her eyes. "What would you know about it?"

"Don't do that," he said.

"Do what? Call you out on your bullshit?" she snarled. The sudden mood swing exploded without warning, but Noah refused to back down.

"How about if I call you out on yours?" he snapped, standing and looming next to the chair. "What the hell happened to you today, Skye? What the hell happened in Afghanistan to send you into a panic attack in the middle of Wal-mart?"

"Nothing," she insisted, looking away, the fight gone from her eyes.

"Bullshit," he said.

Her head snapped back to him, her eyes wide, the fight back in them as if he'd just pushed a button.

That was good. Noah wanted a fight. "It wasn't nothing and you aren't fine. We all know it, your parents, your brothers, Luke, me. We all see you falling apart and you're not doing a goddamned thing to help yourself. That stops right now."

Skye rolled her eyes. "There he is, the righteous hero, trying to fix the broken soldier."

"If that's how you want to see it, fine, but we both know I'm not the bad guy here."

Skye had no response, sipping her coffee and avoiding eye contact as the silence thundered between them.

This woman who had returned home just a few weeks ago was a stranger. The Skye he knew and loved never backed down, demanding things go her way. Sometimes she would bend, but that proved rare. This woman in front of him gave up too easily. Convinced the old Skye was buried inside her, Noah just had to keep pushing the right buttons to free her.

"I saw the pictures on your bed," he said, stoking fire.

Based on Skye's glare, he hadn't just stoked the fire, but threw gasoline on it. "Is that how it's going to be? You poking through my stuff behind my back?"

"I wasn't poking. I was putting the groceries away. It looked like a hurricane had blasted through the room."

She shook her head again but didn't speak and didn't look at him. Not ready to give up, Noah held out his hand. "Come on."

Skye glared at his hand before looking at him.

"You started something today that you obviously can't finish alone. Let's do it together."

"What if I don't want to?" she scowled.

"I don't give a shit what you want. You need to face whatever is down there. I'm going to be right there by your side. You will survive this. I promise."

Skye finished her coffee and stood without taking Noah's hand. She stepped right up to him, her lips curved into a smirk. "When did you grow a pair?"

Noah laughed. "When you lost your set," he joked right back.

Chapter 16

In these hands I held the gun
But it's too late for dying.
Now there's nothing worth hiding.
I've lost love, lived with shame.
I was humbled by my fall from grace.
On the steps of decision
It's revenge or forgiveness.
-Learn To Love, Bon Jovi

Secrets.

Skye had hoped to keep them locked and buried so deep that the secrets would eventually fade into darkness. As usual, hope left her hanging high and dry. Noah's persistence and perseverance hadn't diminished over the years. He wouldn't to let things go and since Skye didn't have an ounce of fight left, she had to relent this time.

"Let's start with something simple," Noah said, moving to the bathroom door where her dress uniform hung. "Where do you want this?"

Since *burn it* would earn his disapproval, Skye shrugged and tried to blink back the tears. "I have no idea."

"Luke said something about separation anxiety. Does looking at this uniform trigger that?" he asked.

"You playing shrink now?" she chuckled despite the tears.

"Whatever it takes," he said, nonplussed. "Talk to me, Skye. Why does looking at this uniform bring tears to your eyes?"

She swiped at them, trying to make those tears disappear, but they were as relentless as Noah and his newfound mission. "The army was my career. I liked it. Some days it sucked. Some days I was ready to walk away." Like when she had to take orders from a newbie officer who was greener than the uniform, or from a senior NCO with a stick up her ass or a chip on his shoulder. Then there were the ass-holes whose egos were so big, a two-ton truck was the only thing that could stand the weight.

But, there was also camaraderie, pride, a sense of belonging she'd never felt anywhere else — except with Noah.

"I didn't want to be discharged. They didn't give me the choice, said with my injuries I wasn't deployable." It was bullshit. Even amputees were able to serve. All of Skye's limbs were intact, she just needed time to learn to compensate for her injuries.

"Where did you keep this before?" he asked.

"In a closet."

That was one thing lacking in this apartment. The small closet under the stairs didn't have a pole or any other means of hanging clothes.

"I never finished the closet," Noah said, as if reading her thoughts. "Okay, that's on me. I'll get something installed in there. For now, why don't we hang this in the laundry room? We can put a trash bag over it as a dust cover if you want."

Skye nodded, prompting Noah to take the uniform out of the apartment. A small burden seemed to lift, leaving Skye feeling lighter and more balanced. That was until she turned to the pictures scattered all over the bed.

A chill raced up her spine. She couldn't do this. Every picture served as a reminder of something lost, something she'd been forced to leave behind.

"Tell me about the pictures," Noah prompted as he stood next to her, his shoulder brushing hers.

There was a familiar comfort in that innocent touch, one that made her heart beat a little faster.

"These are memories," she sighed.

"They look like good memories," he said, giving her shoulder a gentle nudge.

"They were."

"You had all these in frames?"

Skye nodded, the tears fighting their way into her eyes. While the pain hummed with only a dull roar, the fog she loved had worn off while she slept. The longing to have it back pulsed through her veins, desperate for the false euphoria that clouded the memories and the reality of who she'd become.

"Why did you take them out?" Noah asked.

Skye shook her head as a sob escaped. She didn't fight it, hoping if she let it go maybe Noah would cut her some slack and let this go.

As Noah's arm moved across her shoulder, he turned and pulled her against his solid body. Clinging to the security he offered, Skye cried into his chest, doing a bang-up job of hiding while the emotions jumped into the driver's seat and gunned it. Noah's warm and enduring strength soothed her like a drug, one Skye was desperate to OD on.

She gasped a few times, a feeble attempt to catch her breath. It was only when the well dried up that the crying came to a slow halt.

Noah continued to hold her, his warmth pushing away the chill of the break-down. She turned her head, snuggling against his chest and taking a few moments to just enjoy his spicy scent and strong body.

"Better?" he asked.

"Not really," she sighed, stepping out of his arms. "Oh, God, I soaked your shirt."

He looked down and shrugged before reaching one arm behind his head and tugging the shirt off. Finding a dry spot of cotton, Noah wiped her cheeks.

He smelled so good, his musky deodorant mixing with his natural scent. It was how a man was supposed to smell, strong and enticing. Skye met his gaze, those dark eyes like a storm, sparking with the threat of something she didn't dare embrace or even acknowledge.

"Skye," he whispered, melting her heart. With his hand cupping her nape, he pulled her to him and planted a chaste kiss to her forehead.

As he walked across the room, Skye stared, completely enamored with his fit body. She'd seen him without a shirt more times than she could remember, but didn't remember him ever looking this good.

He disappeared from the apartment, returning moments later. He slid a different shirt over his head, one he must have grabbed from the laundry room.

"When did you get ..." hot is what she wanted to ask, but needed to keep their friendship on an even keel. "So buff?" she finished.

Noah smiled as if he'd read her thoughts and approved. "I joined the gym a few years ago. If I work out five days a week, I can eat whatever the hell I want without having to shop in the big man's store."

"Well," she cleared her throat, "you look good."

"I can lose the shirt, you know, if it'll help get you through this," he teased.

Noah without a shirt offered a nice distraction, but she feared where things might lead if he took it off again. Skye's heart wasn't just broken, it had been shattered and crushed — add the guilt and she didn't have the makings of a good girlfriend. Since Noah didn't do casual relationships, she needed to push any wayward thoughts aside and focus on strengthening their friendship, not making it more complicated.

Unsure what to say, Skye turned to the pictures. "I was going to buy an album to put these in, but I didn't make it that far on my little shopping trip."

Noah chuckled as he stood next to her, his shoulder brushing hers again. "So what you're really saying is the thought of scrapbooking sent you into a panic."

Skye laughed because even though that's not what happened, it wasn't a far stretch to think it could have. "I don't have a creative bone in my body," she admitted.

"That's not true," Noah stepped forward and scooped up one of the pictures. "This shows creativity and maybe a bit of raw talent."

"Shut up," she joked.

Noah held the picture out. "I'm serious, Skye. The way you framed this scene, the colors, the light — it's perfect, beautiful."

It was one of her favorite pictures, a shot of the sun shining through the aspens in Kenosha Pass. The scenic vistas in the mountains and the beautiful hiking trails were among the many reasons she'd loved being stationed at Ft. Carson.

"It's just a snapshot," she said.

"It's more than that. You could sell some of these on stock photo sites, generate some income, or, even better, make calendars and prints. Open your own online store. I could show you how."

"Oh, I don't think so." Skye couldn't put herself out there like that. Taking pictures was just a hobby. She had no skill.

"Just think about it. In the meantime, why don't we collect these and ask your mother to put them in an album for you?"

"What?" she asked, sure he'd lost his mind.

"Your mom loves to scrapbook and she wants to feel like she's helping you. She gets to do something she loves and you don't have to lower yourself to something you hate doing."

It sounded reasonable, but there was one small problem. "She'll never let me hear the end of it. Remember the album she did for me when we graduated? For years she asked if I still looked at it, if it survived the moves. Ugh, the woman is insufferable."

"She loves you and it makes her happy. It's a good solution. Otherwise, I can hit the store and get you some supplies."

Skye had to admit she wasn't all that disappointed about not making it to the crafty section of the store. "Fine. You're right. I don't want to do it and Ma would love it. I'll suck it up."

They gathered the pictures and put them into a small box. "Let's do the same with these," Noah said, rifling through the framed awards on the dresser."

Skye agreed and they spent the next ten minutes removing them all from the frames and placing awards in the box with the photos.

Then he picked up the box with the Purple Heart. "What about this?" he asked.

"You can put it in the garbage," she said, walking into the other half of the apartment and away from the symbol of all her guilt and shame. She dug into her bag, pulling out the bottle of pills. Before she got to the sink, Noah put his hand over hers.

"Don't, Skye. You pass out whenever you take one of those. Don't do that just to avoid this." He held out the open box, but Skye couldn't look at it. All her life purple had been her favorite color. Now she couldn't stand to look at it.

"My hip hurts," she said, tugging her hand free and shaking the bottle. "I need this."

"I've seen you in pain," he started.

"I'm always in pain," she snarled.

"But some days it's manageable. Am I wrong?"

She shook her head, hating that he'd figured this out.

"Right now, it's manageable. I can tell by the way you stand and walk. Taking one of those isn't going to do anything except

128

knock you out."

That was a bad thing? "Don't pretend to know about my pain," she said, her body tensing for battle.

"I'm not trying to pick a fight," he said, holding up his hands. "I'm just trying to understand."

Skye shook her head. "You can't possibly understand."

Noah tapped the black box against his palm. "Right, because I've never been to war, because I've never left Sunset Valley."

It's what Skye had said, what she had believed, but as Noah threw the words back in her face, they didn't seem to fit.

"Because you're not me," she said.

"Then tell me. Why aren't you proud of this, Skye? Why does it make you run?"

The panic strangled her, stealing her breaths as sweat cooled her burning forehead.

"Tell me," Noah persisted. "Tell me what happened over there."

Skye had kept the secret so long, it surprised her how it surged to the surface. She tried to fight it back, get it to retreat, but maybe if she told Noah, he'd back off and stop making her feel things she didn't want to feel. "I killed them. I was driving. They were my responsibility, but I wasn't paying attention and I killed them. Rafe, Specialist McMann, PFC Pinnock. They're dead because I didn't do my job."

She grabbed the medal from Noah's hand and stormed across the room, tossing it in the garbage bin near her bed.

"You didn't kill them, Skye. You were attacked."

"Because I wasn't paying attention," she yelled. She wanted to break something, punch someone, take a dive into a cold lake and hold her breath until she couldn't hold it and had no choice but to draw the cold water into her lungs and drown.

She wanted the pain in her leg and side to throb with the same anger that pumped through her veins. She wanted it to ache with such vengeance that Noah would see the physical signs and not judge her for taking the painkillers. She wanted to get lost in the fog.

"We're done here," she said, storming back across the room.

"Don't quit now," he said. "You put a crack in the giant wall you've built around yourself. If we have to tear it down brick by brick, we will."

"There's no we, Noah. I'm the one who screwed up. I'm the one with blood on my hands." The one who had no career and no usable skills in the civilian world. Noah needed to stop being the eternal optimist and get a taste of reality.

"There's always a we. Always."

Chapter 17

Corporate countries go to war
Behind the lies they're fighting for
And black from an old king's soul won his round.
How can someone take a life
In the name of God and say it's right.
-Bullet, Bon Jovi

Bitterness.

There wasn't always a *we*. There hadn't been in five years, not since he'd told her he loved Maddie and wouldn't leave when Skye asked him to.

As if that pill wasn't bitter enough, now Skye had nothing, no man to love, no career to keep her level-headed, no dreams for the future.

The last five years had been all about the war. For whatever reason, she'd managed to dodge deployments in her first seven years in the army, but that kind of luck couldn't last forever. She'd no sooner returned from that first deployment when she got orders to Ft. Hood and geared up for another deployment.

Skye didn't even know what the hell they were fighting for. The war had been going for too many years to count. It should have ended years ago, but the government kept sending the cavalry on a merry-go-round instead of on a mission that had a conclusion.

Skye fought though, because she'd sworn the oath, and never uttered a single complaint about being deployed. Some days were harder than others, when all she wanted was a comfortable bed and blankets that didn't have sand woven into the fabric. There were also days when it felt like she'd made a difference. The innocent people of Afghanistan weren't all that different. They were families, just trying to keep food on the table and love in their hearts.

Now, though, it all seemed a waste. Twelve years of her life dedicated to her country and all she had to show for it was a pile of medals, a scar-ridden body, and an empty soul.

Well, she did have a healthy supply of guilt and shame. Maybe that counted for something.

"Skye," Noah sighed from behind her. She'd forgotten he loomed just a breath away. Of course, he'd been the one to stir the pot, to bring all the guilt and shame to the surface, to make her remember she'd lost everything.

She turned around, ready to ask him to leave, and found him standing with that damned black box in his hand. Despite every light in the basement illuminating the open space, darkness threatened to close in and steal her resolve once more.

No one wanted a Purple Heart, at least no one with a firm head on her shoulders. No one wanted to go to war either, but the government had insisted on her participation. The Purple Heart was just the icing on the cake.

"I get that you don't want this right now," he said, holding it in his strong hand, "but someday you'll regret it if you just toss it out with the garbage."

Noah always had to be the voice of reason. Always. She chuckled at that thought.

Always.

It was more than a word, at least between her and Noah. Like he'd said the day she shattered all of his picture frames, it held a promise.

The words from the Bon Jovi song played in her mind. In the song, *always* spoke of an intimate promise. It held more than that for two friends who had spent their entire lives ignoring their attraction to each other. As she looked at Noah, the man who looked the same as he always had, the shaved hair, the trimmed goatee, the casual t-shirt and jeans, she saw someone different than the boy she'd made that blood on blood promise with. He managed to send her shattered heart aflutter even with that serious gaze.

As Skye traced the scar on her hand, the symbol of their friendship and the evidence of their promise, a million questions raced through her head. How would things be different if they'd gone out in high school? Would Skye have joined the army? Would Noah have gone with her?

Would she be broken and battered? Bitter and angry? Would the shame and guilt still have taken up permanent residence in her soul?

"You keep it," she said, nodding at the box.

"Me keeping it doesn't help you," Noah said.

Skye didn't see how keeping it in her possession would help, but the fight ran dry. She couldn't keep going round and round with Noah, not with his relentless tactics. "Just give it to my mother with all the other ... mementos," she said with a generous shot of sarcasm. "I'm sure she can figure out something creative to do with it."

Noah shook his head. "I'm not giving this stuff to your mother. You are."

Jesus, was he trying to push her over the edge?

"I'll be your getaway driver, though. You want to head over now?"

Skye snagged the black box from Noah and tossed it in the

cardboard box with everything else. Focusing on the mission at hand, she grabbed the collection of haunting memories and limped to the door, her hip and leg reminding Skye of her limitations.

As she pushed on the door handle, she realized Noah didn't follow. "What about the things in here?" he asked. Peering back into the apartment, she found his hand on the box from Afghanistan.

She hadn't sorted through the box yet but knew what lurked within the variegated walls. Aside from Rafe's dog tags and the photo, there were a few other photos she'd printed to hang at her desk and toss away when her tour in the desert ended. "There's nothing in there for my mother to use," she told Noah.

"What about the picture of Rafe and the dog tags?" he asked.

Hearing Rafe's name on Noah's voice sent a chill down her spine. Had she not risked it all for Noah five years ago, she would have told him about Rafe, would have trusted him to keep it secret. Once their friendship took a turn though, there was no going back — at least, that's what she'd thought. Noah was here now, a rock in his unwavering support. It felt like a time warp, like Skye had never exposed her heart that day and lost. "Please don't mention Rafe to my mother."

"Skye," he said, shaking his head.

"Please, Noah. He's dead. It's done. She'll want details and I can't ..."

"I don't agree with keeping this a secret, but I'll do it because you asked me to."

"Thank you," she said, relief creating a funnel that drained the building anxiety. She didn't want to argue with Noah and needed to bring this stuff to her mother's now, before losing her nerve and tossing a match on it instead.

After they pulled out of the driveway, Noah gave her a quick look and breathed a sigh that warned Skye of bad news.

"What?" she demanded.

"Your mother knows about what happened at Wal-mart.

Apparently, her neighbor was there."

Mrs. Foster had always been a gossip-monger, but she wasn't the only one in the town. Skye imagined everyone in Sunset Valley had heard she'd suffered a heart attack and was on life support.

"You should have told me before," she snarled.

"Why, so you could use that as an excuse not to go? You can't avoid your mother forever, Skye. She just wants to see you happy."

Maybe that was true, but that didn't mean Amelia made things easy. She liked things her way regardless of what anyone else wanted.

Sighing, she sat back and stewed on how to deal with her mother's worry, because that is what they'd be walking into.

Bon Jovi erased the silence during the drive. Noah sang along with every song. Before long, the beat and words wound their way into Skye's soul, tamping out the bitterness and soothing the anger.

Skye had forgotten how powerful music could be. Even though she'd been reminded at the concert, the music had been lost in everything else that transpired since that night.

She'd taken an iPod to Afghanistan, relying on playlists to lift her spirits when the deployment became a burden, or to keep her up when things weren't going well. Rafe had made fun of her obsessive love of Bon Jovi, but eventually embraced it. While he didn't love the music the way Noah did, he appreciated the thoughtful lyrics and rhythmic beat.

When *One Wild Night* came on, Noah bumped her arm as he jammed in the driver's seat. "Come on, I know you know the words."

It was such a fun and fast rhythm that Skye couldn't help herself. She bounced in her seat, too, singing off-key because she couldn't carry a tune to save her life. Noah never gave her shit about it even though he had a perfect singing voice.

Skye's spirits fell, though, when *Keep the Faith* played, because the lyrics were right, there were wars that couldn't be won, and it was so hard to hang on with no one to lean on.

"Hey," Noah said, drawing her out from the pity party. "Come on, you can't keep the faith if you don't sing along."

Skye couldn't bring herself to do it, but she did tune out the words to focus on the music. The powerful beat had her left foot tapping and rocking out.

When *Something for the Pain* played, Skye burst into laughter. Boy, did she need something for the pain, especially as they pulled into her parent's driveway.

"Are you coming in?" she asked Noah.

He laughed. "Are you kidding? If I don't, you mother will unleash one of her legendary guilt trips on me. I would never willingly subject myself to one of those."

He had a point. Amelia liked things a certain way, and Skye's friends had always been required to come into the house and say hello, even if they were just picking Skye up.

Skye carried the box even though Noah offered. She needed something to keep her hands steady. This was no big deal. It wasn't. So why was she shaking?

"Skye, oh, honey. Are you okay?" Amelia said when they walked into the kitchen where she watered the jungle of plants in the front window.

"Hi, Ma. I'm fine." Skye said, putting the box on the table to give her mother a hug. Amelia held on a little longer than necessary, but she'd been doing that ever since visiting Skye in the hospital.

Noah hugged Amelia too and they all sat at the table. "Noah said you'd call. If I'd known you were coming over, I would have made brownies or something. Do you want coffee?"

"No, thanks," Skye responded. "We're not staying long."

"Oh," Amelia sighed.

Skye didn't let Amelia's disappointment deter the mission. "Ma, I have all these pictures and awards and stuff. I wondered if you would put them into albums. I hate doing that, but I know you love to."

Amelia's face lit up like she'd just won the lottery. "Really? You want me to make a scrapbook for you?" She tugged the box across the table and peered inside.

"Just an album," Skye insisted, but already knew her mother wouldn't do something that simple. "Whatever you want to do," she added in compromise.

"Oh, Skye, this means so much to me, that you would trust me with your army memories."

Skye wanted to say it was no big deal, but she'd never let her mother near any of her personal belongings like this, so she couldn't just shrug it off.

"Look at all these awards. I had no idea … oh," she gasped, pulling the black box out. "Your Purple Heart."

"Right, well we need to go." Skye stood and hoped her mother wouldn't argue about them leaving.

"Are you sure you can't stay?" Amelia asked, but Skye witnessed the eagerness to get started on this new project, so took the opportunity to make a quick escape.

They said their good-byes, Amelia once again hugging Skye long and tight. Skye found little comfort in the embrace and wondered what kind of person that made her.

Once back in the car, Noah headed in the opposite direction from his house. "Where are we going?" she asked.

"It's a surprise."

Skye hated surprises and Noah knew it, obviously going the extra mile to torture her today.

It didn't take long to figure it out, though. Once he turned down an old dirt road, she knew their destination. "The boat launch?" she asked.

"Can't get anything by you," he quipped.

"There's nothing else down this road," she reminded him. "We need a six pack, and your dad's cigars."

Noah laughed. "I know, right? We should have raided your dad's mini-fridge before we left their house."

The boat launch was a popular party spot when growing up. Fortunately, the chief preferred to let teens go with a warning rather than arrest them. Skye hoped the new chief practiced the same principles. Given how much Luke skirted the law as a teen, she couldn't imagine him being much of a hard-ass.

So early in the season, the empty parking area was no surprise. "It's too cold to go skinning dipping," she said, not that it was an option. As kids, they only skinny dipped in the dark, when no one could see all the good stuff. Now, Skye wouldn't risk it at all. Her scars were enough for her to look at. The thought of anyone else seeing them, especially Noah, inspired a shiver.

"You're such a party pooper," he chuckled.

"Right. Tell me you're not shriveling up just thinking about how cold that water is."

He pinned her with a serious look as he put the car in park. "I can assure you, I am not shriveling."

The heat in his voice shot straight to her core, her thighs squeezing together with hopeful anticipation and sending a thrill straight up her spine. Skye shook it off. She and Noah were patching up their friendship, but she couldn't take the leap with him that she'd wanted all those years ago. Rafe would be alive if she hadn't been so careless. If he was, maybe she'd be with him now, instead of Noah.

Doubt joined the emotional storm as she struggled to get out of the car. Maybe when they returned from deployment it wouldn't have worked with Rafe. Skye had found it hard to believe he would give up his career just to be with her. Skye hadn't been willing to give up hers to be with him.

The guilt reared its ugly head as she and Noah walked to the end of the dock. He spread a blanket that he'd grabbed from the backseat and they dangled their legs off the dock's edge. Skye could only swing her good leg, reminding her of the bitterness she'd wallowed in all day.

"Why are we here?" she asked, unable to bear the growing silence.

"For truth," he said. "You're not telling me everything. I want to know the whole story, Skye, not just the parts you think I want to hear."

Chapter 18

I don't want to see the day
I'd say these words to you.
I didn't want to have to explain
Sometimes heroes have to lose.
It's killing me to see you cry.
-River Runs Dry, Bon Jovi

Honesty.

Before they went to Amelia's, Skye had opened up, talking about what happened, giving Noah insight into all she'd endured. Then she slammed the door shut. As the silence extended between them, Noah could see her retreating again. He couldn't let that happen, not when there were some truths she had yet to share.

"So, Rafe was in your platoon," he muttered more than asked, trying not to sound bitter. He should be happy that Skye found love, but with her being home, Noah had hoped she would find it with him.

Skye shook her head. "First Lieutenant Rafe Warren," she said, the stoic tone of her voice revealing far more than he knew she wanted it to. "He was my platoon leader."

Noah studied her, unable to put a voice to his questions without sounding accusatory. While Skye hadn't been one to follow the rules as a kid, she did in the army. She'd been so proud of her accomplishments, always sharing them with Noah and even bragging about how she'd grown up, learned she didn't need to be wild and rebellious to make a name for herself. Getting involved with her platoon leader didn't sound like something she would do. "Isn't that—"

"Fraternization?" she interrupted. "Yeah. We could have gotten in some serious shit for being together, but we had plans. He was going to leave active duty, join the reserves. If we weren't in the same unit, we couldn't get in trouble."

Her voice trailed off, like she wanted to say something more but couldn't find the words. Maybe she didn't want to say anything more and chose to keep the words close to the vest. That seemed closer to reality given how shut off she'd been since coming home.

"Skye," he prodded, hoping she would continue. She didn't respond, just sat there, swinging her leg and looking out over the calm water.

Noah gave her time because he didn't want to be a dick. They'd waged these silent wars before, a lifetime ago. Back then, Skye always caved. She preferred a fight over silence. Noah preferred the fight too, mostly because he couldn't understand the silence. A quiet Skye was just a storm brewing in the distance.

"It was serious, with you and Rafe?"

The tears streaming down her cheeks wrecked him, but to move forward, she needed to talk this out.

"The stupid, stupid man," she sobbed. "We were on patrol. I can't even remember the name of the village. It looked just like all the others, houses in shambles, garbage everywhere, stray dogs wandering the sand-covered streets."

Noah couldn't fathom the carnage and poverty she'd witnessed. She had always described her work as a desk job, had even assured him before that first deployment that she'd be safe behind the fenceline of the army base.

Skye wiped away the tears, her head shaking. "He pulled me aside when we got back to the vehicle. He couldn't get down on one knee, didn't have a ring. He gave me one of his dog tags, asked me to marry him."

"Oh, Skye," Noah said, his arm moving around her as he scooted closer. She tried to shrug him off, but Noah held on.

"That's why I wasn't paying attention. I was giddy."

"I don't know anything about IEDs, but aren't they designed so you don't see them? How can you know you would have seen it?"

"I don't," she conceded. "But I should have died too. There were four of us in that vehicle. Why am I the only one who survived?"

Above everything else, Skye was a kind, caring person. It didn't surprise Noah that she blamed herself. "You're not responsible, Skye. Being happy because someone loved you isn't what caused the explosion."

She pushed back on the dock and struggled to stand. When Noah tried to help, she shoved at him.

"I want to go home," she demanded.

Noah grabbed her hand as she started off, stopping her momentum. "Not until you admit it isn't your fault."

She looked at him, the storm raging in her eyes. It was wrong to want to kiss her, especially if she was mourning her fiance, but the compulsion gripped Noah so firmly he couldn't stop himself from closing in on her personal space. Her hair was like silk as he smoothed a hand over it, stopping at her nape and holding her steady as his mouth lowered to hers.

To his surprise she didn't push him away.

Noah had dreamed of this for years, fantasized about it more times than he could remember. Her lips were soft, warm, welcoming, the sweet connection shooting straight to his heart.

Skye deepened the kiss, her arms going around Noah's shoulders and pulling herself closer. When her tongue swept across his lips, they parted as if being commanded, his tongue meeting hers in an explosion of love and lust and need. Her breasts crushed against his chest made his heart beat even more wildly, the hand that had been holding hers moving to the small of her back.

Her body writhed against his, a sexy little moan vibrating against his tongue. Every carnal instinct urged him to cup her ass and pull her closer, but Noah forced himself to be reasonable and pulled himself away.

"Skye," he sighed.

"Isn't that what you want? To make love to me so I can forget about the pain? To fuck the guilt away?"

"That's not—"

"Bullshit, Noah. You always want to fix things. I told you before, I can't be fixed. Getting me to talk about what happened changes nothing, but maybe a quick poke will make it all better."

She was the one who pushed the kiss further than it should have gone. Noah wasn't innocent, he was a man, after all, who wanted Skye more than he wanted his next breath, but he wouldn't take advantage of her.

"When we make love, it'll be for love, for us, not because you think I'm trying to make some noble gesture or *fix you*," he said, putting air quotes around the last part. Helping wasn't fixing and he had grown tired of Skye accusing him of that. "You got that?"

"When?" she smirked.

Jesus, he wanted to kiss that smirk right off her face and hold her soft body in his arms again. "There's no *if* for me, Skye. I love you and I'm not giving up on you or us."

That seemed to take the steam out of her fight and fired up the side of her that liked to run. She walked to the car, her gait determined despite the limp.

Fight or flight, it didn't matter. Noah loved her and after

feeling her lips and tasting her, he wanted her more than he ever had. It was going to take the patience of a saint to get her to admit she needed help, but Noah was more determined than ever.

Chapter 19

Tonight I'll dust myself off,
Tonight I'll suck my gut in.
I'll face the night and I'll pretend
I got something to believe in.
-Something to Believe In, Bon Jovi

Lies.

They filled every syllable Noah uttered and every bit of hope that stirred in Skye's heart.

She wanted to believe him, so much so she could taste the hope that lingered on her tongue. After that kiss, she wanted to jump right to the *when*, but Skye didn't deserve it and Noah deserved more than she could offer.

She had killed Rafe, plain and simple.

The bigger truth hurt even more. Rafe shouldn't have been on that patrol. The only reason he was beyond the safety of the gates was because of Skye. He'd made a vow to keep her safe, so if he wasn't assigned to the same patrol, he swapped with someone. That day, he had swapped.

Skye had been selfish enough not to deter him. She didn't mind the patrols, but having Rafe by her side made them more than tolerable. Their time together was limited because of the mission and their schedules, so she would take it where she could get it. Even if it was a patrol that could go from routine to catastrophic in the blink of an eye.

Because of her limp and physical limitations, it only took a few steps for Noah to catch up with her. "Skye," he pleaded.

"What do you want from me?" she demanded, exasperated with this man and the whole day.

"Admit it wasn't your fault."

Tired of his hope, of all his perfect solutions, Skye surrendered. "Fine. It wasn't my fault," she growled, faking a confidence she hoped would convince Noah to back the hell off.

"Skye," he said, that plea in his voice making her want to stomp and scream and beg him to leave her alone.

Except stomping would only piss off her leg and hip.

She stopped, facing him only to see hopeful desperation on his face. It melted the ice around her heart, at least what was left of the ice after that kiss.

She licked her lips thinking about how his had felt against hers, how he had tasted when their tongues met, how she wanted that again.

Skye didn't want to hurt Noah. The one thing she knew for sure was that giving in to this thing bubbling between them would hurt him beyond repair.

"I promise to try," she compromised, wondering where this new set of tears pooling in her eyes had come from. "That's the best I can do right now."

"Thank you," he said, his fingers brushing her cheek.

His lips pressed to hers for just a moment, awakening that desire she shouldn't be feeling. On it's coattails came the guilt, because being with Noah felt like a betrayal to Rafe. It didn't matter that he was dead.

You have to stop kissing me like that.

But, Noah's affectionate smile wouldn't allow the words to cross her lips.

"Want to go out for dinner? Any place you want," he offered.

She was about to say no. Skye didn't want to go on a date with Noah and the tight budget didn't allow for dinner out. Before she could find the words to explain that, her phone interrupted.

Seeing it was Vaughn on the caller ID fired up her frustration. "Hello," she said with a fake smile.

"Where the hell are you? I've been sitting on your patio for over an hour."

"You have shitty phone etiquette," she responded.

"Sorry," he said with a healthy dollop of sarcasm. "Hi, Sarge. How are you?"

Skye rolled her eyes and bit back an angry retort. "What do you want?" she asked, keeping it simple.

"I have news. Great news. When will you be home?"

"Noah and I were going out to dinner," she said, because dinner with Noah had to be safer than great news from her brother.

"Oh, really?" Vaughn sang. "How's *that* going?"

Well, shit. She didn't want to give her brother the wrong impression. Besides, the best way to get him to leave her alone was to face the music. "Forget it. We'll be there in fifteen minutes."

She disconnected before her brother could respond. "Vaughn has some sort of great news. He's waiting at your house."

"All right, I'll make dinner then. Think Vaughn will mind if I swing by the store on the way home?"

"Do you think I care if Vaughn minds?" she laughed.

Ten minutes later, Noah parked at the supermarket. "I'll just wait here," Skye said.

"Is your leg bothering you?" he asked.

Her leg always bothered her and since Noah didn't let her take anything for the pain earlier, the throbbing she'd grown accustomed to persisted. The more daunting issue was the anticipation of another panic attack if she stepped through those doors. "Yes, a little. I don't want to slow you down."

Noah studied her, firing up a good dose vulnerability and self-consciousness. "I don't think it's the pain keeping you from going in there. You can't avoid these stores forever," he said.

"That's not what I'm doing," she lied. "Fine, I'll go in."

The slow pace made Skye crazy even though Noah didn't seem to mind. She wasn't the type of person to stroll through a store. Since childhood, she always stepped with purpose, even if she didn't have one. It's not that she needed to hurry, it was just her way. This slow pace made her desperate to crawl out of her own skin.

Noah filled his basket with everything he needed to make garlic-lemon chicken. Their last stop was for a bottle of wine. Skye wandered across the aisle and grabbed a twelve-pack of the IPA with the highest ABV.

"What's that?" Noah asked.

"Beer," she said.

"Do you think that's a good idea?" The warning in his voice raised her hackles.

"Yeah, actually I do," she snarled. "I haven't celebrated my early retirement yet. I think I should."

"Skye," he said with that heart-wrenching plea again.

She shook her head. Skye needed a break from the roller-coaster of emotions, needed an opportunity to just let the alcohol relieve some of the pressure of adjusting to this new life. "You can join me or you can babysit me. I don't give a shit, but I'm doing this."

The last time Skye tied one on was before she left Ft. Carson, well before that last deployment. Once promoted to staff sergeant, she felt compelled to set an example for the younger soldiers and didn't think it appropriate to get hammered like a lot of the NCOs did. Now, she didn't have any impressionable troops to worry about. She was on her own, all alone.

"At least put the twelve pack down and get a six."

"This is more cost effective," she insisted, just to be stubborn. It might only take two bottles to get drunk, but it would be nice to have a stash for those days when the painkillers didn't kill the pain.

Noah left her alone and she carried the box to the register, paying for it ahead of Noah. When they were back in the car and heading to his house, his silence put her on edge.

It wasn't Skye's job to keep Noah happy. In fact, she lacked the ability to make him happy at all. Maybe in small spurts here and there, but she was wounded, broken, her heart a fragile organ. She didn't deserve Noah's love and couldn't reciprocate, not with everything she'd lost. So, if he got upset because she wanted to get trashed, well, that was his problem, not hers.

To her surprise, Noah parked in his spot by the garage instead of driving around back to the basement. That was fine, Skye could make it down the path with her twelve best friends.

By the time she pulled herself out of the Camry and grabbed the beer, Vaughn had come around the house. "Hey guys," he greeted them.

Noah grunted a greeting and Skye responded with something that oozed with bubbly-happy.

"Uh, what's going on?" Vaughn asked, looking back and forth between them.

"Nothing," she sang, "What's going on with you?"

Vaughn grabbed the twelve-pack. "Is this for me?"

"Not on your life," she responded, heading around the back of the house.

When they got inside, Skye took a seat at the table while her brother stocked the fridge. He popped two bottles open before sitting down.

"Help yourself," she joked, taking a bottle from him.

"Don't mind if I do. Cheers." Vaughn tapped her bottle and

WHISPER TO A SCREAM

took a long drink. "That's good stuff."

Taking a long drink too, Skye enjoyed the strength of the hops. Ever since her tour in Germany, she'd become a beer snob and preferred the strong flavor in IPAs. This one earned a seal of approval.

Above them, Noah cranked up the music, but they could still hear him banging around. "What happened? You two get in a fight or something?"

Skye rolled her eyes and shook her head. "He's just being Noah. What's your great news?" she dared ask.

"I've got a buddy who works at the hospital, manages the billing department. There's an opening and he's willing to interview you. But it has to be tomorrow because they've already closed the billet."

The anger flared up again. When were all these meddling people going to understand Skye didn't need help. "I don't need your help finding a job," she said, slamming the bottle on the table. When beer splashed out, she swiped at it, glaring at her brother.

Vaughn didn't react. The oldest of the Everhart children, he'd dodged Skye's dirty looks and Riley's practical jokes most of his life. "I know you don't need it, but networking is the best way to find one. Do you have your resume ready?"

No, she didn't have her damn resume ready. "I'm not qualified for something like that. I have no experience in billing."

"Give yourself a break, Skye. I'm sure you're more than qualified. Where's your computer? I can show you the job description."

The laptop remained stashed away in a backpack somewhere. She hadn't bothered to take it out, not interested in checking email or social media and fielding all the *"Hi, how are ya's"* or more invasive questions.

"I'm not interested," Skye admitted. Hospital billing sounded like a snooze fest anyway.

"Come on. You can't sit around here moping forever. You

need to get out in the world, earn some money, support yourself. You don't have to stay in a job like this forever. It's just an opportunity you shouldn't pass up."

Skye didn't like that Vaughn's assessment included her moping around. He made her sound like a pathetic piece of shit. Civilian life didn't suit her. She needed time to adjust. Vaughn, however, was too much like their mother, and a lot like Noah, persistent to the point of being annoying. If going on this interview would get him to leave her the hell alone, she'd suck it up. "Fine, I'll go on the stupid interview. What time and where?"

Vaughn wrote down the details. Skye was annoyed it was an early morning appointment, but at least she could get it over with and not waste the whole day. She didn't have any other plans, of course, but that didn't matter.

After taking another long sip of her brew, Skye smiled at her brother. "Want to get hammered with me? Celebrate my homecoming? Noah's cooking dinner."

Vaughn looked at the ceiling as something banged on the floor upstairs. "Sounds like he's wrecking the house. What has his panties all in a bind, anyway?"

Just then Noah stomped downstairs. "You staying for dinner?" he asked Vaughn when he peered through the doorway.

"I'd love to, but only if one of you tell me what's going on."

Skye just smiled and took another drink.

"That's what's going on," Noah said, nodding at Skye. "She shouldn't be drinking."

"Why the hell not? She survived Afghanistan. I think our little Sarge earned the right to a few beers."

"She has PTSD and is taking painkillers. That high alcohol beer is the last thing she needs."

Just to spite Noah, Skye downed the rest of the high ABV bottle. It was tempting to throw the empty container at him, but she dropped it in the recycling bin and grabbed another.

Vaughn watched, his brow raised in question.

"I don't have PTSD and I haven't taken any painkillers in hours. You want another one?"

"No, I'm good, but maybe you should slow down."

"Oh, now you're jumping on the righteous train?" she asked, popping the top and reclaiming her seat.

"No, I just don't want to be the poor bastard holding your hair when you're praying to the porcelain gods later."

"I have hair clips," she said. "Besides, Noah is my self-appointed babysitter. That means he gets to deal with any hurling."

Vaughn laughed, but Noah remained still as a statue, scowling as if that would change her mind.

"I'd love to stay, but really, you should slow it down. You don't want to be hungover for the interview tomorrow."

"Interview?" Noah asked.

Great, one more thing for him to stick his nose in.

"Yeah, got her an interview at the hospital, in the billing department," Vaughn said.

"I'm going to sit on the porch and listen to the music. You two don't need me for this conversation." She grabbed a couple bottles and the opener and stepped past Noah, tempted to bump him but reeling in the childish urge. She walked outside and around to the steps. A few minutes later, Vaughn joined her.

"No lectures," she slurred, a little surprised how quickly the alcohol had kicked in.

Vaughn chuckled. "Noah told me about your panic attack, about the pictures and awards."

Wow, that was a world record for speed informing. "What else did he tell you?" she asked. If he'd told Vaughn about Rafe, she was going to kill him.

"What else is there to tell?" Vaughn asked.

"I invited you to stay here and drink with me, not excavate my soul."

"Good thing I stopped working with big equipment when I left construction," he joked. "Well, except for the big equipment

God endowed me with."

Skye nearly spit out the beer. "That's not what she said," she laughed.

"Believe me, Sarge, that's exactly what she said."

Shaking her head, Skye finished off the bottle. "I refuse to get into a debate about your junk. How come you don't have a girlfriend, anyway?"

Now Vaughn took a long drink. "I'll tell you my story if you tell me yours," he said.

Skye took another drink. Then another. The silence extended between them. She couldn't rehash the story, not when it had bled out mere hours ago. Skye would drink herself into oblivion first. Fortunately, Noah had Bon Jovi playing through the outdoor speakers so she didn't have to fill the silence with noise. While silence between two people was perfectly acceptable, she couldn't stand quiet.

She might not be the type of soldier who woke up and wondered where her weapon was, but the quiet terrified her — or at least the threat of what may shatter the quiet did.

Chapter 20

Better stand tall when
they're calling you out
Don't bend, don't break,
baby, don't back down.
-It's My Life, Bon Jovi

Torture.

Skye shook with the threat of all that lingered in front of her, trying to breathe through the anxiety but failing. She was unprepared and a little hungover, that she would own, but this torment came from the unknown.

Her entire career she'd been in situations that should make a job interview seem like a walk in the park. Soldier of the month boards, soldier of the quarter, NCO of the quarter. Promotion boards. She'd even gone in front of a joint service member of the year board — and won. Sitting across the desk from a civilian should be no big deal.

In lieu of a resume, Skye had brought her DD 214, the military's discharge papers. It listed all of the official awards and she could fill in the gaps with the commendations not listed.

"Vaughn told me you were injured in combat," Connor Bush said as he scrutinized Skye.

"That's right," she responded. She'd kill her brother if she got a pity hire just because her leg and hip had been blown to pieces.

"Can you tell me what happened?"

Skye took a deep breath and focused on the facts. "The humvee I was in hit an IED, sir."

Connor grunted. "Traumatic. Have you been treated for PTSD?"

That seemed like a personal question, one Skye didn't think he was allowed to ask, but since she didn't have PTSD, it wasn't an issue. "I was knocked out in the explosion and woke up in the hospital, so I have no memories of the traumatic event," she explained. "I haven't had PTSD and didn't need to be treated."

He grunted again and Skye wished she had her weapon so she could make him grunt with a butt stroke to the head. "Well, your service record is impressive, I'll grant you that, but I'm going to be honest, I only agreed to interview you as a favor to your brother. He thought this job would be a good fit for you, but frankly, I have concerns about hiring someone fresh from combat. PTSD has a tremendous impact on work performance and attendance."

"Like I said, PTSD isn't an issue."

Connor shook his head. "I've been told that in the past only to have it arise later. I've also hired vets who disclosed their PTSD and treatment, and still saw performance issues. This hospital isn't a charity. It's here to make money and the billing department is an important piece of that. I need good people I can rely on to get the job done."

Skye smiled and stood, doing everything in her power to squash the rage building within. "I appreciate your time, but this job isn't going to be a good fit for me."

"But we haven't even gone over the details of the job," he said, clearly perplexed. Skye got the impression he had no interest in hiring her, or any combat veteran, so she didn't understand the confusion.

"I'm not going to be accused by a man I met ten minutes ago of not only having PTSD, but not being able to crunch some numbers because I've seen combat. I came here because my brother set it up, but I don't need this job or your animosity."

"It's not animosity," he said. "Employee turnover is costly. I want to ensure I hire someone with sticking power."

"Then maybe you should be less of an ass, because if this is how you treat people in an interview, I wouldn't want to work for you every day." Skye picked up the folder with her military papers and walked to the door.

"I would have expected someone who served in the army for over a decade to show a little more respect," Connor said.

She turned on him. "Did you serve?"

He shook his head.

"You've done nothing to earn my respect, sir. Have a nice day," she added, unable to bite back the sarcasm.

Skye walked out, holding her head high and breathing long and deep. When she got home, she'd freak out, but wouldn't give Connor the satisfaction of doing that here. The last thing she needed was to succumb to another panic attack in a public place.

By the time she reached the parking lot, her hands shook so violently she couldn't pull the keys from her purse.

Breathe, she preached silently. *Just breathe.*

Once Skye got hold of the keys, she barreled her way into the car and tore out of the parking lot like the building was on fire.

Only when the siren made her jump did she realize how fast she was driving. With blue lights flashing in the rear view mirror, she pulled over, desperate to bang her head against the steering wheel when Luke got out of the cruiser.

Weren't there any other cops in this town?

She lowered the window, hoping she didn't have to go through the whole rigmarole of showing her license and registration.

"Hi, Skye," he said when he came up to the window. "Driving a little fast, don't you think?"

"Obviously, if you pulled me over," she murmured.

"I clocked you doing fifty in a thirty. Why the hurry?"

"No hurry, Chief, just pissed off and not paying attention."

"Have you been drinking?" he asked.

"It's ten in the morning," she responded, but Luke didn't seem to care about the time. "No, I haven't been drinking."

"Take any meds this morning?"

"Just ibuprofen," she said. After the bullshit of this day, she planned to self-medicate heavily when free of all this torture.

Luke stood there, his intimidating cop pose annoying her more than wearing her down. What was with men today? Was it national *Be An Ass-hole* day?

"Do you want my license and registration?" she asked, "Or can I go?"

"I have to run your license and motor vehicle record," Luke said, "So yeah, I need your license and registration."

Skye dug the license out of her purse and the registration out of the glove box. Watching in the rear view, Luke sat in the cruiser and did his cop thing, as if he'd been born to be chief. Since she'd spent more time deployed than driving in the states the last few years, her record was clean, so his efforts were a waste of time

A few minutes later Luke returned, handing over her things. "Want to talk about what has you so pissed off?" he asked.

"Nope," she said. It was none of his damned business and she had a beer calling her name.

Luke shook his head. "I'm not going to ticket you this time, Skye, but slow the hell down. Twenty over the limit is dangerous and stupid."

"Yes, sir," she said, giving him a mock salute. Noah would

no doubt hear about this before she even got home, so that gave Skye something to look forward to.

Luke shook his head before patting the door. "You're free to go."

She didn't bother thanking him and opted not to peel out even though everything in her screamed go, go, go! Taking great effort to drive the speed limit the rest of the way home, Skye remained aware that the mighty police chief followed until she turned onto her road.

Luck seemed to lean her way when she pulled into the driveway and Noah's car wasn't there. She had no doubt that Luke already called his cousin and Noah would be home soon to make sure she hadn't gone off the deep end, but for now Skye had some peace. With a little more luck, she'd be among the ranks of the inebriated before Noah returned to interrogate her about the interview and the speeding.

Thanks to her brother filling the fridge and her low tolerance for alcohol, there were still plenty of cold bottles. She tossed her purse on the table and grabbed one, taking a long drink before even figuring out her next move.

The bottle of Vicodin rolled out of her bag and teetered on the edge of the table. She picked it up and read the label, already aware of what it said. "Do not take with alcohol."

The Vicodin fog enticed Skye, and last night she'd enjoyed a decent buzz from the beer. Deep down Skye knew it was wrong — maybe even dangerous — to mix the two, but the devil over her shoulder encouraged her to give it a go.

Just one pill.

Just one beer.

There couldn't be any harm in that. She'd get the fog that helped her forget the guilt and shame, and the buzz that made her feel like she could conquer the world. It seemed like a win-win.

She twisted off the cap and grabbed a pill, swallowing it with a long swig. Then she stowed the evidence to avoid providing

Noah with any ammunition when he showed up. Since today appeared to be *National Ass-hole Day*, he was probably already well equipped to harass her.

With another long swallow, she marched forward toward a buzz, feeling prepared to endure the one-two punch with her own one-two.

Grabbing the laptop, Skye figured she'd do that whole resume thing. Without a clue where to start, she brought up a browser and typed "how to write a resume" in the search field.

Writing a resume might be outside her skill set, but the research she could handle. After all, it was just analyzing data, and couldn't be more complex than insurgent communications, sightings, and movements.

She skipped the first four results in the list because they were all ads. The first legitimate article was whether to choose a chronological or functional resume. That seemed like a good place to start.

Skye lifted her bottle for a drink only to find it empty. She hobbled to the fridge for another and focused on the article.

In twelve years, she'd had five assignments, including two deployments, but the job hadn't changed from duty station to duty station. A chronological resume would be redundant, listing the same tasks and skills over and over. Did anyone care where she was assigned? If Connor Bush served as a good example of what she'd have to deal with, then no. In fact, it might be best to keep those assignments out of her resume, as well as anything that screamed combat.

Because she might get accused by one more ass-hole of having PTSD.

If anything, being stateside proved more traumatic than the war. Deployed, she had routine, structure, knew what to expect, even if it was being prepared for the unexpected. Because, really, nothing was unexpected over there. IEDs injured and killed more troops than any other type of attack, but even gun-fire was expected on patrols. During her first deployment, her unit had suffered numerous casualties by the scope of a sniper. It took months, but they finally locked him down and captured him. She'd been proud to be part of the intel team that helped capture the son of a bitch.

The article provided a sample of a functional resume, so she downloaded it and started filling in her information.

When she got to the spot where she had to list her first skill, her muddled brain came to a grinding halt.

Determined to get this done, Skye took a swig and rattled off a bunch of skills in her head. Technical Goddess, Analysis Guru, IED Magnet. Were those marketable in the civilian world?

Sure. Why the hell not.

She filled in the section headings, then replaced the sample bullets with clever descriptions of her daily tasks under each heading.

When trying to figure out what to put for education — or lack of — Noah made an appearance.

"You're drinking?" The question didn't hide his disappointment. "It's just after twelve."

"Oh, hush, little Noah. I had a shitty morning and this is my reward for not killing anyone."

He chuckled, but didn't smile. "Interview didn't go well?"

"That guy was an Alpha-Helo, with a grudge against combat veterans. Or maybe he just doesn't like women. He probably really needs to get laid. All that pent-up testosterone makes you men act like little bitches."

"How much have you had to drink?" Noah asked, shaking his head.

"Oh, Noah," she drawled, "do you need to get laid too? You're awfully uptight."

Chapter 21

You've got to learn to love
The world you're living in.
-Learn to Love, Bon Jovi

Frustration.

In a past life, when Skye wasn't in denial about her PTSD and on the verge of a prescription drug addiction, Noah might find her drunken banter amusing. It's only purpose now was to fire up the frustration that had been stewing since she'd come home.

"What are you doing?" he asked, trying to take the focus off his sexual status and put it back on Skye.

"Watching Internet porn," she shrugged. "It's got me all hot and bothered. Maybe I need to get laid too."

She stood from her chair and moved over to him so fluidly he never would have guessed she had a chronic limp. How much did she have to drink?

Noah made his own move around the table, not so much to avoid her — although that seemed like a good idea — but to see if she was in fact watching porn.

They'd watched porn together in high school, one of those stupid things teens did to see what all the fuss was about. Noah remembered how painful that night had been. He didn't have a girlfriend, but Skye was going out with one of the flunkies she always seemed to attract, so as they watched a bear of a man give it to some blonde, Noah had to pretend to be unaffected even though his raging hard on wanted to forget Skye was his best friend and off-limits.

As he eased around the table, he spotted a document on the screen that looked like a resume. He dropped into the chair for a closer look.

"Internet porn, huh?" he asked.

Skye shrugged. "Internet porn doesn't even make an attempt at a plot. There's nothing to make fun of."

Now she was just trying to cover her tracks. "Skye, this is great," he said. "Mind if I have a look?"

"Whatever yanks your crank," she said and finished off the bottle before going to the fridge. Noah swallowed the compulsion to tell her to stop drinking as she popped open another. The resume was a good sign. If she'd had a shitty interview, he couldn't begrudge her methods for getting over it.

He scrolled to the top of the document, impressed with the professional layout. It's not that he didn't think Skye could pull together a resume, but ever since she'd come home, it didn't seem like she wanted to pull anything together. This resume was a step in the right direction.

As Noah began reading, he realized the resume was as intoxicated as she. The frustration rolled through him as he read the first heading. While she may well be a *Technical Goddess*, no one would take her seriously with it listed on a resume.

He read the bullets and they were pretty good despite the sarcasm. It wouldn't take much tweaking to make them usable.

Noah's frustration wavered a bit, amusement pushing it aside as he read the bullets under the second heading. The third heading shouldn't have made him laugh, but one thing about Skye he'd always loved was her dry sense of humor.

Explosives Expert. Able to sustain direct impact explosion at ground zero range.

It wasn't funny, but at least she was acknowledging the trauma, even if it was with drunken sarcasm.

"You're missing a functional category here."

"What's that?" she asked.

"Thorn in My Side."

Skye laughed, a sweet sound he seldom heard since she'd returned home. She went to the fridge, cracked open another beer, and handed it to Noah before tapping the neck with her bottle. "Maybe I should rewrite the entire resume in Bon Jovi lyrics."

Noah took a long drink because why the hell not? This Skye might be a little buzzed, but she was the closest thing he'd seen in the last few weeks to the Skye he knew and loved.

She walked across the room, no noticeable limp in her steps and dug into one of the boxes stowed away in the corner. She came back with an iPod. "This came in the box from Afghanistan. I don't even know if it works."

Noah stood and put his hand over hers. Her softness and warmth went straight to his heart and to all regions south, awakening the desire he had no control over on a good day. Today was not even close to being a good day. It was a day when his desire had the strength of a thousand armies. "I'll grab mine. I've got a playlist for you."

Maybe it was childish or even tacky to make a playlist for her, but Noah had survived without Skye by his side because the music carried him through. He knew the music might not be the cure, but he believed with all his heart it would help.

He ran upstairs and grabbed his iPod, only to stop in his tracks when he walked back in her apartment.

"Are you taking your pain meds with alcohol?"

"Jesus. Don't you knock?" she snarled, stuffing the bottle in her messenger bag on the table.

Noah wouldn't let her put this on him. "Do you know how dangerous that is? You're taking opiates, for Chrissake. You can't mess around with that shit."

"I know what I'm doing. It's not a big deal. I haven't even had that much to drink."

He'd watched her consume at least two beers in the short time he'd been there and her drink of choice had a high alcohol content. It was a big deal.

"Give me your pills, Skye," he demanded, holding out his hand.

A sardonic smile crossed her face, the mischievous spark in her eye telling him she was ready for a fight. She pulled the blouse away from her chest and tucked the pill bottle inside.

"Come and get them," she challenged.

Well, shit. He wouldn't and she knew it. Noah wasn't the type of man to lay his hands on a woman for any other reason than affection. While fishing for a bottle of pills may be innocent enough, it was not something he was comfortable with, not even with Skye.

"That's a little childish, don't you think."

"One to two pills every four to six hours," she said. "That's what the prescription says and that's what I've been taking. No more than that."

"It also says don't take with alcohol."

"When I take it alone, I need two. With this," she tapped the bottle of beer, "I only need one. It helps."

"It's dangerous," he countered.

She finished off the beer and stepped toward the fridge, but Noah blocked her path. "You are not my keeper. I don't need you babysitting me."

"I care about you," he countered. "Watching out for you isn't babysitting."

"That's just semantics," she said with an eye roll.

"Call it what you want, but you need help. You need to talk to someone." He was ready to drag her kicking and screaming to Maddie's office.

"I talked to you."

"I'm not a therapist," he reminded her.

"No, but you're my friend and I trust you. I'm not going to expose my soul to someone I don't know, worse, to someone who pretends to know what it's like to be in the trenches."

"Did you even research the therapists on that list I gave you?" he asked.

"I don't need to. I'm fine."

It was the last straw. "Goddammit, stop saying that. You are a train speeding down the tracks, out of control and unable to see what's coming at you. Any minute you're going to derail, Skye. You need to stop the forward momentum."

"Maybe I want to derail. I killed three people, Noah. All your fancy analogies and comforting words and all my stupid tears don't change that."

Her walls were back up, fully in place.

"Three soldiers died, during combat operations in a war. Nothing will change that. You taking responsibility for it, that's what needs to change."

Skye threw the beer bottle against the wall, once again going from silent to violent in the blink of an eye. It shattered, the pieces flying back at them like shrapnel. Noah flinched away from the flying glass. When he glanced at Skye, she hadn't moved. He wondered if she'd even flinched.

Noah grabbed the bottle opener off the counter and opened the fridge. Tugging one bottle out, he opened it and poured it down the sink. Skye stood and watched, chuckling with each bottle he drained.

"Feel better?" she asked when he emptied the last one.

He didn't. He expected the stubborn behavior because that was classic Skye, but stupid opened a Pandora's box Noah didn't know how to close. Dumping the beer was only a temporary fix. She would just go to the store and buy more.

"If you're not going to give me your pills, I'm going to call Luke," he said, a desperate threat he hoped would at least put a crack in her defenses.

When she laughed, he knew that attempt failed. "You're going to tattle on me? Now who's being childish?"

"Look at what you just did," he said, pointing at the wet spot on the wall and the glass all over the floor. "You can't tell me you're fine." Taking pills with alcohol might not be illegal, but he hoped the implication might sober her up.

"I could have thrown it at your face," she said.

"Jesus, Skye."

Noah raked his hands across his head, desperate to pull a miracle fix out of his brain. Stopping short of dragging her to therapy, he walked over to the shelf where she kept the car keys and grabbed both sets. "You can have these back when you're sober."

"Oh, so now I'm your hostage?"

"Someone has to be the responsible adult here," he pointed out. "You can't drive when you're drunk and high."

"I'm not high," she snapped before giving a shrug. "I have nowhere to go anyway."

"Sober up and we'll talk about your next steps. Therapy, support group, something. It's your choice, but you're getting help somewhere."

Before she could argue, he stormed upstairs, putting every effort into not slamming the door.

Noah put the keys under his mattress and dropped onto the corner of the bed while he called Luke.

"Hey man," Luke answered.

"Hey. Listen, some shit just went down with Skye. She's mixing her meds with alcohol."

"Son of a bitch," Luke muttered. "I knew I shouldn't have trusted her this morning."

"What the hell are you talking about?" Noah asked.

"She didn't tell you?"

"Tell me what?"

"I pulled her over for speeding," Luke explained. "Let her go with a warning. She said she had only taken ibuprofen. I followed her to your road, just to make sure she went home. Her driving was steady. She wouldn't tell me what pissed her off."

"She had a job interview this morning. Apparently, it didn't go well."

"Is she getting any help yet?" Luke asked.

Noah shook his head, not that Luke could see him. "She's still in denial. I don't know what to do."

"Well, make sure she doesn't go anywhere while she's drinking and try and get her prescription."

"I took her keys, but she shoved the bottle of pills down her bra."

Luke laughed. "Well, that's a classic Skye move. I'm guessing you didn't go digging."

Noah cracked a smile because Luke nailed it as a classic Skye move. "The assertive prick gene was reserved for your branch of the family tree."

"I like my balls right where they are, but I've got a rookie I could send over to fish them out."

The humor of the situation took a dive as Noah's possessive and protective side raised its hackles. No one, not even a cop with good intentions, would put his hands on Skye while Noah drew breath. "Is it illegal, mixing the prescription with alcohol?" Noah asked, hopeful for a legal angle.

"Afraid not, man. It's a medical warning, not a legal issue. Unless she gets behind the wheel, but I'd prefer safety over letting her get busted."

Noah agreed with that.

"Do you think she's a suicide risk?" Luke asked.

"I don't know. She's emotional. I can't keep up with her

mood swings. They shift without warning, sometimes violently."

"It's the PTSD driving that."

"I figured," Noah agreed, leaning forward to stop the anxious twitch in his legs. "How do I get her to get help?"

"I don't have an answer for that. You need to get creative."

"Thanks for nothing. Do you have any other useful advice?" Noah asked.

"Not for free, and I'm pretty sure you can't afford me."

They shared a chuckle and said their good-byes. Noah wasn't any closer to helping Skye than he'd been before the call. He sat down to his computer and started searching out what others had done to help those they loved get help. With any luck, Skye would sober up and see the light, but Noah wasn't holding his breath on that one.

Chapter 22

When life is a bitter pill to swallow
You gotta hold on to what you believe,
Believe that the sun will shine tomorrow
And that your saints and sinners bleed.
-We Weren't Born to Follow, Bon Jovi

Despair.

It rang like the warning sirens of an air raid, so powerful the
need to lash out had Skye wishing for an M4 rifle. She hadn't
touched a weapon since Afghanistan and didn't miss it. Today,
though, she wanted to shoot something, maybe execute a butt-stroke
to someone's head.

Skye sat in her car outside the White Mountain Clinic. She
was scheduled for the first physical therapy session since leaving
the hospital almost two months ago, but couldn't force herself to go
inside. Not even the inner self-talk about the importance and
necessity of PT worked.

The army's form of PT — physical training — appealed to
her more than the pain waiting inside that building. She liked being

fit, having energy, feeling good about her body. It also proved therapeutic on those days when she had to deal with idiots, and there were plenty of those on active duty.

The medical form of PT, though — physical therapy — was brutal. Never in her life had she been a whiner, but those sessions at Walter Reed brought out the worst in her. Learning how to walk again in your thirties, with all the pins and stitches and now the scars and lingering pain, complaining seemed like a rite of passage. During PT, she kept the complaints to herself and did as told despite the pain, because that's the kind of person she was ... or at least the kind of person she had been.

There were exercises and stretches she was supposed to do after leaving the hospital. Skye had been the good little soldier in those first days after being discharged, pushing through the pain to follow the doctor's orders. Once her prescription ran low and the pain didn't subside, she'd stopped following those orders.

Maybe a smidgen of defiance had been a motivator. The army had turned its back on her, telling Skye — SSG Everhart — she was beaten and broken and not useful anymore. Why work hard to be something no one wanted?

She should have died in that explosion, just like Rafe and McMann and Pinnock. Surviving was punishment for breaking the rules and being irresponsible. The pain was penance.

Unfortunately, if she didn't go to PT, an army of people would climb up her ass about it, Noah and her mother leading the troops.

Skye hit the clinic's number in her recent calls. When the receptionist answered, the lie rolled off her tongue with the ease of truth. "This is Skye Everhart. I have an appointment at three but can't make it. I can't drive and I have no one to give me a ride."

The receptionist seemed happy to reschedule the appointment but didn't have an opening for a week.

That worked for Skye. By then she'd either work up the courage to face the pain or come up with another valid lie.

With that out of the way, Skye didn't know what the hell to do with herself. Just the thought of going back to her apartment ratcheted up the despair. Noah hadn't talked to her in days, not since he'd dumped all her beer down the sink. He returned her keys only when satisfied she was sober, but even then he'd done it without saying much. She tried to return his iPod, but he grunted that she should keep it and listen to the playlist he'd made, maybe she'd like it.

Skye didn't blame him for giving up on her. The fact she missed his nagging and judgment was plain absurd.

Losing Noah five years ago had crushed her. She had known the risk, but thought their friendship strong enough to survive if he said no. Maybe their friendship was, but Skye wasn't. It had hurt more than she'd anticipated and the humiliation made it worse. As someone who always got what she wanted, Skye didn't know how to deal with Noah's rejection.

She still didn't.

Bringing up a browser on her phone, she searched out the one person who might be able to tell her how to deal with Noah — and maybe even the storm of emotions she struggled to control at any given moment.

Skye recognized the address that came up in the search and started the car, finally having a mission. It took fifteen minutes to get to Lilac Ridge, where she pulled into a parking space across the street from 314 Main Street.

Once again, Skye found herself sitting in the car, a silent war waged in her head between despair and independence.

It's not that she didn't want help, she just didn't think she needed it. This visit had nothing to do with Skye's alleged issues anyway. She needed Maddie's insight on Noah and how to get over the past, so maybe they could have a future. It'd be a bonus if Maddie knew how to get him to stop trying to fix her, too.

Skye pushed herself out of the car and limped across the street to the Victorian house that served as an office building. She gripped the rail to help her up the steps, the pain more pronounced today. She'd taken a Vicodin, just one with high-octane coffee because she needed to drive, but the one pill did nothing. She made a mental note to grab a six pack on the way home since the alcohol seemed to work better than the stupid prescription.

At the door, Skye debated whether to walk in or ring the doorbell. The house served as an office, not a residence, so she didn't understand why it even had a doorbell. It could be a remnant of when this house had been a home instead of a place where people paid someone to pass judgment.

"This is stupid," Skye muttered and turned around. She'd never subscribed to psychotherapy as a mechanism for help. She'd tried it out at Walter Reed because they forced her to. Skye hated those sessions. It became a game, to see how long she could sit there before breaking down the therapist. Skye won every time.

As always, going down the steps sent shards of agony up her leg. She refused to cry out. Biting down on her lip, she took each step one at a time, focusing on maintaining her balance while gripping the rail.

"Skye?" she heard, only then realizing her eyes were pinched closed. She opened them to find Maddie Carson standing on the sidewalk.

Heat flooded Skye's face as embarrassment seized her body. She stumbled. The vice-grip she held on the rail prevented a total disaster. Instead of falling face-first onto the concrete sidewalk, Skye dropped onto her ass, pain shooting out like the grand finale of a vibrant fireworks show.

Maddie didn't flinch or utter a word. Despite looking a lot smaller than the last time they'd been face to face, the intimidation factor still hit Skye. Even with the extra weight, Maddie had been beautiful. Now, with perfect curves and stoic control, the jealousy Skye tangoed with five years ago took a spin on the dance floor.

"Aren't you going to ask if I need help or if I'm okay?" Skye said.

Maddie chuckled. "Would you be honest if I did?"

No, but Skye didn't say that. Maddie knew. She dealt with mental cases for a living.

"I'm glad you made it home," she said, taking a seat on the steps next to Skye.

"Are you?" Skye asked.

"Of course. You and I don't know each other well, but you were special to Noah and he was special to me, so I cared about what happened to you. Plus, you're a soldier. I respect and admire that."

"Was a soldier," Skye corrected. "Now I'm disabled."

"Are you?" Maddie asked, the words an echo of how Skye had uttered them.

"The army says so," Skye shrugged.

"What do you say?"

She didn't say anything. Skye was broken — in body and spirit — but she deserved to be.

"I should go," Skye said, putting all her focus and energy into standing.

Maddie stood with her. "I was heading over to the stables to spend some time with my horses. Why don't you join me?"

"You were just heading into your office," Skye said, calling her on the obvious lie.

"I left my cell phone in the office. I came back for it. Give me a minute and you can follow me."

"I don't really like horses," Skye said.

"Have you ever spent time around horses?"

Skye shook her head. As a kid she wanted to ride, but her parents never had the money to pay for lessons and once hormones kicked in, Skye preferred chasing boys rather than horses.

"Well, maybe you should give them a chance."

Skye had nothing else to do and running away would make her seem like a coward. "Fine," she said in agreement.

Maddie went inside and a minute later returned with a phone

in hand. "I'm parked around the back."

Skye pointed to her car across the street. "I'm over there."

"You're facing the right direction. Give me a minute and follow me. The stables aren't far."

A minute later Skye recognized Maddie in an old pick-up truck. She waved as she passed and Skye pulled out of the parking space to follow. This was such a dumb idea. What the hell could she say to Noah's ex-girlfriend, the woman he'd chosen over Skye five years ago?

But, Skye followed, maybe because of morbid curiosity. Maybe she was just a glutton for punishment.

A few miles down the road, they turned onto a side street and then another before pulling into a driveway and driving up to a barn. Skye put her best effort into hiding the pain and getting out of the car, not wanting Maddie to know how Skye struggled with something so simple and routine.

Maddie, however, didn't even look at Skye. She walked over to the barn and pushed open the large door. Skye hobbled over to the entrance where Maddie waited without paying her much attention.

"Is this your house?" Skye asked.

"No, it's my parent's house. I grew up here, but I live in town. I come out a couple times a day to take care of the horses."

Skye didn't see any horses in the barn, but spotted a giant of a man in one of the stalls.

"Hey Dad," Maddie said.

The man stepped out of the stall as they approached and gave Maddie a bear hug. "Hey, girlie. You doing a session?"

Maddie shook her head. "No, this is Noah's friend, Skye."

His eyes went wide for a moment before extending his hand. "Thank you for your service," he offered. Skye shook his hand but didn't know how to respond to his gratitude. Fortunately, he filled the awkward silence. "My son is a soldier, too."

Skye nodded, wishing she hadn't come. There was a time

when she could meet new people with ease, but now the awkward exchanges made her uncomfortable. She should have gone back to the basement apartment where the world didn't invade her personal space or force her to abandon her comfort zone.

"I'm going to finish the stalls. The horses are in the turnout. It was nice meeting you, Skye."

"You too, sir," she said, grateful to be moving on.

"Please, call me Hank."

Skye nodded and smiled, surprised at how easy that smile came. She followed Maddie to the other side of the barn and out to where the horses were, her steps feeling a little less strained.

One of them, a beautiful horse with a light gray coat and dark gray mane and tail trotted over to them.

"This is Cleo, my best friend Clarissa's horse. She's very friendly and curious. The other lovely lady is Crystal, my girl. And that big guy there is Sergeant Matty."

"Sergeant Matty?" Skye asked.

"After my brother, Matt."

"Right. You have a twin. Noah told me that."

"It's something Noah and I had in common, both of us dealing with someone we love being in the army and deployed."

Skye just nodded, not sure what to say. Comforting words had never been in Skye's skill set. "They're beautiful," she offered, focusing on the horses.

"Thank you."

"You can pet Cleo if you want. Like I said, she's friendly. She loves making new friends."

Skye followed Maddie's lead, stroking Cleo's long neck. Her fur was softer than Skye would have guessed and the horse seemed to like all the attention.

"Do you do therapy here?" Skye asked, recalling what Hank had asked when they walked in.

"Sometimes. I do equine assisted therapy at a center in Sugar Falls a couple times a month, but I'm working with Clarissa to open our own center up here."

"Is she a therapist too?" Skye asked.

"She's a veterinarian. She loves horses and believes in their ability to help people heal. We've dreamed of doing something like this together since we were kids."

"That's great," Skye offered. She waited for Maddie to say something, to ask why Skye was there or if she was all right, but the silence extended as they both focused on the horse.

"I'm not sure what to do about Noah," Skye admitted, unable to maintain the silence.

Maddie looked at her, a warm smile on her pretty face. Skye wasn't sure she deserved the warmth given she'd tried to steal Noah for herself when he was with Maddie.

"We fight a lot," Skye added when Maddie didn't say anything.

"You've been through hell, I imagine. Now you're adjusting to a new life you didn't choose and Noah has a tendency to want to fix things. I'm sure that makes for a lot of tension and conflict between the two of you."

Skye chuckled. Maddie's summary was spot on. "I know he's trying to help, but he won't accept that I don't need help."

"We all need help, Skye, even those of us who aren't combat veterans."

The silence extended again and Skye was grateful when Sergeant Matty joined them. "He's friendly, too," Maddie offered. "He likes a firm nose rub."

Skye moved over to focus her attention on the larger horse. He was a beautiful brown, his eyes alert and playful. As she held out her hand he nudged it, making Skye laugh. "Wow, he knows what he wants."

"He does. He's a very decisive one."

Chuckling as she rubbed his long nose, Skye wished to be as decisive.

"Are you still in love with Noah?" Maddie asked.

Still. Even though the question held no accusation or contempt, Skye didn't miss the meaning behind that word. "He told you."

"Not until we broke up, but deep inside, I always knew. That's why it could never work between me and Noah. We loved each other, but we were never in love. It took us a long time to acknowledge that."

"I'm not the kind of person who tries to steal another woman's guy." Skye felt the need to defend herself. After it all blew up in her face, she'd not only regretted taking the risk and suffering the humiliation, but had been ashamed of trying to steal Noah's heart from someone else.

"I know that. I don't blame you, Skye. Like I said, I loved Noah. I still do. He's a good man, but he wasn't *the* man for me. I just wish we'd acknowledged that sooner. Then maybe you wouldn't have been hurt."

"I'm fine," Skye said on reflex.

Maddie didn't condemn the words like Noah would. Instead, she smiled, putting Skye at ease again.

"You haven't answered my question yet. Are you still in love with Noah?"

"It's a little more complicated than that."

"Love is always complicated," Maddie said. "But it's also simple."

"I was engaged," Skye said, surprised at the admission. "He died."

"I'm so sorry," Maddie said, moving to the other side of Cleo so she could reach Skye and give her arm a gentle squeeze. "What was his name?"

Skye blinked back the tears. "Rafe," she said.

"So the complicated part is guilt?" Maddie asked.

Nodding, Skye found herself nuzzling the big horse, who seemed more than happy to accept her affection.

Maddie released her hold and gave Sergeant Matty a quick

pat before returning her attention to Cleo.

"How did Rafe die?" Maddie asked.

Skye wiped away the tears and stood so straight and rigid it felt like standing in formation. "The same explosion," she said, hoping Maddie didn't ask more questions.

"Do you believe in the spiritual influences of the universe? Things like coincidence and fate?"

Skye looked at her, trying to analyze the direction of this inquiry, but she was such a wreck, she couldn't wrap her head around it. "I don't know what I believe," she finally admitted.

"I believe you and Noah are meant to be together. For whatever reason, he wasn't ready when you asked him to leave with you. Maybe you weren't ready either. You found love with someone else and that's not a bad thing."

"He died. That's a bad thing."

"He might have died anyway, with or without your love."

Skye didn't believe that. She'd been driving the humvee, paying more attention to Rafe than the road ahead. Plus, Rafe never would have been on that patrol if she hadn't been. Of course, if she hadn't, who knows who would have been on that rotation. IEDs were difficult to detect, especially on the open road.

Claiming he might have died anyway seemed so convenient, an easy excuse to leave the past behind and move on. "So you're saying everything happens for a reason so I shouldn't feel guilty about loving Noah?"

"You've always loved Noah. You tried to forget that for a while, even let someone else in because you were hurt. But you never stopped loving him. You don't have to stop loving Rafe, either. We are capable of infinite love, Skye. We don't have to feel guilty following the path the universe has laid out in front of us."

Skye wanted to believe Maddie's words were all a bunch of alternative psycho-babble, but they seemed to wrap around her heart and give it a gentle, consoling squeeze, just as Maddie had done with Skye's arm. Maybe believing in fate and that everything —

even tragedy — happened for a reason was a stretch, but Skye could easily believe she and Noah were meant to be together. It was easy because it's what she wanted.

Yes, she loved Rafe. He helped her heart heal and taught her about passion in a place where passion wasn't supposed to exist. His death shattered her heart again, but Noah's love seemed to be healing it … at least it would if Skye allowed it.

"I still don't know what to do," she confessed. She needed to let go of the guilt and let Noah in, but he wasn't speaking to her because she was being difficult and stubborn.

"You know what to do," Maddie encouraged. "Follow your heart. Everything else will fall into place."

Skye nodded, giving Sergeant Matty a final pat before stepping away. Maddie followed her through the barn to the cars. "Hang on," she said, stepping to her car and pulling out her purse. She dug through and grabbed a business card. "You can call me anytime, Skye. On the books, call my office, but you can call me off the books, too. This is my personal number." She wrote a number on the back and handed Skye the card.

"Why?" Skye asked.

"I told you, Noah is my friend. He loves you, so that makes you my friend, too. Plus, the horses like you. They don't get nearly as much attention as they'd like."

Skye nodded. "I'll think about it."

"Oh, and here," Maddie said, digging into her pocket. "I found this today, just before I went back to the office for my phone. It was head side up, so it's lucky. I want you to have it."

Skye shook her head. "I don't really believe in those kinds of superstitions."

"You don't need to," Maddie advised. "You need to believe in yourself. Let that penny serve as a reminder to that."

Skye took the penny and dropped into the driver's seat, desperate to see Noah. They needed to move forward, even if it that meant Skye had to swallow her pride and apologize for being so difficult.

Chapter 23

If you don't know if you should stay,
If you don't say what's on your mind,
Baby just, breathe,
There's nowhere else tonight we should be-
You want to make a memory.
-(You Want To) Make A Memory, Bon Jovi

Desire.

Noah tormented himself with the Bon Jovi love songs. Channeling the music from his cell phone through the car stereo seemed like a good idea for the long drive from Boston, but the shuffle setting didn't seem to understand the meaning of random selection.

Maddie would laugh and call it a message from the universe. If that was the case, it was one hell of a message.

With every love song and the car running on auto pilot on the barren interstate, Noah's mind consistently wandered to the most prominent fantasy he had of Skye, with her naked and needy beneath him, her skin soft and warm against his, her body welcoming and passionate.

In truth, his fantasy seemed futile. Skye's silent treatment proved that. When he'd been called to Boston at the last minute to fill in for a colleague, he'd left a note next to the Keurig, asking her to call. Since that's where she got her morning caffeine fix every day, she'd either given up coffee or maintained a tight grip on her stubborn demeanor. Noah would put money on the latter.

He longed for the time when he knew how to deal with Skye's stubbornness. Now he didn't have a clue. Even the two days away didn't provide any clarity. It only fed his desire because it seemed that distance did make the heart — and every other part of his body — grow fonder of the woman he'd always loved.

His phone rang, disrupting the music, the blue tooth feeding the screen on the console. Skye's mother. This should be interesting.

Noah would admit to being overprotective of Skye, but even he thought Amelia took nag to the extreme. "Hello," he said after hitting the answer button.

"Hi, Noah. This is Amelia."

They exchanged the normal pleasantries. Amelia complained that Skye never called, insisting Noah relay the message. She worried about calling, not wanting to wake Skye if she was sleeping. Noah interpreted it as an excuse, Amelia hiding the fear of rejection from her daughter.

"How is she doing, Noah? Vaughn told me she had a job interview the other day. Did you she get the job? It would be great if she started working."

"She's struggling," he said, resisting the urge to utter that Skye was fine. Since he hated hearing that word from Skye, he couldn't use it just to pacify her mother. "It's going to take time," he admitted.

"I just worry. She had her first PT appointment today. They called the house to remind her. I don't know why they have our number, but I'm glad. Since Skye won't tell me what's going on,

I'll take information any way it comes."

"I'm on my way home from Boston. I'll check in with her when I get back and tell her to call you."

"Thank you, Noah. You've always been such a good friend to her."

Noah wanted to be more than her friend, but that too, was going to take time.

"We're also planning a surprise welcome home party. She's been back almost a month. I can't believe we haven't celebrated yet."

"Do you think a surprise party is the best idea?" he asked, hoping Amelia would realize it wasn't.

"She always loved surprises. I'm sure it'll be exactly what she needs, seeing all her old friends, everyone coming together to celebrate her service."

Actually, Skye hated surprises. It was Amelia who loved them. "Amelia—"

"It'll be fine. I promise. It's a week from Sunday. You are responsible for getting her here. One o'clock sharp. Not any earlier."

Skye got that signature stubborn side from her mother. Noah figured that's why the two always knocked heads when Skye was growing up. There was no arguing with her. By now, Amelia had probably invited all of Sunset Valley.

Noah promised to get Skye there and they said their good-byes.

Determined to make a peace offering, Noah hit his favorite Chinese food place on the way home and ordered all the things Skye loved. If the way to someone's heart was through her stomach, Noah had to be on the right path. Spring rolls, beef teriyaki, sweet and sour chicken, won tons, pork fried rice, vegetable lo mien. He added a few other things, realizing they'd be eating Chinese for a week with this feast. If it proved too much, he'd just take it down to the station. Luke and his crew would put it away without a second thought.

When he got home, he left the suitcase in the car and grabbed the large bag of Chinese food. With the assistance of his foot, Noah managed to get into the kitchen. It was only after the door slammed behind him that he realized Skye was asleep in the recliner, Bon Jovi playing softly from the iPod on the arm of the chair.

She jumped at the sound, wide-eyed as she looked around and tried to get her bearings.

"I'm sorry," he said when her gaze landed on him. "If I'd known you were here, I wouldn't have let the door slam."

Shaking herself awake, her arms reached far above her head in a long stretch, pain marring her pretty face when she stretched too far. Noah fought the urge to ask if she was okay because if the word 'fine' crossed her lips, he didn't want to lose his patience or temper.

"Where have you been?" she asked.

"Didn't you read my note?" He turned and found it sitting right where he'd left it.

"What note?" she asked, standing from the chair.

He put the food down and picked up the note. "This one."

"Oh. No. I haven't been up here until today. I thought you were avoiding me."

"I've been in Boston for two days, Skye. Didn't you notice I wasn't around?"

She looked confused, as if just now realizing she hadn't heard a sound up here. "I guess I've been distracted. I'm sorry about the other day."

Had she been drunk, or worse, high, the whole time he was gone? He didn't dare ask, afraid of the answer. He hoped whatever had her distracted was as simple as her being upset about their fight, maybe even feeling guilty for messing around with the prescription and alcohol.

"I'm sorry, too. I need to be more patient, more

understanding."

She smiled, her apology sincere in the soft curve of her mouth. "I know I'm not easy to be around."

"It's not your fault. You've been through a lot. I keep expecting you to be the person I knew before you joined the army."

"We've both changed," she said. "Of course, you're still the voice of reason." She said it with a smile and amusement in her voice.

"The more things change, the more they stay the same," he laughed.

Her smile spread more, a reflection of the smile he'd fallen in love with so long ago. "Is that Chinese I smell?"

Noah nodded. "A peace offering. I don't like fighting with you."

"I don't like fighting with you, either." She stepped into him, her arms going around his waist and holding on. Noah held her, reminding himself the last thing she needed was him putting the moves on her. The kiss a few days ago had rocked him to the core, and she smelled so good, like an ocean breeze seducing him to get lost in the sea. Her warm body coaxed him to hold her tighter, her thick hair so soft beneath his hands it invited him to weave his fingers into the long waves.

When dampness penetrated his shirt, he realized she was crying. "Skye," he pleaded, his heart breaking for the unknown ghosts that had caused the tears.

She shook her head and held on a little tighter. "I don't know why I'm crying," she said. "Just, please, just hold me for a little longer."

"I've got you," he promised, tightening his hold and kissing the top of her head.

They stood there for an eternity, her quiet sobs absorbed by his chest, his heart racing from the way she held on to him. Noah's body burned with the desire he'd tried to ignore for too long. He wouldn't give in to it now, though, not when she needed him to be a rock.

After the sobs petered out and her grip loosened, she stepped back. Noah let her go. "I ruined another shirt," she said.

He looked down to find the large wet spot from her tears smudged with black from the mascara she'd cried away. He opened the top two buttons and tugged the shirt over his head. "You don't have to go to these extremes to get me to strip down. All you have to do is ask."

She laughed and shook her head. "You see right through me." Her smile faded, as if she regretted the words. There was truth to them, they both knew it, and that truth went both ways. He lifted her chin until their eyes met. Because he was only a man and had reached the end of his restraint, Noah lowered his mouth to hers. He held her face in his hands, desperate to touch her. If his hands moved anywhere else, the kiss would become something more than he intended.

Skye's hands landed in his chest, soft and warm, just like her lips. Noah pulled back, just enough to end the kiss, and opened his eyes before Skye did. He loved how she opened hers slowly, as if she hung onto the moment as long as possible. When she smiled, his heart rocketed out of his chest.

"I'm glad you're home," she said.

"Me, too," he agreed, wishing every homecoming offered kisses like this, even if he just went to the store for milk.

He caressed the soft skin of her cheeks, glad to see the tears gone. "I'm going to grab another shirt.

She nodded. "I'll get the food ready."

A few minutes later, dressed in comfortable jeans and the first t-shirt he'd grabbed from the drawer, Noah returned to find all the containers open on the table.

Skye had tossed aside the large army sweatshirt she wore all the time. A loose tank top hung down over another of those long skirts she seemed to like. The outfit covered her yet still left little to the imagination.

Noah swallowed his desire and plastered on a smile to hide what he really wanted. "Let's eat," he offered, but didn't miss how Skye's eyes wandered the length of his body.

They sat down and dug in. Skye took an ample helping of all her favorites. He was happy to see her eating, and glad he'd remembered everything she liked.

"You had PT today, right?" he asked.

She narrowed her gaze, probably wondering how he knew. "Your mother told me."

Now Skye rolled her eyes. "They had a scheduling conflict, changed my appointment to Monday."

It was Noah's turn to study her. She didn't make eye contact when she said it, making him wonder if it really wasn't a big deal or if she lied.

He chose to trust her because he had to. "So you just hung out here?"

She shook her head, but a mouth full of food prevented her from explaining. After she swallowed, she said, "I went to see Maddie."

Noah almost fell out of the chair. Of all the therapists, he thought for sure Maddie would be the last one on Skye's list. "That's great."

"She's nice. I can see why you liked her."

"Maddie's a good person. I imagine she's a good therapist, too." He wanted to ask what they talked about, but if Skye wanted him to know, she'd tell him. If he asked, she might not.

"It wasn't an official visit, or on the books, as she called it."

"No?" Noah asked.

"No. We hung out with her horses and talked about you."

"Me?" Noah and Skye had known each other almost their entire lives, ever since they'd been seated at the same table in kindergarten. They formed an instant friendship and soon became best friends. She was cooler than the boys in their class. Noah figured her tomboy tendencies contributed to that. She liked to throw around a football and dig in the dirt, but also gave great advice. He'd always appreciated Skye's brutal honesty, even when it was a little too brutal. Why on earth she'd want to talk to his ex-girlfriend about him had Noah a little on edge.

It made him crazy when she didn't offer any more details. He didn't know if she was teasing him or had lost her nerve, so he waited.

When she finished eating, she pushed the plate away and sat back in the chair. Her playful expression faded. Noah put his fork down, giving his full attention.

"I'm trying to find my way, Noah. I know this is home, but it's different. I was gone a long time and military life is different than civilian life. I'm trying to deal with all the shit that forced me here, but I need to do it on my terms. I know you want to help, but it's not an easy thing for me to accept. I went to see Maddie because I thought you'd given up on me. I didn't know how to deal with that."

"Jesus, Skye," Noah cursed, pushing his plate away. "I was pissed off, but I'd never give up on you. I swear."

She shook her head and took a deep breath. "And what about us?"

Us. He loved that one little word. It held so much hope. Standing, he held out his scarred hand. "Come here," he said. Skye put her hand in his and he lifted her out of the chair, turning their hands until their mirrored scars pressed together.

Skye closed her fingers between his, locking their hands together.

"What about us?" he asked.

She stepped closer, her other hand splayed over his heart. "I want us," she said.

Her hand moved, the palm brushing his nipple. Her blunt nails were long enough to force a rush of blood and desire to where she drew circles before scraping down his torso. When she moved under his shirt, that warm, soft skin set Noah on fire.

A sexy lilt curved her mouth, filling his heart as she lifted onto her toes and brushed her lips across his. Their scarred hands held tight to each other, her other hand moving around his nape, pulling him closer as her tongue pushed past his lips. Noah's other hand moved around her waist, pulling her against his body. As if the universe was sending another message, a love song played from the iPod.

Skye must have heard it too, because she chuckled as their lips came apart.

"Would it be cliche if I made love to you right now, with this song playing?" he asked, resting his forehead against hers.

Her smile told him everything he needed to know, but her words were sweet music in his ears. "I want to make a memory with you," she whispered, echoing the words of the song.

It was better than a yes. Still holding her hand, he grabbed the iPod and led her to his bedroom. Noah moved slowly to give her time to change her mind. If she had any doubts, they didn't show. "I didn't make a romantic playlist," he confessed when he put the iPod on the dresser, "but if you give me a minute, I can grab a few candles."

"Okay," she said, nodding.

"Don't move, okay? I want to pick up right where we left off." Skye nodded again and Noah went into the guest room where he found a couple candles and a lighter in a drawer. He couldn't remember where they'd come from and he didn't give a shit as long as they created the romantic ambiance Skye deserved.

He was happy to see Skye standing where he'd left her. She licked her lips when he walked into the room and Noah almost dropped the candles, desperate to feel her mouth against his again.

With shaking hands, he got the two candles burning, turning back to her. She was beautiful and sexy in the candlelight, her breasts rising and falling with rapid breaths that mimicked his own.

Noah took her hand, their fingers weaving together again. He positioned Skye's other hand on his nape before moving his to her waist. "I think this is where we left off."

Her little sigh was exactly what he needed to hear to know she wanted this too. As the love song faded to black and another song started, the music and lyrics drifted to the background. It was only Noah and Skye, their lips softly seeking more, their bodies creating a heat that would send them into a tailspin.

Chapter 24

There's a room at the end of the world
Where my secrets go to hide
There's a room at the end of the world
Where I'll wait for you tonight
-Room at the End of the World, Bon Jovi

Need.

Skye commanded every ounce of discipline to keep from ripping Noah's clothes from his body. She wanted to savor his slow touch. A lifetime of fantasy and need pooled low in her body. She'd loved Noah since her teens. She may have kept that secret from the world, but she'd played it out in her mind, a fantasy with a thousand different songs, all with the same melody.

Desperate to feel his skin against hers, she shifted a hand down his strong back, his heat penetrating her skin even through the white t-shirt. When her hand moved under the shirt and against his skin, a fire ignited between them. Skye wanted to push his shirt up and feel more of him, but that required two hands and the connection they shared through those old scars was as potent as the kiss that fluttered all the way to her toes.

Noah's hand moved up her arm and slid over her breast, cupping and massaging the small curve. He was a self-admitted breast man and right now she wished she had more to offer. Losing so much weight since the explosion caused her to decrease an entire cup size. She couldn't afford to lose a cup size to begin with.

The explosion. Skye wanted Noah with such ferocity that she had forgotten about her injuries and scars. As his hand moved down her torso and under the tank top, the repercussions of what they were doing hit her like a bullet at point-blank range.

The light from the candles would allow him to see her, all of her. He would discover the scars she'd kept a secret, the extent of the damage the explosion had rendered. He would see just how hideous she'd become.

Skye tried to push aside the shame and enjoy his touch, but fear gripped her.

"Noah," she said, such a quiet plea she wasn't sure if he heard.

"I've got you."

"Please stop," she pleaded.

He did, in an instant, his touch abandoning her skin as he stepped back to look at her. "Am I hurting you?"

The question broke Skye's heart. She would be the one hurting him. "I, we…" she stumbled, unsure what to say. She didn't want to stop. This was Noah, and she wanted him, wanted the us, the connection, the love.

"Just breathe," he whispered.

"I want this," she said. "But, I don't, I just, I need you to leave my shirt on."

His hands cupped her face, his thumbs brushing away the tears. "Why?"

Skye shook her head. "Because it's what I want. I need you to accept that."

Now Noah shook his head. "No. This, us, it can't happen if

you're going to keep secrets. You need to talk to me, Skye."

"Scars," she choked out. "I have scars. More than you can imagine."

"Show me," he said without hesitation or pity.

She shook her head more adamantly, more tears spilling out. "That's the point. I don't want you to see them."

"You're afraid they're going to scare me off," he said.

"Something like that," she agreed, even though that only scratched the surface.

He went back to caressing her breast over the shirt, teasing her nipple until it was painful and desperate to be freed from the tank top. "I'm not going to make love to half of you, Skye. We do this the way it's meant to be done or we stop now."

There's a room at the end of the world, where my secrets go to hide ...

Skye couldn't ignore the music playing the background, as if something more powerful than just the two of them spoke to what they both wanted.

Where a rose comes back to life ... where young love never dies ... where we never said good-bye ...

"I don't want to stop," she admitted, the lyrics churning up the desire she'd locked away for too long.

"I don't either." Noah pinched her nipple through the fabric and Skye nearly toppled over the edge right there. She wanted him, skin on skin, every inch of him covering every inch of her. The only way to have that was to completely expose herself.

There's a room at the end of the world, where your memories are safe ...

"Please don't pity me," she said in surrender, the music inspiring a smidgen of courage. "Revulsion I can understand, but I can't handle pity."

Noah turned her scarred hand and brought it to his lips, kissing the raised mark.

Where the truth will have its turn...

"I won't be repulsed and I promise no pity. I just want to love you."

Take a look into these eyes ... there's no place I'd rather be tonight ...

His eyes spoke the same promise as his words.

"Okay, but you have to take it off now, before I change my mind."

He nodded once, letting go of her hand so both of his could caress her breasts, making both nipples beg for more. Skye held her breath as hands moved down the fabric, his fingers wrapping around the hem and lifting. She lifted her arms, the cool air hitting her nipples with a vengeance that only made her more desperate for Noah's touch.

It's me and you, in our room at the end of the world ... there's no looking back ...

"These look like burn scars," he said, no pity in his voice.

Skye took a deep breath, scared to utter the words because even this small truth opened a door to other truths she couldn't embrace. Embracing the music, just as she'd always done when faced with decisions and consequences too heavy to handle on her own, Skye let all her fears fade to black.

Don't say no ...

She nodded.

"Do they hurt?"

Just give in ...

She shook her head.

"Promise you'll tell me if I hurt you."

Don't hold back ... just let go ...

She nodded again.

"Say the words, Skye. Promise me."

It's me and you, in our room at the end of the world ...

"I promise," she whispered with the melody.

Where I'll wait for you ...

His right arm went around her waist, tugging her against

him. "You're beautiful," he said, his hand sweeping over the scars and cupping her bare breast.

Dreams are coming true ...

Before the building sob escaped, his mouth captured hers, his tongue pushing past her lips. All of her insecurities faded, pushed aside by the desire to have every part of the man holding her and kissing her so passionately that she melted in his arms.

It's just me and you ...

Skye tugged at his shirt and he stopped kissing her only long enough to pull it over his head and toss it aside. Both of his hands ended up on her ass, cupping her with a gentle grasp and pulling her to him. His skin was hot, the thin layer of hair on his chest and abdomen creating an erotic fiction that had her desperate for more.

His erection pressed against her stomach, the remainder of their clothes creating a frustrating barrier. Skye moved her hands around to the front, releasing the button and lowering the zipper before pushing his jeans and boxers over his hips. When she took his thick length in her hand, he tossed his head back with a groan.

She wanted to take him into her mouth, to taste him and pleasure him until he came undone, but her physical limitations kept both feet firmly planted. Her bad leg wouldn't let her get into the right position.

As Noah's hand stopped her slow strokes, she realized he had other plans.

He pushed the skirt over her hips and once it reached her thighs it dropped to the floor. Noah smiled as he pushed her panties down.

"I want you on the bed," he said, backing her up until her knees hit the mattress.

Skye sat and scooted back with little grace, Noah stalking her on all fours as she moved all the way to the pillows. She'd never imagined him this sexy, but he was so much more than she ever gave him credit for. She'd always known he was compassionate and giving, but never in this way and she knew, just by the way the candlelight flickered in his eyes, that his sole focus was her, as a woman, not as the wounded and broken soldier everyone saw when they looked at her.

With his body braced above hers, his thigh rubbing against her very sensitive core, and his erection pressed to her thigh, Noah kissed her with reverence instead of passion. Skye pushed up on her elbows to demand more, but he wandered from her mouth, kissing her chin and neck until he found her ear and nibbled all around the edge.

Her breath hitched and he chuckled on a groan. "I'm going to love discovering all the things that make you do that," he said, so much gravel in his voice that she barely recognized the words as his.

Kissing his way down the outer column of her neck and across her collar bone, he found a spot that made this pathetic little cry come out of her. She felt his smile against her skin as he nipped and licked there, his lips caressing the spot before he zig-zagged across her chest, his tongue leaving a sensual trail along the swell of her breast.

When he flicked her nipple, that little cry escaped her again. It seemed to spur him on as his tongue circled and flicked, circled and flicked, and then he was pinching her other nipple between his fingers as his teeth tugged at the sensitive nub. Everywhere he touched he created a flurry of sensations Skye had forgotten possible, so arousing and exciting Skye wanted to stay like this forever.

His thigh continued to press against her, an enticing rub that had Skye spiraling to the edge. It had been so long since she'd been touched like this, if she ever had been.

No, it had never been like this because it had never been Noah. This was different, special, and she wanted everything he had to give.

"Noah," she whispered, a quiet plea for more.

"We have all the time in the world," he said, moving over to her other breast and unleashing the same pleasured torment.

She was so close, ready to come without him even being inside her, when he released her nipple and kissed her breast, moving lower. Skye tensed. If he'd been on her left side, she might have laid back and enjoyed the attention, but as he moved across her burn scars, she held her breath, unable even to remember the pleasure he'd just shown her.

"Am I hurting you?" he asked, stopping after a few slow kisses.

"No. I don't really feel anything there. It's just numb, at least on the surface."

"Then breathe, Skye. Let me love you."

Skye took a breath and laid back, focusing on his mouth on her skin instead of the where. Because of all the damage that had been done, she could only feel a light pressure, not the tingling pleasure she'd experienced everywhere else he'd touched her. Noah didn't linger, he kissed his way down, his tongue tracing over the scars on her hips from the shrapnel and surgeries, until his mouth was dangerously close to where she needed him.

"Skye," he whispered, his breath warm against her sensitive flesh just before his tongue was on her. She cried out again, her hips shooting off the bed, begging for more. She was vaguely aware of a shooting pain down her right leg, but the pleasure from how Noah kissed her overshadowed the pain better than any drug ever could.

Between the sensuous scrape of his scruffy face and the warmth of his erotic kiss, Skye tumbled into an abyss. She couldn't even grapple for an ounce of sanity to make the pleasure last. It had been so long since anyone had touched her in a way that wasn't clinical, she launched into an orgasm so intense it almost didn't seem real.

Noah kissed and licked her all the more, his hands moving up her body to tug her nipple between his fingers. She cried out and floated, the pleasure so potent she wondered if this was a sexual overdose.

As she came back down, Noah slowed his affection, his tongue a warm, gentle caress against her sensitive flesh. When she was sure she'd never regain use of her muscles, Noah kissed her left hip, moving his way up the left side of her body, taking the time to lavish her breast before moving to her ear. "Don't move," he whispered and slid off the bed.

With his warmth and strength gone, the cold hit her like a brisk wind, but she found warmth again watching the silhouette of his body in the candlelight.

He opened the drawer in the bed side table, tearing a condom open before rolling it on.

"I don't get a turn to pleasure you?" she asked as he moved back to the bed.

"You're about to," he said, moving over her, his erection pressed against the very place his mouth had just ravaged.

With his weight on her, he brushed the hair from her face, smiling as he lay there. "Am I too heavy?"

"Not at all. I want to feel you inside me."

"I want that too, but I want this first, just to be here with you, skin on skin. You're so beautiful. Making you come like that was better than I ever imagined."

So he'd thought about this too. It was a stupid thought. Of course he'd thought about it, but it warmed her to hear him admit it.

"Remember your promise. If I hurt you, tell me."

She nodded.

"Don't hide your pain for my pleasure Skye."

"I won't," she promised.

Noah lifted his hips, his hand moving between them to position his erection right at her opening. He pushed in slowly, both of them moaning as he filled her.

He stopped when all the way in and Skye smiled, giving him a subtle nod. "I'm okay," she told him knowing he would ask. "You feel good. I don't want to stop."

Opening his mouth, Skye thought he'd say something, but

he bit down and breathed in before placing a gentle kiss to her lips as he withdrew. Skye moved her hands down to his hips, pulling him back in as she lifted her left knee. "Oh, God," he groaned, going in deeper this time.

They moved in a rhythm that seemed to match the beat of the music even though she couldn't focus on what song played.

For as long as she could remember, Skye had wanted this with Noah, the total, complete connection. Their bodies joined, their hearts beating together, their breaths mingling. Her heart threatened to break her rib cage even as she smiled through heavy, erratic breaths. She tried to watch him move in and out, but the pleasure overloaded her senses. Biting her lip, Skye witnessed his struggle to keep his eyes on her too. Then he started moaning, the gruff sound so hot she almost came apart.

"I can't ..." he struggled to say. "God, Skye, you feel so good. I can't hold out."

"I know," she said as she dangled on the edge with him. "Oh, God, please, Noah. Please," she begged, wanting him to let go, to come undone. He grunted and pushed harder, his long, slow thrusts turning to short pulses inside her body, the base of his shaft rubbing against her and pushing Skye over the edge again. Noah groaned her name, pushing in and holding himself all the way inside her. As she clung to his strong body, every pulse of his release echoed against every contraction of her own.

The waves subsided until Noah moved against her again, eliciting aftershocks that rocked her entire body.

It was only when the aftershocks wore off that Skye realized both her legs were tangled around his. She had no idea when she'd moved her right leg or why she hadn't felt it, but had a feeling she was about to make up for missing it.

"Am I hurting you?" he asked.

She shook her head. "No, but I think releasing you from my vice-grip is going to suck."

A little sound crossed his lips, like a satisfied hum as his fingers caressed her right leg. "We should stay like this forever then."

"That'd be nice," she agreed, loving the gentle touch. "Think anyone will wonder what happened to us?"

"Right now, I don't care."

"Good point," she added.

Noah nuzzled her breast, licking and nipping at her nipple, but when her hip started to ache, she couldn't avoid facing the music.

"I'm going to move my leg. Don't freak out if I make a face," Skye warned.

Still as a statue except for the warmth emanating from every inch of skin, Noah kept a watchful eye on her. She winced when straightening the bad knee, but the pain wasn't nearly as bad as expected.

"How did your leg even get there without you noticing?" he asked.

"You had me thoroughly distracted," she laughed. "Maybe sex is a good alternative to physical therapy."

"Who am I to argue about that," he murmured in that sexy, satisfied voice.

Her heart skipped a couple beats knowing she had done that for him.

When he pulled out, Skye missed the feel of him, the intimate connection that brought with it a calming euphoria she wasn't ready to lose.

Noah wasted no time disposing of the condom, returning to the bed and nestling against her, his warmth more comforting than a fleece blanket fresh from the dryer.

One hand lazily played with her breast, keeping the need for him wide awake.

"I know you're a breast man. I'm sorry mine are so small."

He pinched her nipple, sending a siege of desire from the point of impact straight to ground zero. "If size mattered, I'd be the one falling short," he said.

"Hardly. You're the perfect size. Not too big, not at all small. Just right."

Noah's laugh echoed against her skin. "You're perfect too. Every inch of you. I'm going to give us a few minutes to catch our breaths and then ..."

"Then what?" she asked when he didn't finish.

"That place we just went to, where your body erupted all around mine and you cried out my name in that needy, pleasured way, where it was just you and me. I'm going to take you there again, only I'm going to make it hotter and you scream louder."

Chapter 25

When you're young, you always think
The sun is gonna shine
There'll come a day you'll have to say
Hello to goodbye
-Live Before You Die, Bon Jovi

Panic.

It weighed on her chest, heavier than a flak vest and TA-50 gear on a hundred degree day in the desert.

After spending the entire weekend in bed with Noah, Skye had to face the real world again. She despised the real world.

Skye gripped the handle of the door at the front of the White Mountain Clinic. She couldn't open it. Her momentum had come to a complete halt. Inside the door was healing, but there was also pain. She'd been through it before at Walter Reed. It sucked then and it was going to suck now.

Releasing the door, Skye b-lined it back to her car. She stood at the driver's side door, throttled with the same panic that wouldn't let her open the clinic door.

With her eyes pinch closed and efforts focused on steady breaths, Skye tried to push the panic aside. A memory flashed, a camouflage covered arm pulling open a sand-colored door. Her eyes flew open to keep the memory from flashing again. It didn't. Instead, it played like a movie in the window, the reflection of herself and trees in the background fading to an image of SSG Everhart in a kevlar, hair pulled into a tight French braid beneath, a smile displacing the soldier as she climbed into the humvee, focused on the soldier climbing in on the other side.

Then she was driving, looking at the dusty road ahead, at Rafe, back at the dusty road. She remembered the guys in the back talking, grateful they were preoccupied so they didn't see her making googly eyes at their platoon leader, the soldier she loved, the man she had just agreed to marry.

In her mind she heard screams, her own, as the humvee lifted into the air and broke apart. There was heat, pain, blackness.

Shallow, rapid breaths fought for purchase, her body temperature spiking despite the chills. Fisting her cold, clammy hands, Skye struggled to find a switch in her brain to turn off the turmoil. There was nothing, no magic switch, no soothing words. She couldn't even conjure up a memory or image to settle the panic.

All she saw was her reflection in the window, aching eyes filled with pain, her mouth pursed with misery. The reflection blurred, tears pooling but not spilling, as if they fought to protect her from the past she'd so recklessly created.

Moving around to the other side of the car, she climbed into the passenger seat.

Skye had lived her entire thirty years as if invincible. She'd been a daring child, a reckless teen, and even as a soldier, tended to take risks because she believed nothing could take her down. That's why she didn't mind going on patrols.

In combat, the risks were calculated, and while there had been fear, she never once considered not going into a situation or following orders.

Now, as a civilian, broken and scarred, she couldn't command the courage to walk into that stupid clinic for PT or get into the driver's seat and get herself home.

She couldn't even breathe like a normal person.

"Get a grip, Skye," she preached.

Music played from her phone, Bon Jovi's *Blood on Blood*, the ringtone she'd recently set for Noah. He knew she had PT, had even offered to take her. She didn't want him to witness the struggles or unbearable pain she had to work through. Range of motion exercises were the worst, pushing her beyond her limits.

Ignoring the call, Skye traced the scar on her hand, thinking about the past weekend with Noah, how they'd watched movies and made love and got to know each other in a way she'd always wanted but never believed would happen.

There had been love in his eyes, happiness, and a desire that made her heart race and knees go weak. If he saw her at PT, there would be pity, one more thing Skye couldn't handle.

Not long after the music stopped, the voice mail alert beeped. Not minutes later, the text message alert beeped. She knew it was Noah, but the panic strangled and controlled every muscle. It would take time before she could form coherent words or steady her hands enough to text back.

A man passed by the car window, his posture rigid, confident, like a soldier marching in formation. With his chin held high, Skye pegged him as a veteran. No one else walked like that. Seeing his strength, his self-assuredness, Skye felt a pang of jealousy. She wanted that, had once possessed it. It was gone now, torn apart and burned up in the explosion that had cost her everything. Abandoned by everything she'd known and been, all she could do was hyperventilate like a scared girl.

Skye didn't want to sit in the car, watching people come and go, successful in their endeavors to heal. Her basement hideaway beckoned, safe from places like this that would make her remember everything she'd lost.

Calling Noah might be the logical thing to do, but she couldn't. He'd known her for so long, longer than anyone except her family, had never seen her broken and weak, at least not until the incident at Wal-mart. Even that one time was too much. Noah needed to see her strong and resolute, the way she'd always been, not like this.

Her parents would come to the rescue, but then Skye would have to deal with Amelia's overbearing worry.

She thought of Maddie, but the therapist would get Skye talking again, something she didn't want right now.

Luke's judgment intimidated Skye. He'd be disappointed she'd once again let the panic get the best of her.

The last logical option was her brothers. They'd witnessed that pathetic fall in the parking lot. If they saw her like this, it would be her ruin.

Gasping for breath, Skye focused on the worst possible option. Finn.

Deep down, she'd regret it, but his words from Montreal played like a recording, similar to the movie reflected in the window of the moments leading up to the explosion. Finn understood. While calling him would prove him right, Skye could ignore his ego more easily than the pity and worry of her family and Noah.

With shaking hands, she hit Finn in her contacts, holding her breath as it rang.

"Well, hello. How's my favorite soldier?" Skye squirmed hearing the knowledge in his cocky voice.

"I need a ride," she demanded, getting to the point.

"All I have is a motorcycle, darling. You up for that or is it some other kind of ride you're looking for?"

The shiver raced up her spine and back down as the bile surged. "I have my car. I need you to drive me home."

"All right," he drawled. Skye imagined him concocting a deal in his head since the wretch never did anything out of the kindness of his heart. She wasn't even sure he had a heart. "Where are you?"

"The White Mountain Clinic."

He chuckled, the sound making Skye wince. "I'll be there in ten."

Disconnecting the call, Skye reclined in the seat and looked out the window at the blue sky. An occasional cloud passed by but never in front of the sun, keeping the car warm despite the chills shivering through her every couple minutes. It seemed like an eternity before Finn loomed outside the door. His sinister smile made her skin crawl, as if an army of ants decided it was high time to march from fingers to toes.

Finn came around the car and eased into the driver's seat, pushing it back with such abrupt force she jumped. The son of a bitch chuckled and if she had the courage, she'd tell him to fuck off. Instead, She angled her seat straight up and reached for the keys in her bag.

Without saying a word, Finn started the car and headed out of the parking lot. "You're at Carbonneau's?" he asked when they reached the road.

"Yes," Skye whispered between shallow breaths. Please let Noah be out taking pictures. The last thing she needed was for him to see Finn bringing her home.

Maybe this wasn't a good idea. She could have just sat it out, waited for the panic to subside enough to manage driving. What had she been thinking?

"Just drive to your place. I can drive from there."

Finn chuckled. "Boyfriend isn't going to be too happy about this, is he?"

"Noah's not my boyfriend," she responded, the thought putting a crack in her fragile heart.

Was he her boyfriend? Skye didn't know. They hadn't talked about it. They'd always been together, as friends, and the time they'd spent together over the weekend was just like it had always been, the intimacy being the only exception. With that complication now firmly in place, Skye didn't know if they were friends with benefits or something more.

Noah would want something more. He wasn't a friends with benefits kind of man. No, he was always all in with a woman, even when they'd been young and it had been girls.

Maybe he was her boyfriend. It seemed like such a juvenile label. Everything about Noah screamed man, not boy. She'd learned that much about him since returning to sunset Valley. Sexy and caring, he'd loved her with the skill of a man who made a woman's pleasure his priority.

Lovers. That's what they'd become. That simple term seemed less of a betrayal to Rafe's memory.

Skye wasn't stupid. Rafe would want her to move on. If she had any hope of being able to do that without the guilt and shame of the explosion lingering as a constant reminder, it was with Noah.

Finn shot straight past his street en route to Skye's apartment. The panic reared up again. What would she say when Noah saw her with Finn? How would she explain why she hadn't called him?

"Stop at the convenience store," she said as they left the center of town, heading east.

Skye dug into her bag for the last ten dollars she had in cash. After Finn pulled into the parking lot, she handed him the money. "I like IPA. Get me a six pack."

"Bossy," he chuckled, taking the money. "You know I have something that can help your shakes a hell of a lot better than beer."

"I just want beer," she insisted.

With a smug grin, Finn got out. His confident gait ratcheted up her envy again, just as it had when that man walked into the clinic. He didn't waste any time, strutting across the store where he disappeared behind the shelves, reappearing seconds later with a six pack in hand. He paid and was back in the car, grinning at Skye like he had a plan.

"You still want to go to my place?" he asked.

Anger pushed the panic aside. "I never wanted to go to your place."

"We had fun, that day you came over."

"You had fun," she said.

"That's right. You were nursing your wounds that day." He waved the six pack in front of her. "We can bring this to my place, dig into my special stash, and you'll be feeling right as rain in no time."

"I'm fine," she lied. "I just want to go home."

"Your loss," Finn said, putting the beer in her lap and getting the car going.

It didn't take long to get to her place. Her breathing had leveled out even though she still had the shakes, but her body relaxed a bit when she saw Noah's car wasn't there.

"I brought this for you," Finn said, pulling a small, clear bag out of his pocket. "It's a free sample, but if you like it, you know how to find me."

"I don't want it," she said, without a lot of resolve.

"Maybe not, but you need it."

He put it in her hand and got out, leaving the keys in the ignition.

She almost asked how he was going to get home, but knowing Finn, he already had that worked out. Instead, she got out and called his name as he sauntered across the lawn to the path that led to the ATV trail. When he turned, she held up the bag. "Aren't you even going to tell me what this is?"

He chuckled. "It's magic. Take one to three at a time, up to four times a day."

She wasn't going to need any at a time. Skye refused to play around with recreational drugs. She had the prescription, which suited her just fine most of the time. When it didn't, the beer took the edge off.

That was the plan now, to take the edge off.

So what if it wasn't even noon.

She limped to the apartment, locking the door behind her because Finn might still be lurking and she didn't want to leave an open invitation for the creep.

After tossing her messenger bag and the little plastic bag on the table, she cracked open a beer and placed the other five in the fridge.

Limping in circles around the table, she kept her eye on the pills, as if they might come alive. Finn had said they were magic. What kind of magic was contained in little yellow tablets?

Her hands ached from clenching them for so long and her chest still felt like it was weighed down with a cinder block. She'd been sitting so long her hip throbbed, but it was a tolerable pain, much more so than the residual weight of her panic attack.

"Just one," she said, splitting the plastic zipper on the bag and pinching a pill between her fingers.

Finn was a drug dealer. Skye knew that, knew the ramifications. He introduced things to people who were weak to get them hooked, so he could continue to take advantage of those weaknesses for his own profit.

Skye wasn't weak, though. For twelve years she'd been a soldier, strong, resilient. The army still hadn't completely embraced the service of women, but she'd proven her strength time and again. The present circumstances were just a set-back due to the injuries she'd sustained in the explosion. Nothing made her weak or dependent.

Finn had offered something to get her through this set back. If this magic pill would free her from the pain and panic for just a little while, well, she'd earned the reprieve, even deserved it.

Popping the pill into her mouth, Skye swallowed it with a long swig of the IPA. Taking a moment, she wondered if she might sprout wings or if a swarm of locusts would shoot from her mouth.

Nothing happened.

She laughed and took another swig of beer before she settled on the sofa with a book, because she'd earned the time to just relax, too.

Chapter 26

I don't wanna be another wave in the ocean.
I am a rock not just another grain of sand.
I wanna be the one you run to when you need a shoulder.
I ain't a soldier but I'm here to take a stand.
                                        -Because We Can, Bon Jovi

Worry.

Noah shouldn't let it eat away at him, but with the call from Skye's mother that she had missed her PT appointment and Skye not answering his calls, the worry jacked up to full throttle.

Everything seemed fine when he left that morning, her naked body stretched out in his bed, a sleepy yet satisfied smile on her face when they kissed good-bye. Covering for his colleague again, Noah had to shoot pictures of a retail building in North Conway. It should have been a quick job, but the property manager pulled a no-show and it took several calls to get someone there with keys to let him in to the different stores. All the spaces were empty. The building had been vacant for years and recently underwent a renovation. Now the spaces were for sale or lease and Noah's job was to get the photos ready for the portfolio.

To make the day even longer, the woman who showed up was chatty, constantly distracting Noah from his task. Worrying about Skye had distracted him, too.

He had considered calling Luke or her brothers, but that would no doubt piss her off. They'd gained some ground over the weekend. Noah wanted to trust her, to let her deal with everything her way, but it was hard to take a back seat.

As he pulled into the driveway, his stomach reminded him how unhappy it was with his decision to skip lunch. He noticed Skye's car around back, pulled straight in instead of backed in, so he knew she'd left since that morning. Why had she missed PT?

Disappointed she wasn't in his living room, he hoped to find her in his bed, preferably naked, although Noah wouldn't mind peeling her clothes off. Disappointment hit him again when he found the bed empty.

He walked downstairs, trying to be as quiet as possible in case she was sleeping. After knocking lightly on the door casing, he peeked in. The mid-day sun perched high in the sky, but with only two windows in the basement, the apartment sat in shadow. Her messenger bag was on the kitchen table and three beer bottles stood on the side table next to the couch where she was curled up and sleeping.

Dammit.

Something happened today. Finding her asleep like this wasn't unusual, but three beers before two o'clock couldn't be a good thing. Since it was that high ABV stuff she liked, Noah worried about the other problem she had with her prescription.

Curious about the potential abuse, Noah peeked in the messenger bag and found the pills. It was a new prescription, filled less than two weeks ago, but it was almost empty.

Noah did the math, calculating the dosage with the number of days it had been. Then he counted the pills. The result told him one thing, Skye was taking too many of these.

The word *abuse* was pushed aside by the word *addiction* in his mind. He wanted to lash out, to wake her and ask if she was fucking stupid, but his reasonable side kept his feet glued to the floor and his mouth pinned shut.

He poured the pills back in the bottle, but he didn't slip it back into the bag. Skye needed help, whether she would admit it or not, and he couldn't to let this slide. She'd be pissed, but pissed and alive was better than appeased and dead from an overdose.

Something peeking out from under her bag caught what little light came in the windows. Noah moved the purse, finding a small plastic bag with a dozen pills in it.

"What the hell?" he muttered. There was no label, no indication of what the contents were or where it had come from, but Noah knew.

Finn. Son of a bitch.

Noah searched through her purse to make sure there weren't any more rogue packages of pills. When he came up empty, he checked on Skye. Her breaths were steady, like they always were when she slept. He went upstairs and called Luke.

"Hey man," his cousin answered.

"Hey. Can you come by?"

"Social call or official business?" Luke asked.

"Personal business. I need some information only you can provide."

"All right. I'll be there in ten."

While Noah waited, he inspected the little baggie. The pills were non-descript. Yellow tablets with a line through them, but nothing that said what it was.

True to his word, Luke pulled in to the driveway ten minutes later. Noah met him out front, not wanting to wake Skye or give her the opportunity to overhear this conversation. Noah hadn't decided what to do; he supposed that depended on what the pills might be.

He shook hands with Luke. Noah still wasn't used to seeing his once rebellious cousin in uniform, let alone as the police chief.

"What's going on?" Luke asked.

Noah held out the bag. "Ever seen these before?"

Luke raised a brow as he took the bag. "A handful of yellow pills in a plastic bag?"

Noah hesitated because he didn't want to rat Skye out to the police chief, but then he realized Luke, his cousin and friend, would have more insight if he knew the details. "I found this in Skye's apartment. She's passed out, three beer bottles on the table next to the sofa. This was open on the kitchen table. I also counted her Vicodin pills. She's taking more than she should based on the recommended dose and the refill date."

"Fuck …"

Noah couldn't have said it better or more succinct. "Do you know what it is?"

Luke shook his head. "It could be anything. I can take it to the pharmacy and see if they can identify it. Do you know where she got it?"

"I have my suspicions." Noah didn't even want to think about Skye anywhere near that drug dealing prick, but she'd taken Finn to the concert and reeked of his cologne the first day he'd seen her.

He swallowed hard. Thinking about what might have gone down between Skye and Finn made Noah want to punch something — preferably Scott Finnegan.

"Have you seen them together since the concert?" Luke asked. It was no surprise he had the same suspicions.

"No, but I don't stick to her like glue. She doesn't leave much, but I'm also not here twenty-four seven. She was supposed to have PT today, but the clinic called her mother and said she missed the appointment."

"Is she getting help?"

"She talked to Maddie."

Luke raised one eye brow. He didn't know what went down five years ago. He was deployed at the time and when he came home a year ago, Noah didn't feel the need to air that dirty laundry. Luke did know, however, about Noah's past relationship with Maddie.

"It's a step in the right direction," Noah said without offering details.

"And the two of you?" Luke asked.

Noah smiled. How could he not?

Luke laughed and smacked him on the shoulder. "Congratulations, man. 'Bout fucking time."

Noah couldn't argue with that. "Just don't say anything. We haven't exactly established a ..." A what? Formal relationship? Label? With Skye, even though it felt more than right, it was still unchartered territory.

"I'm the police chief, not the town gossip."

"Aren't the two one in the same?" Noah laughed.

"Some days I wonder," Luke chuckled before holding up the bag of pills. "I'll let you know what the pharmacist says about these. In the meantime, keep two eyes on her. Regardless of what these pills are, she's playing with fire."

Noah knew that. It's why he had taken not just the mystery pills, but the prescription bottle. It was going to piss her off to have to come to him whenever she needed a dose, but Noah was committed to helping her through this.

After Luke left, Noah went back inside, moving quietly down the stairs to check on Skye. He found her sitting up on the couch, reading a book.

"Hi," he said after tapping on the doorway.

Her forced smile sent a surge of guilt through him. Did she know he rifled through her bag?

"Hi. How was work?" she asked. He was surprised she didn't lash out, but maybe she hadn't realized what he'd done yet. It gave Noah a chance to come clean.

"It wasn't great. The property manager didn't show up and then the woman who came to unlock the building wanted to chat

215

instead of letting me do my job. I should have been home hours ago. What happened with PT?"

Skye shrugged. "I'd rather not talk about it."

"I know you missed the appointment. I tried calling. I was worried."

"I had my phone off," she said, not meeting his eyes.

"Why'd you miss the appointment? You were ready to go this morning."

She shrugged again, the gesture as annoying as the words *I'm fine*. Noah sat next to her, his arm going around her shoulders as he eased as close as he could. Her body was warm against his and he couldn't resist kissing her, even if for just brief moment.

She sighed against his mouth, her hand cupping his cheek. This could go from innocent to hot in seconds if he let it, but there were issues to discuss so he ended the kiss, releasing his own sigh when he pulled away.

Skye's smile seemed a little less forced now. "I'm not trying to be a jerk here and I don't want to fight, but I'd like to know why you missed your appointment."

"PT hurts — a lot. I just got home, I'm still adjusting and I can't ... I don't ... I'm just not ready for that."

"You don't have to do it alone. I would have gone with you."

"You had work," she sighed.

"I could have rescheduled," he insisted. Hell, the client didn't seem to care about being on time anyway.

Skye pushed off the couch and walked away. "I don't want an audience, all right?"

Her anger had settled in, but Noah didn't take the bait. She might be itching for a fight, but he wanted to keep the peace if he could. "You are the poster child for stubborn."

Moving to the table, she ignored his proclamation and dug into her bag. When she come up empty, she scowled at him. "Going through my things while I'm sleeping is a new low."

Noah refused to feel guilty about what he'd done. Skye was accelerating down a dead end road and it was up to him to get her to stop. He pulled the bottle out of his pocket. "I counted them. You're taking too many."

"I'm taking the recommended dose," she huffed.

"Then you're taking the recommended dose too often because you should have at least twice as many in this bottle."

"I have pain, Noah. You saw the scars."

Seeing them had broken his heart. He had no idea she'd been burned, and the scars on her hip and leg were just as horrifying. "PT may hurt, but it's going to help the pain go away. You need to go and you need to be careful with these," he said, shaking the bottle.

"I am being careful." It was the opportune time to ask about the other pills, but he still hoped Skye would bring up the subject. "Can I have them back? Please."

"When you need a dose, I'll give it to you, but I'm not going to let you have unlimited access. You don't want to add addiction to the list of things you're dealing with."

"I'm not addicted," she sighed. According to Skye, she also didn't have PTSD. Denial seemed to be her best friend.

"Then it's not a problem."

"You're not qualified to be a pharmacist," she said.

"Neither is Finn," he retorted.

She winced and studied the floor for a good long time. Would she admit to buying drugs from him? As the silence passed between them, Noah acquiesced to her stubbornness. "When did you take these last?" he asked.

"I don't know," Skye shrugged. "Before I went to PT, I guess."

"You didn't go to PT," he reminded her.

"Before I left for the appointment," she snarled. He looked at the clock. The appointment was at ten and now it was almost three.

"How many do you take?" he asked.

"Sometimes one, sometimes two. Depends."

"And you're hurting now?" he asked.

"I said I was," she snapped. "One. The pain isn't horrible, so I just need one."

Noah didn't like it. He'd seen her in pain and it didn't look like this. Skye looked exhausted, like she hadn't just woken from a mid-afternoon nap.

He shook one pill out of the bottle and gave it to her. "Not with beer," he said.

With a scowl, she walked to the sink and got a drink of water, swallowing the pill and dumping the rest of the water down the sink. "You need to call the clinic and reschedule your appointment," he said. He couldn't fathom all she had to endure, the changes she had to adapt to. Avoiding it wouldn't change anything, though. Noah was sure he could help her through it if only she'd let him.

Chapter 27

This ain't no game, I play it hard
Kicked around, cut, stitched and scarred
I'll take the hit but not the fall
I know no fear, still standing tall.
-Bounce, Bon Jovi

Cope.

Funny how it rhymed with hope. It proved to be just as evasive too. Hope always abandoned Skye and now she couldn't seem to cope with the hand she'd been dealt or the choices she'd made.

She sure itched for a fight, though. If Noah wanted to pretend to be the gatekeeper to her pain relief, he'd better brace for impact. She was thirty, old enough and more than capable of knowing when and how much medication to take.

Skye itched for a beer, too, and another one of those pills Finn had given her. She didn't even care what they were because they were exactly what Finn had said — magic.

The lingering anxiety had dissolved quickly, leaving Skye

feeling light and relaxed. That's when the exhaustion pulled her in and she didn't resist. Sleeping meant she didn't have to deal with the real world. It had become her new best friend. It didn't judge her the way Noah did, or assume a truth that didn't exist.

Noah hadn't said the word, but Skye could almost see it rattling around his head. It was written all over his face, too, from those concerned eyes to the sad lilt of his mouth.

Addict.

Skye knew many vets struggled with it, especially those with PTSD. Not Skye, though. She had everything except the pain under control. Why couldn't anyone understand that?

"Are you going to take my beer too?" she asked as he sat on the couch and watched her with that assessing gaze.

Noah shook his head. "No, I'm going to trust you to not be stupid."

His words were an even lower blow than snooping through her bag. "You must have work to do," she suggested, desperate for him take his high horse and trot away.

Skye still couldn't believe he didn't say a word about the bag of pills. She had no doubt he'd confiscated them. Where else could they have gone? He admitted to taking her prescription. Why hadn't he mentioned the other pills?

Stealing them was enough to put her on edge, but the curiosity of what he'd done with them had her teetering on the brink of another panic attack. Was he hanging on to them? Did he flush them down the toilet? Was he going to say anything?

The torment threatened to pull her under, into murky waters where she couldn't see, couldn't breathe, couldn't find her way out.

"Let's head out to the lake, take some pictures," Noah suggested.

How could he act like nothing was wrong? She had pills, illegally acquired pills, at least on Finn's part. How could Noah just snag them and not acknowledge it? How could he not accuse her of … being stupid?

"I'd rather just hang out here," she said.

Noah pushed off the couch. "Well, that's too damn bad. We're going. You can stew about it if you want, but I'm not letting you sit here and feel sorry for yourself."

"I don't feel sorry for myself."

"Then it's not a problem. Grab your camera. Let's go."

He didn't give her a chance to argue, just headed for the door and up the stairs.

Skye could ignore him, keep her ass planted on the couch and continue reading. Only one small problem with that plan: she wouldn't read a word. Noah had those pills. She needed to know what he did with them. Even if it meant another fight and more accusations, she had to know.

Maybe if they went to take pictures, he'd say something.

Her camera and all the peripherals were still packed away. Noah had given it to her years ago as a birthday present. It was old but still took fantastic pictures.

She dug under the bed for the camera bag and checked everything. The battery was probably dead, but she had a spare and a car charger packed, so could charge it in the car. Since it was the same camera Noah used, just older, he might have a spare she could borrow.

Noah moved around upstairs. The quiet pad of his steps revealing he wasn't pissed. That was too bad, because she still had some fight scratching at the surface and ready to escape.

Fighting with Noah didn't even make the top 100 list of things Skye liked to do. Their friendship made him an easy target because they were so close and he was there, always there, in her business, in her stuff.

Looking out for her.

Tears slid down her cheek without even the courtesy of a warning. Dammit. She hated this, the crazy emotions and mood swings. Even when PMS-ing, her moods weren't this extreme.

"Get a grip," she preached, which seemed to be her new

mantra, and wiped the tears away.

When she made it upstairs, Noah leaned against the kitchen counter, his camera bag slung across his chest, looking sexy and righteous in equal measure. Without saying anything, Skye stepped outside. Noah followed. In the car, he pumped up the Bon Jovi.

Instead of going to the dock, he went to the park on the lake. After they parked and walked down to the water, he turned and smiled. "Divide and conquer?" he asked.

This was something they'd done since high school when they took a photography class together. After going their separate ways and shooting images for an hour or two, they'd compare shots. It was interesting to see their different interests and perspectives.

By going their separate ways, Skye didn't have to worry about Noah confronting her about those pills.

"Sounds good," she said. He dropped a quick kiss on her cheek and headed left.

Spring flowers had started to bloom, the trees budding. It was a sunny day, only a few clouds. Noah preferred snapping pictures on cloudy days, but Skye preferred the sunshine. It was a challenge to get the right settings and the right angles to allow enough light in but not too much. She liked to play around with how the sun cast shadows and darkened objects in the foreground of the image.

Skye found a birch tree that had an interesting dynamic with its buds and the bright sun. It was blue sky all around, the water like glass extending behind the tree. Skye snapped a few shots in auto mode at different angles, then changed to manual and adjusted the aperture. The sun shone high in the sky, but from a low angle, she could capture it behind the tree.

The problem was getting low enough. She could get down, but back up would be the bigger challenge.

Scoping out the park, Skye wanted to be sure no one watched when she attempted this. A man ran by with his dog. Following his path, Skye realized he had a prosthetic leg. She switched the camera to sports mode and snapped some pictures, first at a distance, then zoomed in. He had to be a veteran. With the confident gait in every step and his shoulders back, he possessed the posture of someone who had learned to stand at attention.

Curious about his story, she continued to watch him until he cleared the small knoll a hundred yards away.

With no one else in sight, Skye dropped without any grace onto the ground. A pain shot through her hip and down her leg upon impact. She cried out because she couldn't help it, but focused on the task.

From a sitting position, she couldn't get the angle she wanted for the shot, so she moved onto her side before rolling onto her stomach and shimmying around. Now the tree lined up exactly how she had envisioned it, the sun peeking through the bare branches, a second image of the tree reflecting off the water. Skye took a number of shots on auto and manual. Satisfied there might be something she could use, she now had to face the daunting task of standing up.

"Shit," she muttered.

Skye removed the bag from her shoulder and stuffed the camera into it. Pushing herself into perfect army front leaning rest position wasn't difficult, but where to go from there remained a mystery. Yoga lessons from a past life paid off when it dawned on her to ease her good leg under into pigeon pose. From there, getting into a sitting position only required a slight roll and twist to the side. Now Skye was stuck again.

Uneven steps padded across the grass, accompanied by the distinct sound of panting.

"Let me help," an unfamiliar voice said. Not even realizing her eyes were pinched closed, Skye opened them to find a hand extended in front of her. She followed the arm and found the runner, his black lab sitting next to him.

The man chuckled. "I can tell by the look on your face that you're going to say you don't need help, but we both know you do.

Suck it up and let me help you."

Spoken like a veteran. Skye didn't argue, just grabbed the guy's hand and let him pull her up.

The whimper that escaped embarrassed her, but no more than needing help from this stranger.

"Thanks," she said.

"No problem."

Skye worried about fending off pick-up lines when she spotted the ring on his left hand.

"Did you get the shot you were after?" he asked, nodding at the camera.

"Yeah," she said.

"Was it worth it?"

She laughed. "I hope so. You army?"

He continued to smile. "Prosthetic leg and service dog give me away, don't they?"

"Actually, it's the way you carry yourself."

He laughed now. "Good to know. That's how I knew you were a vet, too. Is that a combat injury you're dealing with?"

"Afghanistan with the Fourth ID," she said, referring to the army's fourth infantry division. "IED."

"One of those fuckers got me, too. I was First Cav."

"Hard core," she laughed.

"You, too. How much time did you do?"

"Twelve years," Skye said proudly. "Gimp hip and leg got me early retirement. I'd rather be sucking sand."

"Not me. I signed on for four years for the GI Bill. Never thought something like this would happen to me. How long you been out?"

"I spent eight months at Walter Reed. Been back here almost a month. How about you?"

"It's been four years for me."

"You live here in Sunset Valley?" she asked.

"Lilac Ridge. My wife is from there. She's in the guard. We

met in basic, hit it off. I like this park. It's a good place to run, never too busy."

Skye nodded. "Well, thanks again for the hand," she said, stepping away.

"You got any support?" he asked.

She stopped and looked at him.

"You go through shit, you recognize it on someone else. You're wearing your battle stripes like neon lights."

"I—" she started, but didn't know what to say.

"There's a group of us, combat vets. We get together, mostly just hang out, sometimes swap war stories, occasionally air our dirty laundry. It helps."

He handed her a business card. Chad Newell, gunsmith. "You're Chad?" she asked.

"Yep. And you are?"

"Skye," she responded.

Noah came over the knoll then, hesitating for a second before stepping it out. She appreciated his worry even though unnecessary. "This is my support," she said when Noah stood next to her. It felt good to say it. Skye wasn't making things easy for him. She wasn't even making it easy for herself.

"Chad," the man said, holding out his hand to Noah.

"Noah," he responded, shaking Chad's hand.

Chad nodded at the card. "We get together a couple times a month. One is sort of open, significant others are welcome. The other time is just us."

Skye nodded. "Thanks. I'll think about it."

"Are you acknowledging your PTSD yet?" he asked.

Noah laughed, but Skye couldn't bite back her outrage. "Who the hell do you think you are?"

"I think that answers your question," Noah added, sliding his arm around Skye's waist. She wanted to tell him not to touch her, but she liked the warmth and strength of him keeping her safe, protecting and loving her.

"I went two years," Chad said. "Total denial. The VA doesn't have any resources up here for us. The vets group saved me, saved my marriage. You should do more than think about it."

He nodded at Noah and stepped off, leaving Skye a little dumbfounded and a whole lot pissed off.

"Want me to take that?" Noah asked, looking down at the card Skye gripped between her fingers.

"Are you going to babysit everything?" Skye asked.

"Do you know that guy?" Noah asked, ignoring her accusation.

"No. He was running by," she said, leaving out the part about helping her off her ass.

"So you just met him and he pegged you in a matter of minutes? I'm not babysitting, Skye. I'm helping. Mislabel it all you want, but it's not going to move you forward until you acknowledge your problems — just like he said."

The guy didn't have her pegged. He made an assumption based on his own experience, without a lick of intel about what Skye had been through.

"Stop scowling," Noah said, kissing her on the forehead. "Do you want to keep shooting or head back and compare notes?" he asked, dropping the subject.

Skye was too pissed off to take any more pictures. "Head back," she muttered. Noah picked up the camera bag and slung it over her shoulder before taking her hand.

Instead of letting her temper drive another wedge between them, she wove her fingers between his. As their palms came together, Skye was humbled by the simple yet potent connection. His warmth seeped into her, the raging pulse of her temper easing to a slow thrum. The heavy weight that burdened her most days lifted, the slow breaths and slack muscles a welcome relief from the anxiety.

Noah was her support, and while he might be a pain in the ass, he cared enough to say the things she didn't want to hear. Skye didn't believe herself an addict, but maybe PTSD kept her from settling into this new life she'd been forced into.

Chapter 28

I believe, I believe
With every breath that I breathe
You and me can turn a
Whisper to a scream.
-I Believe, Bon Jovi

Believe.

Noah had to, because Skye was worth believing in. He held on to her hand as he drove, wishing she would believe in herself.

His heart had done a back flip when she'd introduced him as her *support* to the guy she'd been talking to in the park. It renewed his energy and resolve to see her through this transition and healing, no matter how challenging she made it.

Skye sighed as he stroked the scar on her palm with his thumb. It had hurt like hell when they'd cut each other. Stoic even as a teen, Skye winced, but didn't cry out or shed a tear. Instead, her beautiful smile radiated, as if she'd known the unbreakable strength of their connection and promise.

"Did you get some decent shots?" he asked, choosing not to

push her on the PTSD issue.

With her had back against the headrest, she turned and looked at him. He glanced at her before focusing on the road, happy to see the anger gone. She looked tired, though, and he wondered about the cause of the fatigue, if the pain or medicine, or maybe both, contributed or if the exertion of walking around the park caused it.

Maybe PTSD held some of the blame. She probably battled depression along with it and based on the research he'd done, fatigue and excessive sleeping were symptoms of depression.

"I think so," she said, her voice quiet. "How about you?"

"I think so, too. It's nice snapping something other than buildings." Noah wasn't any good at snapping pictures of people, but he liked nature shots.

As they drove through town, Noah caught sight of Finn leaving the Family Pharmacy. It was a small store, nestled in one of the spaces in an old brick building on Main Street. Finn stepped onto the crosswalk just this side of the store. Noah had about fifty yards, but didn't slow down.

"What are you doing?" Skye demanded.

"Think anyone would miss him?"

"I don't want to visit you in jail. Come on, Noah," she pleaded, squeezing his hand.

Not interested in jail either, he pressed on the brakes and came to an abrupt stop. Finn gave him a mock salute and they were close enough that Noah saw him wink at Skye.

"I can't wait until the cops bust that piece of shit," he muttered once Finn cleared the crosswalk.

Skye didn't say anything, just turned and looked out the passenger window.

"He preys on people. You know that, right?" he asked.

She pulled her hand away, bringing her left knee to her chest and hugging it.

"Skye," he pleaded.

229

"I know," she snapped. "I know what he is and what he does."

Now was the perfect time to ask about those pills he'd given Luke, but Noah wanted Skye to bring it up. If she accused him of taking them, he'd know for sure addiction was an issue. If he asked her, she'd pull her stubborn card and lie, probably even deny having them. The other response would be letting her anger stew and fester while shutting Noah out. He couldn't risk that.

"Would you miss him?" he asked, not able to let it go.

"Of course not," she muttered but didn't look at him.

They rode the rest of the way home in silence, Noah at a loss for what to say without sounding like a dick.

When they got home, Skye got out of the car, grabbed her camera bag with a huff and started toward the path that led to the basement.

"Don't you want to share your shots?" he asked.

"Not if you're going to be an ass," she said.

Noah caught up with her, not a difficult task considering the pronounced limp. When he caught her arm, she spun on him, an angry fire in her eyes.

"You're right. I'm sorry. I just," love you is what he wanted to say, but worried that was one more thing to make her run, "I care about you, about what happens to you."

He cupped her face and kissed her mouth, hoping if she didn't believe his words she'd at least feel his love.

When she pulled away, Noah rested his forehead against hers. She kept her eyes closed. "I just wish you'd trust me," she whispered.

"I believe in you," he said, but she didn't open her eyes, only shook her head. "Look at me, Skye."

Taking a couple steps back, Noah despised the distance. Skye opened her eyes and the sadness in them nearly knocked him over. "I know this is hard. Coming home and dealing with what happened is the hardest thing you've ever had to do, but you can do it. You're strong. You always have been."

"I don't feel strong," she said.

"You don't have to feel strong if you just believe," he said.

Tears pooled before spilling down her cheeks. Noah closed the distance between them, wrapping his arms around her. "I've got you."

Quiet sobs only fed his resolve. She didn't cry for long. As the sobs tapered off, her hands moved down his back and under his shirt, setting his skin on fire with a need to have her naked and under him. She clamped onto his nipple with her teeth, the barrier of his shirt doing nothing to keep the desire at bay.

"Skye," he whispered, his hands weaving into her silky hair.

She looked up at him, red, glassy eyes flashing with desire.

"I need you." The whispered plea undid him. Noah claimed her mouth. Tasting her tears only drove his own need, wanting to erase the pain and fear and replace it with all the love he had to give.

Her nails bit into his back, making him arch into her. Then she squeezed his ass before her hands moved around to open his belt.

"Jesus, Skye. Slow down," he said as she gripped his raging erection. All Noah could think about was her mouth on him, how hot it would be to have her suck him off.

"I want it rough. I need you to take me hard and fast."

Jesus, if she kept stroking him like that, he was going to come in her hand, right there in the driveway.

He tugged her hand out of his pants and squeezed it in his as he claimed her mouth again.

"Inside," he said, pulling her with him as he backed up to the front door. "Bedroom."

He had to stop kissing her to get the door open. They dropped their camera bags and then clothes started flying. He'd have taken her right there against the front door if he'd had a condom handy.

"Bedroom," he said again, stepping back and grabbing her hand.

Noah fell back on the bed, taking her with him. Stretched out on top of him, she ground against his cock, sexy little mewls and moans vibrating against his lips and tongue, driving him insane.

If he let her go, get herself off like this, he'd come too, and they'd both miss out on the hard and fast she'd demanded.

He rolled them over, pinning her arms above the pillow. With his chest pressed against her breasts and her hips still grinding against his erection, Noah couldn't wait any longer.

Rolling away, he grabbed a condom from the drawer in the nightstand, wasting no time in getting it on.

Skye flipped onto her stomach, looking at him over her shoulder. Noah knew this was her favorite position, something she'd revealed more than once during their friendship. He'd fantasized about taking her like this, but given her injuries, didn't think it was in the cards, at least not now.

"Hard and fast," she demanded.

"I don't want to hurt you," he said, the reality of the situation like a splash of cold water.

"You won't. I need this. Please."

Her words from earlier echoed in his mind. *I just wish you'd trust me.*

He hadn't trusted her, not since discovering the prescription drug abuse and keeping time with Finn. His desire pushed him to trust her now. Maybe it was the wrong motivation, but he wanted to give her exactly what she pleaded for.

Positioning himself behind her, he was careful not to put too much pressure on her injured leg. She lifted her hips just enough to encourage him to keep going and he pushed in with a strong thrust.

"Yes," she cried, her head still turned so he could see her biting down on her lip as she pushed back against him.

Despite the urge to remind her to tell him if he hurt her, he kept his mouth shut. This was Skye, the stubborn, bull-headed woman who did things on her terms. She'd tell him if she wanted to, whether he reminded her or not. A reminder might only inspire silence out of spite.

"Hard and fast," she demanded again.

Buried deep inside her, Noah pressed his body against hers, moving his hands beneath her body. Her breast was soft and warm in his hand, the nipple hard between his fingers. With his other he found her clit, swollen and wet. Noah thrust in and out, Skye's moans all wanton pleasure.

She cried his name, her sex clamping around him, pulling him deeper than he ever imagined. Noah threw his head back and breathed, focusing on her pleasure in order to delay his own.

Once again relaxed, she opened her eyes and looked at him. "More," she said, a command Noah was happy to oblige.

With her hips pushing against his hand, Noah gave her more, thrusting into her again and again, loving the sound of their bodies slapping together.

"Harder, Noah. Please," she pleaded. Noah moved his hands to brace himself above her. This angle allowed him to thrust harder, faster, deeper.

"Yes," she cried, and Noah was lost, her heat surrounding him and bringing him to the edge.

Noah's roar echoed in the room as he came, Skye's body tightening around his again. With a few final thrusts, he was spent, collapsing on her warm, soft skin. He loved the smell of her hair, it's softness caressing his cheek as he kissed the soft skin of her shoulder. She smiled through raspy breaths.

"Is that what you wanted?" he asked with a laugh.

"Oh yeah. I think you pounded the bitch right out of me."

He laughed. She had such a dry sense of humor, one he'd always loved and appreciated. He hadn't seen much of it since she'd been home.

"I might have enjoyed that more than you did," he said.

"Oh, so you like pounding the bitch out of me."

"I like being inside you. Your pleasure is my pleasure. Don't kill me for asking, but are you okay?"

"My hip is throbbing," she admitted to his surprise, "but it was worth it."

"Do you want one of your pain pills?" he asked.

"In a minute. Just stay where you are for a little longer. I like the way you feel."

It was another command he was happy to follow. Nothing measured up to the feeling of being inside Skye, of skin on skin. For Noah, it represented a million fantasies come to life, a dream realized. He hoped it meant the same for Skye.

He wanted to stay like this forever, but he had to deal with the condom and didn't want to be responsible for causing any more pain in her hip. He withdrew slowly, kissing her as he rolled away.

"We need to think about another form of birth control," he said.

"Good idea," she agreed.

Noah took care of the condom and washed up before heading out to the living room to retrieve their clothes. He grabbed one of the pain pills from where he kept the bottle stashed before returning to the bedroom.

Skye had rolled onto her back, the comforter draped over her right side to hide the scars. Noah hated that she was self-conscious about them, but he ignored it, knowing it was a battle he couldn't win.

He dropped their clothes and got a glass of water, handing it and the Vicodin to her.

"We should eat. It's after six."

"I'm starving," she agreed, "but maybe we can come back here for dessert."

He loved the suggestion and hoped he was up to a repeat performance. "Can't get enough of me?" he laughed.

"I have a lifetime of fantasies to indulge," she said.

Noah kissed her. "Me too. That was one of them. I'm going

to get dinner started."

She pushed up. "I'll help."

"Maybe you should take it easy," he suggested.

"I need to move around, otherwise that pill is going to put me to sleep."

Noah liked the thought of her naked and in his bed while he got dinner going, but having Skye next to him in the kitchen was even better. They decided on something easy, baked potatoes and broccoli. Once the potatoes were in the oven, they grabbed their cameras and Noah's laptop and settled on the couch. Noah downloaded his pictures first, then popped Skye's memory card into the computer.

He brought up the first picture in his folder and started moving through them until Skye commented. "I like that one, how you captured the bird right in front of the sun. It looks like a shadow, almost ghostly but full of life."

The shot was a lucky catch. When he'd seen the bird, he pointed the camera at the sun, hoping the bird would pass by it. "I snapped this on auto. I could have gotten better lighting if I'd had more time, but it was one of those quick capture opportunities."

"I like it. Can you play with the lighting in your editing software?" she asked.

"Probably. I can apply some pretty interesting effects, too."

They scrolled through, talking about some of the flowers he'd captured and the four leaf clover he'd found. Noah had forgotten about it after what transpired when he met back up with Skye. He dug his wallet out, finding the clover pressed between a couple business cards.

"That's lucky," Skye said.

"We were there together, so we get to share in the luck."

Skye pursed her lips, compelling Noah to kiss the tension away. When her lips relaxed and she let out one of those sexy little sighs, he put his attention back on the photos.

When they finished looking through his, Noah brought up

Skye's. Even though the only class she'd taken in photography was in high school, she had a natural talent for it. Her pictures were always better than Noah's. She was also more picky about what she snapped, so there were fewer pictures to scroll through.

Noah stopped when he got to a picture of Chad and his dog. "Holy shit, Skye. This is amazing," he said. The man was running, but in complete focus, the background slightly blurred. She'd framed it so he occupied the left side of the image, as though ready to run across the landscape in the rest of the picture. Noah scrolled to the next, where the man and dog were in the center, and the next where they were framed on the right side. "These would make a great collage, put all three in a matted frame."

"Go to the next one," she said. "I want to see how it came out."

In the next picture, she zoomed in, a determination and confidence written all over Chad's face. "I like this," Noah said.

"I don't know …" A sob swallowed her words but before Noah could offer any comfort, she sucked in a deep breath. "I don't know how he does it."

"What's that?"

Skye wiped at the tears streaming down her cheeks. "He had such an easy way about him. He didn't seem at all bothered by the prosthesis." Leaning back in the chair, she shook her head as if in disbelief before waving her hands down her body. "My whole body is intact. I was left with scars, but I didn't lose a leg like he did. I'm a wreck, and he was just a normal person."

Noah put his arm around her, stunned when she shook beneath his hands, as if she struggled to keep her emotions behind a cracking wall. "He's had more time to adjust. You've been home a month."

"And I was in the hospital for eight." Her voice was harsh now, the anger taking a front seat but all the other emotions still trying to gain some ground. "It's been a long time."

Noah held her tighter, resting his chin on her head as he

hoped to calm the frenzy wreaking havoc on her. "Remember what he said? It took him two years before he acknowledged he had PTSD. That's probably the first step in moving forward. I know you think it makes you weak to admit it, but I believe it'll only make you stronger."

Chapter 29

These eyes hold no secrets
I hide no truths.
I am all I am, all I was to you.
The lie and the promise,
the great escape artist,
The weed in your garden
In that place you're still guarding
Where I am not a liar.
-The Fighter, Bon Jovi

Confess.

What started as a whisper in her mind had turned into an urge that struck with such clarity Skye felt like she'd been tossed out of a tornado into an open field under a cloudless sky.

Her mind whispered the word over and over until her vocal chords wanted to scream.

Confess ... confess ... confess ...

Instead of admitting to all the sins she had yet to acknowledge, Skye pushed Noah's hand off the mouse and clicked to the next picture. In this one she'd focused on Chad's prosthetic and the dog.

Her heart raced as the chant continued in her mind. Skye swallowed the lump in her throat, sucking in a deep breath and repeating the drill a few more times before finding her voice. "Do you think they provide service dogs for vets with PTSD? I mean, not just amputees?" The words came out as a whisper, a barely there acknowledgment of the thing haunting ever beat of her ragged heart.

Noah's hand slid across hers, as if he knew the effort it took for her to ask that question, to essentially admit to the one thing everyone else had seen. "They might. We can research it, maybe you can ask Chad."

Skye nodded, the terror of her admission ripping any remaining words from her throat. She prayed for the oven to beep, so she could stuff her mouth full of baked potato and not have to own up to the shit that was eating away at her little by little.

PTSD. It wasn't something any soldier wanted to admit to, let alone own.

Noah believed in her, though. He'd seen her scars, watched her drama, had even confiscated her pills, but he hadn't given up on her.

She stared at the image on the screen, remembering how calm the dog had been. She just sat there next to Chad until he gave her leash a tug and they walked away together. Skye scrolled back to the picture of Chad's face.

Tears spilled down her cheeks again, a reminder of everything she'd lost, that the strong and capable soldier she had once been no longer existed. "I want that," she whispered, choking back another sob, "confidence, determination. I just don't know how to get there. I forgot what it's like to fight."

"You didn't forget. You fight with me at every opportunity." There was humor in voice despite the truth of those words.

"I'm sorry," she said, leaning against him. Hurting Noah wasn't part of her plan, not that she had a plan at all. It just seemed easier than letting him in, and letting everything else she'd been battling out.

Noah kissed the top of her head, his arm holding her tighter, as if he knew she teetered on the edge, ready to fall apart with the next aching teardrop. "I don't want an apology."

She moved then, angling to look at him and hoping gravity would do its job to keep that tear from falling. "What do you want?"

"It's not about what I want. You say you want what he has." He nodded at the image on the screen, drawing Skye's gaze back there.

The lone teardrop spilled, a warm tickle on her cheek. Noah brushed it away with his thumb. "You can't do it alone, Skye. You told him I was your support, but you need more than just me. You need to go to PT, you need to talk to someone — a professional, and you need a support group."

An invisible weight pressed against her chest, pushing another sob from her. It brought more tears, too many, more than Noah could ever wipe away. "I'm scared," she admitted, pressing her forehead to his chest. The steady beat of his heart offered an invitation of peace, a rhythm to calm her racing heart. She counted the beats, breathing in for four, and out for four, until her pulse no longer threatened to push her over the edge.

She turned, pressing her ear to his chest, letting the rhythm help her find some strength to admit the truth. Noah caressed her arm with the same rhythm, a cadence that comforted her and promised relief if she'd just open up. With a deep breath, she let the words come in the same cadence. "I panicked today. That's why I didn't go to PT. It was worse than the panic attack I had before. I don't know how to stop it."

Noah cursed and Skye's guilt reared up. Noah would have helped. He would have dropped what he was doing and rescued her. Instead, she'd called the absolute worst person she could think of.

Finn had helped, though. He'd given her those pills, and like he'd said, it'd been magic. Skye could ask Noah now what he'd done with them, explain how they'd helped and maybe he'd give them back. Of course, she'd have to admit where she got them. After seeing him almost run Finn down today, she couldn't tell him, couldn't be responsible for Noah hurting Finn and getting himself into trouble.

"Tomorrow, get a new PT appointment. Call someone on that list Maddie sent me — or hell, call Maddie. Maybe give this guy a call, too," he suggested, pointing at the picture on the screen. "Find out when their next get together is. I have a couple days of computer work ahead of me, so I'll be here to see you through it, but you're the one who has to pick up the phone."

The oven beeped before Skye agreed to Noah's to-do list. Deep down, she knew he was right. She had to do all those things, but every single one of them terrified her. PT would unleash a hell like no other. What if the panic took her in front of everyone at the clinic? Talking to Maddie had been fine because they only talked about Noah, and not even all that much. Talking about Rafe, about the explosion, it would just drudge up all the feelings Skye had managed to bury.

They ate in silence, something that had never seemed awkward between them, but now was a painful experience.

"Aren't you hungry?" Noah asked. Skye looked down and realized she'd been poking away at the potato, but hadn't eaten any.

"Just tired, I guess." The half lie was also a half truth. Emotionally, she'd had enough of this day. "I think I'll just go read, maybe fall asleep. I'm going to need another dose of Vicodin."

"It hasn't even been two hours since your last," he said, the drug police standing in judgment again.

Accusing him of taking his self-appointed role too seriously would get Skye nowhere. "It says take 1-2 every 4 hours. If I only take one, I take another after a couple hours."

Her routine included taking two for a dose after taking only one, but she didn't expect Noah to understand. He'd just throw more accusations at her.

"Are you in pain?" he asked.

"You know what, forget it. I'll take ibuprofen instead."

She dumped the potato in the garbage and dropped the plate in the sink, opting out of clean-up to get away from Noah and his accusations.

"Skye," he pleaded as she stormed away. While marching down the stairs, she heard his footsteps behind her.

When she reached the bottom, Skye turned on him, using the rail to catch herself before tumbling to the floor. "What? Are you going to monitor my over-the-counter use, too?"

"Have you noticed your mood swings?" he said through a disapproving and judgmental frown. "You go from eerily quiet to seething bitch in a nanosecond."

"So?" she snarled, preferring the seething bitch to the pathetic, quiet girl who burst into tears for no reason.

"That's not you, Skye. If you need a painkiller, I'll give you one, but if you can get by on ibuprofen, maybe you should try that."

Her throat tightened, the burn of tears drowning her aching eyes. Grappling for purchase on the seething bitch, Skye turned away, hoping Noah didn't catch the watery eyes.

"Shit," he muttered, his hands landing on her shoulders and stopping her retreat.

Skye took a couple deep breaths and pushed the tears away. She was so sick of all these emotions. "Seething bitch to crybaby in a nanosecond, too."

Noah moved around her. "Crying doesn't make you a baby. It's a way to relieve stress and anger. Crying is good."

"Crying sucks," she muttered.

"You want to tell me what the trigger was?" he asked.

She shook her head, but the word wanted out and when she opened her mouth to breathe, it escaped. "You think I'm an addict."

Noah shook his head, but she didn't believe the gesture. "I think you're at risk."

At risk, addict, they were the same thing, all a sign of

weakness, a sign she couldn't cope with her stupid issues. The truth was painful because of course, she couldn't. Between the fear and guilt and panic attacks, Skye was a train wreck, desperate for anything to make her numb, even pills provided by a drug dealer.

Pills provided by a drug dealer. A predator. "I think you're right," she whispered only to wish she could take the words back.

"Come here," he said, pulling her to his body. She went easily, a moth to a flame, selfishly absorbing his warmth and strength. The tears faded for only moments before they started up again, and Skye held on to Noah for all she was worth.

The revelation didn't sit well with her. Now that it was out, she couldn't take it back, couldn't continue to deny it.

Noah kissed her temple. "Why do you take it if you're not in pain?"

She looked up at him, ready for a fight, but saw only concern, not anger or judgment. "It puts me in a daze, a kind of fog. My brain doesn't really work, so there are no memories to torment me. No emotions."

"Maybe it fogs the memories, but not your emotions. You're all over the grid, all the time."

"You don't pull any punches, do you?" she laughed.

Noah laughed too. "That's what best friends are for, right?"

Skye's hands went around his nape, pulling him down so she could kiss him. He was so good to her, honest and ruthless, not giving up even though he should.

"Stay with me tonight," he insisted. "Grab your book and get in your pajamas if you want, though I won't stop you from sleeping naked."

She nodded, wanting the same thing. Alone was a scary place, like the darkness under the bed when she was a kid, where the monsters lurked and threatened. "I'll be up in a few."

Noah retreated up the stairs, leaving Skye to change into a giant sweatshirt and fleece pants. She grabbed her book and was about to head back up when she decided to scavenge for that bag of pills. Noah hadn't said anything about them, so maybe he hadn't taken them. It's possible the fog of sleep and Vicodin and the magic pill had made her overlook the bag. Skye felt around inside her messenger bag and when she came up short, dumped it on the table.

There were no pills. She pulled the cushions off the couch, thinking maybe, she'd taken the bag with her when she sat down. Reaching down into the depths of the couch, even pushing it back to search underneath, turned up nothing.

Addict, the voice in her mind whispered, inspiring a shiver that raced down her spine and back up.

The pills weren't there because Noah had taken them. He had done that because he cared. Skye was an addict, desperate for a pill she couldn't even name.

She left the cushions on the floor and the contents of the messenger bag spilled across the table. Burdened steps carried her upstairs, like a ghost mourning the loss of its soul.

When she got to Noah's room, he was already in bed reading. She slid under the covers next to him, once again selfishly absorbing his warmth.

"What's wrong?" he asked.

"Another mood swing," she said, finding a new excuse he would likely buy. "Sometimes I can't explain it."

She opened the book, but after reading the same paragraph three times, clapped it shut and kissed Noah goodnight.

"Will it bother you if I keep reading?" he asked.

Skye shook her head and closed her eyes.

Darkness filled the room when she opened them again. The digital clock said it was just after midnight. Noah's breaths were quiet but she felt the rise and fall of his chest beneath her hand.

She'd been asleep for a few hours, but instead of feeling rested, restlessness stirred in every muscle. Her hip throbbed and she rolled onto her back to see if that would relax the tension in her battered muscles. Light from the clock and moonlight creeping in around the edge of the curtains illuminated the room in a dim glow.

Flat on her back, there was nothing else to look at but the ceiling.

Sleep had been her new best friend during the day, but unless she was … doped up, she couldn't make it through the night. Sometimes she awoke from a nightmare in a cold sweat. Others, like tonight, was the throb of her gimp hip that pulled her out of sleep. Until today, she handled the problem by tossing back another pain pill. Now, Noah had them stashed and under his direct control.

To avoid another interrogation that might inspire her temper to wake up, too, Skye opted to slide out of bed in stealth mode. With one of his strong, warm arms draped across her body, she risked waking him, but could always claim to be going to the bathroom. That seemed easy enough to fake.

Skye managed to slide away and out of bed without disturbing him. Her search started in the bathroom, just in case he did wake up. She checked the medicine cabinet for the prescription and the bag from Finn, but they weren't there. Too obvious. Noah was smarter than that. No way would he put the pills some place so obvious and accessible. He'd accused her of being an addict and having PTSD. He may as well have called her desperate.

Groaning, she realized that's what Finn had said. A desperate little junkie, he'd called her. She'd been pissed at the time. She realized now how close it hit to home, just more proof he understood what she endured every day.

After searching the vanity and between the towels on the wire shelf, and even lifting the cover of the tank at the back of the toilet, Skye moved into the kitchen. Maybe he'd hidden the pills with all the spices.

Her search of the kitchen cupboards turned up nothing, so she moved to the living room. He had replaced the frames she'd shattered during her little tantrum a couple weeks ago, but he wasn't using any of the frames to hide her prescription. The desperation even drove her hands into the pockets of Noah's coats hanging near the front door. Nothing.

Movement down the hall propelled Skye to the recliner.

Moments later, Noah came into the living room. "Are you all right?" he asked.

"Couldn't sleep. My hip hurts."

"You should have woken me. Do you need your meds?" he asked.

Skye nodded. "I need two, please."

"All right. Why don't you head back to bed and I'll grab them," he suggested.

He wanted to get rid of her to keep the hiding spot a secret. Skye was smart too, too smart to fall for that. "It's going to take a while for them to kick in. I don't want to keep you up with my tossing and turning."

After giving her a quick kiss, he said, "Sit tight. I'll be right back."

Because of the chair's angle, Skye couldn't see if he went into the bedroom or the office, but made a mental note to check both next time he left the house.

Addict, that little voice in her mind scolded, but Skye ignored the whisper. Needing the pills to get through the day was an issue. Needing them to get through the night was necessity.

A minute later Noah returned with two pills. He got a glass of water and lingered, making Skye feel like a specimen under a microscope.

"I'll be in soon," she assured him. "You don't have to wait up."

"I won't be able to sleep," he said, holding out his hand. "We may as well toss and turn together."

She took his hand instead of arguing. Noah pulled her out of the chair and against his body, kissing her until her knees went weak and the rest of her body turned to pliable puddy. "Mmm, I'm wide awake now," he said, the combination of sleep and desire making his voice sound all sexy.

"Are you trying to kill me with sex?" she joked.

"Maybe making up for lost time, but definitely not trying to kill you. I like having you around. It feels right."

She nodded because despite everything else that felt wrong in her life, Noah was the one thing that felt right. "Yeah, for me too."

Chapter 30

Hitched a ride with forgiveness
In that river of emotion, I went down, a third time.
I spent the night with the living
Took a chance, looked inside
Didn't know who I'd find.
Standing on the corner of the long goodbye
-One Step Closer, Bon Jovi

Terror.

As Skye's entire body shook, she had no idea how to get from Point A — the car, to Point B — the clinic. No amount of army training in navigation would help. All that waited inside was pain and misery as they manipulated her leg and forced her muscles to do things they had forgotten how to do.

She didn't mind the limp and most days the pain was bearable. So what if people whispered? Going out in public was overrated anyway.

"You ready?" Noah asked. She'd been brave enough to make the call a few days ago, but not brave enough to make it inside on her own, so he'd insisted on driving.

The alternative to Noah's escort was another panic attack where she'd end up calling Finn for a rescue. Of course, that wouldn't be so bad if he offered another bag of those magic pills. Skye would do a better job of hiding them next time.

Next time. That thought echoed with the surety of an addict. "Shit," she muttered.

"The sooner you go, the sooner you're done," Noah offered, but he didn't get it. The sooner she went in, the sooner she'd suffer the torture those physical terrorists had planned for her.

"Fine," she snarled, and got out of the car. Without waiting for Noah, Skye stomped across the parking lot, pain shooting up her leg and into her hip each time that right foot hit the pavement.

It didn't take long for Noah to catch up. He didn't have a gimp leg and hip and the screaming pain to go along with it.

"Jesus, Skye, what the hell are you doing?" he asked when she reached the door.

"Going to my appointment," she said, rolling her eyes.

Noah brushed the hair from her face. "You're sweating and breathing like you just ran a marathon."

Whether it had become the norm or because her give a shit meter was tapped out, Skye hadn't noticed. If she'd had one of those magic pills, it wouldn't matter. Normal would be like everyone else's normal.

"You are not going in with me," she said, gripping the door handle.

"Waiting room only. I promise." Noah grabbed the handle on the other door and opened it. Skye rolled her eyes again at his chivalry but limped inside and to the reception desk. She was sure the woman behind the tempered glass silently assessed her, mentally flagging her as a pain in the ass for missing two appointments.

Skye stood with her shoulders back and chin up, as if standing at attention, and waited for her orders. She figured she'd have to wait, but the woman sent her to the end of the hall.

She nearly fell over after entering the large, open room. It had a beautiful view of the mountains and Starlight Lake in the distance, a bright airy space that couldn't have been more horrifying if it had been the run-down home hiding an insurgent gunman in Afghanistan.

Everyone would see her here, see the struggle and the pain she couldn't hide.

"You must be Skye," a woman said.

"This is where you do therapy?" Skye asked.

"Some of it. We have some private spaces as well. Let's go in this room over here and review your history."

Skye didn't like it. It wasn't any different than the PT room at Walter Reed as far as set-up went, but at Walter Reed, everyone was a veteran, most had been in combat. The encouragement rang with honesty, the camaraderie only those serving understood. Civilians wouldn't understand what she had survived. Once they knew she was a veteran, they'd look at her with pity.

Skye despised pity.

The woman introduced herself as Maria, a physical therapy assistant, and explained about the team and the methods. Then they went over Skye's history, meds, current level of pain.

"Are you being treated for PTSD?" Maria asked.

"I don't have PTSD," Skye declared.

Maria smiled, wearing her doubt like a badge of honor.

"I was treated at Walter Reed. I'm fine now," Skye clarified.

"You seem to have some anxiety about being here," Maria pointed out.

"That doesn't mean I have PTSD." The cream-colored walls started to close in. Skye took a breath and held it for five seconds before letting it out in a slow release.

"I don't mean to offend you," Maria continued as Skye controlled every breath, "but we see a lot of combat veterans. Most are like you, with the same anxiety, and most haven't been treated for PTSD. That hinders the healing process."

What did she want Skye to say about that? "You expect people to do PT out in the open like that for everyone to see and you're surprised we have anxiety about it?"

"I think you'll be surprised at how relaxing the environment is out there. I'd like to get you started on the treadmill, to evaluate your leg and hip."

Skye swallowed her attitude and complied, following Maria out to the large room. There were a series of treadmills against one wall, facing the large windows. They stopped next to one.

"On a scale from one to ten, what is your pain level right now?"

The hard core soldier she'd been would have said zero, but Skye thought about Noah just down the hall and all of his encouraging words. Skye could be difficult — stubborn — on a good day. She couldn't even summon a word to describe herself on a bad day. Yet Noah stood by her, believed in her. For him, she had to be honest. "About a six. The best I ever get to is three or four." Skye's pain only ever got that low when she had a steady stream of painkillers and alcohol pumping through her veins.

Maria made some notes and pointed to the treadmill. "Get on and set it to a pace that's comfortable for you."

Following those orders like a good soldier, Skye climbed on the machine, hitting the start button and upping the speed until reaching a pace that didn't make her look pathetic but also didn't offer a challenge.

In less than ten minutes, her hip started to throb. A few minutes later, the shooting pains started in her leg.

"You can stop the machine," Maria instructed. "What's your pain level?"

Skye glared at the woman.

"Your gait changed, so did your expression. Those are clear signals that your pain increased."

"Eight," Skye growled.

"And you took Vicodin this morning?" Maria asked even though they'd already covered that when going over her history.

"Two tablets, two hours ago," Skye confirmed.

"You may be developing a tolerance. You should see your doctor, see about getting a different prescription to manage your pain."

Or she could just call Finn and see what he had to offer. Seemed like less of a hassle and Finn wouldn't judge her the way this woman did.

"You can step off the treadmill," Maria said, still making notes. Skye stretched and leaned toward the woman, desperate to know what she wrote, wondering if she accused Skye of having PTSD and being a drug addict.

"When you go home, take a hot shower or bath, then ice your hip, twenty minutes every couple hours. That'll help with the pain."

"That's it? Just walking?" Skye asked.

"For today, yes. I'm not going to lie to you, Skye, it's going to get harder before it gets easier. You're in rough shape. You haven't had therapy in almost three months, so it's like starting from square one. If you stick with it, the pain will go away, so will the limp."

That's what all the medical professionals said, but they didn't have to endure the pain. Once Skye healed enough at Walter Reed to start therapy, she never reached the point where it got easier. It got harder and harder with each session. When discharged under orders to continue PT, she'd pretty much given them the single finger salute, taking a well-earned break.

Maria handed her a sheet of paper. "These are your appointments for the next two months. The frequency could change depending on your progress, but this is what you should plan for. I'll see you Monday."

Skye's eyes widened when she took the paper. Three times a week for two months? That was one more session a week than she'd done at Walter Reed.

Before she could ask what the hell, Maria walked away, preparing for the next gimp.

Skye crushed the paper in her palm and limped down the hall, giving Noah a quick, "Let's go," as she headed straight for the door.

"How'd it go?" he asked when they got outside.

"Great. Time of my life," she groaned.

"Do you need to make your next appointment?"

He grated on her fucking nerves sometimes. "No, they do that without asking. I'm booked out for the next two months." She regretted holding out the paper as soon as he took it, wishing she had somehow hidden it instead. Without her messenger bag or pockets in the yoga pants, the only hiding place was down her shirt. That hadn't occurred to her until now.

Noah got wise and kept his trap shut, folding the paper and putting it in his pocket. He led her to the car, opening the door and closing it once she was in because he didn't even think she could manage that on her own. Skye was a helpless baby, apparently. A drug-addicted, PTSD-suffering cripple.

When Noah got in the car, he plugged his phone into the center console and got the music going. Skye reached over and cranked it up, preferring to lose herself in rhythm and lyrics than engage in any more useless conversation.

She closed her eyes, wishing for sleep to stake its claim. Given how much her hip throbbed, the empty wish would be ignored. "I need a Vicodin," she demanded.

"It hasn't been four hours."

"I don't fucking care. I hurt."

Her demands didn't deter Noah. "There's ibuprofen in the glove box. Take a few of those."

If the Vicodin wasn't working, ibuprofen had no hope of busting through the pain.

Skye went back to the music, ignoring Noah while she

formulated a plan. If he wanted to be the prescription Nazi, she needed to find another way to get what she needed.

After the third consecutive song that rang with hope and determination, Skye hit the power button. God, how far had she fallen if the music wasn't even speaking to her?

Only minutes later, Noah pulled into the driveway. Skye burst out of the car and trudged to the apartment.

"Do you need anything?" Noah asked, not following.

"I need to be alone," she growled.

What she needed was for Noah to leave her alone so she could carry out her new plans.

After dragging her broken body into the dark apartment, Skye got into the shower as instructed. The hot water did little for the pain. Dressed again in yoga pants and a big sweatshirt, Skye sat on the couch and called her last resort.

"Hello, darling," Finn drawled, making the bile rise in her throat.

"Can we meet up?" she asked, remaining vague in case Noah eavesdropped.

"I'd love to. What do you need?"

"Something stronger."

"I've got just the thing. When do you want to stop by?"

"No, I'm not going to your place. I want to meet someplace else."

"No can do, darl. You come here or there's no deal."

Shit. "Fine. I'm on my way."

Skye grabbed her bag and keys and headed out. With her hip still throbbing, she couldn't move fast and hoped Noah wouldn't spot her leaving. Worse than another inquisition would be the disappointment on his face if he suspected what she was up to.

She made it to the car without incident and headed out. It took ten minutes to get into town and another five to Finn's house. He opened the door before she knocked.

"Welcome back," he said, too pleased to see her.

"Can we just get this over with?" Skye demanded.

"Come on in," he insisted. "I don't do business on the porch."

Bile rose in her throat, fear and loathing ratcheting up. She'd been in worse situations, so swallowed the rising anxiety and followed Finn.

In his living room, he leaned against the desk, as casual and cocky as ever. "Vicodin isn't cutting it?" he asked.

She shook her head. "I've developed a tolerance."

"I'm sure your doctor would prescribe you something else."

"It'll take weeks to get an appointment. I need something now. I have money this time."

Finn smirked. "I liked our last deal. I'd be willing to do that again."

Skye shook her head again. "I'm not."

Laughing, he opened a box on the desk. "Heroin is the best thing to help you. It's fast, cheap, and effective."

"I'm not taking illegal drugs."

Finn's laughter echoed throughout the room. "You realize the irony of that statement, right?"

"Shut-up, Finn. Do you have something else, something I could get from the doctor?"

"Vicodin is pretty potent shit. If you're not willing to take H, morphine is the best I can do."

"Is that in pill form?" she asked.

"You bet."

"I'll take that. Oh, and whatever you gave me the other day. I need more of those."

"You didn't go through all that already?" His concern surprised Skye. Why would Finn care? As a drug dealer, if she needed more, it only served his business.

"No."

Finn looked at her, as if waiting for an explanation. Skye wasn't prepared to do that and found herself at a loss.

"I'm not giving you more until you tell me what happened to the gift I gave you."

"They disappeared when I was sleeping. I think Noah took them."

Finn lurched at her so quickly she didn't have time to step back. He gripped her neck, angling her head to look at him. "You need to keep a hold of the shit I give you. That prick probably handed it over to his cousin and that adds up to trouble for me. You feel me?"

"Let go of me," she snarled.

He released her with a shove. Skye stumbled back and hit the wall. Pain exploded from her hip and head, like a thousand fire ants unleashing hell.

What was she doing? Finn was trouble, what they were doing, illegal. Realization dawned like a sunrise over the Hindu Kish mountains in Afghanistan. This road would only lead to disaster. After living with the pain for what felt like an eternity, Skye could survive long enough to see the doctor. In the meantime, she'd appeal to Noah's sympathetic side.

"Forget it," she said, pushing off the wall and heading for the door.

"You came to me, Skye. Every time, you've come to me."

She walked out and ignored his statement, expecting him to claim she'd be back. He didn't say a word, didn't follow, and Skye was grateful for that small miracle.

Chapter 31

I can't save me from my sins
Innocence my long lost friend
No wind no rain can wash away
These hallowed words
My mouth won't pray
- Life Is Beautiful, Bon Jovi

Memories.

Like a waterfall crashing onto the rocks, images of Rafe flashed through her mind. Skye hadn't thought about him as much lately, probably because of Noah, but now it felt like he was with her, bringing not just the happiness they'd shared, but the guilt she'd lived with since he'd died.

For two days she'd secluded herself in the apartment, ashamed about going to Finn, afraid to face Noah. One look and he'd see right through her, know what she'd done.

To her surprise, Noah left her alone. He checked on her a couple times a day, but didn't stay, his absence digging out that hollow place in her heart where memories of Rafe lingered.

Noah lived right upstairs, but she missed him, as much as she missed Rafe.

A glutton for punishment, Skye went to Facebook for the first time since coming home and brought up Rafe's page. The hope that it had been deactivated fizzled when she found recent posts honoring him.

Skye scrolled through, reading each post but not interacting. She didn't want anyone to know she stalked the dead. The discharge and Rafe's death meant no consequences if anyone found out about their relationship, but Skye needed to keep it close to the vest. Keeping their secret meant locking down the memories, only letting them come to light in her mind, not because someone else talked about it.

The more honest conclusion whispered of the shame that came with breaking the rules and falling for her platoon leader.

Tears poured as Skye looked at the tributes and pictures. When Noah knocked on the door frame, she jumped and slammed the laptop closed as he stepped in to the apartment.

"Hi. Am I interrupting?" he asked. His voice was calm, but narrowed eyes gave away the curiosity.

"Just looking at porn again," she joked, wiping the tears.

"Porn makes you cry?"

"It was really bad porn."

Noah sat next to her, his body flush against hers from shoulder to knee. He didn't put his arm around her in that natural and affectionate way he normally did. Skye tried not to read too much into it, but it hurt, as if Noah had given up on her, given up on them.

He nudged her a little. "Want to show me what you were looking at?" he asked.

"No," she answered.

"Why not?"

"Because it's none of your business." Yep, quiet to bitch in a nanosecond.

"Maybe not, but I haven't been a very good friend the last few days. I thought giving you space is what you needed, but I'm not so sure."

"I did need space," she admitted.

"So what are you hiding on here?" he asked, tapping the computer.

It'd be so easy to fight with him, to go on the defensive and tell him to mind his own business, but the mental fortitude to put up a fight had made a stealthy retreat, overtaken by a vengeful exhaustion. She opened the laptop and showed him the page.

"Oh," he sighed. "Do you mind if I have a look?"

"Free country," she muttered, leaning back on the couch.

Skye closed her eyes at first, but when Noah chuckled, she opened them to see what he was reading. Someone Skye didn't know wrote about going through basic training together, how Rafe was the consummate overachiever, always making the rest of them look like schleps. He went on to say what a natural leader Rafe was, how he'd been appointed the trainee platoon sergeant and led the platoon to work as a team despite clashing personalities and other differences.

"That's so true. Our platoon had some conflicts, but he brought us all together."

They continued to scroll through the timeline, to before the explosion. Rafe posted occasionally, pictures from pick up basketball games, sunsets, the occasional hike. Nothing mission-related, nothing about her.

Then there were posts from other people, letting him know he was loved and missed. "You never met his family?" Noah asked.

"No. He was assigned to our unit a few months before we deployed. Things didn't spark between us until we were working in close quarters during the deployment."

"Have you tried to contact them?"

"To what end? He's dead. They probably didn't even know about me."

Noah shook his head. "There's no way he proposed without telling his family about you. Look at these pictures, Skye. He was close with his family."

Rafe talked about how close they were. "Maybe," she admitted. "But I still don't see the point of contacting them. It'll only cause more pain."

"Closure. You need it and maybe they do too. If they know about you, they'd want to meet you. If they didn't know about you, they'd want to know he was happy, that he'd found someone."

Noah was always the logical one, but what did he have to gain? "This doesn't bother you?"

"What? That you have a past that doesn't include me?"

When Skye nodded, his arm went around her, pulling her against him. She loved the strength of his body, the warmth and comfort he shared so easily with her. "It bothers me that you shut me out, not that you found someone to love and who loved you back."

The guilt of shutting him out stabbed her heart. Her pride had been stepped on, her ego bruised. Letting that come between them had been stupid, but she couldn't undo the past.

She couldn't undo any of it, not the five years she'd lost with Noah, not the explosion that had killed Rafe. "I don't know. It's been so long." She'd spent a couple weeks in Germany, and it'd been two months since her discharge after eight months at Walter Reed. Almost a year since the explosion, yet it seemed like just yesterday when she and Rafe had shared that last secret smile after he'd proposed.

"When you left that last time, after asking me to go with you, I was devastated. You wouldn't return my calls or message me back. I lost my best friend and didn't even get a chance to fight for you. Five years, Skye. I didn't have closure on that for five damn years and it was the hardest five years of my life. You need closure with Rafe. Without it, you're going to suffer and it is going to impact every relationship you have. You're only going to get that closure through his family."

Skye needed to know if Rafe did tell his family. She'd told no one, because Noah wasn't the only one she'd shut out the last time she left Sunset Valley. She'd closed her heart to everyone and everything she'd known as an excuse to stay away. Skye didn't see how she'd ever be able to face Noah after taking the risk with him and losing. Sunset Valley was too small to avoid him. He proved that when she did come home.

"Okay," she said, taking the computer from him. "If I don't do it now, I might chicken out."

After finding a picture of Rafe and his mother, taken just before he arrived at Ft. Hood, Skye clicked on the woman's name and then the message button. She started by introducing herself, explaining that she'd served in Afghanistan with Rafe. "I don't know what to say about the explosion. Will she hate me if she knows I survived and her son didn't?"

"The explosion wasn't your fault," Noah insisted. "You didn't make the bomb, you didn't bury it."

No, but she'd been the only one to survive it.

She opted not to write anything about the explosion, just told his mother what a good man he was and offered her condolences.

After sending the message, Skye put the computer down as if it might explode. "I hope I don't regret this," she said, pushing off the couch.

Noah followed, wrapping his arms around her. "Whatever happens, I'm with you," he promised.

Her computer beeped with the distinct sound of a message and Skye's heart dropped into her stomach. "Oh, God, you don't think that's her, do you?"

"It might be. Do you want me to check?"

She shook her head. With no idea what Rafe's mother might say, Skye didn't want to leave it to chance. "It might not be her," she said, though after such a long hiatus from social media, she couldn't imagine who else it would be.

Leaving Noah's hold, she crossed the room and checked the computer. Confirming it was from Rafe's mother, Skye held her breath and sat down to read the message.

Skye, thank you so much for contacting me. Rafe told me about you. I'd like to talk to you. Please call me.

The next part of the message included her phone number, going on about how important it was that Skye call her.

Skye's stomach turned over and over.

"What is it?" Noah asked, crossing the room. "You just went ghost-white."

"She wants me to call her."

Noah read the message and squeezed her hand. "That's good." He grabbed her cell phone off the table next to the computer and handed it to Skye.

She eyed it like it posed a lethal threat, but Noah didn't back down. "No time like the present," he said.

Skye took it and dialed the number, her hands shaking and clammy. It rang three times before a woman answered. "May I speak with Mrs. Thompson, please."

"This is she," the woman said.

"Ma'am, this is Skye Everhart."

"Oh goodness, you don't waste any time, do you?" Despite the amusement in the woman's voice, Skye remained on edge.

"If this is a bad time, I can call back."

"Oh, no, this is the perfect time. I just wasn't sure you'd call."

"You said it was important," Skye reminded her.

"It is, but first tell me about yourself, about you and Rafe."

"How much do you know?" Skye asked. This was so awkward, talking about the man she had loved to his mother while the man she now shared a bed with sat next to her.

"I know you were in his platoon. He called on occasion, but couldn't say much and worried about email being monitored, so he wrote letters. He loved you very much."

"I loved him too," Skye said, hoping she didn't hurt Noah in the process.

"This must be hard for you," Mrs. Thompson said.

"I, I," Skye stammered, desperate for the woman to know the truth, "I was in the explosion, too. I was driving."

"Oh, honey, I'm so sorry. How bad were you injured?"

"I'm in one piece," she said. "I was in the hospital for a long time. Otherwise I would have been there, for his service, to pay my respects."

"Oh, I know that. I'm just glad you're all right."

Skye wasn't sure she deserved the woman's affection, but also knew she wasn't all right. Her body might be in one piece, but mentally, Skye teetered on the edge, a live grenade with a loose pin that could fall out at any moment.

She wanted to end the call, but didn't know how. She'd never done anything like this before and it was so far outside her comfort zone that Skye felt paralyzed.

"I have some things for you, things Rafe wanted you to have if … if he didn't come home." The woman's sob pulled one from Skye as well.

"I, ma'am, I think you should know, I'm, well, I'm with someone," Skye said. She needed to be honest, to not let this woman think her a saint.

"I'm glad. Rafe would want that. He was just a teen when his father died and I was alone for a long time. Rafe always encouraged me to move on, find someone to love. He always said that someone like me deserved to be happy."

Someone like you.

Rafe's reverent words whispered in her memories, reminding Skye how special he always made her feel. "He used to say that to me, too."

"He was a good man, my son. Honest and proud, good head on his shoulders. He could lead a herd of cats through raging water."

Skye laughed at the truth of that analogy.

"He was loyal, to his country, to his family, to those he loved, but he was also a realist. He wouldn't want you to be alone."

Skye squeezed Noah's hand, realizing how alike he and Rafe were. It was probably why she'd been drawn to him, why she'd broken the rules to be with him.

"Thank you for talking to me," Skye said.

"I should be thanking you. You made my son happy and loved him. That's all a mother can ever ask for. Now tell me where I can send these things and promise you'll stay in touch."

Skye gave Mrs. Thompson her address and whispered the promise even though she wasn't sure she could keep it.

Chapter 32

Take a look in these tired eyes
They're coming back to life
I know I can change
Got hope in my veins
I'm telling you I ain't going back to the pain.
-Can I Be Happy Now, Bon Jovi

Determination.

Anxiety pulsed through her veins, but determination pushed her feet forward. Skye sucked in a deep breath and let it out with a slow cadence. She did not want to have Sunday dinner at her parent's house, did not want to fall prey to her mother's inquisition or her brothers' antics. If her father looked at her with that same pity he'd been wearing since he first visited at Walter Reed, she might snap.

With Noah by her side, his hand warm and steady in hers, their scars a persistent reminder of the bond they shared, Skye's determination won the battle. It was only an afternoon, only her family. It's not like she was marching into a village full of

265

insurgents and IEDs.

Noah stopped, the concern on his face breaking her heart. Why couldn't Skye do something as simple as dinner with her family without drawing that kind of concern.

"I can't do this to you," he said. "Your mother might kill me, but I can't let you walk in there without you knowing what is really going on."

"What are you talking about?" she asked, stepping closer to him.

"It's not Sunday dinner. It's a surprise welcome home party."

A boulder dropped onto Skye's chest, pushing all the air from her lungs and threatening to knock her to the ground.

Noah grabbed her, holding her tight against his body. "I'm sorry. I told her it was a bad idea, but you know how she is."

Even if Skye could think of something to say that wasn't a string of curses and accusations, the words would have remained lodged in her throat.

Things like this had driven a wedge between Skye and her mother years ago. People always accused Skye of being stubborn, and okay, maybe she was, but she had learned from the master. Amelia never budged. Once she got something in her head, it was her way or the highway. It didn't matter what other people wanted or needed.

"I can't walk in there like this." Her whole body vibrated with anxiety, shallow breaths fighting to escape, skin glistening with the cold sweat of fear.

"Just breathe. I've got you," Noah said, as she clung to him.

With a cheek pressed to his chest, she breathed in the enticing smell of him and wished they could just escape back to his house.

They couldn't, though. They'd both have to face the wrath of her mother, a woman who not only held a grudge but earned her crown as the queen of guilt trips. "Are you going to let me drink?"

she asked.

Noah laughed. "I don't think a couple beers will do much harm, but no painkillers with it."

She'd pass out if she took any painkillers, feeding the humiliation she was guaranteed to experience in that house. "Who is in there?"

Noah shook his head. "I don't know. I stayed right out of it. My only job was to get you here."

Skye laughed despite the anxiety. "She would have made a great drill sergeant."

She held on to Noah, who held on to her just as tight. With one finger, he traced a circle at her nape and that simple gesture soothed her. Skye counted the circles, matching her breathing to the slow trace of his finger.

By the time she counted twenty-two circles, Skye's breathing leveled out. Releasing a sigh, she stepped back to let Noah know she was okay, but he still held on. Placing a sweet kiss to her forehead, he sighed too, as if he wished to go back to his house and pursue the passion that lingered between them.

"You ready?" he asked.

Skye searched deep for that determination she'd embraced just minutes ago. This was her parent's house, the place where she'd grown up, where her room hadn't changed at all in the twelve years she'd been gone. That room offered a place she could escape to if the anxiety spiked beyond control. "Maybe we need a signal or a code word, in case I need to get out of there."

"Good idea. Just say my name and grab these," he suggested, tracing his fingers along the dog tag chain around her neck. She'd been wearing Rafe's dog tags since calling his mother yesterday.

"I could say your name for any number of reasons," she said.

Noah shook his head. "I'll know, Skye. Believe me, if you need to get out of there, I'll know."

Which translated to her not hiding the panic very well.

She stepped out of Noah's comforting hold and took his hand. "Thank you for telling me. I promise to act surprised."

"Thanks," he laughed.

Breathing slow and steady, Skye led Noah up the sidewalk to the house. As she stepped into the kitchen, Skye braced for the onslaught of surprises and cheers, but there was no one in the kitchen.

"Hello," Skye called.

"Back here," Riley bellowed. They headed through the house and out the back door where the barrage of "surprise" and "welcome home" filled the back yard.

The open space was better than being trapped in the kitchen with all these people. Skye plastered on a smile and gripped Noah's hand, dragging him along as she stepped onto the deck to greet the thirty or so guests.

Her parents were the first to greet her, both of them wearing big smiles. "Were you surprised?" Amelia asked.

"I was, Ma. Thanks, this is great." It may not be great, but it wasn't horrible, either. As long as Noah stuck close, she'd be fine, make a little conversation, catch up with people she hadn't seen in over five years. It was all good.

She hugged her mother and then her dad and started making the rounds, saying hello to everyone, even thanking them for coming.

Luke was there, not in uniform, as were a few of her high school friends, cousins, aunts and uncles, and friends of her parents. Noah's parents had even surprised her. Skye didn't know they'd returned from their winter in Florida.

With shaking hands, she gripped Noah's hand. Too many questions, the same ones over and over, some she hadn't expected, some she had, it all took hold. Skye found herself unable to form responses. The noise seemed to ring and echo as Skye just nodded. She was ready to run to her room when Amelia invited everyone to dig in. Skye used that as an excuse to claim one of the lawn chairs, grateful the herd was hungry.

Noah was accosted by his parents. Skye was about to close her eyes when Riley approached.

"Hey," he said, his smile as carefree as ever. His ridiculous Hawaiian shirt, covered with half naked cartoon women, made her laugh.

"Hi."

"How's the leg?"

"Fine."

"Good. So, you and Noah?" he asked, nodding at where Noah stood with his parents at the buffet table.

Skye chuckled. Riley's curiosity always seemed to drive him but after all the people she'd spoken to, her brother was the first one to ask about Noah.

She wasn't sure what to say, since she and Noah hadn't talked about their relationship, but they'd been holding hands until Skye sat and Noah went to get food, so it didn't take a genius to figure out they were together.

"Yeah, me and Noah."

"It's about time."

Skye laughed. As far as she knew, no one knew what had happened five years ago. When her mother had asked, Skye claimed they had a fight, and she was sure Noah hadn't said otherwise. He knew how much Skye didn't like Amelia getting into her business and trying to fix things. It tended to have the opposite effect.

"He's a good person," Skye said, though he was so much more. He gave her hope, supported her despite the anger and frustration she took out on him.

"You're a good person, too." Riley could say that because he didn't know the demons she fought, or the things she'd done to battle them.

"You should go grab some food before it's all gone," she said, not wanting to debate her status as a person.

"Right, yeah. You want me to grab something for you?"

"No, I'll head over there in a few." Her appetite had taken a nose-dive when Noah offered the heads-up about the party. Skye also worried whether or not she'd be able to get out of the chair without attracting attention.

"Oh, hey, I have some fireworks. Mom said I shouldn't shoot them off, what with the PTSD and all, but I figured I'd ask."

Instead of claiming she didn't have PTSD, Skye shook her head. She was determined to move forward, to stop letting that damn explosion dictate her life. Maybe shock therapy would be the best thing for her.

"I'm pretty sure I can tell the difference between fireworks and gunfire," she told Riley. Maybe without any forewarning they would startle her, but here in her parents' backyard, with Riley asking permission, she didn't worry about it.

"So I can shoot them off?" he asked.

"Just don't set the house on fire," she chuckled.

Riley's excitement radiated in his smile. It felt good to make her brother happy. He'd always been a bit of a pyromaniac, evidenced by the scar on his arm from a misfired bottle rocket when he was a teen. That incident earned him a trip to the emergency room, followed by a month of being grounded.

Not long after Riley hit the table, Noah joined Skye in the chair her brother had vacated. "You want me to get you something?" he asked.

Skye figured she better get off her ass before everyone at the party asked that same question. She looked around to make sure no one watched before pushing out of the chair and stumbling. Noah stood with her, grabbing her arm to hold her steady. "Thanks," she said.

"My pleasure," he smiled, his gaze dropping to her mouth.

"Riley asked about us," she told him.

"Yeah? What'd you say?"

"I wasn't sure what to say. We haven't talked about it."

"We're together, Skye, at least that's how I see it. You've known me long enough to know I'm not a casual sex kind of guy."

"I know. That's something I always respected about you." It was also something she'd admired, especially when she'd gone through her casual sex phase. Noah had never approved, even though he never said it outright.

"How do you see things?" he asked.

She kissed him, a gentle brush of her lips against his. "We're together," she agreed. It felt good to say it, even better to know it. This is what Skye had wanted for so long, up until she met Rafe. "I'm going to grab some food."

The vultures had cleared and miraculously some food remained. Skye filled her plate with a burger, macaroni salad, and potato chips and grabbed a beer from the cooler before reclaiming the seat next to Noah.

"Did you know your parents were back?" she asked, surprised he hadn't mentioned it.

Noah nodded. "They drove in yesterday and wanted to surprise you, so I was sworn to secrecy."

His parents owned a small cabin on Starlight Lake, where they spent the summers. "Did you tell them about us?" she asked.

"Yeah," he said, stroking her hand. "I told Mom not to make a big deal out of it even though I know she wants to."

Skye appreciated that. She loved Noah's parents, but being back in Sunset Valley was difficult enough without dealing with unrealistic expectations from their parents about their new relationship.

As the sun dropped, daylight giving way to dusk, Skye enjoyed the casual conversations. Being with her friends and family turned out to be a lot easier than she'd imagined, though she was still grateful Noah had let her in on the surprise.

No one seemed surprised or even asked about her and Noah as they sat there and held hands. Skye's leg stiffened from sitting too long, so when Liz Hall came to talk to Noah about doing contract work for her website development business, Skye pushed out of the chair to move around a bit.

"You need anything?" Noah asked.

"I just need to walk around. I'm all right." She kissed him, then stepped off, leaving him to his conversation with Liz.

Vaughn met her at the bottom of the steps. "Mind if I join you?"

"Not at all," she responded, though hoped he didn't have another interview lined up. Skye wanted to find a job, but needed to do it on her own, figure out what she wanted to do. She also needed to get the PT routine under control and figure out her capabilities after a session. The first day of PT wasn't bad, but that only scratched the surface of what they were going to make her do.

It's all part of the healing process, she preached silently. Skye wanted to heal, for herself and for Noah. Skye despised the sudden mood swings and pain. Noah was a saint for sticking by her, especially since he served as an easy target to her angst.

"You seem good," Vaughn said.

"Today's a good day," she responded. The good days seemed few and far between, but she'd take them when they came and maybe with a little effort on her part, there would be more of them.

Vaughn put his arm around her shoulder. "I'm not sure if I've mentioned this, but I'm glad you made it home alive."

"Thanks. Me too." She'd never intended to move back to Sunset Valley. Growing up, the town was too small, everyone in everyone else's business, spreading rumors and exaggerating truths, passing judgment. Skye had hated it, but today, being with her friends and family was nice. She felt a little like Dorothy, thinking there was no place like home.

Riley crossed their path, pushing a cart that had to be full of fireworks. She loved how her brothers hadn't changed, even if they could still be pains in the ass sometimes.

"What's he up to?" Vaughn asked.

"Fireworks," Skye said.

Vaughn stopped and turned to her. "You okay with that?"

"Yeah, it's fine."

"You sure? Because you just came from an active war zone."

"I didn't just come from deployment. I've been stateside almost a year," she reminded him.

"Still. I've heard stories."

"Well, I'm fine," Skye insisted. She'd been lucky on both deployments, never being up close and personal with any gunfire. Shots often echoed in the distance, but the only close-up gunfire she'd ever been exposed to was at the range.

They watched as Riley set up a few canisters at the back of the yard. The solar lights that lined the flower beds provided enough illumination for them to see his movements, but the sky was dark enough that it would be the perfect backdrop.

Skye smiled as Riley focused on his task. He had struggled in school, first diagnosed with ADHD, then later with anxiety disorder. He had trouble staying on task on everything except Legos and fireworks. Skye had similar issues in school, but managed to focus enough to get the work done when she needed to. She preferred to hang out with her friends and since she'd been a bit boy crazy as a teen, her priorities were never on school.

Riley lit the first canister and moved down the line. Moments later, the first one launched with a whistle.

The first bang hit Skye right in her solar plexus. Her breath seized in her chest as her entire body shook with the force. When the second bang sounded, she cried out.

"Fuck," her brother cursed. "Jesus Christ, Skye." Tunnel vision stole her sight as garbled voices accompanied the ringing in her ears. Noah looked at her with fear in his eyes and then he was gone. She followed his shadowed form across the lawn and gasped as he punched Riley in the face.

Shaking her head, Skye pushed away from Vaughn. "No,

stop!" she yelled, but she fell to the ground, crying out when landing on her gimp hip.

Skye was afraid to open her eyes, terrified that everyone would be staring. Next thing she knew, she was being lifted, her body jostling. She turned into the person holding her, recognizing Noah's cologne and wrapping her arms around him.

"I've got you," he whispered through the chaos in her mind.

"I'm sorry," she sobbed.

"No. You have nothing to be sorry about."

With loud steps, he carried her up the stairs. Skye opened her eyes when he set her on the bed. Tears muddled her vision, but she recognized Riley and Vaughn at the door.

"I'm so sorry, Skye," Riley muttered. His face looked like he'd gone a round with Ronda Rousey, the left eye swollen, his nose and cheek cut and bloody. "I wouldn't have ... but ... Jesus, you said it was okay."

"It's not your fault," she assured her brother. "I don't know what happened."

"You have PTSD," Noah snapped, his voice thick with anger. "That's what the hell happened."

Skye shook her head. "I didn't ... I don't ..." she threw her head back, frustrated she couldn't put words to the swarm of emotions wreaking havoc in her. "I thought it would be fine."

"You're not fine," Noah spat. "The sooner you own that, the sooner we can get you the help you need."

We. The simple word sent a jolt of regret through her. "I'm sorry," she sighed, closing her eyes as the tears spilled.

"Are you all right?" Vaughn asked.

Skye nodded. "Yeah. I don't know what happened. I mean, I watched him set them up and everything. I don't know why I reacted like that."

"Noah's right, you know," Vaughn preached. "It doesn't take a genius to know this is a symptom of PTSD. You need to stop being so damned stubborn and get some help."

They all made it sound so easy. They didn't understand the stigma of a soldier asking for help.

Of course, she didn't have the honor of being a soldier anymore. She was just a broken body and spirit hobbling around, trying to find her way in a world she no longer understood.

"Can we go home?" she asked Noah.

He nodded, not saying a word, which cut as deep as the anger radiating off him. He turned and focused that anger on Riley. When he pointed at her brother, Skye realized Noah's hand was as bruised as her ego. "You. Make sure no one's hanging around downstairs."

"I'll help," Vaughn said, shoving Riley out of the room. There was no reprieve, though, because Skye's parents came right in.

"I'll have a talk with your brother later," her father said.

"He asked permission. I told him it was fine," Skye explained, wishing everyone would cut Riley a little slack.

"Skye, how long are you going to deny your issues?" Amelia asked. "Missing PT, now this. You need help."

Skye swallowed the frustration. She'd already been lectured, something she could take coming from Noah and her brothers, but hearing it from her mother just made her want to leave town and never look back.

"I went to PT," she said, turning to Noah. "Tell her."

Noah nodded once.

"He needs ice for his hand," Skye said.

"I'm fine," he snarled, not looking at her. "She wants to go home."

"This is her home," Amelia said.

Ken put his arm around Amelia's shoulder, pulling her to the door. "Let her go with Noah."

Shaking her head, the hurt in her eyes stabbed Skye's heart with guilt. "Ma," she said.

Amelia looked at her and Skye wished they had been closer.

"Thanks for the party. It was nice."

The smile did little to relieve Skye's guilt because the damage was done. Moving into Noah's basement hurt Amelia, but Skye continued to dish it out by avoiding her. She just didn't know how to have a friendly relationship with the woman, but maybe she wasn't trying hard enough.

When her parents left, Vaughn reappeared. "Coast is clear down there. You need help?"

"I can walk," she said. "Thank you."

Noah continued to scowl, giving her the silent treatment not just to the car, but all the way home.

"Do you want to watch a movie?" she asked when they pulled into the driveway.

Noah shrugged. Skye rolled her eyes.

"How long are you going to be mad at me?" she asked.

"I'm not mad at you," he said.

"Don't be mad at Riley either. I told him it was okay to shoot off the fireworks."

"And that's what I'm mad about. It was stupid, Skye."

She didn't want to fight, but Noah seemed to want one and she wasn't the type of person to back down. "It was stupid or I was stupid?"

Chapter 33

This road was paved by the
hopeless and the hungry.
This road was paved
by the winds of change.
Walking beside the guilty
and the innocent,
How will you raise your hand
when they call your name?
-We Weren't Born to Follow, Bon Jovi

Patience.

Noah reached the end of his rope, searching deep inside for an ounce of something other than frustration and anger.

He came up empty. "You have been consistent about making bad decisions ever since you came home," he said after pulling the car into the driveway.

"Well, with everyone wanting to make decisions for me, maybe I've forgotten what making a good decision feels like."

"We are trying to help your stubborn ass," he argued.

"Maybe my stubborn ass doesn't want help! I told you I had to do this my way and you agreed. If you can't deal with that, then go to hell, Noah."

She limped down the path to her apartment, leaving Noah to feel like shit because Skye wasn't the only one making bad decisions. He had to own his part.

Noah stormed through his front door, slamming it behind him. Moments later the door down the hall slammed.

Uneven steps drew closer until Skye stood in the kitchen, a look of hate on her face.

"I don't think you're stupid," he said. He thought for sure she would cross the room and slap him, but instead she opened the freezer and snatched a bag of frozen peas.

"Sit," she ordered. He bet she was an effective leader in the army, more so when she was pissed. The look on her face and the roar in her voice demanded obedience. Noah would be the one making a stupid decision if he didn't do as commanded.

She took his hand and looked at it. It hurt, but he didn't realize it was bruised until now. "Wiggle your fingers," she said a little more gently.

Noah did and then obeyed her next command to make a fist.

"Does it hurt?"

"A little," he admitted, opting for honesty in order to set a good example.

"Good. That was stupid. You have to stop punching people." He'd punched all of two people his entire life, both in the past month and both because of what they'd done to Skye.

Noah never condoned violence as a solution, but when it came to Skye, he'd do anything to keep her safe.

"I'm not going to apologize. I don't care that you gave Riley permission. He still shouldn't have done it."

"He's still just a kid at heart," she said.

"I don't give a shit, Skye. He's old enough to know better — hell, he's older than we are." Riley had never been all that bright.

Noah liked him, he was a good guy, but had never grown up.

"Well, I'm not going to apologize for trying to be normal, like everyone else."

Noah shook his head. "You're not like everyone else," he said more harshly than he intended. "You've been through hell."

"Everyone's been through hell. Just because I was deployed doesn't make me special."

"You're right," Noah agreed. He dropped the bag of peas and pushed out of the chair, stepping right up to Skye. He cupped her face, loving the softness of her skin against his. "There are so many other things that make you special — your independence, your kind heart, your dedication. Jesus, the way you look at me."

He brushed her lips with his, but when she sighed, his control snapped. Holding her right where he wanted her, Noah pushed his tongue past her lips, his desire ratcheting up when her tongue met his.

With his patience gone and his need surging to the surface, all Noah could think about was getting Skye naked and beneath him as he thrust inside her until they both forgot about her injuries and PTSD. It wouldn't solve anything, though, and as she'd mentioned earlier, they hadn't talked about their relationship, what they wanted from each other, or where they wanted to take things. Telling her they were together wasn't enough.

"Skye," he sighed, resting his forehead against hers as he tried to catch his breath.

She sighed too and it was like the anger they'd been slinging around wilted under the power of that kiss.

"Whenever I'm being an unbearable bitch, just kiss me. It seems to work."

Like techni-color kisses, he thought, the Bon Jovi lyrics playing in his head. "I can handle that. I might even encourage you to be an unbearable bitch just so I have an excuse."

"I don't need encouragement and you don't need an excuse."

Because he didn't, he kissed her again, this time with a little less demand, but the passion still sparked between them. Skye held on, her kiss encouraging him to take things to the next level.

Noah didn't give in. He wanted to talk, to be sure they were on the same page. "Can we talk?" he asked.

"I'd rather take this to the bedroom," she said, kissing his jawline and moving over to his ear where she gave him an erotic tug with her teeth.

"We can, after we talk."

"If it's about PTSD—"

"It's about us," he interrupted before her temper flared. "You said we haven't talked about us yet. I think we should."

"Okay," she agreed, a smile softening her expression. "We can do that naked."

"You have a one track mind," he laughed.

"That's because you do me good, Noah Carbonneau," she said, smacking his butt.

His ego took that and filed it for later.

"We should sit," he offered. If they stood here in the kitchen, with a direct line to the bedroom, he might cave in and drag her down the hall without saying a word.

They sat on the couch facing each other, her right leg extended to the floor while her left leg curled in.

"So," she started. "You wanted to talk."

Right, he supposed this was his show. "We're together. For me that means there's no one else for either of us."

She nodded. "I know. It means that for me too."

"It also means complete honesty."

He didn't miss her flinch. "I'm not kidding, Skye. Full disclosure on your pain and your struggles. If I'm not with you and the panic hits, you call me. I'll get to you, no matter what but you need to promise me you'll get help, a counselor or a support group. I don't care which, but you need to do it this week."

The scowl came right on cue, but Noah wouldn't back down

just to make her happy in the moment. "We're best friends. That doesn't change. What we have now only makes that stronger and I'm not going to be the guy who stands by and let's you take the easy road instead of the right road."

She gave him a mock salute. "Anything else, sir?"

Noah scooted closer, cupping her face and stroking her soft skin with his thumb. "Just one more thing," he said as she nuzzled his hand. "I love you."

When her breath caught and eyes widened, Noah knew he'd risked too much. Five years ago, she had said the same words to him, but a lot had happened since then. She'd fallen in love with someone else, even gotten engaged, and still nursed that loss.

It was too late to take the words back, not that he wanted to. He'd asked her for full disclosure and honesty. He needed to give the same.

When she'd been brave enough to risk it all those years ago, he'd been stunned stupid. It seemed he'd done the same to her since all she did was stare at him.

"You don't have to say you love me, Skye, but please say something."

"Something," she said, breaking the tension.

Noah couldn't swallow the chuckle, but he held back on laughing because he didn't want to lose the moment.

Skye traced the scar on his hand. "You mean everything to me. I just don't know how to be the person you want me to be."

"Just be you," he said.

Her sad smile ripped his heart in half. "I don't know who I am."

"All those things that make you special, that's who you are."

Chapter 34

Let's close our eyes and just disappear
Slip through the cracks no looking back
We'll get a million miles away from here
And let the past just fade to black
-Brokenpromiseland, Bon Jovi

Surrender.

As Skye hobbled out of the clinic on crutches, her humiliation intact, one word rang in her head.

Finn.

He understood her. He knew what she needed. He didn't judge.

Skye tossed the crutches in the back and dropped into the driver's seat with a groan. It was her third PT appointment this week. She wouldn't survive another week, not without help.

Noah still kept her prescription in his super secret hiding spot, not that it helped all that much anyway. Mostly it just knocked her out. Right now, Skye preferred that option. She didn't know how to talk to him, not since he said he loved her.

What was there to love? Skye couldn't manage the pain, couldn't own the PTSD that seemed to own her, robbing her of the ability to admit she loved him too.

Not that Skye should love him. The last man she loved died because of her carelessness. That past haunted her again as the package Rafe's mother sent sat on Skye's front seat. Terror prevented her from opening it. Noah would look through it if she asked, but it's not like this was a spider that needed to be captured and rehomed. It was more like the boogie man, the unknown lurking around a dark corner, ready to attack.

Those pills Finn had given her might help relieve the anxiety. The painkillers he had too, to take care of the pain from PT. Then maybe she could face what lurked in the box — face Noah too. Maybe even tell him what he deserved to hear.

She drove to Finn's, desperate for some sort of reprieve from reality. Cars and trucks packed the driveway. Skye hated the crutches, but the PT assistant had worked her leg hard today and she couldn't walk without help.

After knocking on the door, Finn answered with that smug smile. "Hello, darling. To what do I owe this pleasure?"

The man made her skin crawl but he had what she needed, so Skye would just have to suck it up and drive on. "I need some painkillers and anxiety meds."

"Still pushing for the pills, huh? Come in, join the party."

Skye hesitated. The last time she went into that house, he put her in a choke hold and shoved her against a wall.

"Just get what I need and bring it out here. I have cash."

Finn chuckled. "I told you before, I don't do business on the porch."

Shaking her head, Skye stood her ground.

"You came to me, Skye. What you need is inside. Those are my terms." He walked in the house, the old screen door tapping on the casing.

As always, Finn's words rang with too much truth. What she

283

needed was inside that house. Last time she'd left empty handed. Skye couldn't do that again.

With determination, as much as the crutches would allow, Skye hobbled into the house. It only took the door tapping closed behind her for the regret to take hold. There were people everywhere, drinking and smoking. She turned to leave and preserve what little self-esteem she had, but relief beckoned from within the house, turning her once again.

"Can we do this exchange somewhere more private?" she asked as Finn loomed in front of her.

He continued to smirk. "Of course. Follow me."

As Skye followed him through the house, no one paid her any attention. There was a group of four men talking sports around the island in Finn's kitchen, a couple on the other side of the room engaged in a heated discussion. The living room was a sex fest, three couples and one threesome that comprised of two men and a woman, all in various stages of dress and activity.

"Isn't it kind of early for a party?" she asked as they entered a bedroom. He closed the door behind her, closing them off from the others. While it was the privacy she'd asked for, it made her more uncomfortable than being in the more public rooms.

"My friends like to unwind after a long week at work."

Unwinding was an understatement based on what she'd seen. "Can we just get this done?" she demanded.

"Make yourself comfortable. I'll go get the product."

"Pills," she reminded him. "I don't want heroin." Even saying the word didn't feel right.

Finn continued to smirk as he turned and headed out of the room.

The bedroom was tidy, the bed made, all of his clothes put away. He didn't have much for decor, just a couple framed pictures of motorcycles on the walls. She noticed a stack of porn magazines under the table next to his bed. A large television was mounted to the wall opposite the bed. She guessed he had a stash of porn movies hidden somewhere.

Finn seemed to be gone forever. Skye had almost talked herself out this when he came back in the room.

He opened a box, dropping two bags of pills and two bags of powder on the bed.

"I told you I don't want heroin," she said, ready to leave, but the allure of those pills kept her ass planted on the edge of the bed.

Finn held out his hand and smiled, not that smug grin she was used to, but a curve that was warm and friendly. "Hear me out. Please."

"Fine," she snapped, knowing it didn't matter. Yes, getting prescription drugs from Finn was illegal, but they were drugs she could get legally if she had the patience. She was so tired of doctors and hospitals and clinics, she was willing to pay for the relief.

"These are run of the mill prescriptions. This is Valium, to help with your anxiety. This is Percocet, for your pain. Valium will run you ten dollars a pill, minimum ten pills. You're dropping a Ben on this alone."

Was he serious? A hundred bucks just for ten pills?

"The Percs are a little cheaper, four bucks a pill, minimum twenty-five, so that's another Benjamin."

"Jesus," she muttered.

"Right here, you are dropping two hundred," he paused as Skye weighed the benefit versus the cost. "There are less expensive alternatives."

"Finn," she warned, not willing to go down that road. She could call the doctor, just like the PT assistant had said, ask for something new.

Getting the last prescription had been a battle and getting an appointment would take time.

"Just hear me out, darling."

Skye rolled her eyes but let him talk. "This is 250mg of heroin. It has about the same number of doses as those, but it's only $50. More bang for your buck."

"I'm not interested in shooting up," she countered, hoping to put him off the topic.

"That's the glory of this, you have options. Shooting up gives the most intense high, but you can smoke it or snort it, too."

Skye shook her head. He was so casual about it, like it was no big deal. "I wouldn't even know how to, or how much."

"That's why you have me, darling. I'm a full service business man. I'll take you through it your first time, and as many times as you need until you're comfortable on your own."

Skye wasn't even comfortable taking the pills, how could she ever do something like smoke heroin?

"What's that?" she asked, nodding at the last bag.

"This is a dime bag of cocaine. You mix this with the heroin, that's called a speedball. Intense rush, but none of the anxiety you'll get when you come down from the heroin."

"I don't want to get high," she reminded him. "I just need to manage my pain and anxiety."

"Pain makes you low. Anxiety makes you low. You take these," he said, shaking the bags of pills, "to counter that low. That's getting high. Doesn't matter if it's a prescription or street drugs, same effect. It's just more socially accepted through these channels."

"I'll just take the pills," she said.

"Just give it a try. One time, on the house."

"Why is this so important to you?" she asked.

"You're hurting. I see that. No one else wants to help. What's that army saying, suck it up? That's probably what you're telling yourself too, but you don't have to."

She tapped the two bags of powder. She didn't know a lot about illegal drugs because she'd never been interested in experimenting, never had a need for that kind of high, but she knew the risks. "These are illegal, addictive, and easy to O.D. on."

Finn smiled and shook the bags of pills again. "So are these. I promise, you'll feel so good, you'll not just walk out of here, you'll float."

"No needles," she said, her curiosity and desperation leading her down the path of surrender.

He pulled foil, a lighter, and a straw out of the box and talked her through the steps as he got it all set up. "I'll handle this end, you use the straw to inhale the smoke."

Skye's heart raced, a whisper in her mind telling her to walk away, but a louder, stronger voice encouraging her to give this a try. What was the harm in just trying it? She'd get a lot of satisfaction out of proving Finn wrong. Since she wasn't shooting up, just breathing in a little smoke, it was no big deal.

The mental encouragement didn't slow her pulse, so she focused on following Finn's commands. As the smoke filled her throat, Skye expected to be hit with something magical, or at the very least, feel like she'd walked through a gas chamber without a mask.

But nothing seemed to happen. She looked at Finn, raising her brow.

"It'll take a few minutes to hit," he said. "It's faster when you shoot up."

She'd never know because she had no intentions of shooting up, or ever smoking again. She just needed to prove to Finn he was wrong, heroin wasn't the magical cure to her problems.

It didn't take long before the drug started to work. It wasn't unlike when she took the Vicodin, that happy, light feeling giving her a dose of euphoria she struggled to feel on her own.

"You might want to sit back, darling," Finn suggested, propping the pillows and helping her scoot back on the bed.

Skye closed her eyes and melted into the pillows, letting the euphoria take its hold and carry her away from this new reality she couldn't quite adapt to.

"Feels good, doesn't it," Finn drawled, his voice close but quiet.

Skye nodded, her head lolling around with that light feeling floating through her body. "Yes," she said.

Her thoughts drifted to Noah, his warm smile, eyes dark with desire. It was like they were together, his breath on her skin, his hand on her breast. "Yes," she sighed, feeling his warm lips on her neck.

On the nights she spent in his bed, they took turns waking each other, just like this, with soft kisses and gentle strokes.

He pushed her shirt over her head and the cold air cooled her hot body.

"Jesus Christ," he said, his voice different, not Noah's at all. Skye opened her eyes to find Finn looking down at her.

"Finn? What? Where's Noah?"

He chuckled. "It's just you and me."

Skye shook her head. "No, Noah was here, kissing me."

Finn huffed. "I'll try not to let that bruise my ego."

Skye's eyes darted around, searching the room, her mind, anything, for answers.

"That's some serious shit you're wearing," Finn muttered. She followed his gaze to her bare torso and scars. "No wonder you needed me."

Oh, God, was her shirt off? What the hell was she doing? "Where's my shirt?" she tried to demand but it came out as a whimper as her head lolled again.

"On the floor," Finn said, looming over her.

"No. I'm with Noah."

"Tonight you're with me," he said, that smug grin firmly in place.

She blinked, her lids heavy, her head falling back on the pillows. "Don't touch me," she said, but there wasn't a lot of bite in the words.

"I scratched your itch, darling. It's your turn to scratch mine."

Skye scooted back, trying to get away. "No. You said it was on the house."

Blinking a few times, it took great effort to keep her head up. It felt huge, bobbing around, like it wanted to roll right off her neck. Finn didn't seem to notice. He tugged his shirt over his head, revealing a very fit body. If she wasn't with Noah, and this body belonged to anyone else, Skye might be game, but this was all wrong. Everything about being here was wrong.

"I need to go," she said, trying to push him away. He didn't budge.

"You're higher than a kite. I can't let you leave like that. Cops could pull you over, or worse, you could cause an accident."

"What do you care?" she asked. "You got what you wanted. I did your drugs. Now leave me alone."

"I haven't quite gotten everything I want," he drawled.

"You're going to rape me?" she asked, still not able to get her muscles to work.

"You were more than willing a few minutes ago. You were moaning, begging for more."

"I thought you were Noah," she said, falling back into the pillows. How long did this last? She needed to leave, to get away from Finn, from the people having sex in his living room. Oh, god, were they high too?

"You're the one who wanted to go someplace private, Skye. You want this, as much as you wanted the drugs. I didn't have to convince you."

Before Skye could deny it or defend herself, a knock at the door had Finn cursing. Skye couldn't open her eyes to see who it was. "Shit, man, sorry, but the fucking cops are here."

"Fuck," Finn muttered. The mattress shifted and she assumed he had gotten off the bed. Skye needed to get up, get her shirt on, get out of there. If Luke found her at Finn's, like this, he'd arrest her, or worse, tell Noah.

Noah would never trust her again.

Why should he? Isn't that what she wanted? Skye didn't deserve his love. Who the hell knows why he stuck around this long anyway. Oh, that's right, because she was a mental case and he liked to fix things. Skye was Noah's little pet project.

She opened her eyes, the room blurry and warped, and managed to scoot to the edge of the bed. The door was closed, but Finn was gone. Skye needed a drink. Water, beer, anything. Her mouth felt like she'd been sucking on cotton.

Leaning down to grab her shirt ended up being a bad decision. As if she'd had too much to drink, she lurched, vomiting all over the floor. To add to the humiliation, the door opened then, followed by a string of curses.

It sounded like Luke. Through her blurred vision, it looked like Luke, the blob of dark blue a clear indication.

When she stopped hurling, he crouched beside her. "You all done?"

"I don't know," she admitted. It had snuck up on her. "I'm not drunk, I don't know why I hurled."

"Your high as a fucking kite, Skye, that's why you hurled. Come on, let's get you cleaned up and out of here."

Luke helped her up, pausing to open Finn's dresser and pull out a shirt, but he didn't give it to her. He led her across the living room and through another door. "Get in the shower. You have vomit all over you."

Skye did as she was told without stripping out of her remaining clothes. "Where's Finn?" she asked.

"Why the fuck do you care?" he asked.

"I just," she just what? Wanted to make sure he wasn't going to rape her? Maybe she wanted to make sure their business relationship was intact so she could come crawling back and ask for more?

When Luke turned on the cold water, Skye cried out. She reached for the knob to turn up the temperature but Luke's commanding voice stopped her. "Leave it."

After a few minutes of silence, he told her to turn around. The shock of the cold water on her back wasn't any less potent.

After he turned off the water, he tossed the shirt at her. "Put that on."

"Can I at least dry off?" she asked.

"You can air dry. Let's go."

He held her arm as he led her out. The dozen people who had been at the party stood in the driveway, two uniformed officers standing in front of them.

"It's all clear, Chief," one of the officers said as they approached. "Just alcohol. No drugs, not even drug paraphernalia. We checked IDs and everyone's of age."

Skye tried to hold her head up, refusing to leave in shame even though it pulsed through her veins more potently than the drugs. Finn wore that smug grin again. "See you soon, darling," he drawled.

"Where are your keys?" Luke asked.

"Ah, I'm not sure. In my bag, with the crutches," she said, remembering how she hobbled through Finn's house to the bedroom.

Luke turned to the officer. "Go find her bag and crutches. Wait here for Vaughn. He'll drive the car home."

"You called my brother?" she asked. "I'm surprised you didn't rat me out to Noah."

"I did," Luke said, holding the back door of the cruiser open. She climbed into the SUV and closed her eyes, wishing to go back to the PT appointment and change the outcome of this cluster fuck.

"Where are we going?" she asked when he turned left out of the driveway, the opposite direction to Noah's house.

"To the hospital. I'm going to make sure you're not overdosing."

"I'm not," she said.

"Forgive me if I don't trust your word on that."

Skye shut her mouth because she didn't have any fight in her. As the euphoria continued to fade, the panic spiked. What had Luke said to Noah? How would she make him understand how much she needed the reprieve? Would he forgive her?

"I didn't have sex with Finn," she said, praying Luke didn't give Noah all the details.

Luke answered with silence. The hospital wasn't far, but the drive took a lifetime. When Luke pulled up to the emergency room drop-off where Noah waited, a lifetime wasn't long enough.

She refused to hang her head in shame. Responsibility for her decisions rested solely on her shoulders, just like everything else. Luke opened the door and helped Skye out. Noah stood his ground, the hurt so potent in his eyes Skye's heart dropped into her stomach, awakening the nausea she thought she'd left behind at Finn's.

Chapter 35

If you ain't got someone,
you're afraid to lose
Everybody needs just one, someone...
to tell them the truth
Maybe I'm a dreamer,
but I still believe
I believe in hope, I believe the change
can get us off our knees
-What Do You Got, Bon Jovi

Truth.

It slammed Noah hard as Luke helped Skye out of the cruiser. He'd been trying to define their own truth, that Noah's love held the power to get Skye past her pain and trauma. That truth was a lie.

The new truth blinded him as Skye's head lolled and she stumbled. Noah had done more harm than good.

"I have no idea what she's on or how much. We couldn't find any evidence of drugs and no one's talking." Luke's anger

293

pierced Noah's patience, rearing up his own anger and guilt.

How could he have let things go this far?

"What do I do?" he asked as Luke handed Skye off.

"Get her checked in. I'll move the car and be back to tell them what I know."

Skye put her arm around him, taking a deep breath as she rested her head on his chest. "Smells like you this time," she said.

Noah lifted her chin, her eyes opening to reveal pin-holes for pupils. He'd done enough reading about drug addiction to recognize what Luke already confirmed, she was high.

"Noah," she whispered and smiled. "It is you."

"What do you mean, this time?" he asked.

"Finn tricked me, made me think he was you."

Son of a bitch. If that ass-hole laid a hand on her, Noah would kill him. "Did he hurt you?"

"Nah-uh. Luke swooped in, all cop like," she said, her arms spread out as she moved like a soaring bird. "I hate being rescued, but I'll make an exception this one time." She tapped his sternum with each word.

"What did Finn give you?" he asked, trying to keep his anger on a short leash.

"Ssshhh," she said, her finger over her lips. "If I tell, you'll be mad." She pinched his cheeks between her fingers. "I don't like mad Noah. I like horny Noah."

"Let's get you inside," he said, stepping toward the entrance. It took ten minutes to get her checked in and they brought her back right away. The nurses said she wasn't at risk for overdose, but they wanted to monitor her. Skye dropped in and out of sleep for the next couple hours, flirty and suggestive when awake. If he didn't know better, he'd think she was drunk, but even this behavior seemed different than her normal *had a few beers* merriment.

She *was* different. Whether the explosion had changed her, or being deployed, or what had happened five years ago — maybe all of it — she had changed. Maybe Noah had changed too.

The circumstances didn't matter. What mattered was getting Skye through this sober. She couldn't mess around with drugs, prescription or worse, but talking to her now, when she was barely coherent, served no purpose.

The guilt poked at Noah. He'd taken her pills away, given what turned out to be Valium to Luke and distributed her Vicodin prescription according to the dosage instructions. Maybe if he'd talked to her about the anxiety she experienced and actually tried to help instead of being the drug police, she wouldn't have gone to Finn again. Whatever drug she'd taken there, it was stronger than anything he'd seen her on.

"We're working on her discharge," the nurse said, peering around the curtain. "She can sleep it off at home."

"Thanks," Noah said.

"I've already been discharged. The army doesn't want broken soldiers. I'm not Army Strong anymore."

Noah wondered if that was Skye's new truth — why she never fought to recover from everything that had happened to her. "Screw Army Strong," he said, giving her arm a squeeze. "You're Skye Strong."

"Skye Stupid," she muttered.

"Stupid is a choice," he pointed out.

"Mmmmm," she mumbled.

Was that agreement or argument?

With her discharge were strict orders for water and no drugs, and the suggestion that she see a doctor and get counseling. She nodded, probably more to appease the nurse than in agreement, but Noah was going to lay it out for her when the drugs were out of her system.

They road home without talking, the playlist he'd made for her playing softly through the speakers. Noah wondered if she'd even listened to it.

Her shallow breaths worried him, but when he pulled into his driveway and turned off the car, he realized she was crying.

Noah took her hand, stroking her palm with his thumb to try and soothe her. "Let's go inside," he said and she nodded, still not saying a word.

Skye went straight to the bathroom, and Noah went to the kitchen to get her water. The shower came on and while it was tempting to join her, he couldn't get the thought of Finn touching her out of his head. He knocked on the door and cracked it open when she didn't say anything.

"Are you okay?" he asked.

"I don't think I'm ever going to be okay," she sobbed.

"Is there anything I can do?"

Her mirthless laugh frustrated him. "You're doing it, being my friend, putting up with my bull shit."

Noah didn't have much friend left in him. Skye going to Finn pushed Noah to the end of his rope. "I'm pretty damned sick of your bull shit, Skye. You promised to get help and you end up at Finn's. Jesus, if Luke hadn't shown up, who the hell knows what would have happened to you."

The reality scared the shit out of him. Finn touching her, taking advantage of her, Skye overdosing. The horrors were endless, but they all led to a tragic end.

"Maybe you'd be better off if—"

Noah flung the curtain open. "Bull shit," he bellowed, not letting her finish. "You're in a shitty place, I get that, but no one, not me, not your family, not anyone in this world would be better off without you. You need help, Skye, but more than that, you need to admit it."

"I know," she whispered, hanging her head. Her body started shaking with the sobs she seemed to be holding back. Noah stepped into the shower, fully clothed, and wrapped his arms around her shaking body.

"Come on, let it out," he encouraged.

He didn't expect her to, so when she sobbed into his chest with the force an explosion, Noah was floored. He held her tighter, hoping she understood he'd never let her go.

When the sobs petered out, she looked up at him, the sadness in her eyes ripping him apart. "Your clothes are soaked," she said.

"I don't care."

She offered a smile, one that didn't reach her eyes or show any of the happiness she had once had. "I need to wash up," she said.

"Okay. I'm going to get these clothes in the wash. See you in the bedroom?"

With narrowed eyes she asked, "you want me to stay with you, after everything that's happened?"

"Always, Skye. I believe in you, in us, and I'm not going to lose you now or let you go just because you're dealing with stuff I can't even imagine." He kissed her palm before closing the curtain. The bathroom was drenched from the spray of water, but that was a problem for another time. Stripping out of his clothes, he tossed them in the hamper, wrapped a towel around his waist, took the load downstairs, and tossed everything in the washing machine. Through the door he spotted Skye's car outside and noticed a box and keys sitting on the floor just inside the door.

He crouched to inspect the box, recognizing the name on the return address as Rafe's mother. Noah suspected receiving this box might have been what pushed Skye over the edge.

He left it there, not wanting to overwhelm her even more and went into her apartment where he grabbed her some clothes. Then he went upstairs to his bedroom and threw on a pair of boxers and a t-shirt.

Skye took forever in the shower. He checked on her twice, just to be sure she was still conscious. She claimed she needed to wash the stench of her mistakes away. Noah's hackles raised at the thought of that stench being Finn.

Noah didn't want to accuse her of anything. She'd been high after all, her brain not capable of making good decisions, but he had to know if she'd slept with Finn. He didn't know what it would mean for them if she had, but they couldn't move forward without the truth on the table.

After an hour in the shower, Skye came into the bedroom, wrapped in a towel, looking tragic and sad. She dressed in the t-shirt and yoga pants he'd grabbed for her but didn't slide under the covers.

"I think I should stay at my own place," she said.

"Why?"

Skye didn't answer, just stood there and shook her head, avoiding his gaze. After a long pause Noah asked the question tearing him apart. "Did you have sex with him?"

She shook her head. "No. He tried to, and I was so messed up I thought it was you, but then I told him to stop."

"Did he?"

"Not really. I'm not sure I could have fought him off. Physically, I'm pretty limited and mentally, well, I was too messed up to fight back."

"You need to tell Luke," Noah said. Dealing drugs wasn't okay by any means, but rape, that crossed another line.

"I know. I will, but ..." her words trailed off, stopping Noah's heart in his chest.

"But what?"

Skye shook her head and stared at the floor. Noah didn't like the direction of the conversation, but she held a truth that needed to be spoken.

"What, Skye?" he urged.

"I did ..."

Her whole body shook, but Noah couldn't comfort her because he shook as violently. "Did what?"

Her gaze shifted to the ceiling and she curled her lips between her teeth. Noah wanted to pry the truth from her, but put all his energy into keeping the anger on a leash. "Did what, Skye?"

"I had sex with him," she yelled, throwing her head back

before looking at the floor again. "Right after I came home. It was before you and I even saw each other. I didn't have any money and my prescription was out, so …"

Noah saw red before everything blurred, angry tears filling his eyes. Finn preyed on people. He'd always been good at it, but Noah's loathing turned inside. He'd given Skye time when she came home before going to see her. Maybe if he hadn't …

Not meeting his gaze, she took a deep breath and shook her head. "It was disgusting. I didn't even take my clothes off because I didn't want him to see me. I hated every second of it, but I didn't see any other way."

Of course she didn't see any other way because she was too damned stubborn to ask Noah for help. Instead, she ran off to her drug-dealing ex-boyfriend who was looking to score more than just his next payday.

Quiet sobs broke the silence screaming between them. "I'm sorry."

Noah wanted to drive across town, find Finn and tear him apart one piece at a time in the most painful way possible. Then he wanted to burn that house down, and all of the drugs with it. Instead, he pushed off the bed and crossed the room, pulling Skye into his arms.

"I won't blame you if you hate me," she said, her arms still at her sides. "The things I've done, they're unforgivable."

"Forgiveness is a choice," Noah whispered, digging deep for the courage to heed his own words. She'd been with Finn in high school, he knew that, but even back then it pissed him off. Noah understood she went to Finn now out of desperation.

"What did he give you?" he asked again, hoping now that she'd come off the high she might tell him.

"Heroin," she whispered.

"Shit, Skye."

"I know. It was stupid."

"And dangerous," he added.

Skye shrugged. "It's not like I shot up. I smoked it, and not even that much."

Excuses. He read about how addicts had an excuse and explanation for everything. They could justify anything. Noah refused to fall for any of it. Addiction was serious. No amount of excuses or justification made it right.

He kissed the top of her head, wishing like hell things had been different five years ago. If he'd left with her, maybe none of this would have happened. "Nothing you've done is irreparable, Skye. I've played my part too. I'm not even sure you have any control over the decisions you're making. What you're going through is some serious stuff."

"PTSD, drug addiction," she said, acknowledging it for the first time.

"And grief. You lost someone you love on top of everything else." When she didn't say anything, Noah took the opportunity to own up to his part. Skye wasn't the only one at fault. Noah had pushed her too hard. It seemed all his efforts to help her through the pain and trauma only served to push her closer to the edge. "I'm sorry, too, Skye. I shouldn't have taken your pills. I should have found a better way to help you."

She pulled away, looking at him with red, tear-filled eyes. "This isn't your responsibility. I'm glad you're sticking by me, but the responsibility, the blame, it's all on me."

"I'm with you, no matter what, but you have to be the one to ask for help. I can't force it on you anymore."

Chapter 36

I've lived, I've loved, I've lost,
I've paid some dues, baby
We've been to hell and back again
Through it all you're always my best friend
For all the words I didn't say and
all the things I didn't do
Tonight I'm gonna find a way
-All About Lovin' You, Bon Jovi

Love.

She didn't deserve it, and with the reality of losing it exploding like an IED around her, Skye was desperate to hang on to it.

She had reached a new all-time low, not just going to Finn but giving in to his destructive charms. The high had been everything he promised and she wanted it again.

What would Noah say to that? He was being supportive, but Skye worried she would take him down with her.

He wanted honesty, had laid that out as a rule of them being together. She had to tell him, because if she took him down with her, it had to be his choice to hang on.

"I liked it, the heroin," she admitted. "I wish I could say I don't want to do it again, but I do."

Noah's body tensed against hers, proving she was successful in opening a whole new door to judgment and disappointment.

"I'm just going to go downstairs," she said, pushing away from him. He couldn't comfort her with that much tension vibrating from his body and Skye was in no position to comfort him.

"You can't just drop a bomb like that and walk away," he said.

Skye glared at him, the shrapnel of that analogy tearing her apart from the inside. "That's not funny."

Noah's hand scraped across his head before he gripped it with both hands. "Nothing about this is funny. Jesus, Skye, you just told me you had sex with Finn and then you tell me you liked getting high."

"You asked for honesty," she reminded him. "I can't win. I keep things locked up and you get mad. I tell you the truth and you get mad."

"I'm mad at what you said, not at you," he said.

"Mad is mad. This isn't easy for me."

She stormed out of the room, tearing the basement door open and attempting to slam it behind her.

The door didn't slam, though and without looking behind her, she knew Noah loomed, watching her retreat down the stairs.

Her angry steps came to an abrupt halt when she reached the bottom. The box she'd left in the passenger seat of her car blocked the path to her apartment.

"Shit," she muttered as Noah's footsteps closed in on her.

Kicking the box aside, she chose to step around it instead of picking it up. Skye went to the refrigerator, only to find it empty. She muttered a string of curses, trying to remember if she'd drank all the beer or if Noah had dumped them all down the drain again.

As she settled on the couch, Noah took a seat at one of the chairs around the dining table. "Tell me, what was so great about it?" he asked.

"So great about what?" she snarled.

"Getting high. You said you liked it. Why?"

Skye glared at him despite the gentle tone of his voice.

He stared right back, no anger in his expression. Instead, there was resignation, as if the hope he'd been carrying for both of them had left him stranded and alone.

Skye knew there was no hope for her. She'd even warned Noah to stay away so she wouldn't take him down with her. He should have listened.

"Tell me, Skye. Help me understand why I'm not enough for you."

Shaking her head, she tried not to focus on her breaking heart. "This isn't about you, Noah."

"Then tell me."

Skye sucked in a deep breath and closed her eyes, remembering the moment when the drug hit her system. "It was like being whisked away on a cloud. The pain, the guilt, it was all gone and I was just floating, like nothing could hurt me."

"Finn would have hurt you," he reminded her.

"I know," she sighed, opening her eyes. "I know that. I knew it then too, but I didn't care. I haven't cared about anything, not since the explosion."

His eyes glassed over.

"Except you, Noah. I care about you."

Noah continued to sit there, assessing Skye with those sad eyes, making it clear he didn't believe her honest words. Skye leaned forward, her elbows resting on her knees, burying her face in her hands as the tears took hold again.

Seconds later, the couch cushion sank as Noah sat next to her, his arm moving around her shoulder and pulling her to him. "Finn's going to keep preying on you if you let him."

That's because Finn was a drug dealer. He was in business to make money, but he still had that bad-boy charm she'd been attracted to when she was a naive teen. She knew what his game was about now, but she didn't have the strength or willpower to see past it. "He says all the right things, and I know it's all bull shit, but, God, I can't explain it."

"He's saying what you want to hear, not what you need to hear." The anger and disappointment made Skye want to disappear, just go up in a poof of smoke and fade away until she was nothing but a distant memory.

"I guess," she said, not willing to admit it. Admitting any of this, that she was an addict, that she had PTSD, that she liked getting high, it was more traumatic than the explosion she'd survived.

"This isn't who I want to be," she sighed.

"Then don't. Everything is a choice, Skye. The easy way isn't always the right way."

"Says the person who isn't nursing a bum hip and leg." She tried to keep her tone light. Noah wasn't to blame, but he also didn't understand what she had to endure every day.

"Or PTSD," he added.

"That too," she sighed. Turning to him, she was relieved to see the sadness had left his eyes. "What do you get out of this?"

"I don't get anything out of it," he retorted.

"Come on, Noah. You always like fixing people. It's who you are. Me, though, I'm not even sure I'm fixable."

He shot off the couch, taking a few steps before he turned to face her once more. "I don't fix people, I help. You have to stop thinking about yourself as someone who needs fixing and realize the first step to healing is asking for help."

"You're avoiding the question," she pointed out.

"I love you," he said with a surety and confidence that made her heart beat a little faster. "That's what I get out of it."

While those words were sweet music, they still didn't

answer the question. Noah loving her is what Skye got out of it. For Noah to get something out of it, she had to love him back.

Skye needed to say it, to tell him she loved him too, but it seemed so inappropriate given what she'd done.

He narrowed his eyes and tilted his head.

"What?" she asked.

"It looked like you were about to say something."

Skye shook her head. "No, I'm just ready to go to sleep."

It had been light out when she left the house to go to PT. It was still light when Luke swooped in and rescued her from the big, bad drug dealer. By the time they left the hospital, darkness had fallen, a cloudy sky making the night even darker.

"I need to stay with you," Noah said. "Seeing you like that, it scared the hell out of me. I need to hold you, to feel your breaths, the beat of your heart. Please don't deny me that."

She didn't want to be alone either and even though she didn't deserve Noah, she was grateful he continued to stick by her.

"I want you to stay," she said, needing him as much as he needed her.

They always slept in Noah's bed, but Skye didn't have the strength to climb the stairs one more time. After pushing off the couch, she held out her hand. Noah took it, his palm warm against hers, his fingers filling her with strength as they wove between hers.

She'd told him she was ready for sleep to avoid admitting more truth, but as they slid under the covers, exhaustion settled in, sweeping her away more quickly than the heroin had. Skye didn't fight it. Instead, she nestled against Noah's body. He was the only good thing in her life. As sleep claimed her, she sent out a silent prayer that the rest of the bull-shit she'd been forced to live with was all just a bad dream.

$Chapter\ 37$

It's my life
It's now or never
I ain't gonna live forever
I just wanna live while I'm alive.
-It's My Life, Bon Jovi

Control.

Skye was determined to take it back, to start living life on her terms and not be a victim of her pain and guilt, and that little thing called PTSD.

Noah had gotten out of bed hours ago, kissing her temple and asking if she needed anything. She still needed sleep and didn't want him to leave, but he was a morning person, so she let him go. Approaching noon, Skye had dragged herself out of bed and taken a long, hot shower, hoping he would come down and she could entice him back to bed.

He never made an appearance.

Skye pushed aside the worry and decided to head upstairs. Everything was quiet, so she didn't expect to find him, but maybe he'd left a note next to the coffee maker.

She almost jumped out of her skin when she found Noah's mother sitting in the recliner, Noah's computer on her lap.

"Skye," Rachel squealed, putting the computer aside and rushing out of the chair.

The woman embraced Skye in one of her famous bear hugs, rocking back and forth with joy. "Thank God you made it home. How are you, honey?"

Taking a deep breath when Rachel released her and her lungs were able to expand again, Skye was about to utter, "Everything's fine," when she recognized it for the lie it had always been. Taking control meant being honest and the first words to cross her lips couldn't counter her determination.

"Things have been difficult," she said to the woman who had been a second mother to Skye since elementary school.

"Oh, honey, I'm so sorry. Is there anything I can do? I know soldiers need tons of support when they come home. Luke sure did."

"Just keep those hugs at the ready," Skye said, smiling at Rachel.

Rachel gave Skye's shoulder a squeeze. "I promise, and anything else you need, just ask. Okay?"

Skye nodded, unsure of what else she could say. "Where's Noah?" she asked.

"Oh, he's off with all the men, Tom, Luke, your dad, your brothers. Riley needed some help at the orchard, tearing down a small barn, I think."

"Demolition," Skye laughed, pushing away the paranoia that this gathering was something more.

"Men are so strange," Rachel said, laughing along with Skye. "I'm here to get you. The women are tasked with making dinner, but your mother thought it would be nice if we all spent the afternoon together. She said she hasn't seen much of you since you moved into Noah's basement."

That was another thing Skye wanted to work on, spending more time with her family. While it might be happening a little sooner than she was ready for, jumping head first in the deep end might be the best way to kick start her coping mechanisms.

"Sounds great," Skye said, her suspicions growing. "But you could have called."

"We don't have Internet at the cabin yet. I wanted to catch up on Facebook and Candy Crush."

It sounded like a convenient excuse, but Skye chose not to pursue it. Rachel had always been kind to Skye and the woman didn't have a manipulative bone in her body, unlike Amelia.

"I'll meet you there," Skye said.

"I can drive. It'll give us time to catch up."

"You've already gone out of your way," Skye offered. "If I drive myself, I can get home later."

Rachel smiled. "Noah can bring you home later."

Skye couldn't argue with that, even if it did seem like Rachel was keeping an eye on her. "Okay, well, just let me get my shoes."

She hobbled downstairs and changed out of the yoga pants and sweatshirt that weren't appropriate for going out in public, even if public was just her mother's house. After slipping into loose jeans and a light oversized sweater, Skye slipped into a pair of Danskos and headed back upstairs.

"It's nice seeing you and Noah together," Rachel said when they set off. "You two were always thick as thieves."

Skye laughed, wondering if Rachel knew that was the title of a Bon Jovi song.

"He was lost, you know, after you left last time. Once he and Maddie broke up, I know he regretted not leaving with you."

Her cheeks burned with embarrassment. Skye had never asked Noah if he told anyone. She never would have guessed his mother knew.

"Oh, don't be embarrassed, honey," Rachel said, patting

Skye's knee. "That was brave, telling him how you felt."

"Who else knows?" she asked.

Rachel gave her knee another pat. "Just me. Like I said, Noah had a hard time. Amelia told me the two of you had some sort of falling out. It took a lot of digging before Noah finally told me what happened. He's always loved you."

Skye had always loved him too, something she needed to tell him.

"Noah's a good person," Skye offered.

"So are you, honey," Rachel responded. She wouldn't be saying that if she knew what Skye had done last night, how she'd been struggling since returning to Sunset Valley.

When they pulled up in front of the Everhart abode, she didn't miss the fact Noah's car was parked out front. As she took inventory, she noticed Riley's Jeep and Vaughn's Shelby, too. "What's going on?" Skye asked.

"Let's just head inside," Rachel said, still smiling and cheerful.

Skye's suspicions ratcheted up, along with the anxiety. A rush of adrenaline reminded her of the patrols in Afghanistan, when they swept a building in one of the outlying towns where insurgents were rumored to be organizing their forces.

The difference now was Skye didn't have any weapons, nor any Kevlar to protect her from whatever waited inside.

She walked in the kitchen to find all the men, as Rachel had referred to them, and her mother gathered around the large table.

"Shit," she muttered as they all looked at her. Riley was closest and he stood, wrapping his arms around Skye and hugging her so tight it rivaled one of Rachel's hugs.

Skye hugged him back, surprised by the affection.

"What's going on?" Skye dared ask when Riley let her go.

"It's called an intervention, honey," Rachel said, patting Skye's shoulder.

Skye's eyes darted around before resting on Noah. With a

churning stomach, she fisted her hands, trying to settle her ragged breaths before the panic took hold. "You ratted me out?"

"I did," Luke and Vaughn said in perfect sync.

"We didn't give him a choice," Vaughn added, clapping Noah on the shoulder.

"It was my idea," Rachel said from next to Skye. "Luke came to me and I went to Noah. This isn't something either one of you can get through alone. You both need family."

"You lied to me," Skye said to Rachel, surprised by her actions.

"I stretched the truth. The men are planning to tear down a barn at the orchard and we are making them dinner, but this had to be first."

Amelia put a cup of coffee at the empty spot between Noah and Luke, her eyes glassy and her hands shaking. "Will you be okay sitting at the table or should we move to the living room?"

Skye didn't want to do this here, nor in the living room, but a small part of her breathed a sigh of relief that she couldn't hide from it any longer. "I'm fine, Ma," Skye said, moving to the spot reserved for her.

"You're not fine," her mother snapped before she sobbed. "I'm sorry, I shouldn't …"

Skye pinched her lips between her teeth, biting back her own tears as she dropped into the chair. She'd rather face a hundred insurgents than be at this table, but there was no easy escape.

Noah's words from last night echoed in her mind. *The easy way isn't always the right way.*

"Where should we start?" her dad asked, turning to Rachel, who had taken the empty seat between him and her husband, Tom. To Tom's left was Riley, then Luke and Skye. Noah sat to her left, Vaughn next to him, and her mother completed the circle.

"Skye," Rachel said, her voice supportive. "Why don't you tell us what's going on?"

"Seems like all of you already know," Skye said, looking for an out. If everyone already knew, there was no need for her to air all that dirty laundry. "Why else would we all be sitting here?"

"We have pieces of the story," her dad said, folding his hands on the table in the way he'd always done as a high school principal. "We'll be better equipped to develop a plan to help you if we know the whole story."

"I don't …" Skye said, desperate to run, to be anywhere but here.

"We're not your enemy," he added.

"Then why does it feel like I've been sent to the principal's office?" she asked.

That earned a couple chuckles from the younger generation around the table.

Noah, however, didn't laugh. He gave her hand a gentle squeeze, encouraging her to take this leap of faith. "Why don't you start with your injuries," he suggested. "No one realizes how extensive they are."

Skye sucked in a deep breath digging for some courage. "You know about my leg and hip," she started, wringing her hands on the table in front of her. From her periphery, she could see everyone watching, but she focused on working out the tension from her hands as she continued. "That's where the pain is. It comes and goes, is worse when I'm active. What you don't know is I also suffered third degree burns. I had a couple surgeries where they replaced the burned skin with grafts. There's nerve damage there, so it's numb. Sometimes if I overextend my torso, it bothers me, but mostly it's my hip and leg."

"Why didn't you tell us? Why didn't anyone tells us when we were at the hospital with you?" Amelia asked.

"Because I didn't want you to know," Skye snapped. She extended her fingers on the table, feeling her toes mimic the motion in an attempt to reel in the festering anger.

More tears spilled down her mother's cheeks, inspiring a good dose of guilt to join the angst. Skye's lungs felt tiny, as if they were a cashmere sweater put through the dryer on high heat and shrinking until rendered useless. She sucked in a breath through her nose, but it only added to the ache in her chest. "I told the doctor not to tell you because that, right there," she pointed at her mother, "that pity, that's what I didn't want."

"It's not pity," her father growled, a signature warning that his temper was flaring. He always kept a tight grip on it. It was only when Skye or one of her brothers crossed a line that he unleashed the Everhart anger.

Skye, however, was undeterred. She lived with that anger, stared it in the face every single day. She'd faced worse things than the Everhart temper. The pity, though, that she couldn't handle. Since it sat sidesaddle with disappointment, Skye was ready to double-time it right out of this house, right out of Sunset Valley. She'd take another tour in Afghanistan over the pity and disappointment staring back at her from every face in this room.

"Then what is it?" Skye hollered back.

"Love."

When Skye rolled her eyes, her father's fists slammed down on the table, making everyone around jump. "Are you so goddamned stubborn that you can't see that? Because I know your mother and I didn't raise an idiot."

"Fine," she bellowed, pushing the chair back with such force it fell over. She ignored the biting pain in her hip as she stood as tall as a soldier should and lifted the right side of her sweater to reveal her scarred torso.

Her mother gasped, eyes once again filling with tears. Skye let them have a good long look before she dropped her sweater and fell back into the chair, which Noah had put upright. She wiped her own tears with shaking hands as Noah's arm moved around her shoulder.

"Breathe," he whispered in her ear. Skye closed her eyes, picturing herself in formation, marching alongside other soldiers to the cadence of left, left, left, right, left. She breathed in with each imagined heel strike of that cadence, then out, reeling in the humiliation and anger. Noah's caress moved in perfect rhythm.

"Why were you at Finn's last night?" Vaughn asked.

"I guess I developed a tolerance to the Vicodin, so I went through my prescription faster than I should have." The statement was a cop-out, Skye knew it, but she'd just shown everyone her burn scars. She wasn't ready to face further disapproval for her apparent addiction, let alone own her part in it. With her eyes closed so she didn't get lost in the disappointed expressions surrounding her, she continued, her next statement an even bigger cop-out. "I ran into Finn, he said he could help. He got me more Vicodin and later, after the panic attack at Wal-mart, he gave me something to help with the anxiety I've been having."

"It was Valium," Luke added. Her eyes flew open. She chewed on her bottom lip in order to keep from demanding how he knew that.

"I gave them to him," Noah admitted.

"You went through my stuff," she accused, narrowing her eyes at him.

"I'm not going to apologize. You weren't just taking more than you should have been, you were mixing narcotics with alcohol. It's stupid and dangerous, so yeah, I went through your bag. Those pills weren't labeled. No way was I letting you keep them."

Sky pushed back from the table again. This time the chair didn't topple over, but her father stood too, fury wafting off him like the heat emanating from scorching sand in the desert.

"Sit down," he demanded.

"I'm not one of your students," she countered, surprised he hadn't added a 'young lady' to his command. "You can't order me around."

"You are my daughter and you are in my house and you will sit down and tell us the rest of your story so we can figure out the best way to help you." His stern voice left no room for negotiation, but Skye hadn't been labeled stubborn for doing as she was told.

"What if I don't want help?" she bellowed, a sob riding on those words.

Noah wrapped his hand around her fist, loosening the stranglehold she had on nothing but air and weaving his fingers between hers. "Skye, please," he pleaded.

Through pooling tears, she looked at him as he stood next to her, his dark eyes glassy.

Skye never wanted to hurt Noah, never wanted to hurt anyone in her family. She hadn't wanted any of this, the pain, the desperation, the loss. She hadn't even wanted to come home.

"Please," Noah whispered, the plea wrenching her heart so tight, it strangled the strength to stand and fight. She dropped into the chair. Noah followed suit, keeping a gentle hold on her hand as his thumb caressed her prickly skin.

Vaughn's hand landed on her shoulder, giving her a subtle squeeze that encouraged her to continue on.

Skye couldn't speak, though. The words got lodged in her throat as soon as she opened her mouth. Her mother got up from the table, returning a minute later with a wet washcloth and a box of tissues. Skye swallowed the humiliation of her outburst and everything else she'd done and wiped her face, taking a few extra moments to let the cool cloth sooth her aching eyes.

"You were going to tell us why you went to Finn's last night," Vaughn reminded her.

Skye was so done with this intervention. She didn't want to air her dirty laundry, but based on her father's commands and Noah's pleas, she wasn't going to be able to leave without putting it all on the line.

"The Vicodin stopped working," she admitted, staring at the wet washcloth wrung between her fingers and palm. "Going to Finn just seemed easier than waiting for another appointment at the VA."

Once again, she could see the disapproving gazes from her periphery. The disappointment permeated the room, so potent it sucked the air from Skye's lungs.

They already knew the rest of the story, they had to. Even if they didn't, Skye couldn't utter the words. As a teen, when Amelia had found her cigarettes, Skye had tried to lie her way out of it. Except now, she wasn't a teen. She was an adult, responsible for her actions. She'd woken up this morning wanting to gain control back of her life. To do that, she had to tell them, to be completely honest. "He talked me into trying heroin," she admitted, slumping in the chair.

Her mother gasped again and Skye gripped the wet cloth, looking for the strength to survive this inquisition. She'd never be able to look any of them in the eye again, not after doing something so horrid.

She tried to pull her hand away from Noah, but he gripped it tighter, not letting her retreat.

"What's your plan now?" Ken asked, ever the one who demanded a solution.

"I don't want to be a drug addict," she mumbled, the words harder to utter than she ever would have thought.

"You already are," Luke said. "You need to get sober and stay sober. You need to get help."

"What can we do?" Vaughn asked.

Skye shrugged. This was unchartered territory. She wasn't good at asking for help, but as she dared a glance at the people around her, for the first time since she'd entered this room, or even returned to Sunset Valley, she saw the truth. They wanted to help. They wanted Skye to not just be here in Sunset Valley, but to finally come home. "I don't have a clue."

"I don't think you should be alone," Noah said, focusing on her and not the people around the table. "I know you think it's babysitting, but if you're feeling low and desperate enough to give in, you need someone there to keep you from doing that. If you can't trust us with that, you need to consider rehab."

The thought of rehab sent a shiver down her spine. It sounded more like a prison sentence than an opportunity to take control. As much as she didn't like it though, Noah was right. She had wanted to drive her own car today, just so she had the option to swing by Finn's if she needed it.

As the word *addict* echoed in her mind, she nodded her agreement, unable to put words to it. She couldn't have control of her life and be an addict; she was smart enough to understand that. Having someone with her at all times seemed the lesser of the evils.

"I need to find a job before I go stir-crazy." Because if someone was going to be with her all the time, she most certainly would go stir-crazy without a mission. "I also want to try out that veteran's support group," she admitted. "Do you still have Chad's card?"

"I have it at home," Noah said.

Skye nodded before once again daring to look at the people around the table, her family. She'd hurt them by going down this road. She wasn't sure she could ever repair the damage, but she wanted to try.

"I need help with the orchard, marketing and stuff," Riley offered. "Noah suggested you might take some pictures and get a website going for me?"

"I don't have any experience," she started until Noah squeezed her hand.

"I don't give a shit about experience. I'm desperate and you're desperate. If we put our heads together, we can figure it out."

Skye nodded. It sounded easy enough. She'd put together enough websites during her time in the army to be able to figure out what to do for Riley.

"Liz Hall is also looking for some part-time help. She has too many clients and can't keep up with it all," Noah said. "I was going to mention it sooner, but it never seemed like the right time."

"I'll talk to her, see if it's something I can do," Skye said. She had doubts, but arguing them at this table would get her nowhere. At the welcome home party, she'd talked to Liz briefly. They'd been friends in school, so it would be nice to reform that bond again. Liz owned a website design business and still seemed pretty down to earth. It was worth having the conversation, at the very least, even if she didn't have enough experience.

"We're with you, sis," Riley said. "You didn't survive that explosion just so you could come home and die."

"Whatever you need," Vaughn added, "Whenever you need it."

The emotions hit her like a tidal wave. Her brothers had always teased her growing up. She'd never expected this show of support.

Through the blur of tears, she glanced at her dad, a warm smile on his face as he nodded. "Whatever you need, sweetheart. You come to any of us at this table if you're in trouble. We'll get you the help you need."

Skye nodded, swallowing the rush of emotions and digging deep for the courage she needed to utter the last piece of truth she'd kept from them.

"There's one more thing," she said, gripping the dog tags beneath her sweater.

"What is it?" Amelia asked.

Noah nodded. "You should tell them," he whispered.

"I was ... with someone, in Afghanistan. Rafe. He was my platoon leader, so we had to keep it secret. That's why I never said anything."

"Where is Rafe now?" her dad asked.

Skye pinched her lips between her teeth again, swallowing the sob that threatened. "He died, in the explosion. We were on the same patrol, in the humvee together."

Everyone around the table took their turn offering heartfelt condolences, but they did nothing to soothe Skye's aching heart.

"There's more," she said, taking another deep breath. "He, uh, while we were on patrol, he asked me to marry him. Once we were stateside, he was going to request to be reassigned until his time in service was met. Then he planned to go reserves. He had it all figured out, but then I hit that IED and he was killed."

"It's not your fault," her dad said without hesitation, the sternness in his voice demanding she agree.

"I'm trying to come to terms with that," she admitted. "It's not easy."

Ken nodded too. "I'm proud of you, Skye."

"I am too, honey," Amelia added. Everyone else took a turn uttering the words, the storm swirling into a mass of confusion and doubt in Skye's chest.

"Proud of me? How? After all I've done."

Her father chuckled, a stark contrast to the anger and disappointment that had rolled off him earlier. Amelia tended to hold a grudge, but Ken was skilled at tackling a problem and letting it go. "You were never one to ask for help or admit when you were wrong. We forced your hand today. Telling us all of this wasn't easy, I know that, but it's a step in the right direction."

"We just want you to be happy and healthy," her mother added. "We want you to finally come home."

Chapter 38

We gotta hold on
Ready or not
You live for the fight
When that's all that you've got.
-Livin' on a Prayer, Bon Jovi

Sober.

It made sense to Skye that the first three letters in the word spelled sob. Whenever she denied herself a pain pill she didn't need or a beer, she found the sobs were more frequent and more violent.

Noah stayed by her side, taking her to PT, taking her to see Maddie's horses, even taking her to an eclectic new age shop where she bought a book about aromatherapy and a few oils to get started on a holistic healing remedy.

It seemed like voodoo to Skye, but somehow when they put a few drops of the oils in a diffuser, her anxiety mellowed. Noah had started doing aromatherapy massage on her hip and leg and she spent a lot of time icing it, both of which seemed to help.

It wasn't enough, though. Skye knew it was wrong, but she

fantasized about sneaking out, about meeting Finn and getting high again. She'd only done it once, and aside from throwing up and being molested, it had been exactly what she needed.

"You sure you want to do this now?" Noah asked, sitting down at her small dining table, the box from Rafe's mom looming between them.

"I've already put it off too long. We have an hour before we need to leave for Chad's. That should be plenty of time."

"I just don't want you to feel overwhelmed. Going through this box and hitting your support group for the first time … it's a lot, Skye."

"I know, but I need to do this."

Noah nodded, grabbing the scissors and cutting the tape on the box.

"Wait," she said, putting her hand over his before he flipped the top open. "I love you," she said, her first time uttering the words she should have said weeks ago.

Noah smiled, bringing her hand to his lips.

"I just, whatever is in that box, I need you to know that I love you."

"I know, Skye. I love you, too."

She nodded and sucked in a deep breath. "Okay, I'm ready. Open it."

Noah opened the flaps and Skye peered in, afraid to get too close, as if some sort of explosive lingered inside.

"Looks like a letter from Mrs. Thompson," Noah said. "Do you want me to read it to you?"

Skye nodded, her eyes too blurry with unshed tears to be able to read it herself.

"Dear Skye, Rafe asked me to send these things to you if he didn't make it back from Afghanistan. He seemed to do a lot of Internet shopping while deployed. Sometimes I wondered if he had an actual mission. These are gifts from his heart, for the woman he loved.

"Losing him was hard, but knowing he loved someone enough to want to spend the rest of his life with her, that gives me so much comfort. I hope you will stay in touch, and maybe sometime we can meet, but of course I'll understand if you don't want to. We all grieve in our own ways. Be well. Sylvia Thompson."

Skye took another deep breath and nodded again, a silent command for Noah to take the next thing out of the box.

"It looks like another letter," Noah said, showing her the envelope. She recognized Rafe's writing in the four letters that spelled her name.

"Read it," she encouraged, desperate to march forward with this mission.

Noah opened the envelope with care and pulled out the folded paper. With a deep breath and glassy eyes, he started on Rafe's words.

"Dear Skye, The first time I saw you, leading your soldiers in PT and pushing them to find new limits, I knew I was going to break the rules to be with you. I've never known someone like you, someone with an incredible spark, a fierce determination that burns with every task you take on."

Noah chuckled while giving her a quick glance and smirk. Skye smiled, knowing Rafe's words reflected how Noah felt about her too.

"You lead with your heart, a unique and noble trait in a soldier, and perfectly executed. The army is lucky to have you not only in its ranks, but as a leader, inspiring soldiers to shoot for the stars. If you're reading this letter, it means I didn't make it back."

Noah paused, clearing his throat.

"I have no regrets about my time in the army, even if it means I made the ultimate sacrifice so many talk about. I'm proud to serve my country, to make a difference in the world, even if just a small one. I write this letter knowing I'm going to marry you, so I just hope I had the chance to ask before all hell broke loose."

Pausing again, Noah looked up, the question in his eyes.

Skye nodded for him to continue.

"I wish we had had more time together, beyond the fences and the desert sands, time to visit all the places we talked about, time to meet each other's family and friends. You are the love of my life, Skye Brooke Everhart. As your platoon leader, I have one last command for you. You need live your life, just as you always have, leading with your heart, kicking ass and taking names."

Noah chuckled again, shaking his head in amusement as he looked at the paper.

"What are those Bon Jovi lyrics you love so much? It's my life, it's now or never. I ain't gonna live forever. None of us do. Don't mourn for me, at least not too long. Take life by the horns and find love again. You deserve it and I want you to be happy and to be loved. That's an order, staff sergeant. All my love, Rafe."

Noah slid the letter across the table, his own eyes glassy with unshed tears.

Skye didn't touch the letter. "What's next?" she asked, ready to plow through the contents of the box. She'd take the time to process it all later.

"You sure. That was …"

"I need to keep going," she insisted. "What's next?"

Noah pulled out something wrapped in paper. He unwrapped it carefully and chuckled, setting the large glass stein on the table. "Guy knew the direct way to your heart."

The stein had the Bon Jovi logo on it. Noah continued to pull things out of the box, a messenger bag, a couple t-shirts, a sweatshirt, all Bon Jovi.

"He used to make fun of me, how much I love Bon Jovi," she said, looking at all the fan gear.

"Skye, there's one more thing in the box," Noah said, his voice quiet and serious.

"What is it?" she asked.

"I, I'm not sure, but you need to take it out." He pushed the box toward her and Skye stood from her chair to find a small jewelry box.

She reached in slowly, as if putting her hand in a box full of sleeping snakes, and extracted the small box. Shaking it, she heard the rattle of a chain inside.

"It's a necklace," she told Noah, who obviously worried it was an engagement ring. "He told me he planned to buy a ring when we got home, that he planned to propose the way a man should, on one knee," she explained.

Unable to read the emotions on Noah's face, she gripped the box and smiled at him. "I love you, Noah," she assured him.

"I love you, too. I'm not jealous, it's just, I don't know, I wish I could have met him. That letter was pretty powerful. All this stuff, he loved you a lot."

"He was a good man," she said. "So are you."

Noah nodded at the box. "You should open that."

Skye lifted the lid and gasped, the tears once again stinging her eyes. Pinching her lips between her teeth did nothing to keep the tears from falling. There was a necklace, a small key pendant, but it wasn't the only thing in the box. "He always said I owned the key to his heart," she said, pulling the necklace from the box to show Noah.

"Pretty," he said.

"It's not the only thing in the box," she admitted, brushing her finger over the round diamond at the center with two smaller diamonds lining the white gold band.

"Show me," Noah insisted.

Her heart dropped like a brick, turning her stomach over and over as the tears spilled down her cheeks. She couldn't imagine how difficult this must be for him, seeing all these gifts from a man she had promised her heart to. "I shouldn't have made you stay," she admitted.

"I want to be here, Skye. It's a ring, right? An engagement ring?"

She nodded, too terrified that it would tear Noah apart if she took the ring out of the box. Without turning it, she pushed the box across the table. He had to make the decision to look at the ring, at the promise she and Rafe had shared before it was ripped away.

"It's beautiful," he said after turning the box. His gaze lifted as he licked his lips. "Do you want to put it on?"

The man was a saint, standing by her, watching her go through this box that contained little pieces of love from another man.

"Not the ring, no." She'd never be able to put it on. All it would do is remind her of what she'd lost and how hard she had to fight to find her way in this new life. "But I would like to wear the necklace."

The necklace seemed less of a betrayal to Noah while still honoring what she and Rafe had shared.

Noah nodded as he stood from the chair and came around the table. "Let me help you put it on," he offered.

He lifted her hair, a simple yet intimate gesture that had her breath hitching and her heart beating a little faster. Skye brought the dainty chain around and clipped it, letting the pendant fall over her shirt. She pressed her fingers against it and closed her eyes, remembering the man behind all these precious gifts.

Breathing in a long, deep breath, Skye rose out of the chair and turned to the man standing before her now, another man she wasn't sure she deserved. "I will always love Rafe and will always wish he had lived, but I'm so glad you and I found our way to each other. I may not deserve you, but I love you and I need you, Noah. Always."

His smile reached his glassy eyes as she lifted onto her toes, her eyes closing as their lips met in a soft caress.

"I love you too, Skye. Always," he said against her lips.

Skye sighed when the kiss ended, sad for what she'd lost but grateful for what she'd found in the aftermath of the tragedy.

"It's almost time to go. You probably want to wash the mascara off your cheeks," he said, tracing the line of dried-up tears on her cheek.

Laughing, Skye nuzzled against his hand. "Life was easier when I didn't wear make-up," she said.

After grabbing one of the new Bon Jovi shirts, Skye retreated to the bathroom where she washed her tear-soaked face and reapplied mascara and eye shadow around her bloodshot eyes. She hoped the guys in Chad's group didn't judge her for being such a cry-baby.

"You ready to go?" Noah asked when she came out of the bathroom.

She nodded, not at all ready but knowing this was another necessary step. "I just want to switch my stuff over to this bag. It's too cool not to use," she said, picking up the Bon Jovi messenger bag.

Noah chuckled. "You want me to grab that picture you framed?"

Skye nodded. "Yeah, it's on my desk." She'd taken the three images of Chad running, placing the one with him at the left of the image on top, the one with him in the middle in the middle, and the one with him at the right of the image on the bottom and printed it as a single image, placing it in a simple black frame. "I hope he doesn't think it's weird," Skye admitted as she stuffed her new bag full of the crap she always carried around, absent any pills.

She had quit the pills cold turkey, the beer too. It had been two weeks since the incident at Finn's. Most days she struggled to keep herself from going there and begging him for more, but she was seldom alone, Noah ensuring if he wasn't around, Skye had someone to spend time with.

It wasn't as horrible as she'd imagined, and no one, not even her mother, asked if she was okay or insisted she talk about her issues. She'd seen Maddie and the horses twice, and even though Skye had told Maddie it was on the books, the therapist let Skye lead the conversations.

"You have the directions?" she asked as Noah handed her

the framed picture and she put it in her bag.

Noah laughed. "I don't need them. All I need is an address. The GPS will do the rest."

They held hands as they walked to the car. "Relax. Chad seems cool. I'm sure the other guys are too."

"Yeah," she said, hoping Noah was right.

Keeping to her promises, she had called Chad, asking if the invite was still open to join his little group of merry men. He said she was always welcome, so that's where she was off to.

Chapter 39

Close your eyes and you will see
That you are all you really need.
　　　　　　　　-I Believe, Bon Jovi

Redemption.

Skye was on the path, but she knew it was a long road ahead. She had never had a problem meeting new people. The explosion changed that, changed everything about her. She'd lost her confidence and every new experience terrified her. She wouldn't even have Noah there for support since this was one of the vets-only gatherings. Skye had wanted to wait for when the significant others were invited, but Noah encouraged her to go now. Given how he'd stuck by her, she owed it to him to keep moving forward.

"I was waiting for the right time to tell you," she said, squeezing Noah's hand as they headed to Lilac Ridge.

"Tell me what?" he asked.

She smiled, letting him know it was good news. "Liz called this morning. She offered me the job. I start Monday."

Noah's eyes widened, his smile making her heart flutter. "That's great, Skye. Congratulations."

"Thanks. I never pictured myself developing websites or doing photography, but I'm excited. I might even sign up for some courses at the community college. I have the G.I. Bill, I may as well use it."

Noah nodded. "That's a great idea. I can teach you to use photo editing software, too. I use a few different programs."

"Can we do that naked?" she joked.

"I'm not sure we'd accomplish anything if we did it naked," he laughed. "But I'm willing to give it a try."

"I've been playing around with different website providers, trying to find the best one for Riley's orchard. It's easier than I thought it'd be."

"That's good. You should have it mastered in no time."

She hoped so. "I still can't believe Riley bought an orchard. Though, honestly, that's a better fit for him than accounting. He must go stir crazy sitting at a desk crunching numbers all day."

"It's a good investment. That orchard has always done well. I'm glad someone local bought it," Noah added. "Oh, looks like this is it," he said as the GPS told them they'd reached their destination.

The garage door was open, four men lounging in lawn chairs in the driveway. A couple of them held water bottles, the other two holding soda cans. Chad told her it was an alcohol free zone. "Can you at least walk me over there?" she asked, her nerves so tight she felt like the stretched rubber band of a sling shot.

"Of course," Noah said, giving her hand a squeeze. "Just be you, Skye. Talk about what's comfortable. You don't have to dive into the deep end head first."

"I'm not sure I know how to do it any other way," she admitted.

Noah chuckled and squeezed her hand again. "I'm with you. I may not be here physically, but I'm only a text or phone call away."

Skye nodded and squeezed his hand back. "Now or never," she said, letting go and opening the door.

Chad started down the driveway, meeting her just as Noah came up beside her. "Skye, so glad you came," he said, holding out his hand. Skye shook it before he offered it to Noah. "Good to see you, too, man. Come meet the guys."

Chad stepped off, heading back toward the garage where the other three men stood.

"Guys, this is Skye Everhart," Chad said.

"Clint Avery," the first man said, giving her a mock salute, "19D, Cav Scout."

"Shane Ellis," the next said, holding out his hand. Skye reached forward to shake it. "Working dog handler, 31K. Coolest MOS in the army."

"Shane helped me find this girl," Chad said, giving his dog a pet. "Her name's Sasha, by the way."

"Pete Mitchell," the third guy said, "but unlike the guy in Top Gun, I was a SatComms Operator."

Skye nodded. "35N, Intel Analyst. Worked with a lot of 25S's," she said, acknowledging Pete's MOS by its code. She turned to Clint. "Worked with a lot of Cav Scouts, too."

"You know we're going to make fun of you for being intel, right?"

"Bring it, grunt," she retorted.

All the men laughed. "I think we've got a spit fire on our hands," Pete said.

Noah laughed too. "You have no idea."

"Guys, this is Noah," Chad said. They all said their hellos and shook Noah's hand before Chad turned his attention back to him. "You're welcome to go inside and hang out with my wife or come back in a couple hours. Choice is yours. Maggie doesn't mind the company, but be warned, she might put you to work. She's pregnant and nesting."

"I'm pretty handy," Noah offered, turning to Skye. "If you'd rather I leave, I can take off."

Skye shook her head. "Go help Maggie," she said, knowing he didn't want to go far and grateful to have him nearby even though these guys made her feel more relaxed than she'd been in a long time. Chad led Noah to the house while Skye lingered outside the garage.

"What's your poison?" Clint asked. "We've got everything from root beer to diet soda."

Skye would kill for a beer, but that wouldn't get her anywhere, and since this was a no alcohol zone, wasn't an option anyway. She'd been sober for two weeks and while it didn't seem like long, to her it felt like an eternity. "A Coke," she said.

"Coke it is," Clint said.

"None of you drink?" she asked. In the army, it seemed everyone drank.

"I've been sober six months," Pete said, holding up his Coke. "I liked taking my painkillers with whiskey."

Skye nodded, surprised how open he was.

"I gave up heroin for beer, lesser of two evils and all that." Clint said as he opened the fridge. "But I don't drink here out of respect."

Now she shook her head, surprise morphing into shock. She glanced at Pete who also held a Coke. "All of the above," he grunted.

"Me too," Skye whispered, feeling obligated to air her dirty laundry. "I've only been sober two weeks," she added. "It sucks."

"Amen," they all said.

"What are we praying about?" Chad asked as he rejoined the group.

"Skye thinks sobriety sucks," Clint offered.

"Amen," Chad added. "Beats being dead, though."

"Amen," they all said again, holding up their respective drinks.

Skye settled into an empty chair and took a long drink of the soda Clint had fetched from the mini fridge.

"You quit cold turkey?" Pete asked.

Skye nodded. "Yeah, my family staged an intervention."

"Any withdrawal symptoms?" Shane asked.

"I have trouble sleeping," she admitted, hoping they didn't want her to talk about the struggle she had every day to not give in to the temptation.

"Restless legs?" Shane asked.

She shouldn't have been surprised he knew, after all, he'd admitted to doing exactly what she had done. She nodded.

"Try soda water before you go to bed. I cut it with ginger ale so it doesn't taste like ass. It seems to calm my legs down."

Skye nodded. "I'll try that. Thanks."

Conversation turned from their respective vices to baseball and Skye made a mental note to start watching some games. If she was going to hang with these guys, she needed to keep up with their interests. Rafe was a Blue Jays fan and while Skye grew up a Red Sox fan just like the four soldiers around her, she thought it'd be fun to throw a wrench in the mix.

"Oh," Skye said during a lull in the conversation. "I have something for you."

She flipped open her messenger bag, smiling as the Bon Jovi logo and Rafe's smile flashed through her mind. "That day in the park, I snapped a few pictures of you running. I hope you don't mind."

"Stalker much?" Clint laughed. Skye knew she was going to have to stay on her toes around that guy.

After handing Chad the frame, she held her breath, hoping he didn't peg her as a stalker.

"Holy shit, this is incredible," Chad said. "Guys, check this." He turned the frame around and the other men leaned in.

"Fuck, man, that's, shit, that's just wow," Clint said. Skye chuckled to herself, feeling like she'd gotten one on him.

"You took these?" Shane asked.

Skye nodded. "It's a hobby."

"That's no hobby," Pete added. "I've seen pics like this on Facebook." He pulled up his pant leg to reveal a prosthetic leg that wasn't much different from Chad's. "Would you do me?"

"Excuse me?" Skye choked out.

"Snap pictures, shit, not, no. You've got your guy in there, I wouldn't, I'm not. Shit," Pete muttered.

The other three guys laughed. "Pete's the shy one of the bunch, has a tendency to stick his prosthetic foot in his mouth," Shane said.

"This was just random," Skye said of the pictures.

"It's fucking cool, Miss Intel," Clint drawled, pulling up his left pant leg. "You can do me, too."

Skye laughed because these guys were just like the soldiers she'd worked and played with over the last twelve years. She turned to Shane. "Do you have one too or am I the only one here without a strap-on?"

Shane lifted his shirt, revealing burn scars that weren't much different from Skye's except for how much more real estate they covered. "Fake hip," he said.

Her eyes widened. "Me too," she said, standing and lifting her shirt to show her own scars. "I've got a dozen pins in my leg too."

"Fucking A," Clint said. "That's some impressive brass right there."

"You guys mind if I bring Maggie out to show her this?" Chad asked.

"Go for it, man," Shane said, Pete and Clint in agreement.

"Maaaaaggggggieeeeeee," he yelled, his voice echoing off the houses. The window on the side of the house facing the garage opened, a pretty woman with long black hair leaning out.

"Seriously?" she said.

"Come down here, babe. You gotta see this."

The woman rolled her eyes before disappearing from the

window. A few minutes later, a very pregnant woman walked with steps more confident than Skye's toward the group. "Babe, you gotta see this," Chad said, putting his arm around the woman and guiding her to his chair. When she was settled, he handed the frame over. Maggie gasped.

"Wow, this is amazing," she cooed.

"Right? Skye took those."

Maggie looked at Skye, her eyes wide. "Are you a professional photographer?"

Skye shook her head. "It's just a hobby."

"I've been telling her since high school she had talent," Noah said, standing next to Skye's chair.

Her face was hot with embarrassment. She'd expected to be called a stalker, but didn't expect this kind of response.

"I'm thinking calendar," Clint said. "I'd go the full monty. We can donate funds to the group where Wick-man got Sasha."

"Like someone would pay to see your naked ass," Shane drawled.

Clint stripped out of his shirt to reveal a tight six pack, skin all tanned and taut. Skye's blush increased.

"If her red face is any indication, women would empty their purses to have this hanging on their walls," Clint said while nodding at Skye and pounding his very firm chest.

"I'm not a professional. I just point and shoot," she said.

"That's what he said," Maggie laughed and Skye instantly liked the woman. "These pics are amazing and I hate to say it, but Clint's right. People would pay for these."

"I agree," Noah added. "You should do this, Skye. See where it goes."

"Huah," the other four men bellowed in perfect army agreement. Between the encouraging look on Noah's face and the cheers from her new squad, Skye was inspired, thinking maybe as a veteran with her own combat injuries and ghosts, she could capture something other photographers couldn't.

She nodded. "Okay, I'll give it a go on one condition."

"Name it," Shane and Pete echoed in perfect cadence.

"If Clint goes the full monty, every single one of you have to be there."

$$Chapter\ 40$$

When your world comes crashing down
Like you've lost every round
Stand your ground and
ring the bells of freedom.
-Bells of Freedom, Bon Jovi

Fearless.

Never in a million years would Skye have pictured herself shooting pictures of naked combat veterans who suffered losses so similar yet so much different than hers.

"I don't know how to do this," she whispered to Noah, who had spent countless hours over the last two weeks helping her research techniques to photograph combat veterans. Despite all the blog posts they'd read and photos they'd studied, nothing helped.

"Just go with your instincts," he said. "Keep the faith."

She laughed. "Yeah, let's crank that up," she said.

Noah nodded, pulling his iPod from the pocket of his sweatshirt.

"Okay," Skye said. While she wanted to say, "strip it on

down," she called on all of her military discipline to keep it professional. "You ready?"

Clint got that cocky smile on his face before he dropped the terry robe.

"I don't think starting with the naked guy was the best decision," Skye said.

Noah laughed. "You dive into everything head first."

"Right," she drawled, wishing for a drink.

"Look at him, Skye. Not his, you know, but everything else. See the soldier, the warrior."

Skye took a deep breath and did what Noah said, her gaze moving from Clint's … you know … to his prosthetic leg and back up. His torso was covered in tattoos and Skye would bet her next breath every single one of them had meaning.

They were at Starlight Lake, at the secluded dock where they partied as kids. The sun approached the horizon. The light would be a challenge, but Skye had a plan.

"Tell me about your tattoos," she said, bringing the camera up to peer through the view finder.

Clint tapped the Superman tattoo on his left bicep. "This was my first, on my eighteenth birthday. Thought I was invincible, the Man of Steel."

Skye snapped as Clint talked, the shutter like a drumbeat to the rhythm of his words.

"These," he said, brushing his hand across the lines on his torso, "they remind me I'm not invincible. I get a new one every month I don't give in to the siren's call. Keeps me strong."

"Fist your hands," Skye said, "look out over the lake." She wasn't sure how Clint would respond to her commands, but he followed them without uttering a word.

"You got any tats, Ms. Intel?" he asked.

"Not a fan of needles," she admitted, switching to sports mode on the camera and holding the button down. The shutter sounded like an automatic weapon, capturing Clint in the crosshairs.

"I need the tripod," she whispered to Noah, knowing she wasn't going to be able to hold it steady enough to catch the sun as it settled against the mountains.

Noah set it up as Skye tried to crouch to get a different angle. A shooting pain reminded her of her limitations. "Fuck it," she said and dropped onto her ass without an ounce of grace.

"Ten points for style," Clint said with a chuckle.

"Look over my shoulder," she said, "bring your left leg out front, like you're marching in formation."

Once again he followed her commands, the confidence on his face and in his posture much like Chad's had been that day she'd secretly snapped photos while he ran.

"Are you able to do push-ups?" she asked.

Clint snickered like it was a stupid question. "Are you?"

"Drop and give me twenty," she said as she twisted around and got on her stomach. The sun was low, the light reflecting off the water and creating an eerie glow. "Great," she said, "just angle your body away from me a bit so I don't have to crop out your personal weapon."

He laughed again but did as she asked, angling away so his genitals weren't in the picture. His body was perfect except for the prosthetic leg, but Skye realized as he knocked out push-up after push-up with little effort that the prosthesis took nothing away from his strength or his perfection.

She wasn't sure how many shots she snapped when she realized the sun was in the perfect spot, just about to kiss the mountains.

"Let's do a little sun and moon," she said. "Noah can you help me up?"

He did and Skye positioned the camera on the tripod as Clint got to his feet. "Just face the lake," she directed.

The man was a natural, as if born to model. Skye found she didn't even care that he was naked anymore. She just focused on the next shot and hoped to hell some of the pictures came out.

Clint stood in a position that was somewhere between attention and at ease, his legs apart and his arms at his sides. She snapped a few shots from behind, some full body, some at full zoom, zeroed in on his prosthesis and moving up his body. Then she moved around, capturing similar shots from different angles with the setting sun.

After the sun disappeared behind the mountains, Skye gazed at her watch, shocked to see ninety minutes had passed.

"Think you got anything good?" Clint asked, his signature arrogance gone, replaced with a childlike curiosity.

Skye scrolled through the pics, nodding her head. "I think so. I want to see them on the computer, see if I can enhance them with the software."

Clint chuckled, the arrogance back in his voice. "No enhancements necessary. I'm the model of perfection."

Skye ignored him and focused on the ideas running through her head. "I've got some great shots but I'd love to do this in the morning, or maybe inside where I have more control of the light."

"Didn't peg you for a control freak," Clint laughed and turned to Noah, cupping himself. "You might want to keep your eye on her, I think your girl just wants to see me naked again."

"Only because she's never seen a dick that small," Noah retorted without missing a beat.

"Noah," Skye gasped.

Clint chuckled as he put his robe on. "Well played, man."

When Clint extended his hand, Noah shook his hand. "I'm not shaking the hand that just groped your junk."

Clint laughed again and Skye was ready to get away from all the testosterone.

"Let's go home, boys," she drawled, putting her camera in the bag. She was anxious to get these pics on the computer and see what she could do with the editing software to enhance them.

"Who's next?" Clint asked as they headed to the cars.

"Chad and Maggie. She wants some baby belly pictures. That's Thursday. Then Pete and Shane are Saturday before the squad meeting," she explained.

"Rock-n-roll," Clint drawled. "Can't wait to see what you put together. It's going to be epic."

Clint grabbed clothes from the front seat of his truck, stripping out of the robe with as much modesty as he had during the shoot. He had a beautiful body, but Skye turned her attention to the man she adored. "Thanks for being here. I'm not sure I could have handled all that alone."

"He's a little crazy," Noah agreed.

Chapter 41

Thank you for loving me
For being my eyes when I couldn't see for
Parting my lips when I couldn't breathe
-Thank You for Loving Me, Bon Jovi

Happiness.

Faster than an improvised explosive device, Skye had gone from feeling sorry for herself and detesting this life that had been forced upon her to embracing everything she'd been blessed with.

Between the website work she was doing for Liz and Riley and the photos she was taking of her new squad mates, she didn't have time for all the other emotions that had assaulted her when she first came home. PT still sucked but not as much as it had when she first started.

Today was the first day she was able to walk out of PT without a limp. Progress.

Riley had dropped her off at the appointment because Noah was snapping photos of a property in Lilac Ridge that was going to auction. He assured her he'd be done before her appointment was over and true to his word, she found him reading Sports Illustrated on the bench just outside the clinic.

"Hey," he said, rolling the magazine and standing to kiss her. "You're not limping."

"I know," she laughed, spinning around. "I'm not ready to go dancing, but I feel good. I want to celebrate."

"Yeah?" Noah said, the happiness vibrating through her reflecting on his handsome face.

"Can we go to that new Thai place in town? Maggie and Liz both say it's fantastic."

"It's been there almost four years, Skye. It's not new."

"It's new to me," she laughed.

"Do you need to go home or should we head straight there?" he asked.

"I'm starving. PT makes me hungry."

"Well, at least it doesn't make you hangry," he laughed. While her mood swings had mellowed, they hadn't completely retreated, but Noah continued to stick by her and call her on the bull shit.

Noah held out his hand and Skye traced the scar on his palm before tangling her fingers with his. "We should get matching tattoos," she said as they walked to the car.

"You have at that. I'll pass," he said. Noah always had a ridiculous fear of needles, worse than Skye's fear of them. He didn't have a problem with her slicing his hand with a hunting knife, but any sort of needle and he turned ghost white. "I wouldn't be opposed to matching rings, though."

Her heart did a hop, skip, and jump. "I wouldn't be opposed to that either," she said, squeezing his hand.

"Good to know," he drawled, opening her door, which she accepted as a polite gesture from a gentleman and not because she was a hopeless, broken soldier.

A million thoughts ran through Skye's head as they drove to the restaurant. She tried not to look too far into the future because she'd learned that life was easier one day at a time, but the thought of sharing her life — the rest of her life — with Noah made her heart sing a tune she hadn't sung since before the explosion.

She wondered if he was thinking about it too as they drove in silence, not even any music playing through the stereo.

Skye wasn't ready to get married. Every day was still a struggle, maybe a little less of a struggle because of Noah's support, but she owed it to him to be independent and strong before she promised him forever.

"About the ring thing," she said, hoping he didn't have an immediate plan.

"I know you're not ready," he said, not letting her finish. "I'm not in any hurry. We're together now, and someday I want to watch you walk down the aisle, but only when it's right."

"How is it you know me so well?" she asked.

"Same way you know me so well," he said. He left it at that, but Skye understood. They couldn't define their bond. It had been strong since they were kids, stronger than anything she'd ever felt, even the allure of the fog that kept the ghosts from haunting her.

"I love you," she said, tracing his scar once more. "Thanks for sticking with me."

"I love you, too. Thanks for sticking with me. I know it hasn't been easy for you."

"It hasn't, but it gets a little easier every day."

They were lucky enough to get a parking space right in front of the restaurant. Skye took her time unbuckling so Noah could open the door for her again. She knew he liked that and she was happy to do anything she could to make him happy.

They were seated immediately and after the server took their drink orders, Noah gave her a mischievous smile. "I have something for you."

"Okay," she said, curious because they'd just had the whole she wasn't ready to get married conversation.

He pulled a long, narrow jewelry box from his jacket and

slid it across the table. "Open it," he commanded.

Skye grabbed the box and lifted the lid, gasping when she saw the charm bracelet inside.

"It was two months ago today when my mother staged that whole intervention. I was so scared it wouldn't work, but you stepped up that day, Skye. You took responsibility and have been so strong ever since."

"I'm strong because of you," she said.

"No, you're strong because of the person you are. You got lost along the way, but you've reclaimed who you are. When Clint talked about his tattoos, I wanted you to have something to mark your milestones. I'm not a fan of ink, but I thought this would be something to remind you of everything you've accomplished, as well as add to."

"It's beautiful," she said, pulling the bracelet out of the box.

"It's white gold. I hope you don't mind, but I put the pendant from the necklace Rafe sent you on there. I noticed you weren't wearing it."

Skye brushed her finger over the key, surprised to see it on there. She had tucked the engagement ring away in a box of other mementos she hadn't figured out what to do with. While she didn't want to wear it, she wasn't ready to let it go. All things in due time.

"There's also a dog tag on there with your name. That represents your time in the army."

"What does the heart represent?" she asked.

"Me, us. Our love. We've always loved each other. I know that love has saved me. I hope it is one of the things that keeps you going, too."

"It is," she said, nodding as she ran her finger over the heart.

"The four leaf clover is the one I found the day we snapped pictures. I sent it away to have it embossed in white gold. It's for luck."

"Oh, Noah, it's beautiful. I love this."

Skye took her time looking at each charm, gasping when she

found the red square with a smiley face. It matched cover image for her favorite Bon Jovi album, *Have a Nice Day*.

"I know that's your favorite," he said.

That album spoke to her, even when she didn't want it to. "I should have listened to the music more, maybe it wouldn't have been so hard when I came home."

He reached across the table and squeezed her hand.

"I don't crave it anymore, the fog. I'm still scared and things are still foreign and intimidating, but I don't feel the need to hide. Thank you for pushing me to get help. The squad is great. They make me feel at home. So does Maddie with the horses. I've almost forgotten she was your girlfriend."

"Maddie's a good person," he said.

"She is," Skye agreed. She still didn't talk a lot during their sessions, but being with the horses put her at ease. She was spending more and more time with Maggie, too, and they'd been talking about a double date, but she was so close to having the baby, she just didn't have the energy.

"We can keep adding to that, with every new milestone," he said, taking the bracelet from her and wrapping it around her wrist. When it was latched, he brought her wrist to his mouth and kissed her through the bracelet.

"I like that idea," she admitted. In the army, there had always been a goal. Win a board, get promoted, gain a leadership position, find the enemy. When thrown out in the civilian world, Skye didn't have a grasp on anything, let alone setting goals. Now she had some direction, a goal to stay sober, a goal to work through the pain, a goal to use photography to help other veterans like her. She was even setting goals with her new found career, and planned to take classes when the fall semester started.

"I'm so proud of you. I know it's still a long road ahead, but if you work as hard as you have the last two months, there's nothing you can't do."

The pride in his voice made her blush. She'd been so stupid, relying on those prescriptions and turning to Finn for help. Skye didn't know how she would have survived without Noah and her family.

"The photography thing is taking off," he said, when he released her wrist and grasped her hand. "I was thinking, and there's no pressure here because I know it's fast. You spend most of your nights with me anyway, and I still have the guest room upstairs if you need your own space, so why not convert your apartment to a working studio. You can get some equipment, lighting, props, whatever."

Skye's eyes widened because she had been thinking about that too but had been too scared to broach the subject. "It's not too soon. I want to be with you and you've been great about giving me space. I'd love to use the apartment as a studio. I have one condition, though."

"Name it," he said, his hand squeezing hers.

"You work with me. I'm not comfortable doing the naked guy thing alone and you give me confidence. Plus, you're really good with a camera. I want this to be a partnership."

Noah nodded. "Shooting people isn't my thing, but I like being your grip," he chuckled, "in more ways than one."

"I love your dirty mind," she laughed. "And I love you, Noah. It means so much that you stuck by me."

He turned her hand over and traced the scar, the intimacy calming her and exciting her at the same time. "Always, Skye. I will always be here for you."

The End

Dear Reader,

Writing this story was the most emotional journey I've embarked on with a book thus far. The concept was forged from a couple different story ideas that came together after my 13th Bon Jovi concert in Montreal in November 2013. It wasn't until I met Jon Bon Jovi in July 2015 and asked permission to use the lyrics that the dream of this book became an active project. I wrote the first draft in November 2015 and after publishing three other books, I was able to come back and see this story through revision, editing, and proofreading.

While I didn't face combat operations during my five years in the U.S. Army, I needed to tell this story for all of the combat soldiers who face the very real issues of PTSD and drug addiction. I was happy to see Skye through to a happily ever after, but there are many veterans who aren't as lucky. I'm a believer in the healing power of music, but some veterans need more than just the music and a family-staged intervention.

22 veterans commit suicide every day. The number of veterans facing PTSD and drug-addiction are staggering and the lack of resources is heartbreaking. There is no single solution to stop the tragic outcome many veterans find, but I hope this story can inspire a spark of hope for at least one person to keep the faith.

Always,

Susan

Books by Susan Ann Wall

Puget Sound ~ Alive With Love Series
The Sound of Consequence (April 2013)

The Sound of Betrayal (August 2013)

The Sound of Suspicion (January 2014)

The Sound of Deception (June 2014)

The Sound of Circumstance (December 2015)

The Sound of Reluctance (Coming Soon)

Fighting Back for Love Series
Relay For Love (May 2011)

A Flame Burns Inside (January 2012)

Worth the Fight (Coming Soon)

Superstitious Brides Series
Marrying for Love (January 2016)

For the Love of Chocolate (February 2016)

3rd Trip to the Altar (Coming Soon)

Devon Taggart Suspense Series
Broken Strings (April 2016)

Sunset Valley Women's Fiction Series
Whisper to a Scream

Too Many Daughters (Coming Soon)

Multi-Author Anthologies

Book Boyfriends Cafe *Summer Lovin'* (May 2015)
14 summer romances from USA Today and National Bestselling authors (includes Relay For Love)

Book Boyfriends Cafe *Tall, Dark, & Loaded* (January 2016)
6 billionaire romances from USA Today and National Bestselling authors (includes Marrying for Love)

Love Notes Country Music-Themed Collection (April 2016)
8 country-music themed novels and novellas from USA Today and National Bestselling authors (includes Broken Strings)

Summer Solstice: When Friends Become Lovers (June 2016)
9 friends to lovers romances from USA Today and National Bestselling authors (includes The Sound of Deception)

~~~

Photograph by BLC Photography

Big dreamer and certifiable overachiever Susan Ann Wall embraces life at full speed and volume. She's a beer and tea snob, can be bribed with dark chocolate, and the #1 thing on her bucket list is to be the center of a Bon Jovi flash mob.

Susan is a multi-genre author of racy, rule-breaking romance, women's fiction, and erotic fiction (her erotic titles are published as Ann Victor). Her bragging rights include nine books in three different series, three perfect children, adopting two amazing rescue dogs, and a happily ever after that started while serving in the U.S. Army and has spanned two decades (which is crazy since she's not a day over 29).

In her next life, Susan plans to be a 5 foot 10, size 8 rock star married to a chiropractor and will not be terrified of large bridges, spiders, or quiet people (shiver).

You can find Susan online at:
www.susanannwall.com
Facebook: Author Susan Ann Wall
Twitter: @susanannwall

www.ingramcontent.com/pod-product-compliance
Lightning Source LLC
Chambersburg PA
CBHW071516260626
47170CB00002B/392